PRAISE FOR
RAYMOND E. FEIST'S
MASTERPIECE OF FANTASY
THE RIFTWAR SAGA

MAGICIAN: APPRENTICE
MAGICIAN: MASTER

"The best new fantasy in years . . . has a chance of putting its author firmly on the throne next to Tolkien—and keeping him there."

—*The Dragon Magazine*

SILVERTHORN

"As exciting and absorbing as *Magician* in every way . . . one of the outstanding fantasy offerings of the season."

—Andre Norton

A DARKNESS AT SETHANON

"Feist writes skillfully and his imagination is prolific."

—*Rave Reviews*

AND FOR HIS OTHER RIFTWAR NOVELS

PRINCE OF THE BLOOD

"Has just about everything a fantasy fan could ask for."

—UPI

THE KING'S BUCCANEER

"A superior, rousing adventure."

—*Publishers Weekly*

FAERIE TALE

"A contemporary novel of masterful horror replete with magic, fantasy, and more than a little stylish eroticism."

—*The Washington Post*

BY RAYMOND E. FEIST

*Magician: Apprentice
*Magician: Master
*Silverthorn
*A Darkness at Sethanon

*Daughter of the Empire (with Janny Wurts)
*Servant of the Empire (with Janny Wurts)
*Mistress of the Empire (with Janny Wurts)

*Prince of the Blood
*The King's Buccaneer

*Faerie Tale

Shadow of a Dark Queen
Rise of a Merchant Prince
Rage of a Demon King
Shards of a Broken Crown

Krondor: The Betrayal
Krondor: The Assassins
Krondor: Tear of the Gods

Honoured Enemy (with William R. Forstchen)
Murder in Lamut (with Joel Rosenberg)
Jimmy the Hand (with S. M. Stirling)

Talon of the Silver Hawk
King of Foxes
Exile's Return

*Starred titles available from Bantam Books

Magician: Apprentice

Raymond E. Feist

The Author's Preferred Edition

BANTAM BOOKS

New York Toronto London Sydney Auckland

MAGICIAN: APPRENTICE
A Bantam Spectra Book

PUBLISHING HISTORY
Doubleday hardcover edition published November 1982
Bantam edition / January 1986
Revised Doubleday edition / November 1992
Revised Bantam edition / January 1994
Bantam reissue edition / July 2004

Published by
Bantam Dell
A Division of Random House, Inc.
New York, New York

ISBN 0-553-56494-3

Manufactured in the United States of America
Published simultaneously in Canada

OPM   31 30 29 28 27 26 25 24 23

This book is dedicated to the memory of my father,
FELIX E. FEIST,
in all ways, a magician

Acknowledgments

Many people have provided me with incalculable aid in bringing this novel into existence. I would like to offer my heartfelt thanks to:

The Friday Nighters: April and Stephen Abrams; Steve Barett; David Brin; Anita and Jon Everson; Dave Guinasso; Conan LaMotte; Tim LeSelle; Ethan Munson; Bob Potter; Rich Spahl; Alan Springer; and Lori and Jeff Velten, for their useful criticism, enthusiasm, support, belief, wise counsel, wonderful ideas, and most of all, their friendship.

Billie and Russ Blake, and Lilian and Mike Fessier, for always being willing to help.

Harold Matson, my agent, for taking a chance on me.

Adrian Zackheim, my editor, for asking rather than demanding, and for working so hard to build a good book.

Kate Cronin, assistant to the editor, for having a sense of humor and for so gracefully putting up with all my nonsense.

Elaine Chubb, copy editor, for having such a gentle touch and for caring so much about the words.
And Barbara A. Feist, my mother, for all of the above and more.

RAYMOND E. FEIST
San Diego, California
July 1982

Acknowledgment to the Revised Edition

On this occasion, the publication of the author's preferred edition, I would like to add the following names to the preceding list, people who, though not known to me at the time I made the foregoing acknowledgment, proved invaluable aid to me in bringing *Magician* to the public and contributed materially to my success:

Mary Ellen Curley, who took over from Katie and kept us all on course.

Peter Schneider, whose enthusiasm for the work gave me a valued ally within Doubleday and a close friend for the last decade.

Lou Aronica, who bought it even when he really didn't want to do reprints, and for giving me the chance to return to my first work and "rewrite it one more time."

Pat Lobrutto, who helped before it was his job, and who took over at a tough time, and whose friendship endures beyond our business relationship.

Janna Silverstein, who despite her short tenure as my editor has shown an uncanny knack for knowing when to leave me alone and when to stay in touch.

Nick Austin, John Booth, Jonathan Lloyd, Malcolm Edwards, and everyone at Granada, now HarperCollins Books, who made the work an international bestseller. Abner Stein, my British agent, who sold it to Nick in the first place.

Janny Wurts, for being my friend, and who, by working with me on the Empire Trilogy, gave me a completely different perspective on the Tsurani; she helped turn The Game of the Council from a vague concept to a murderously real arena of human conflict. Kelewan and Tsuranuanni are as much her inventions as mine. I drew the outlines and she colored in the details.

And Jonathan Matson, who received the torch from a great man's hand and continued without faltering, for wise counsel and friendship. The acorn fell very close to the tree.

And most of all, my wife Kathlyn S. Starbuck, who understands my pain and joy in this craft because she toils in the same vineyard, and who is always there even when I don't deserve to have her there, and who makes things make sense through her love.

RAYMOND E. FEIST
San Diego, California
April 1991

Foreword to the Revised Edition

It is with some hesitation and a great deal of trepidation that an author approaches the task of revising an earlier edition of fiction. This is especially true if the book was his first effort, judged successful by most standards, and continuously in print for a decade.

Magician was all this, and more. In late 1977 I decided to try my hand at writing, part-time, while I was an employee of the University of California, San Diego. It is now some fifteen years later, and I have been a full-time writer for the last fourteen years, successful in this craft beyond my wildest dreams. *Magician*, the first novel in what became known as *The Riftwar Saga*, was a book that quickly took on a life of its own. I hesitate to admit this publicly, but the truth is that part of the success of the book was my ignorance of what makes a commercially successful novel. My willingness to plunge blindly forward into a tale spanning two dissimilar worlds, covering twelve years in the lives of several major and dozens of minor characters, breaking numerous rules of plotting along the way, seemed to find kindred souls among readers the world over. After a decade in print, my best judgment is that the appeal of the book is based upon its being what was known once as a "ripping yarn." I had little ambition beyond spinning a good story, one that satisfied my sense of wonder, adventure, and whimsy. It turned out that several million readers—many of whom read translations in languages I can't even begin to comprehend—found it one that satisfied their tastes for such a yarn as well.

But insofar as it was a first effort, some pressures of the marketplace did manifest themselves during the creation of the final book. *Magician* is by anyone's measure a large book. When the penultimate manuscript version sat upon my editor's desk, I was informed that some fifty thousand words would have to be cut. And cut I did. Mostly line by line, but a few scenes were either truncated or excised.

While I could live out my life with the original manuscript as published being the only edition ever read, I have always felt that some of the material cut added a certain resonance, a counterpoint if you will, to key elements of the tale. The relationships between characters, the additional details of an alien world, the minor moments of reflection and mirth that act to balance the more frenetic activity of conflict and adventure, all these things were "close but not quite what I had in mind."

In any event, to celebrate the tenth anniversary of the original publication of *Magician*, I have been permitted to return to this work, to reconstruct and change, to add and cut as I see fit, to bring forth what is known in publishing as the "Author's Preferred Edition" of the work. So, with the old admonition, "If it ain't broke, don't fix it," ringing in my ears, I return to the first work I undertook, back when I had no pretensions of craft, no stature as a bestselling author, and basically no idea of what I was doing. My desire is to restore some of those excised bits, some of the minor detail that I felt added to the heft of the narrative, as well as the weight of the book. Other material was more directly related to the books that follow, setting some of the background for the mythic underpinning of the Riftwar. The slightly lengthy discussion of lore between Tully and Kulgan in Chapter Three, as well as some of the things revealed to Pug on the Tower of Testing were clearly in this area. My editor wasn't sold on the idea of a sequel, then, so some of this was cut. Returning it may be self-indulgent, but as this was material I felt belonged in the original book, it has been restored.

To those readers who have already discovered *Magician*, who wonder if it's in their interests to purchase this edition, I would like to reassure them that nothing profound has been changed. No characters previously dead are now alive, no battles lost are now won, and two boys still find the same destiny. I ask you to feel no compulsion to read this new volume, for your memory of the original work is as valid, perhaps more so, than mine. But if you wish to return to the world of Pug and Tomas, to rediscover old friends and forgotten adventure, then consider this edition your opportunity to see a bit more than the last time. And to the new reader, welcome. I trust you'll find this work to your satisfaction.

It is with profound gratitude I wish to thank you all, new readers and old acquaintances, for without your support and encouragement, ten years of "ripping yarns" could not have been possible. If I have the opportunity to provide you with a small part of the pleasure I feel in being able to share my fanciful adventures with you, we are equally rewarded, for by your embracing my works you have allowed me to fashion more. Without you there would have been no *Silverthorn, A Darkness at Sethanon, Faerie Tale,* and no *Empire Trilogy.* The letters get read, if not answered—even if they sometimes take months to reach me—and the kind remarks, in passing at public appearances, have enriched me beyond measure. But most of all, you gave me the freedom to practice a craft that was begun to "see if I could do it," while working at the Residence Halls of John Muir College at UCSD.

So, thank you. I guess "I did it." And with this work, I hope you'll agree that *this time* I did it a little more elegantly, with a little more color, weight, and resonance.

RAYMOND E. FEIST
San Diego, California
August 1991

Magician:
Apprentice

A boy's will is the wind's will,
And the thoughts of youth are
long, long thoughts.

—LONGFELLOW,
My Lost Youth

1

Storm

The storm had broken.

Pug danced along the edge of the rocks, his feet finding scant purchase as he made his way among the tide pools. His dark eyes darted about as he peered into each pool under the cliff face, seeking the spiny creatures driven into the shallows by the recently passed storm. His boyish muscles bunched under his light shirt as he shifted the sack of sandcrawlers, rockclaws, and crabs plucked from this water garden.

The afternoon sun sent sparkles through the sea spray swirling around him, as the west wind blew his sun-streaked brown hair about. Pug set his sack down, checked to make sure it was securely tied, then squatted on a clear patch of sand. The sack was not quite full, but Pug relished the extra hour or so that he could relax. Megar the cook wouldn't trouble him about the time as long as the sack was almost full. Resting with his back against a large rock, Pug was soon dozing in the sun's warmth.

A cool wet spray woke him hours later. He opened his eyes with a start, knowing he had stayed much too long. Westward, over the sea, dark thunderheads were forming above the black outline of the Six Sisters, the small islands on the horizon. The roiling, surging clouds, with rain trailing below like some sooty veil, heralded another of the sudden storms common to this part of the coast in early summer. To the south, the high bluffs of Sailor's Grief reared up against the sky, as waves crashed against the base of that rocky pinnacle. Whitecaps started to form behind the breakers, a sure sign the storm would quickly strike. Pug knew he was in danger, for the storms of summer could drown anyone on the beaches, or if severe enough, on the low ground beyond.

He picked up his sack and started north, toward the castle. As he moved among the pools, he felt the coolness in the wind turn to a deeper, wetter cold. The day began to be broken by a patchwork of shadows as the first clouds passed before the sun, bright colors fading to shades of grey. Out to sea, lightning flashed against the blackness of the clouds, and the distant boom of thunder rode over the noise of the waves.

Pug picked up speed when he came to the first stretch of open beach. The storm was coming in faster than he would have thought possible, driving the rising tide before it. By the time he reached the second stretch of tide pools, there was barely ten feet of dry sand between water's edge and cliffs.

Pug hurried as fast as was safe across the rocks, twice nearly catching his foot. As he reached the next expanse of sand, he mistimed his jump from the last rock and landed poorly. He fell to the sand, grasping his ankle. As if waiting for the mishap, the tide surged forward, covering him for a moment. He reached out blindly and felt his sack carried away. Frantically grabbing at it, Pug lunged forward, only to have his ankle fail. He went under, gulping water. He raised his head, sputtering and coughing. He started to stand when a second wave, higher than the last, hit him in the chest, knocking him backward. Pug had grown up playing in the waves and was an experienced swimmer, but the pain of his ankle and the battering of the waves were bringing him to the edge of panic. He fought it off and came up for air as the wave receded. He half swam, half scrambled toward the cliff face, knowing the water would be only inches deep there.

Pug reached the cliffs and leaned against them, keeping as much weight off the injured ankle as possible. He inched along the rock wall, while each wave brought the water higher. When Pug finally reached a place where he could make his way upward, water was swirling at his waist. He had to use all his strength to pull himself up to the path. He lay panting a moment, then started to crawl up the pathway, unwilling to trust his balky ankle on this rocky footing.

The first drops of rain began to fall as he scrambled along, bruising knees and shins on the rocks, until he reached the grassy top of the bluffs. Pug fell forward exhausted, panting from the exertion of the climb. The scattered drops grew into a light but steady rain.

When he had caught his breath, Pug sat up and examined the swollen ankle. It was tender to the touch, but he was reassured when he could move it: it was not broken. He would have to limp the entire way back, but with the threat of drowning on the beach behind him, he felt relatively buoyant.

Pug would be a drenched, chilled wretch when he reached the town. He would have to find a lodging there, for the gates of the castle would be closed for the night, and with his tender ankle he would not attempt to climb the wall behind the stables. Besides, should he

wait and slip into the keep the next day, only Megar
would have words for him, but if he was caught coming
over the wall, Swordmaster Fannon or Horsemaster Algon would surely have a lot worse in store for him than
words.

While he rested, the rain took on an insistent
quality and the sky darkened as the late-afternoon sun
was completely engulfed in storm clouds. His momentary relief was replaced with anger at himself for losing
the sack of sandcrawlers. His displeasure doubled when
he considered his folly at falling asleep. Had he remained awake, he would have made the return trip
unhurriedly, would not have sprained his ankle, and
would have had time to explore the streambed above
the bluffs for the smooth stones he prized so dearly for
slinging. Now there would be no stones, and it would
be at least another week before he could return. If
Megar didn't send another boy instead, which was
likely now that he was returning empty-handed.

Pug's attention shifted to the discomfort of sitting
in the rain, and he decided it was time to move on. He
stood and tested his ankle. It protested such treatment,
but he could get along on it. He limped over the grass
to where he had left his belongings and picked up his
rucksack, staff, and sling. He swore an oath he had
heard soldiers at the keep use when he found the rucksack ripped apart and his bread and cheese missing.
Raccoons, or possibly sand lizards, he thought. He
tossed the now useless sack aside and wondered at his
misfortune.

Taking a deep breath, he leaned on his staff as he
started across the low rolling hills that divided the
bluffs from the road. Stands of small trees were scattered over the landscape, and Pug regretted there wasn't
more substantial shelter nearby, for there was none

upon the bluffs. He would be no wetter for trudging to town than for staying under a tree.

The wind picked up, and Pug felt the first cold bite against his wet back. He shivered and hurried his pace as well as he could. The small trees started to bend before the wind, and Pug felt as if a great hand were pushing at his back. Reaching the road, he turned north. He heard the eerie sound of the great forest off to the east, the wind whistling through the branches of the ancient oaks, adding to its already foreboding aspect. The dark glades of the forest were probably no more perilous than the King's road, but remembered tales of outlaws and other, less human, malefactors stirred the hairs on the boy's neck.

Cutting across the King's road, Pug gained a little shelter in the gully that ran alongside it. The wind intensified and rain stung his eyes, bringing tears to already wet cheeks. A gust caught him, and he stumbled off balance for a moment. Water was gathering in the roadside gully, and he had to step carefully to keep from losing his footing in unexpectedly deep puddles.

For nearly an hour he made his way through the ever growing storm. The road turned northwest, bringing him almost full face into the howling wind. Pug leaned into the wind, his shirt whipping out behind him. He swallowed hard, to force down the choking panic rising within him. He knew he was in danger now, for the storm was gaining in fury far beyond normal for this time of year. Great ragged bolts of lightning lit the dark landscape, briefly outlining the trees and road in harsh, brilliant white and opaque black. The dazzling afterimages, black and white reversed, stayed with him for a moment each time, confusing his senses. Enormous thunder peals sounding overhead felt like physical blows. Now his fear of the storm outweighed his fear of imagined brigands and goblins. He decided to walk among the trees near the road; the wind would be lessened somewhat by the boles of the oaks.

As Pug closed upon the forest, a crashing sound brought him to a halt. In the gloom of the storm he could barely make out the form of a black forest boar as it burst out of the undergrowth. The pig tumbled from the brush, lost its footing, then scrambled to its feet a few yards away. Pug could see it clearly as it stood there regarding him, swinging its head from side to side. Two large tusks seemed to glow in the dim light as they dripped rainwater. Fear made its eyes wide, and it pawed at the ground. The forest pigs were bad-tempered at best, but normally avoided humans. This one was panic-stricken by the storm, and Pug knew if it charged he could be badly gored, even killed.

Standing stock-still, Pug made ready to swing his staff, but hoped the pig would return to the woods. The boar's head raised, testing the boy's smell on the wind. Its pink eyes seemed to glow as it trembled with indecision. A sound made it turn toward the trees for a moment, then it dropped its head and charged.

Pug swung his staff, bringing it down in a glancing blow to the side of the pig's head, turning it. The pig slid sideways in the muddy footing, hitting Pug in the legs. He went down as the pig slipped past. Lying on the ground, Pug saw the boar skitter about as it turned to charge again. Suddenly the pig was upon him, and Pug had no time to stand. He thrust the staff before him in a vain attempt to turn the animal again. The boar dodged the staff and Pug tried to roll away, but a weight fell across his body. Pug covered his face with his hands, keeping his arms close to his chest, expecting to be gored.

After a moment he realized the pig was still. Uncovering his face, he discovered the pig lying across his lower legs, a black-feathered, cloth-yard arrow protruding from its side. Pug looked toward the forest. A man garbed in brown leather was standing near the edge of the trees, quickly wrapping a yeoman's longbow with an oilcloth cover. Once the valuable weapon was protected from further abuse by the weather, the man crossed to stand over the boy and beast.

He was cloaked and hooded, his face hidden. He knelt next to Pug and shouted over the sound of the wind, "Are you 'right, boy?" as he lifted the dead boar easily from Pug's legs. "Bones broken?"

"I don't think so," Pug yelled back, taking account of himself. His right side smarted, and his legs felt equally bruised. With his ankle still tender, he was feeling ill-used today, but nothing seemed broken or permanently damaged.

Large, meaty hands lifted him to his feet. "Here," the man commanded, handing him his staff and the bow. Pug took them while the stranger quickly gutted the boar with a large hunter's knife. He completed his work and turned to Pug. "Come with me, boy. You had best lodge with my master and me. It's not far, but we'd best hurry. This storm'll get worse afore it's over. Can you walk?"

Taking an unsteady step, Pug nodded. Without a word the man shouldered the pig and took his bow. "Come," he said, as he turned toward the forest. He set off at a brisk pace, which Pug had to scramble to match.

The forest cut the fury of the storm so little that conversation was impossible. A lightning flash lit the scene for a moment, and Pug caught a glimpse of the man's face. Pug tried to remember if he had seen the stranger before. He had the look common to the hunters and foresters that lived in the forest of Crydee: large-shouldered, tall, and solidly built. He had dark hair and beard and the raw, weather-beaten appearance of one who spends most of his time outdoors.

For a few fanciful moments the boy wondered if he might be some member of an outlaw band, hiding in the heart of the forest. He gave up the notion, for no outlaw would trouble himself with an obviously penniless keep boy.

Remembering the man had mentioned having a master, Pug suspected he was a franklin, one who lived on the estate of a landholder. He would be in the holder's service, but not bound to him as a bondsman. The franklins were freeborn, giving a share of crop or herd in exchange for the use of land. He must be freeborn. No bondsman would be allowed to carry a longbow, for they were much too valuable—and dangerous. Still, Pug couldn't remember any landholdings in the forest. It was a mystery to the boy, but the toll of the day's abuses was quickly driving away any curiosity.

AFTER WHAT SEEMED to be hours, the man walked into a thicket of trees. Pug nearly lost him in the darkness, for the sun had set some time before, taking with it what faint light the storm had allowed. He followed the man more from the sound of his footfalls and an awareness of his presence than from sight. Pug sensed he was on a path through the trees, for his footsteps met no resisting brush or detritus. From where they had been moments before, the path would be difficult to find in the daylight, impossible at night, unless it was already known. Soon they entered a clearing, in the midst of which sat a small stone cottage. Light shone through a single window, and smoke rose from the chimney. They crossed the clearing, and Pug wondered at the storm's relative mildness in this one spot in the forest.

Once before the door, the man stood to one side and said, "You go in, boy. I must dress the pig."

Nodding dumbly, Pug pushed open the wooden door and stepped in.

"Close that door, boy! You'll give me a chill and cause me my death."

Pug jumped to obey, slamming the door harder than he intended.

He turned, taking in the scene before him. The interior of the cottage was a small single room. Against one wall was the fireplace, with a good-size hearth before it. A bright, cheery fire burned, casting a warm glow. Next to the fireplace a table sat, behind which a heavyset, yellow-robed figure rested on a bench. His grey hair and beard nearly covered his entire head, except for a pair of vivid blue eyes that twinkled in the firelight. A long pipe emerged from the beard, producing heroic clouds of pale smoke.

Pug knew the man. "Master Kulgan . . . ," he began, for the man was the Duke's magician and adviser, a familiar face around the castle keep.

Kulgan leveled a gaze at Pug, then said in a deep voice, given to rich rolling sounds and powerful tones, "So you know me, then?"

"Yes, sir. From the castle."

"What is your name, boy from the keep?"

"Pug, Master Kulgan."

"Now I remember you." The magician absently waved his hand. "Do not call me 'Master,' Pug— though I am rightly called a master of my arts," he said with a merry crinkling around his eyes. "I am higher-born than you, it is true, but not by much. Come, there is a blanket hanging by the fire, and you are drenched. Hang your clothes to dry, then sit there." He pointed to a bench opposite him.

Pug did as he was bid, keeping an eye on the

magician the entire time. He was a member of the Duke's court, but still a magician, an object of suspicion, generally held in low esteem by the common folk. If a farmer had a cow calve a monster, or blight strike the crops, villagers were apt to ascribe it to the work of some magician lurking in nearby shadows. In times not too far past they would have stoned Kulgan from Crydee as like as not. His position with the Duke earned him the tolerance of the townsfolk now, but old fears died slowly.

After his garments were hung, Pug sat down. He started when he saw a pair of red eyes regarding him from just beyond the magician's table. A scaled head rose up above the tabletop and studied the boy.

Kulgan laughed at the boy's discomfort. "Come, boy. Fantus will not eat you." He dropped his hand to the head of the creature, who sat next to him on his bench, and rubbed above its eye ridges. It closed its eyes and gave forth a soft crooning sound, not unlike the purring of a cat.

Pug shut his mouth, which had popped open with surprise, then asked, "Is he truly a dragon, sir?"

The magician laughed, a rich, good-natured sound. "Betimes he thinks he is, boy. Fantus is a fire-drake, cousin to the dragon, though of smaller stature." The creature opened one eye and fastened it on the magician. "But of equal heart," Kulgan quickly added, and the drake closed his eye again. Kulgan spoke softly, in conspiratorial tones. "He is very clever, so mind what you say to him. He is a creature of finely fashioned sensibilities."

Pug nodded that he would. "Can he breathe fire?" he asked, eyes wide with wonder. To any boy of thirteen, even a cousin to a dragon was worthy of awe.

"When the mood suits him, he can belch out a flame or two, though he seems rarely in the mood. I think it is due to the rich diet I supply him with, boy. He has not had to hunt for years, so he is something out of practice in the ways of drakes. In truth, I spoil him shamelessly."

Pug found the notion somehow reassuring. If the magician cared enough to spoil this creature, no matter how outlandish, then he seemed somehow more human, less mysterious. Pug studied Fantus, admiring how the fire brought golden highlights to his emerald scales. About the size of a small hound, the drake possessed a long, sinuous neck atop which rested an alligatorlike head. His wings were folded across his back, and two clawed feet extended before him, aimlessly pawing the air, while Kulgan scratched behind bony eye ridges. His long tail swung back and forth, inches above the floor.

The door opened and the big bowman entered, holding a dressed and spitted loin of pork before him. Without a word he crossed to the fireplace and set the meat to cook. Fantus raised his head, using his long neck to good advantage to peek over the table. With a flick of his forked tongue, the drake jumped down and, in stately fashion, ambled over to the hearth. He selected a warm spot before the fire and curled up to doze away the wait before dinner.

The franklin unfastened his cloak and hung it on a peg by the door. "Storm will pass afore dawn, I'm thinking." He returned to the fire and prepared a basting of wine and herbs for the pig. Pug was startled to see a large scar that ran down the left side of the man's face, showing red and angry in the firelight.

Kulgan waved his pipe in the franklin's direction. "Knowing my tight-lipped man here, you'll not have made his proper acquaintance. Meecham, this boy is Pug, from the keep at Castle Crydee." Meecham gave a brief nod, then returned to tending the roasting loin.

Pug nodded back, though a bit late for Meecham to notice. "I never thought to thank you for saving me from the boar."

Meecham replied, "There's no need for thanks, boy. Had I not startled the beast, it's unlikely it would have charged you." He left the hearth and crossed over to another part of the room, took some brown dough from a cloth-covered bucket, and started kneading.

"Well, sir," said Pug to Kulgan, "it was his arrow that killed the pig. It was indeed fortunate that he was following the animal."

Kulgan laughed. "The poor creature, who is our most welcome guest for dinner, happened to be as much a victim of circumstance as yourself."

Pug looked perplexed. "I don't follow, sir."

Kulgan stood and took down an object from the topmost shelf on his bookcase and placed it on the table before the boy. It was wrapped in a cover of dark blue velvet, so Pug knew at once it must be a prize of great value for such an expensive material to be used for covering. Kulgan removed the velvet, revealing an orb of crystal that gleamed in the firelight. Pug gave an *ah* of pleasure at the beauty of it, for it was without apparent flaw and splendid in its simplicity of form.

Kulgan pointed to the sphere of glass. "This device was fashioned as a gift by Althafain of Carse, a most puissant artificer of magic, who thought me worthy of such a present, as I have done him a favor or two in the past—but that is of little matter. Having just this day returned from the company of Master Althafain, I was testing his token. Look deep into the orb, Pug."

Pug fixed his eyes on the ball and tried to follow the flicker of firelight that seemed to play deep within its structure. The reflections of the room, multiplied a hundredfold, merged and danced as his eyes tried to fasten upon each aspect within the orb. They flowed and blended, then grew cloudy and obscure. A soft white glow at the center of the ball replaced the red of firelight, and Pug felt his gaze become trapped by its pleasing warmth. Like the warmth of the kitchen at the keep, he thought absently.

Suddenly the milky white within the ball vanished, and Pug could see an image of the kitchen before his eyes. Fat Alfan the cook was making pastries, licking the sweet crumbs from his fingers. This brought the wrath of Megar, the head cook, down upon his head, for Megar considered it a disgusting habit. Pug laughed at the scene, one he had witnessed before many times, and it vanished. Suddenly he felt tired.

Kulgan wrapped the orb in the cloth and put it away. "You did well, boy," he said thoughtfully. He stood watching the boy for a moment, as if considering something, then sat down. "I would not have suspected you of being able to fashion such a clear image in one try, but you seem to be more than you first appear to be."

"Sir?"

"Never mind, Pug." He paused for a moment, then said, "I was using that toy for the first time, judging how far I could send my sight, when I spied you making for the road. From your limp and bruised condition, I judged that you would never reach the town, so I sent Meecham to fetch you."

Pug looked embarrassed by the unusual attention, color rising to his cheeks. He said, with a thirteen-year-old's high estimation of his own ability, "You needn't have done that, sir. I would have reached the town in due time."

Kulgan smiled. "Perhaps, but then again, perhaps not. The storm is unseasonably severe and perilous for traveling."

Pug listened to the soft tattoo of rain on the roof

of the cottage. The storm seemed to have slackened, and Pug doubted the magician's words. As if reading the boy's thought, Kulgan said, "Doubt me not, Pug. This glade is protected by more than the great boles. Should you pass beyond the circle of oaks that marks the edge of my holding, you would feel the storm's fury. Meecham, how do you gauge this wind?"

Meecham put down the bread dough he was kneading and thought for a moment. "Near as bad as the storm that beached six ships three years back." He paused for a moment, as if reconsidering the estimate, then nodded his endorsement. "Yes, nearly as bad, though it won't blow so long."

Pug thought back three years to the storm that had blown a Quegan trading fleet bound for Crydee onto the rocks of Sailor's Grief. At its height, the guards on the castle walls were forced to stay in the towers, lest they be blown down. If this storm was that severe, then Kulgan's magic was impressive, for outside the cottage it sounded no worse than a spring rain.

Kulgan sat back on the bench, occupied with trying to light his extinguished pipe. As he produced a large cloud of sweet white smoke, Pug's attention wandered to a case of books standing behind the magician. His lips moved silently as he tried to discern what was written on the bindings, but could not.

Kulgan lifted an eyebrow and said, "So you can read, aye?"

Pug started, alarmed that he might have offended the magician by intruding on his domain. Kulgan, sensing his embarrassment, said, "It is all right, boy. It is no crime to know letters."

Pug felt his discomfort diminish. "I can read a little, sir. Megar the cook has shown me how to read the tallies on the stores laid away for the kitchen in the cellars. I know some numbers, as well."

"Numbers, too," the magician exclaimed good-naturedly. "Well, you are something of a rare bird." He reached behind himself and pulled out one volume, bound in red-brown leather, from the shelf. He opened it, squinting at one page, then another, and at last found a page that seemed to meet his requirements. He turned the open book around and lay it upon the table before Pug. Kulgan pointed to a page illuminated by a magnificent design of snakes, flowers, and twining vines in a colorful design around a large letter in the upper left corner. "Read this, boy."

Pug had never seen anything remotely like it. His lessons had been on plain parchment with letters fashioned in Megar's blunt script, using a charcoal stick. He sat, fascinated by the details of the work, then realized the magician was staring at him. Regaining his wits, he began to read.

"And then there came a sum . . . summons from . . ." He looked at the word, stumbling over the complex combinations that were new to him. ". . . Zacara." He paused, looking at Kulgan to see if he was correct. The magician nodded for him to continue. "For the north was to be forgot . . . forgotten, lest the heart of the empire lan . . . languish and all be lost. And though of Bosania from birth, those soldiers still were loyal to Great Kesh in their service. So for her great need, they took up their arms and put on their armor and quit Bosania, taking ship to the south, to save all from destruction."

Kulgan said, "That's enough," and gently closed the cover of the book. "You are well gifted with letters for a keep boy."

"This book, sir, what is it?" asked Pug, as Kulgan took it from him. "I have never seen anything like it."

Kulgan looked at Pug for a moment, with a gaze that made him uncomfortable again, then smiled, breaking the tension. As he put the book back, he said, "It is a history of this land, boy. It was given as a gift by the abbot of an Ishapian monastery. It is a translation of a Keshian text, over a hundred years old."

Pug nodded and said, "It all sounded very strange. What does it tell of?"

Kulgan once more looked at Pug as if trying to see something inside of the boy, then said, "A long time ago, Pug, all these lands, from the Endless Sea across the Grey Tower Mountains to the Bitter Sea, were part of the Empire of Great Kesh. Far to the east existed a small kingdom, on one small island called Rillanon. It grew to engulf its neighboring island kingdoms, and it became the Kingdom of the Isles. Later it expanded again to the mainland, and while it is still the Kingdom of Isles, most of us simply call it 'the Kingdom.' We, who live in Crydee, are part of the Kingdom, though we live as far from the capital city of Rillanon as one can and still be within its boundaries.

"Once, many long years ago, the Empire of Great Kesh abandoned these lands, for it was engaged in a long and bloody conflict with its neighbors to the south, the Keshian Confederacy."

Pug was caught up in the grandeur of lost empires, but hungry enough to notice Meecham was putting several small loaves of dark bread in hearth oven. He turned his attention back to the magician. "Who were the Keshian Con— . . . ?"

"The Keshian Confederacy," Kulgan finished for the boy. "It is a group of small nations who had existed as tributaries to Great Kesh for centuries. A dozen years before that book was written, they united against their oppressor. Each alone was insufficient to contest with Great Kesh, but united they proved its match. Too close a match, for the war dragged on year after year. The Empire was forced to strip its northern provinces of their legions and send them south, leaving the north open to the advances of the new, younger Kingdom.

"It was Duke Borric's grandfather, youngest son of the King, who brought the army westward, extending the Western Realm. Since then all of what was once the old imperial province of Bosania, except for the Free Cities of Natal, has been called the Duchy of Crydee."

Pug thought for a moment, then said, "I think I would like to travel to this Great Kesh someday."

Meecham snorted, something close to a laugh. "And what would you be traveling as, a freebooter?"

Pug felt his face flush. Freebooters were landless men, mercenaries who fought for pay, and who were regarded as being only one cut above outlaws.

Kulgan said, "Perhaps you might someday, Pug. The way is long and full of peril, but it is not unheard of for a brave and hearty soul to survive the journey. Stranger things have been known to happen."

The talk at the table turned to more common topics, for the magician had been at the southern keep at Carse for over a month and wanted the gossip of Crydee. When the bread was done baking, Meecham served it hot, carved the pork loin, and brought out plates of cheese and greens. Pug had never eaten so well in his life. Even when he had worked in the kitchen, his position as keep boy earned him only meager fare. Twice during dinner, Pug found the magician regarding him intently.

When the meal was over, Meecham cleared the table, then began washing the dishes with clean sand and fresh water, while Kulgan and Pug sat talking. A single scrap of meat remained on the table, which Kulgan tossed over to Fantus, who lay before the fire. The drake opened one eye to regard the morsel. He pondered the choice between his comfortable resting place and the juicy scrap for a moment, then moved the necessary six inches to gulp down the prize and closed his eye again.

Kulgan lit his pipe, and once he was satisfied with its production of smoke, he said, "What are your plans when you reach manhood, boy?"

Pug was fighting off sleep, but Kulgan's question brought him alert again. The time of Choosing, when the boys of the town and keep were taken into apprenticeship, was close, and Pug became excited as he said, "This Midsummer's Day I hope to take the Duke's service under Swordmaster Fannon."

Kulgan regarded his slight guest. "I would have thought you still a year or two away from apprenticeship, Pug."

Meecham gave out a sound somewhere between a laugh and a grunt. "Bit small to be lugging around sword and shield, aren't you, boy?"

Pug flushed. He was the smallest boy of his age in the castle. "Megar the cook said I may be late coming to my growth," he said with a faint note of defiance. "No one knows who my parents were, so they have no notion of what to expect."

"Orphan, is it?" asked Meecham, raising one eyebrow, his most expressive gesture yet.

Pug nodded. "I was left with the Priests of Dala, in the mountain abbey, by a woman who claimed she found me in the road. They brought me to the keep, for they had no way to care for me."

"Yes," injected Kulgan, "I remember when those who worship the Shield of the Weak first brought you to the castle. You were no more than a baby fresh from the teat. It is only through the Duke's kindness that you are a freeman today. He felt it a lesser evil to free a bondsman's son than to bond a freeman's. Without proof, it was his right to have you declared bondsman."

Meecham said in a noncommittal tone, "A good man, the Duke."

Pug had heard the story of his origin a hundred times before from Magya in the kitchen of the castle. He felt completely wrung out and could barely keep his eyes open. Kulgan noticed and signaled Meecham. The tall franklin took some blankets from a shelf and prepared a sleeping pallet. By the time he finished, Pug had fallen asleep with his head on the table. The large man's hands lifted him gently from the stool and placed him on the blankets, then covered him.

Fantus opened his eyes and regarded the sleeping boy. With a wolfish yawn, he scrambled over next to Pug and snuggled in close. Pug shifted his weight in his sleep and draped one arm over the drake's neck. The firedrake gave an approving rumble, deep in his throat, and closed his eyes again.

2

Apprentice

The forest was quiet.

The slight afternoon breeze stirred the tall oaks and cut the day's heat, while rustling the leaves only slightly. Birds who would raise a raucous chorus at sunrise and sundown were mostly quiet at this time of morning. The faint tang of sea salt mixed with the sweet smell of flowers and pungency of decaying leaves.

Pug and Tomas walked slowly along the path, with the aimless weaving steps of boys who have no particular place to go and ample time to get there. Pug shied a small rock at an imagined target, then turned to look at his companion. "You don't think your mother was mad, do you?" he asked.

Tomas smiled. "No, she understands how things are. She's seen other boys the day of Choosing. And truthfully, we were more of hindrance than a help in the kitchen today."

Pug nodded. He had spilled a precious pot of honey as he carried it to Alfan, the pastry cook. Then he had dumped an entire tray of fresh bread loaves as he took them from the oven. "I made something of a fool of myself today, Tomas."

Tomas laughed. He was a tall boy, with sandy hair and bright blue eyes. With his quick smile, he was well liked in the keep, in spite of a boyish tendency to find trouble. He was Pug's closest friend, more brother than friend, and for that reason Pug earned some measure of acceptance from the other boys, for they all regarded Tomas as their unofficial leader.

Tomas said, "You were no more the fool than I. At least you didn't forget to hang the beef sides high." Pug grinned. "Anyway, the Duke's hounds are happy." He snickered, then laughed. "She is angry, isn't she?"

Tomas laughed along with his friend. "She's mad. Still, the dogs only ate a little before she shooed them off. Besides, she's mostly mad at Father. She claims the Choosing's only an excuse for all the Craftmasters to sit around smoking pipes, drinking ale, and swapping tales all day. She says they already know who will choose which boy."

Pug said, "From what the other women say, she's not alone in that opinion." Then he grinned at Tomas. "Probably not wrong, either."

Tomas lost his smile. "She truly doesn't like it when he's not in the kitchen to oversee things. I think she knows this, which is why she tossed us out of the keep for the morning, so she wouldn't take out her temper on us. Or at least you," he added with a questioning smile. "I swear you're her favorite."

Pug's grin returned and he laughed again. "Well, I do cause less trouble."

With a playful punch to the arm, Tomas said, "You mean you get caught less often."

Pug pulled his sling out from within his shirt. "If

we came back with a brace of partridge or quail, she might regain some of her good temper."

Tomas smiled. "She might," he agreed, taking out his own sling. Both boys were excellent slingers, Tomas being undoubted champion among the boys, edging Pug by only a little. It was unlikely either could bring down a bird on the wing, but should they find one at rest, there was a fair chance they might hit it. Besides, it would give them something to do to pass the hours and perhaps for a time forget the Choosing.

With exaggerated stealth they crept along, playing the part of hunters. Tomas led the way as they left the footpath, heading for the watering pool they knew lay not too far distant. It was improbable they would spot game this time of the day unless they simply blundered across it, but if any were to be found, it most likely would be near the pool. The woods to the northeast of the town of Crydee were less forbidding than the great forest to the south. Many years of harvesting trees for lumber had given the green glades a sunlit airiness not found in the deep haunts of the southern forest. The keep boys had often played here over the years. With small imagination, the woods were transformed into a wondrous place, a green world of high adventure. Some of the greatest deeds known had taken place here. Daring escapes, dread quests, and mightily contested battles had been witnessed by the silent trees as the boys gave vent to their youthful dreams of coming manhood. Foul creatures, mighty monsters, and base outlaws had all been fought and vanquished, often accompanied by the death of a great hero, with appropriate last words to his mourning companions, all managed with just enough time left to return to the keep for supper.

Tomas reached a small rise that overlooked the pool, screened off by young beech saplings, and pulled aside some brush so they could mount a vigil. He stopped, awed, and softly said, "Pug, look!" Standing at the edge of the pool was a stag, head held high as he sought the source of something that disturbed his drinking. He was an old animal, the hair around his muzzle nearly all white, and his head crowned by magnificent antlers.

Pug counted quickly. "He has fourteen points."

Tomas nodded agreement. "He must be the oldest buck in the forest." The stag turned his attention in the boys' direction, flicking an ear nervously. They froze, not wishing to frighten off such a beautiful creature. For a long, silent minute the stag studied the rise, nostrils flaring, then slowly lowered his head to the pool and drank.

Tomas gripped Pug's shoulder and inclined his head to one side. Pug followed Tomas's motion and saw a figure walking silently into the clearing. He was a tall man dressed in leather clothing, dyed forest green. Across his back hung a longbow and at his belt a hunter's knife. His green cloak's hood was thrown back, and he walked toward the stag with a steady, even step. Tomas said, "It's Martin."

Pug also recognized the Duke's Huntmaster. An orphan like Pug, Martin had come to be known as Longbow by those in the castle, as he had few equals with that weapon. Something of a mystery, Martin Longbow was still well liked by the boys, for while he was aloof with the adults in the castle, he was always friendly and accessible to the boys. As Huntmaster, he was also the Duke's Forester. His duties absented him from the castle for days, even weeks at a time, as he kept his trackers busy looking for signs of poaching, possible fire dangers, migrating goblins, or outlaws camping in the woods. But when he was in the castle, and not organizing a hunt for the Duke, he always had time for the boys. His dark eyes were always merry when they pestered him with questions of woodlore or for tales of the lands near the boundaries of Crydee. He seemed to possess unending patience, which set him apart from most of the Craftmasters in the town and keep.

Martin came up to the stag, gently reached out, and touched his neck. The great head swung up, and the stag nuzzled Martin's arm. Softly Martin said, "If you walk out slowly, without speaking, he might let you approach."

Pug and Tomas exchanged startled glances, then stepped into the clearing. They walked slowly around the edge of the pool, the stag following their movements with his head, trembling slightly. Martin patted him reassuringly and he quieted. Tomas and Pug came to stand beside the hunter, and Martin said, "Reach out and touch him, slowly so as not to frighten him."

Tomas reached out first, and the stag trembled beneath his fingers. Pug began to reach out, and the stag retreated a step. Martin crooned to the stag in a language Pug had never heard before, and the animal stood still. Pug touched him and marveled at the feel of his coat—so like the cured hides he had touched before, yet so different for the feel of life pulsing under his fingertips.

Suddenly the stag backed off and turned. Then, with a single bounding leap, he was gone among the trees. Martin Longbow chuckled and said, "Just as well. It wouldn't do to have him become too friendly with men. Those antlers would quickly end up over some poacher's fireplace."

Tomas whispered, "He's beautiful, Martin."

Longbow nodded, his eyes still fastened upon the spot where the stag had vanished into the woods. "That he is, Tomas."

Pug said, "I thought you hunted stags, Martin. How—"

Martin said, "Old Whitebeard and I have something of an understanding, Pug. I hunt only bachelor stags, without does, or does too old to calve. When Whitebeard loses his harem to some younger buck someday, I may take him. Now each leaves the other to his own way. The day will come when I will look at him down the shaft of an arrow." He smiled at the boys. "I won't know until then if I shall let the shaft fly. Perhaps I will, perhaps not." He fell silent for a time, as if the thought of Whitebeard's becoming old was saddening, then as a light breeze rustled the branches said, "Now, what brings two such bold hunters into the Duke's woods in the early morning? There must be a thousand things left undone with the Midsummer festival this afternoon."

Tomas answered. "My mother tossed us out of the kitchen. We were more trouble than not. With the Choosing today . . ." His voice died away, and he felt suddenly embarrassed. Much of Martin's mysterious reputation stemmed from when he first came to Crydee. At his time for the Choosing, he had been placed directly with the old Huntmaster by the Duke, rather than standing before the assembled Craftmasters with the other boys his age. This violation of one of the oldest traditions known had offended many people in town, though none would dare openly express such feelings to Lord Borric. As was natural, Martin became the object of their ire, rather than the Duke. Over the years Martin had more than justified Lord Borric's decision, but still most people were troubled by the Duke's special treatment of him that one day. Even after twelve years some people still regarded Martin Longbow as being different and, as such, worthy of distrust.

Tomas said, "I'm sorry, Martin."

Martin nodded in acknowledgment, but without humor. "I understand, Tomas. I may not have had to endure your uncertainty, but I have seen many others wait for the day of Choosing. And for four years I myself have stood with the other Masters, so I know a little of your worry."

A thought struck Pug and he blurted, "But you're not with the other Craftmasters."

Martin shook his head, a rueful expression playing across his even features. "I had thought that, in light of your worry, you might fail to observe the obvious. But you've a sharp wit about you, Pug."

Tomas didn't understand what they were saying for a moment, then comprehension dawned. "Then you'll select no apprentices!"

Martin raised a finger to his lips. "Not a word, lad. No, with young Garret chosen last year, I've a full company of trackers."

Tomas was disappointed. He wished more than anything to take service with Swordmaster Fannon, but should he not be chosen as a soldier, then he would prefer the life of a forester, under Martin. Now his second choice was denied him. After a moment of dark brooding, he brightened: perhaps Martin didn't choose him because Fannon already had.

Seeing his friend entering a cycle of elation and depression as he considered all the possibilities, Pug said, "You haven't been in the keep for nearly a month, Martin." He put away the sling he still held and asked, "Where have you kept yourself?"

Martin looked at Pug as the boy instantly regretted his question. As friendly as Martin could be, he was still Huntmaster, a member of the Duke's household, and keep boys did not make a habit of questioning the comings and goings of the Duke's staff.

Martin relieved Pug's embarrassment with a slight smile. "I've been to Elvandar. Queen Aglaranna has ended her twenty years of mourning the death of her husband, the Elf King. There was a great celebration."

Pug was surprised by the answer. To him, as to most people in Crydee, the elves were little more than legend. But Martin had spent his youth near the elven forests and was one of the few humans to come and go through those forests to the north at will. It was another thing that set Martin Longbow apart from others. While Martin had shared elvish lore with the boys before, this was the first time in Pug's memory he had spoken of his relationship to the elves. Pug stammered, "You feasted with the Elf Queen?"

Martin assumed a pose of modest inconsequence. "Well, I sat at the table farthest from the throne, but yes; I was there." Seeing the unasked questions in their eyes, he continued. "You know as a boy I was raised by the monks of Silban's Abbey, near the elven forest. I played with elven children, and before I came here, I hunted with Prince Calin and his cousin, Galain."

Tomas nearly jumped with excitement. Elves were a subject holding particular fascination for him. "Did you know King Aidan?"

Martin's expression clouded, and his eyes narrowed, his manner suddenly becoming stiff. Tomas saw Martin's reaction and said, "I'm sorry, Martin. Did I say something wrong?"

Martin waved away the apology. "No fault of yours, Tomas," he said, his manner softening somewhat. "The elves do not use the names of those who have gone to the Blessed Isles, especially those who have died untimely. They believe to do so recalls those spoken of from their journey there, denying them their final rest. I respect their beliefs.

"Well, to answer you, no, I never met him. He

was killed when I was only a small boy. But I have heard the stories of his deeds, and he was a good and wise King by all accounts." Martin looked about. "It approaches noon. We should return to the keep."

He began to walk toward the path, and the boys fell in beside him.

"What was the feast like, Martin?" asked Tomas.

Pug sighed as the hunter began to speak of the marvels of Elvandar. He was also fascinated by tales of the elves, but to nowhere near the degree Tomas was. Tomas could endure hours of tales of the people of the elven forests, regardless of the speaker's credibility. At least, Pug considered, in the Huntmaster they had a dependable eyewitness. Martin's voice droned on, and Pug's attention wandered, as he again found himself pondering the Choosing. No matter that he told himself worry was useless: he worried. He found he was facing the approaching of this afternoon with something akin to dread.

THE BOYS STOOD in the courtyard. It was Midsummer, the day that ended one year and marked the beginning of another. Today everyone in the castle would be counted one year older. For the milling boys this was significant, for today was the last day of their boyhood. Today was the Choosing.

Pug tugged at the collar of his new tunic. It wasn't really new, being one of Tomas's old ones, but it was the newest Pug had ever owned. Magya, Tomas's mother, had taken it in for the smaller boy, to ensure he was presentable before the Duke and his court. Magya and her husband, Megar the cook, were as close to being parents to the orphan as anyone in the keep. They tended his ills, saw that he was fed, and boxed his ears when he deserved it. They also loved him as if he were Tomas's brother.

Pug looked around. The other boys all wore their best, for this was one of the most important days of their young lives. Each would stand before the assembled Craftmasters and members of the Duke's staff, and each would be considered for an apprentice's post. It was a ritual, its origins lost in time, for the choices had already been made. The crafters and the Duke's staff had spent many hours discussing each boy's merits with one another and knew which boys they would call.

The practice of having the boys between eight and thirteen years of age work in the crafts and services had proved a wise course over the years in fitting the best suited to each craft. In addition, it provided a pool of semiskilled individuals for the other crafts should the need arise. The drawback to the system was that certain boys were not chosen for a craft or staff position. Occasionally there would be too many boys for a single position, or no lad judged fit even though there was an opening. Even when the number of boys and openings seemed well matched, as it did this year, there were no guarantees. For those who stood in doubt, it was an anxious time.

Pug scuffed his bare feet absently in the dust. Unlike Tomas, who seemed to do well at anything he tried, Pug was often guilty of trying too hard and bungling his tasks. He looked around and noticed that a few of the other boys also showed signs of tension. Some were joking roughly, pretending no concern over whether they were chosen or not. Others stood like Pug, lost in their thoughts, trying not to dwell on what they would do should they not be chosen.

If he was not chosen, Pug—like the others—would be free to leave Crydee to try to find a craft in another town or city. If he stayed, he would have to either farm the Duke's land as a franklin, or work one of the town's fishing boats. Both prospects were equally unattractive, but he couldn't imagine leaving Crydee.

Pug remembered what Megar had told him, the night before. The old cook had cautioned him about fretting too much over the Choosing. After all, he had pointed out, there were many apprentices who never advanced to the rank of journeyman, and when all things were taken into account, there were more men without craft in Crydee than with. Megar had glossed over the fact that many fishers' and farmers' sons forsook the Choosing, electing to follow their fathers. Pug wondered if Megar was so removed from his own Choosing he couldn't remember that the boys who were not chosen would stand before the assembled company of Craftmasters, householders, and newly chosen apprentices, under their gaze until the last name was called and they were dismissed in shame.

Biting his lower lip, Pug tried to hide his nervousness. He was not the sort to jump from the heights of Sailor's Grief should he not be chosen, as some had done in the past, but he couldn't bear the idea of facing those who had been chosen.

Tomas, who stood next to his shorter friend, threw Pug a smile. He knew Pug was fretting, but could not feel entirely sympathetic as his own excitement mounted. His father had admitted that he would be the first called by Swordmaster Fannon. Moreover, the Swordmaster had confided that should Tomas do well in training, he might be found a place in the Duke's personal guard. It would be a signal honor and would improve Tomas's chance for advancement, even earning him an officer's rank after fifteen or twenty years in the guard.

He poked Pug in the ribs with an elbow, for the Duke's herald had come out upon the balcony overlooking the courtyard. The herald signaled to a guard, who opened the small door in the great gate, and the Craftmasters entered. They crossed to stand at the foot of the broad stairs of the keep. As was traditional, they stood with their backs to the boys, waiting upon the Duke.

The large oaken doors of the keep began to swing out ponderously, and several guards in the Duke's brown and gold darted through to take up their positions on the steps. Upon each tabard was emblazoned the golden gull of Crydee, and above that a small golden crown, marking the Duke a member of the royal family.

The herald shouted, "Hearken to me! His Grace, Borric conDoin, third Duke of Crydee, Prince of the Kingdom; Lord of Crydee, Carse, and Tulan; Warden of the West; Knight-General of the King's Armies; heir presumptive to the throne of Rillanon." The Duke stood patiently while the list of offices was completed, then stepped forward into the sunlight.

Past fifty, the Duke of Crydee still moved with the fluid grace and powerful step of a born warrior. Except for the grey at the temples of his dark brown hair, he looked younger than his age by twenty years. He was dressed from neck to boot in black, as he had been for the last seven years, for he still mourned the loss of his beloved wife, Catherine. At his side hung a black-scabbarded sword with a silver hilt, and upon his hand his ducal signet ring, the only ornamentation he permitted himself.

The herald raised his voice. "Their Royal Highnesses, the Princes Lyam conDoin and Arutha conDoin, heirs to the House of Crydee; Knight-Captains of the King's Army of the West; Princes of the royal house of Rillanon."

Both sons stepped forward to stand behind their father. The two young men were six and four years older than the apprentices, the Duke having wed late, but the difference between the awkward candidates for apprenticeship and the sons of the Duke was much more than a few years in age. Both Princes appeared calm and self-possessed.

Lyam, the older, stood on his father's right, a blond, powerfully built man. His open smile was the image of his mother's, and he looked always on the verge of laughter. He was dressed in a bright blue tunic and yellow leggings and wore a closely trimmed beard, as blond as his shoulder-length hair.

Arutha was to shadows and night as Lyam was to light and day. He stood nearly as tall as his brother and father, but while they were powerfully built, he was rangy to the point of gauntness. He wore a brown tunic and russet leggings. His hair was dark and his face clean-shaven. Everything about Arutha gave one the feeling of quickness. His strength was in his speed: speed with the rapier, speed with wit. His humor was dry and often sharp. While Lyam was openly loved by the Duke's subjects, Arutha was respected and admired for his ability, but not regarded with warmth by the people.

Together the two sons seemed to capture most of the complex nature of their sire, for the Duke was capable of both Lyam's robust humor and Arutha's dark moods. They were nearly opposites in temperament, but both capable men who would benefit the Duchy and Kingdom in years to come. The Duke loved both his sons.

The herald again spoke. "The Princess Carline, daughter of the royal house."

The slim and graceful girl who made her entrance was the same age as the boys who stood below, but already beginning to show the poise and grace of one born to rule and the beauty of her late mother. Her soft yellow gown contrasted strikingly with her nearly black hair. Her eyes were Lyam's blue, as their mother's had been, and Lyam beamed when his sister took their father's arm. Even Arutha ventured one of his rare half smiles, for his sister was dear to him also.

Many boys in the keep harbored a secret love for the Princess, a fact she often turned to her advantage when there was mischief afoot. But even her presence could not drive the day's business from their minds.

The Duke's court then entered. Pug and Tomas could see that all the members of the Duke's staff were present, including Kulgan. Pug had glimpsed him in the castle from time to time since the night of the storm, and they had exchanged words once, Kulgan inquiring as to his well-being, but mostly the magician was absent from sight. Pug was a little surprised to see the magician, for he was not properly considered a full member of the Duke's household, but rather a sometime adviser. Most of the time Kulgan was ensconced in his tower, hidden from view as he did whatever magicians do in such places.

The magician was deep in conversation with Father Tully, a priest of Astalon the Builder and one of the Duke's oldest aides. Tully had been adviser to the Duke's father and had seemed old then. He now appeared ancient—at least to Pug's youthful perspective —but his eyes betrayed no sign of senility. Many a keep boy had been impaled upon the pointed gaze of those clear grey eyes. His wit and tongue were equally youthful, and more than once a keep boy had wished for a session with Horsemaster Algon's leather strap rather than a tongue-lashing from Father Tully. The white-haired priest could nearly strip the skin from a miscreant's back with his caustic words.

Nearby stood one who had experienced Tully's wrath upon occasion, Squire Roland, son of Baron

Tolburt of Tulan, one of the Duke's vassals. He was companion to both Princes, being the only other boy of noble birth in the keep. His father had sent him to Crydee the year before, to learn something of the management of the Duchy and the ways of the Duke's court. In the rather rough frontier court Roland discovered a home away from home. He was already something of a rogue when he arrived, but his infectious sense of humor and ready wit often eased much of the anger that resulted from his prankish ways. It was Roland, more often than not, who was Princess Carline's accomplice in whatever mischief she was embarked upon. With light brown hair and blue eyes, Roland stood tall for his age. He was a year older than the gathered boys and had played often with them over the last year, as Lyam and Arutha were frequently busy with court duties. Tomas and he had been boyish rivals at first, then fast friends, with Pug becoming his friend by default, because where Tomas was, Pug was certain to be nearby. Roland saw Pug fidgeting near the edge of the assembled boys and gave him a slight nod and wink. Pug grinned briefly, for while he was as often the butt of Roland's jokes as any other, he still found himself liking the wild young Squire.

After all his court was in attendance, the Duke spoke. "Yesterday was the last day of the eleventh year of the reign of our Lord King, Rodric the Fourth. Today is the Festival of Banapis. The following day will find these boys gathered here counted among the men of Crydee, boys no longer, but apprentices and freemen. At this time it is proper for me to inquire if any among you wishes to be released from service to the Duchy. Are there any among you who so wish?" The question was formal in nature and no response was expected, for few ever wished to leave Crydee. But one boy did step forward.

The herald asked, "Who seeks release of his service?"

The boy looked down, clearly nervous. Clearing his throat, he said, "I am Robert, son of Hugen." Pug knew him, but not well. He was a netmender's son, a town boy, and they rarely mixed with the keep boys. Pug had played with him upon a few occasions and had a sense the lad was well regarded. It was a rare thing to refuse service, and Pug was as curious as any to hear the reasons.

The Duke spoke kindly. "What is your purpose, Robert, son of Hugen?"

"Your grace, my father is unable to take me into his craft, for my four brothers are well able to ascend to the craft as journeymen and masters after him, as are many other netmender's sons. My eldest brother is now married and has a son of his own, so my family no longer has room for me in the house. If I may not stay with my family and practice my father's craft, I beg your grace's leave to take service as a sailor."

The Duke considered the matter. Robert was not the first village boy to be called by the lure of the sea. "Have you found a master willing to take you into his company?"

"Yes, Your Grace. Captain Gregson, master of the ship *Green Deep* from Margrave's Port is willing."

"I know this man," said the Duke. Smiling slightly he said, "He is a good and fair man. I recommend you into his service and wish you well in your travels. You will be welcomed at Crydee whenever you return with your ship."

Robert bowed, a little stiffly, and left the courtyard, his part in the Choosing done. Pug wondered at Robert's adventuresome choice. In less than a minute the boy had renounced his ties with his family and home and was now a citizen of a city he had never seen.

It was custom that a sailor was considered to owe his loyalty to the city that was his ship's home port. Margrave's Port was one of the Free Cities of Natal, on the Bitter Sea, and was now Robert's home.

The Duke indicated the herald should continue.

The herald announced the first of the Craftmasters, Sailmaker Holm, who called the names of three boys. All three took service, and none seemed displeased. The Choosing went smoothly, as no boy refused service. Each boy went to stand next to his new master.

As the afternoon wore on and the number of boys diminished, Pug became more and more uncomfortable. Soon there were only two boys besides Pug and Tomas standing in the center of the court. All the Craftmasters had called their apprentices, and only two of the Duke's household staff beside the Swordmaster had not been heard from. Pug studied the group on the top of the steps, his heart pounding with anxiety. The two Princes regarded the boys, Lyam with a friendly smile, Arutha brooding on some thought or another. The Princess Carline was bored by the entire affair and took little pains to hide the fact, as she was whispering to Roland. This brought a disapproving look from Lady Marna, her governess.

Horsemaster Algon came forth, his brown-and-golden tabard bearing a small horsehead embroidered over his left breast. The Horsemaster called the name of Rulf, son of Dick, and the stocky son of the Duke's stableman walked over to stand behind the master. When he turned, he smiled condescendingly at Pug. The two boys had never gotten along, the pock-scarred boy spending many hours taunting and tormenting Pug. While they both worked in the stable under Dick, the stableman had looked the other way whenever his son sprang a trap on Pug, and the orphan was always held responsible for any difficulty that arose. It had been a terrible period for Pug, and the boy had vowed to refuse service rather than face the prospect of working next to Rulf the rest of his life.

Housecarl Samuel called the other boy, Geoffry, who would become a member of the castle's serving staff, leaving Pug and Tomas standing alone. Swordmaster Fannon then stepped forward, and Pug felt his heart stand still as the old soldier called, "Tomas, son of Megar."

There was a pause, and Pug waited to hear his own name called, but Fannon stepped back and Tomas crossed over to stand alongside him. Pug felt dwarfed by the gaze of all upon him. The courtyard was now larger than he had ever remembered it, and he felt ill fashioned and poorly dressed. His heart sank in his chest as he realized that there was no Craftmaster or staff member present who had not taken an apprentice. He would be the only boy uncalled. Fighting back tears, he waited for the Duke to dismiss the company.

As the Duke started to speak, sympathy for the boy showing clearly in his face, he was interrupted by another voice. "Your Grace, if you would be so kind."

All eyes turned to see Kulgan the magician step forward. "I have need of an apprentice and would call Pug, orphan of the keep, to service."

A wave of murmuring swept through the assembled Craftmasters. A few voices could be heard saying it wasn't proper for a magician to participate in the Choosing. The Duke silenced them with a sweep of his gaze, his face stern. No Craftmaster would challenge the Duke of Crydee, the third-ranking noble in the Kingdom, over the standing of one boy. Slowly all eyes returned to regard the boy.

The Duke said, "As Kulgan is a recognized master of his craft, it is his right to choose. Pug, orphan of the keep, will you take service?" Pug stood rigid. He had imagined himself leading the King's army into battle as a Knight-Lieutenant, or discovering someday he was the lost son of nobility. In his boyish imaginings he had sailed ships, hunted great monsters, and saved the nation. In quieter moments of reflection he had wondered if he would spend his life building ships, making pottery, or learning the trader's skill, and speculated on how well he would do in each of those crafts. But the one thing he never thought of, the one dream that had never captured his fantasies, was that of becoming a magician.

He snapped out of his shocked state, aware the Duke patiently awaited his response. He looked at the faces of those before him. Father Tully gave him one of his rare smiles, as did Prince Arutha. Prince Lyam nodded a slight yes, and Kulgan regarded him intently. There were signs of worry upon the magician's face, and suddenly Pug decided. It might not be an entirely proper calling, but any craft was better than none. He stepped forward and caught his own heel with his other foot, and landed face down in the dust. Picking himself up, he half scrambled, half ran to the magician's side. The misstep broke the tension, and the Duke's booming laughter filled the courtyard. Flushing with embarrassment, Pug stood behind Kulgan. He looked around the broad girth of his new master and found the Duke watching, his expression tempered by a kind nod at the blushing Pug. The Duke turned back to those who stood waiting for the Choosing to end.

"I declare that each boy present is now the charge of his master, to obey him in all matters within the laws of the Kingdom, and each shall be judged a true and proper man of Crydee. Let the apprentices attend their masters. Until the feasting, I bid you all good day." He turned and presented his left arm to his daughter. She placed her hand lightly upon it and they passed into the keep between the ranks of the courtiers, who drew aside. The two Princes followed, and the others of the court. Pug saw Tomas leave in the direction of the guard barracks, behind Master Fannon.

He turned his attention back to Kulgan, who was standing lost in thought. After a moment the magician said, "I trust neither of us has made a mistake this day."

"Sir?" Pug asked, not understanding the magician's meaning. Kulgan waved one hand absently, causing his pale yellow robe to move like waves rippling over the sea. "It is no matter, boy. What's done is done. Let us make the best of things."

He placed his hand on the boy's shoulder. "Come, let us retire to the tower where I reside. There is a small room below my own that should do for you. I had intended it for some project or another, but have never managed to find the time to prepare it."

Pug stood in awe. "A room of my own?" Such a thing for an apprentice was unheard of. Most apprentices slept in the workrooms of their master, or protected herds, or the like. Only when an apprentice became a journeyman was it usual for him to take private quarters.

Kulgan arched one bushy eyebrow. "Of course. Can't have you underfoot all the time. I would never get anything done. Besides, magic requires solitude for contemplation. You will need to be untroubled as much as or perhaps more than I will." He took out his long, thin pipe from a fold of his robe and started to stuff it full of tabac from a pouch that had also come from within the robe.

"Let's not bother with too much discussion of duties and such, boy. For in truth, I am not prepared for you. But in short order I will have things well in hand. Until then we can use the time by becoming acquainted with one another. Agreed?" Pug was startled. He had little notion of what a magician was about, in spite of the night spent with Kulgan weeks ago, but he readily knew what Craftmasters were like, and none would have thought to inquire whether or not an apprentice agreed with his plans. Not knowing what to say, Pug just nodded.

"Good, then," said Kulgan, "let us be off to the tower to find you some new clothes, and then we will spend the balance of the day feasting. Later there will be ample time to learn how to be master and apprentice." With a smile for the boy, the stout magician turned Pug around and led him away.

THE LATE AFTERNOON was clear and bright, with a gentle breeze from the sea cooling the summer heat. Throughout the keep of Castle Crydee, and the town below, preparations for the Festival of Banapis were in progress.

Banapis was the oldest known holiday, its origins lost in antiquity. It was held each Midsummer's Day, a day belonging to neither the past nor the coming year. Banapis, known by other names in other nations, was celebrated over the entire world of Midkemia according to legend. It was believed by some that the festival was borrowed from the elves and dwarves, for the long-lived races were said to have celebrated the feast of Midsummer as far back as the memory of both races could recall. Most authorities disputed this allegation, citing no reason other than the unlikelihood of humans borrowing anything from the elven or dwarven folk. It was rumored that even the denizens of the Northlands, the goblin tribes and the clans of the Brotherhood of the Dark Path, celebrated Banapis, though no one had ever reported seeing such a celebration.

The courtyard was busy. Huge tables had been erected to hold the myriad varieties of foods that had been in preparation for over a week. Giant barrels of dwarven ale, imported from Stone Mountain, had been hauled out of the cellars and were resting on protesting, overburdened wood frames. The workmen, alarmed at the fragile appearance of the barrel ricks, were quickly emptying some of the contents. Megar came out of the kitchen and angrily shooed them away. "Leave off, there will be none left for the evening meal at this rate! Back to the kitchen, dolts! There is much work to be done yet."

The workers went off, grumbling, and Megar filled a tankard to ensure the ale was at proper temperature. After he drained it dry and satisfied himself that all was as it should be, he returned to the kitchen.

There was no formal beginning to the feast. Traditionally, people and food, wine and ale, all accumulated until they reached a certain density, then all at once the festivities would be in full swing.

Pug ran from the kitchen. His room in the northmost tower, the magician's tower as it had become known, provided him with a shortcut through the kitchen, which he used rather than the main doors of the keep. He beamed as he sped across the courtyard in his new tunic and trousers. He had never worn such finery and was in a hurry to show his friend Tomas.

He found Tomas leaving the soldiers' commons, nearly as much in a hurry as Pug. When the two met, they both spoke at once.

"Look at the new tunic—" said Pug.

"Look at my soldier's tabard—" said Tomas.

Both stopped and broke into laughter.

Tomas regained his composure first. "Those are very fine clothes, Pug," he said, fingering the expensive material of Pug's red tunic. "And the color suits you."

Pug returned the compliment, for Tomas did cut a striking figure in his brown-and-gold tabard. It was of little consequence that he wore his regular homespun tunic and trouser underneath. He would not receive a soldier's uniform until Master Fannon was satisfied with his worthiness as a man-at-arms.

The two friends wandered from one heavily laden table to another. Pug's mouth watered from the rich fragrances in the air. They came to a table heaped with meat pies, steam rising from their hot crusts, pungent cheeses, and hot bread. At the table a young kitchen boy was stationed with a shoo-fly. His job was to keep pests from the food, whether of the insect variety or the chronically hungry apprentice variety. Like most other situations involving boys, the relationship between this guardian of the feast and the older apprentices was closely bound by tradition. It was considered ill-mannered and in poor taste merely to threaten or bully the smaller boy into parting with food before the start of the feast. But it was considered fair to use guile, stealth, or speed in gaining a prize from the table.

Pug and Tomas observed with interest as the boy, named Jon, delivered a wicked whack to the hand of one young apprentice seeking to snag a large pie. With a nod of his head, Tomas sent Pug to the far side of the table. Pug ambled across Jon's field of vision, and the boy watched him carefully. Pug moved abruptly, a feint toward the table, and Jon leaned in his direction. Then suddenly Tomas snatched a puff-pastry from the table and was gone before the shoo-fly lash began to descend. As they ran from the table, Pug and Tomas could hear the distressed cries of the boy whose table they had plundered.

Tomas gave Pug half the pie when they were safely away, and the smaller apprentice laughed. "You're the quickest hand in the castle, I bet."

"Or young Jon was slow of eye for keeping it on you."

They shared a laugh. Pug popped his half of the pie into his mouth. It was delicately seasoned, and the contrast between the salty pork filling and the sweet puff-pastry crust was delicious.

The sound of pipes and drums came from the side courtyard as the Duke's musicians approached the main courtyard. By the time they had emerged around the keep, a silent message seemed to pass through the crowd. Suddenly the kitchen boys were busy handing out wooden platters for the celebrants to heap food upon, and mugs of ale and wine were being drawn from the barrels.

The boys dashed to a place in line at the first table. Pug and Tomas used their size and quickness to good advantage, darting through the throng, snagging food of every description and a large mug of foamy ale each.

They found a relatively quiet corner and fell to with ravenous hunger. Pug tasted his first drink of ale and was surprised at the robust, slightly bitter taste. It seemed to warm him as it went down, and after another experimental taste he decided that he liked it.

Pug could see the Duke and his family mingling with the common folk. Other members of his court could also be seen standing in line before the tables. There was no ceremony, ritual, or rank observed this afternoon. Each was served as he arrived, for Midsummer's Day was the time when all would equally share in the bounties of the harvest.

Pug caught a glimpse of the Princess and felt his chest tighten a little. She looked radiant as many of the boys in the courtyard complimented her on her appearance. She wore a lovely gown of deep blue and a simple, broad-brimmed hat of the same color. She thanked each author of a flattering remark and used her dark eyelashes and bright smile to good advantage, leaving a wake of infatuated boys behind.

Jugglers and clowns made their appearance in the courtyard, the first of many groups of traveling performers who were in the town for the festival. The actors of another company had set up a stage in the town square and would give a performance in the evening. Until the early hours of the next morning the festivities would continue. Pug knew that many of the boys the year before had to be excused duty the day following Banapis, for their heads and stomachs were in no condition for honest work. He was sure that scene would be repeated tomorrow.

Pug looked forward to the evening, for it was the custom for new apprentices to visit many of the houses in the town, receiving congratulations and mugs of ale. It was also a ripe time for meeting the town girls. While dalliance was not unknown, it was frowned upon. But mothers tended to be less vigilant during Banapis. Now that the boys had crafts, they were viewed less as bothersome pests and more as potential sons-in-law, and there had been more than one case of a mother looking the other way while a daughter used her natural gifts to snare a young husband. Pug, being of small stature and youthful appearance, got little notice from the girls of the keep. Tomas, however, was more and more the object of girlish flirtation as he grew in size and good looks, and lately Pug had begun to be aware that his friend was being sized up by one or another of the castle girls. Pug was still young enough to think the whole thing silly, but old enough to be fascinated by it.

Pug chewed an improbable mouthful and looked around. People from the town and keep passed, offering congratulations on the boys' apprenticeship and wishing them a good new year. Pug felt a deep sense of rightness about everything. He was an apprentice, even if Kulgan seemed completely unsure of what to do with him. He was well fed, and on his way to being slightly intoxicated—which contributed to his sense of well-being. And, most important, he was among friends. There can't be much more to life than this, he thought.

3

Keep

P̶ug sat sulking on his sleeping pallet.

Fantus the firedrake pushed his head forward, inviting Pug to scratch him behind his eye ridges. Seeing that he would get little satisfaction, the drake made his way to the tower window and with a snort of displeasure, complete with a small puff of black smoke, launched himself in flight. Pug didn't notice the creature's leaving, so engrossed was he in his own world of troubles. Since he had taken on the position of Kulgan's apprentice fourteen months ago, everything he had done seemed to go wrong.

He lay back on the pallet, covering his eyes with a forearm; he could smell the salty sea breeze that blew in through his window and feel the sun's warmth across his legs. Everything in his life had taken a turn for the better since his apprenticeship, except the single most important thing, his studies.

For months Kulgan had been laboring to teach him the fundamentals of the magician's arts, but there was always something that caused his efforts to go awry. In the theories of spell casting, Pug was a quick study, grasping the basic concepts well. But each time he attempted to use his knowledge, something seemed to hold him back. It was as if a part of his mind refused to follow through with the magic, as if a block existed that prevented him from passing a certain point in the spell. Each time he tried he could feel himself approach that point, and like a rider of a balky horse, he couldn't seem to force himself over the hurdle.

Kulgan dismissed his worries, saying that it would all sort itself out in time. The stout magician was always sympathetic with the boy, never reprimanding him for not doing better, for he knew the boy was trying.

Pug was brought out of his reverie by someone's opening the door. Looking up, he saw Father Tully entering, a large book under his arm. The cleric's white robes rustled as he closed the door. Pug sat up.

"Pug, it's time for your writing lesson—" He stopped himself when he saw the downcast expression of the boy. "What's the matter, lad?"

Pug had come to like the old priest of Astalon. He was a strict master, but a fair one. He would praise the boy for his success as often as scold him for his failures. He had a quick mind and a sense of humor and was open to questions, no matter how stupid Pug thought they might sound.

Coming to his feet, Pug sighed. "I don't know, Father. It's just that things don't seem to be going right. Everything I try I manage to make a mess of."

"Pug, it can't be all black," the priest said, placing a hand on Pug's shoulder. "Why don't you tell me what is troubling you, and we can practice writing some other time." He moved to a stool by the window and adjusted his robes around him as he sat. As he placed the large book at his feet, he studied the boy.

Pug had grown over the last year, but was still small. His shoulders were beginning to broaden a bit, and his face was showing signs of the man he would someday be. He was a dejected figure in his homespun tunic and trousers, his mood as grey as the material he wore. His room, which was usually neat and orderly, was a mess of scrolls and books, reflecting the disorder in his mind.

Pug sat quietly for a moment, but when the priest said nothing, started to speak. "Do you remember my telling you that Kulgan was trying to teach me the three basic cantrips to calm the mind, so that the working of spells could be practiced without stress? Well, the truth is that I mastered those exercises months ago. I can bring my mind to a state of calm in moments now, with little effort. But that is as far as it goes. After that, everything seems to fall apart."

"What do you mean?"

"The next thing to learn is to discipline the mind to do things that are not natural for it, such as think on one thing to the exclusion of everything else, or not to think of something, which is quite hard once you've been told what it is. I can do those things most of the time, but now and again I feel like there are some forces inside my head, crashing about, demanding that I do things in a different way. It's like there was something else happening in my head than what Kulgan told me to expect.

"Each time I try one of the simple spells Kulgan has taught me, like making an object move, or lifting myself off the ground, these things in my head come flooding in on my concentration, and I lose my control. I can't even master the simplest spell." Pug felt himself tremble, for this was the first chance he had had to speak about this to anyone besides Kulgan. "Kulgan simply says to keep at it and not worry." Nearing tears, he continued. "I have talent. Kulgan said he knew it from the first time we met, when I used the crystal. You've told me that I have talent. But I just can't make the spells work the way they're supposed to. I get so confused by it all."

"Pug," said the priest, "magic has many properties, and we understand little of how it works, even those of us who practice it. In the temples we are taught that magic is a gift from the gods, and we accept that on faith. We do not understand how this can be so, but we do not question. Each order has its own province of magic, with no two quite alike. I am capable of magic that those who follow their orders are not. But none can say why.

"Magicians deal in a different sort of magic, and their practices are very different from our practices in the temples. Much of what they do, we cannot. It is they who study the art of magic, seeking its nature and workings, but even they cannot explain how magic works. They only know how to work it, and pass that knowledge along to their students, as Kulgan is doing with you."

"Trying to do with me, Father. I think he may have misjudged me."

"I think not, Pug. I have some knowledge of these things, and since you have become Kulgan's pupil, I have felt the power growing in you. Perhaps you will come to it late, as others have, but I am sure you will find the proper path."

Pug was not comforted. He didn't question the priest's wisdom or his opinion, but he did feel he could be mistaken. "I hope you're right, Father. I just don't understand what's wrong with me."

"I think I know what's wrong," came a voice from

the door. Startled, Pug and Father Tully turned to see Kulgan standing in the doorway. His blue eyes were set in lines of concern, and his thick grey brows formed a V over the bridge of his nose. Neither Pug nor Tully had heard the door open. Kulgan hiked his long green robe and stepped into the room, leaving the door open.

"Come here, Pug," said the magician with a small wave of his hand. Pug went over to the magician, who placed both hands on his shoulders. "Boys who sit in their rooms day after day worrying about why things don't work make things not work. I am giving you the day for yourself. As it is Sixthday, there should be plenty of other boys to help you in whatever sort of trouble boys can find." He smiled, and his pupil was filled with relief. "You need a rest from study. Now go." So saying, he fetched a playful cuff to the boy's head, sending him running down the stairs. Crossing over to the pallet, Kulgan lowered his heavy frame to it and looked at the priest. "Boys," said Kulgan, shaking his head. "You hold a festival, give them a badge of craft, and suddenly they expect to be men. But they're still boys, and no matter how hard they try, they still act like boys, not men." He took out his pipe and began filling it. "Magicians are considered young and inexperienced at thirty, but in all other crafts thirty would mark a man a journeyman or master, most likely readying his own son for the Choosing." He put a taper to the coals still smouldering in Pug's fire pot and lit his pipe.

Tully nodded. "I understand, Kulgan. The priesthood also is an old man's calling. At Pug's age I still had thirteen years of being an acolyte before me." The old priest leaned forward. "Kulgan, what of the boy's problem?"

"The boy's right, you know," Kulgan stated flatly. "There is no explanation for why he cannot perform the skills I've tried to teach. The things he can do with scrolls and devices amaze me. The boy has such gifts for these things, I would have wagered he had the makings of a magician of mighty arts. But this inability to use his inner powers . . ."

"Do you think you can find a solution?"

"I hope so. I would hate to have to release him from apprenticeship. It would go harder on him than had I never chosen him." His face showed his genuine concern. "It is confusing, Tully. I think you'll agree he has the potential for a great talent. As soon as I saw him use the crystal in my hut that night, I knew for the first time in years I might have at last found my apprentice. When no master chose him, I knew fate had set our paths to cross. But there is something else inside that boy's head, something I've never met before, something powerful. I don't know what it is, Tully, but it rejects my exercises, as if they were somehow . . . not correct, or . . . ill suited to him. I don't know if I can explain what I've encountered with Pug any better. There is no simple explanation for it."

"Have you thought about what the boy said?" asked the priest, a look of thoughtful concern on his face.

"You mean about my having been mistaken?"

Tully nodded. Kulgan dismissed the question with a wave of his hand. "Tully, you know as much about the nature of magic as I do, perhaps more. Your god is not called the God Who Brought Order for nothing. Your sect unraveled much about what orders this universe. Do you for one moment doubt the boy has talent?"

"Talent, no. But his ability is the question for the moment."

"Well put, as usual. Well, then, have you any

ideas? Should we make a cleric out of the boy, perhaps?"

Tully sat back, a disapproving expression upon his face. "You know the priesthood is a calling, Kulgan," he said stiffly.

"Put your back down, Tully. I was making a joke." He sighed. "Still, if he hasn't the calling of a priest, nor the knack of a magician's craft, what can we make of this natural ability of his?"

Tully pondered the question in silence for a moment, then said, "Have you thought of the lost art?"

Kulgan's eyes widened. "That old legend?" Tully nodded. "I doubt there is a magician alive who at one time or another hasn't reflected on the legend of the lost art. If it had existed, it would explain away many of the shortcomings of our craft." Then he fixed Tully with a narrowed eye, showing his disapproval. "But legends are common enough. Turn up any rock on the beach and you'll find one. I for one prefer to look for real answers to our shortcomings, not blame them on ancient superstitions."

Tully's expression became stern and his tone scolding. "We of the temple do not count it legend, Kulgan! It is considered part of the revealed truth, taught by the gods to the first men."

Nettled by Tully's tone, Kulgan snapped, "So was the notion the world was flat, until Rolendirk—a magician, I'll remind you—sent his magic sight high enough to disclose the curvature of the horizon, clearly demonstrating the world to be a sphere! It was a fact known by almost every sailor and fisherman who'd ever seen a sail appear upon the horizon before the rest of the ship since the beginning of time!" His voice rose to a near shout.

Seeing Tully was stung by the reference to ancient church canon long since abandoned, Kulgan softened his tone. "No disrespect to you, Tully. But don't try to teach an old thief to steal. I know your order chops logic with the best of them, and that half your brother clerics fall into laughing fits when they hear those deadly serious young acolytes debate theological issues set aside a century ago. Besides which, isn't the legend of the lost art an Ishapian dogma?"

Now it was Tully's turn to fix Kulgan with a disapproving eye. With a tone of amused exasperation, he said, "Your education in religion is still lacking, Kulgan, despite a somewhat unforgiving insight into the inner workings of my order." He smiled a little. "You're right about the moot gospel courts, though. Most of us find them so amusing because we remember how painfully grim we were about them when we were acolytes." Then turning serious, he said, "But I am serious when I say your education is lacking. The Ishapians have some strange beliefs, it's true, and they are an insular group, but they are also the oldest order known and are recognized as the senior church in questions pertaining to interdenominational differences."

"Religious wars, you mean," said Kulgan with an amused snort.

Tully ignored the comment. "The Ishapians are caretakers for the oldest lore and history in the Kingdom, and they have the most extensive library in the Kingdom. I have visited the library at their temple in Krondor, and it is most impressive."

Kulgan smiled and with a slight tone of condescension said, "As have I, Tully, and I have browsed the shelves at the Abbey of Sarth, which is ten times as large. What's the point?"

Leaning forward, Tully said, "The point is this: say what you will about the Ishapians, but when they put forth something as history, not lore, they can usually produce ancient tomes to support their claims."

"No," said Kulgan, waving aside Tully's comments with a dismissive wave. "I do not make light of your beliefs, or any other man's, but I cannot accept this nonsense about lost arts. I might be willing to believe Pug could be somehow more attuned to some aspect of magic I'm ignorant of, perhaps something involving spirit conjuration or illusion—areas I will happily admit I know little about—but I cannot accept that he will never learn to master his craft because the long-vanished god of magic died during the Chaos Wars! No, that there is unknown lore, I accept. There are too many shortcomings in our craft even to begin to think our understanding of magic is remotely complete. But if Pug can't learn magic, it is only because I have failed as a teacher."

Tully now glared at Kulgan, suddenly aware the magician was not pondering Pug's possible shortcomings but his own. "Now you are being foolish. You are a gifted man, and were I to have been the one to discover Pug's talent, I could not imagine a better teacher to place him with than yourself. But there can be no failing if you do not know what he needs to be taught." Kulgan began to sputter an objection, but Tully cut him off. "No, let me continue. What we lack is understanding. You seem to forget there have been others like Pug, wild talents who could not master their gifts, others who failed as priests and magicians."

Kulgan puffed on his pipe, his brow knitted in concentration. Suddenly he began to chuckle, then laugh. Tully looked sharply at the magician. Kulgan waved offhandedly with his pipe. "I was just struck by the thought that should a swineherd fail to teach his son the family calling, he could blame it upon the demise of the gods of pigs."

Tully's eyes went wide at the near-blasphemous thought, then he too laughed, a short bark. "That's one for the moot gospel courts!" Both men laughed a long, tension-releasing laugh at that. Tully sighed and stood up. "Still, do not close your mind entirely to what I've said, Kulgan. It may be Pug is one of those wild talents. And you may have to reconcile yourself for letting him go."

Kulgan shook his head sadly at the thought. "I refuse to believe there is any simple explanation for those other failures, Tully. Or for Pug's difficulties, as well. The fault was in each man or woman, not in the nature of the universe. I have often felt where we fail with Pug is in understanding how to reach him. Perhaps I would be well advised to seek another master for him, place him with one better able to harness his abilities."

Tully sighed. "I have spoken my mind of this question, Kulgan. Other than what I've said, I cannot advise you. Still, as they say, a poor master's better than no master at all. How would the boy have fared if no one had chosen to teach him?"

Kulgan bolted upright from his seat. "What did you say?"

"I said, how would the boy have fared if no one had chosen to teach him?"

Kulgan's eyes seemed to lose focus as he stared into space. He began puffing furiously upon his pipe. After watching for a moment, Tully said, "What is it, Kulgan?"

Kulgan said, "I'm not sure, Tully, but you may have given me an idea."

"What sort of idea?"

Kulgan waved off the question. "I'm not entirely sure. Give me time to ponder. But consider your question, and ask yourself this: how did the first magicians learn to use their power?"

Tully sat back down, and both men began to consider the question in silence. Through the window they could hear the sound of boys at play, filling the courtyard of the keep.

EVERY SIXTHDAY, THE boys and girls who worked in the castle were allowed to spend the afternoon as they saw fit. The boys, apprentice age and younger, were a loud and boisterous lot. The girls worked in the service of the ladies of the castle, cleaning and sewing, as well as helping in the kitchen. They all gave a full week's work, dawn to dusk and more, each day, but—on the sixth day of the week they gathered in the courtyard of the castle, near the Princess's garden. Most of the boys played a rough game of tag, involving the capture of a ball of leather, stuffed hard with rags, by one side, amid shoves and shouts, kicks and occasional fistfights. All wore their oldest clothes, for rips, bloodstains, and mudstains were common.

The girls would sit along the low wall by the Princess's garden, occupying themselves with gossip about the ladies of the Duke's court. They nearly always put on their best skirts and blouses, and their hair shone from washing and brushing. Both groups made a great display of ignoring each other, and both were equally unconvincing.

Pug ran to where the game was in progress. As was usual, Tomas was in the thick of the fray, sandy hair flying like a banner, shouting and laughing above the noise. Amid elbows and kicks he sounded savagely joyous, as if the incidental pain made the contest all the more worthwhile. He ran through the pack, kicking the ball high in the air, trying to avoid the feet of those who sought to trip him. No one was quite sure how the game had come into existence, or exactly what the rules were, but the boys played with battlefield intensity, as their fathers had years before.

Pug ran onto the field and placed a foot before Rulf just as he was about to hit Tomas from behind. Rulf went down in a tangle of bodies, and Tomas broke free. He ran toward the goal and, dropping the ball in front of himself, kicked it into a large overturned barrel, scoring for his side. While other boys yelled in celebration, Rulf leaped to his feet and pushed aside another boy to place himself directly in front of Pug. Glaring out from under thick brows, he spat at Pug, "Try that again and I'll break your legs, sand squint!" The sand squint was a bird of notoriously foul habits— not the least of which was leaving eggs in other birds' nests so that its offspring were raised by other birds. Pug was not about to let any insult of Rulf's pass unchallenged. With the frustrations of the last few months only a little below the surface, Pug was feeling particularly thin-skinned this day.

With a leap he flew at Rulf's head, throwing his left arm around the stockier boy's neck. He drove his right fist into Rulf's face and could feel Rulf's nose squash under the first blow. Quickly both boys were rolling on the ground. Rulf's greater weight began to tell, and soon he sat astride Pug's chest, driving his fat fists into the smaller boy's face.

Tomas stood by helpless, for as much as he wanted to aid his friend, the boys' code of honor was as strict and inviolate as any noble's. Should he intervene on his friend's behalf, Pug would never live down the shame. Tomas jumped up and down, urging Pug on, grimacing each time Pug was struck, as if he felt the blows himself.

Pug tried to squirm out from under the larger boy, causing many of his blows to slip by, striking dirt instead of Pug's face. Enough of them were hitting the mark, however, so that Pug soon began to feel a queer detachment from the whole procedure. He thought it strange that everybody sounded so far away, and that Rulf's blows seemed not to hurt. His vision was beginning to fill with red and yellow colors, when he felt the weight lifted from his chest.

After a brief moment things came into focus, and Pug saw Prince Arutha standing over him, his hand firmly grasping Rulf's collar. While not as powerful a figure as his brother or father, the Prince was still able to hold Rulf high enough so that the stableboy's toes barely touched the ground. The Prince smiled, but without humor. "I think the boy has had enough," he said quietly, eyes glaring. "Don't you agree?" His cold tone made it clear he wasn't asking for an opinion. Blood still ran down Rulf's face from Pug's initial blow as he choked out a sound the Prince took to mean agreement. Arutha let go of Rulf's collar, and the stableboy fell backward, to the laughter of the onlookers. The Prince reached down and helped Pug to his feet.

Holding the wobbly boy steady, Arutha said, "I admire your courage, youngster, but we can't have the wits beaten out of the Duchy's finest young magician, can we?" His tone was only slightly mocking, and Pug was too numb to do more than stand and stare at the younger son of the Duke. The Prince gave him a slight smile and handed him over to Tomas, who had come up next to Pug, a wet cloth in hand.

Pug came out of his fog as Tomas scrubbed his face with the cloth, and felt even worse when he saw the Princess and Roland standing only a few feet away as Prince Arutha returned to their side. To take a beating before the girls of the keep was bad enough; to be punished by a lout like Rulf in front of the Princess was a catastrophe.

Emitting a groan that had little to do with his

physical state, Pug tried to look as much like someone else as he could. Tomas grabbed him roughly. "Try not to squirm around so much. You're not all that bad off. Most of this blood is Rulf's anyway. By tomorrow his nose will look like an angry red cabbage."

"So will my head."

"Nothing so bad. A black eye, perhaps two, with a swollen cheek thrown in to the bargain. On the whole, you did rather well, but next time you want to tangle with Rulf, wait until you've put on a little more size, will you?" Pug watched as the Prince led his sister away from the site of battle. Roland gave him a wide grin, and Pug wished himself dead.

PUG AND TOMAS walked out of the kitchen, dinner plates in hand. It was a warm night, and they preferred the cooling ocean breeze to the heat of the scullery. They sat on the porch, and Pug moved his jaw from side to side, feeling it pop in and out. He experimented with a bite of lamb and put his plate to one side.

Tomas watched him. "Can't eat?"

Pug nodded. "Jaw hurts too much." He leaned forward, resting his elbows on his knees and chin on his fists. "I should have kept my temper. Then I would have done better."

Tomas spoke from around a mouthful of food. "Master Fannon says a soldier must keep a cool head at all times or he'll lose it."

Pug sighed. "Kulgan said something like that. I have some drills I can do that make me relax. I should have used them."

Tomas gulped a heroic portion of his meal. "Practicing in your room is one thing. Putting that sort of business into use while someone is insulting you to your face is quite another. I would have done the same thing, I suppose."

"But you would have won."

"Probably. Which is why Rulf would never have come at me." His manner showed he wasn't being boastful, merely stating things as they were. "Still, you did all right. Old cabbage nose will think twice before picking on you again, I'm sure, and that's what the whole thing is about, anyway."

Pug said, "What do you mean?"

Tomas put down his plate and belched. With a satisfied look at the sound of it, he said, "With bullies it's always the same: whether or not you can best them doesn't matter. What is important is whether or not you'll stand up to them. Rulf may be big, but he's a coward under all the bluster. He'll turn his attention to the younger boys now and push them around a bit. I don't think he'll want any part of you again. He doesn't like the price." Tomas gave Pug a broad and warm smile. "That first punch you gave him was a beaut. Right square on the beak."

Pug felt a little better. Tomas eyed Pug's untouched dinner. "You going to eat that?"

Pug looked at his plate. It was fully laden with hot lamb, greens, and potatoes. In spite of the rich smell, Pug felt no appetite. "No, you can have it."

Tomas scooped up the platter and began shoving the food into his mouth. Pug smiled. Tomas had never been known to stint on food.

Pug returned his gaze to the castle wall. "I felt like such a fool."

Tomas stopped eating, with a handful of meat halfway to his mouth. He studied Pug for a moment. "You too?"

"Me too, what?"

Tomas laughed. "You're embarrassed because the Princess saw Rulf give you a thrashing."

Pug bridled. "It wasn't a thrashing. I gave as well as I got!"

Tomas whooped. "There! I knew it. It's the Princess."

Pug sat back in resignation. "I suppose it is."

Tomas said nothing, and Pug looked over at him. He was busy finishing off Pug's dinner. Finally Pug said, "And I suppose you don't like her?"

Tomas shrugged. Between bites he said, "Our Lady Carline is pretty enough, but I know my place. I have my eye on someone else, anyway."

Pug sat up. "Who?" he asked, his curiosity piqued.

"I'm not saying," Tomas said with a sly smile.

Pug laughed. "It's Neala, right?"

Tomas's jaw dropped. "How did you know?"

Pug tried to look mysterious. "We magicians have our ways."

Tomas snorted. "Some magician. You're no more a magician than I am a Knight-Captain of the King's army. Tell me, how did you know?"

Pug laughed. "It's no mystery. Every time you see her, you puff up in that tabard of yours and preen like a bantam rooster."

Tomas looked troubled. "You don't think she's on to me, do you?"

Pug smiled like a well-fed cat. "She's not on to you, I'm sure." He paused. "If she's blind, and all the other girls in the keep haven't pointed it out to her a hundred times already."

A woebegone look crossed Tomas's face. "What must the girl think?"

Pug said, "Who knows what girls think? From everything I can tell, she probably likes it."

Tomas looked thoughtfully at his plate. "Do you ever think about taking a wife?"

Pug blinked like an owl caught in a bright light. "I . . . I never thought about it. I don't know if magicians marry. I don't think they do."

"Nor soldiers, mostly. But Master Fannon says a soldier who thinks about his family is not thinking about his job." Tomas was silent for a minute.

Pug said, "It doesn't seem to hamper Sergeant Gardan or some of the other soldiers."

Tomas snorted, as if those exceptions merely proved his point. "I sometimes try to imagine what it would be like to have a family."

"You have a family, stupid. I'm the orphan here."

"I mean a wife, rock head." Tomas gave Pug his best "you're too stupid to live" look. "And children someday, not a mother and father."

Pug shrugged. The conversation was turning to provinces that disturbed him. He never thought about these things, being less anxious to grow up than Tomas. He said, "I expect we'll get married and have children if it's what we're supposed to do."

Tomas looked very seriously at Pug, so the younger boy didn't make light of the subject. "I've imagined a small room somewhere in the castle, and . . . I can't imagine who the girl would be." He chewed his food. "There's something wrong with it, I think."

"Wrong?"

"As if there's something else I'm not understanding . . . I don't know."

Pug said, "Well, if you don't, how am I supposed to?"

Tomas suddenly changed the topic of conversation. "We're friends, aren't we?"

Pug was taken by surprise. "Of course we're friends. You're like a brother. Your parents have treated me like their own son. Why would you ask something like that?"

Tomas put down his plate, troubled. "I don't know. It's just that sometimes I think this will all somehow change. You're going to be a magician, maybe travel over the world, seeing other magicians in faraway lands. I'm going to be a soldier, bound to follow my lord's orders. I'll probably never see more than a little part of the Kingdom, and that only as an escort in the Duke's personal guard, if I'm lucky."

Pug became alarmed. He had never seen Tomas so serious about anything. The older boy was always the first to laugh and seemed never to have a worry. "I don't care what you think, Tomas," said Pug. "Nothing will change. We will be friends no matter what."

Tomas smiled at that. "I hope you're right." He sat back, and the two boys watched the stars over the sea and the lights from the town, framed like a picture by the castle gate.

PUG TRIED TO wash his face the next morning, but found the task too arduous to complete. His left eye was swollen completely shut, his right only half-open. Great bluish lumps decorated his visage, and his jaw popped when he moved it from side to side. Fantus lay on Pug's pallet, red eyes gleaming as the morning sun poured in through the tower window.

The door to the boy's room swung open, and Kulgan stepped through, his stout frame covered in a green robe. Pausing to regard the boy for a moment, he sat on the pallet and scratched the drake behind the eye ridges, bringing a pleased rumble from deep within Fantus's throat. "I see you didn't spend yesterday sitting about idly," he said.

"I had a bit of trouble, sir."

"Well, fighting is the province of boys as well as

grown men, but I trust that the other boy looks at least as bad. It would be a shame to have had none of the pleasure of giving as well as receiving."

"You're making sport of me."

"Only a little, Pug. The truth is that in my own youth I had my share of scraps, but the time for boyish fighting is past. You must put your energies to better use."

"I know, Kulgan, but I have been so frustrated lately that when that clod Rulf said what he did about my being an orphan, all the anger came boiling up out of me."

"Well, knowing your own part in this is a good sign that you're becoming a man. Most boys would have tried to justify their actions, by shifting blame or by claiming some moral imperative to fight."

Pug pulled over the stool and sat down, facing the magician. Kulgan took out his pipe and started to fill it. "Pug, I think in your case we may have been going about the matter of your education in the wrong way." Searching for a taper to light in the small fire that burned in a night pot and finding none, Kulgan's face clouded as he concentrated for a minute; then a small flame erupted from the index finger of his right hand. Applying it to the pipe, he soon had the room half-filled with great clouds of white smoke. The flame disappeared with a wave of his hand. "A handy skill, if you like the pipe."

"I would give anything to be able to do even that much," Pug said in disgust.

"As I was saying, I think that we may have been going about this in the wrong way. Perhaps we should consider a different approach to your education."

"What do you mean?"

"Pug, the first magicians long ago had no teachers

in the arts of magic. They evolved the skills that we've learned today. Some of the old skills, such as smelling the changes in the weather, or the ability to find water with a stick, go back to our earliest beginnings. I have been thinking that for a time I am going to leave you to your own devices. Study what you want in the books that I have. Keep up with your other work, learning the scribe's arts from Tully, but I will not trouble you with any lessons for a while. I will, of course, answer any question you have. But I think for the time being you need to sort yourself out."

Crestfallen, Pug asked, "Am I beyond help?"

Kulgan smiled reassuringly. "Not in the least. There have been cases of magicians having slow starts before. Your apprenticeship is for nine more years, remember. Don't be put off by the failures of the last few months.

"By the way, would you care to learn to ride?"

Pug's mood did a complete turnabout, and he cried, "Oh, yes! May I?"

"The Duke has decided that he would like a boy to ride with the Princess from time to time. His sons have many duties now that they are grown, and he feels you would be a good choice for when they are too busy to accompany her."

Pug's head was spinning. Not only was he to learn to ride, a skill limited to the nobility for the most part, but to be in the company of the Princess as well! "When do I start?"

"This very day. Morning chapel is almost done." Being Firstday, those inclined went to devotions either in the Keep's chapel, or in the small temple down in the town. The rest of the day was given to light work, only that needed to put food on the Duke's table. The boys and girls might get an extra half day on Sixthday, but their elders rested only on Firstday. "Go to Horse-master Algon; he has been instructed by the Duke and will begin your lessons now."

Without a further word, Pug leaped up and sped for the stables.

4

Assault

*P*ug *rode in* silence.

His horse ambled along the bluffs that overlooked the sea. The warm breeze carried the scent of
flowers, and to the east the trees of the forest swayed
slowly. The summer sun caused a heat shimmer over
the ocean. Above the waves, gulls could be seen hanging in the air, then diving to the water as they sought
food. Overhead, large white clouds drifted.

Pug remembered this morning, as he watched the
back of the Princess on her fine white palfrey. He had
been kept waiting in the stables for nearly two hours
before the Princess appeared with her father. The Duke
had lectured Pug at length on his responsibility toward
the lady of the castle. Pug had stood mute throughout
as the Duke repeated all of Horsemaster Algon's instructions of the night before. The master of the stables
had been instructing him for a week and judged him
ready to ride with the Princess—if barely.

Pug had followed her out of the gate, still marveling at his unexpected fortune. He was exuberant, in spite of having spent the night tossing and then skipping breakfast.

Now his mood was changing from boyish adulation to outright irritation. The Princess refused to respond to any of his polite attempts at conversation, except to order him about. Her tone was imperious and rude, and she insisted on calling him "boy," ignoring several courteous reminders that his name was Pug. She acted little like the poised young woman of the court now, and resembled nothing as much as a spoiled, petulant child.

He had felt awkward at first as he sat atop the old grey dray horse that had been judged sufficient for one of his skills. The mare had a calm nature and showed no inclination to move faster than absolutely necessary.

Pug wore his bright red tunic, the one that Kulgan had given to him, but still looked poorly attired next to the Princess. She was dressed in a simple but exquisite yellow riding dress trimmed in black, and a matching hat. Even sitting sidesaddle, Carline looked like one born to ride, while Pug felt as if he should be walking behind his mare with a plow between. Pug's horse had an irritating tendency to want to stop every dozen feet to crop grass or nibble at shrubbery, ignoring Pug's frantic kicks to the side, while the Princess's excellently trained horse responded instantly to the slightest touch of her crop. She rode along in silence, ignoring the grunts of exertion from the boy behind, who attempted by force of will as much as horsemanship to keep his recalcitrant mount moving.

Pug felt the first stirring of hunger, his dreams of romance surrendering to his normal, fifteen-year-old's appetite. As they rode, his thoughts turned more and more to the basket of lunch that hung from his saddle horn. After what seemed like an eternity to Pug, the Princess turned to him. "Boy, what is your craft?"

Startled by the question after the long silence, Pug stammered his reply. "I . . . I'm apprenticed to Master Kulgan."

She fixed him with a gaze that would have suited her had an insect been found crawling across a dinner plate. "Oh. You're that boy." Whatever brief spark of interest there had been went out, and she turned away from him. They rode awhile longer, then the Princess said, "Boy, we stop here."

Pug pulled up his mare, and before he could reach the Princess's side, she was nimbly down, not waiting for his hand as Master Algon had instructed him she would. She handed him the reins of her horse and walked to the edge of the cliffs.

She stared out to sea for a minute, then, without looking at Pug, said, "Do you think I am beautiful?"

Pug stood in silence, not knowing what to say. She turned and looked at him. "Well?"

Pug said, "Yes, Your Highness."

"Very beautiful?"

"Yes, Your Highness. Very beautiful."

The Princess seemed to consider this for a moment, then returned her attention to the vista below. "It is important for me to be beautiful, boy. Lady Marna says that I must be the most beautiful lady in the Kingdom, for I must find a powerful husband someday, and only the most beautiful ladies in the Kingdom can choose. The homely ones must take whoever will ask for them. She says that I will have many suitors, for Father is very important." She turned, and for a brief moment Pug thought he saw a look of apprehension pass over her lovely features. "Have you many friends, boy?"

Pug shrugged. "Some, Your Highness."

She studied him for a moment, then said, "That must be nice," absently brushing aside a wisp of hair that had come loose from under her broad-brimmed riding hat. Something in her seemed so wounded and alone that moment, that Pug found his heart in his throat again. Obviously his expression revealed something to the Princess, for suddenly her eyes narrowed and her mood shifted from thoughtful to regal. In her most commanding voice she announced, "We will have lunch now." Pug quickly staked the horses and unslung the basket. He placed it on the ground and opened it.

Carline stepped over and said, "I will prepare the meal, boy. I'll not have clumsy hands overturning dishes and spilling wine." Pug took a step back as she knelt and began unpacking the lunch. Rich odors of cheese and bread assailed Pug's nostrils, and his mouth watered.

The Princess looked up at him. "Walk the horses over the hill to the stream and water them. You may eat as we ride back. I'll call you when I have eaten." Suppressing a groan, Pug took the horses' reins and started walking. He kicked at some loose stones, emotions conflicting within him as he led the horses along. He knew he wasn't supposed to leave the girl, but he couldn't very well disobey her either. There was no one else in sight, and trouble was unlikely this far from the forest. Additionally he was glad to be away from Carline for a little while.

He reached the stream and unsaddled the mounts; he brushed away the damp saddle and girth marks, then left their reins upon the ground. The palfrey was trained to ground-tie, and the draft horse showed no inclination to wander far. They cropped grass while Pug found a comfortable spot to sit. He considered the situation and found himself perplexed. Carline was still the loveliest girl he had ever seen, but her manner was quickly taking the sheen off his fascination. For the moment his stomach was of larger concern than the girl of his dreams. He thought perhaps there was more to this love business than he had imagined.

He amused himself for a while by speculation on that. When he grew bored, he went to look for stones in the water. He hadn't had much opportunity to practice with his sling of late, and now was a good time. He found several smooth stones and took out his sling. He practiced by picking out targets among the small trees some distance off, startling the birds in residence there. He hit several clusters of bitter berries, missing only one target out of six. Satisfied his aim was still as good as always, he tucked his sling in his belt. He found several more stones that looked especially promising and put them in his pouch. He judged the girl must be nearly through, and he started toward the horses to saddle them so that when she called, he'd be ready.

As he reached the Princess's horse, a scream sounded from the other side of the hill. He dropped the Princess's saddle and raced to the crest and, when he cleared the ridge, stopped in shock. The hair on his neck and arms stood on end.

The Princess was running, and close in pursuit were a pair of trolls. Trolls usually didn't venture this far from the forest, and Pug was unprepared for the sight of them. They were humanlike, but short and broad, with long, thick arms that hung nearly to the ground. They ran on all fours as often as not, looking like some comic parody of an ape, their bodies covered by thick grey hide and their lips drawn back, revealing long fangs. The ugly creatures rarely troubled a group of humans, but they would attack a lone traveler from time to time.

Pug hesitated for a moment, pulling his sling from his belt and loading a stone; then he charged down the hill, whirling his sling above his head. The creatures had nearly overtaken the Princess when he let fly with a stone. It caught the foremost troll in the side of the head, knocking it for a full somersault. The second stumbled into it, and both went down in a tangle. Pug stopped as they regained their feet, their attention diverted from Carline to their attacker. They roared at Pug, then charged. Pug ran back up the hill. He knew that if he could reach the horses, he could outrun them, circle around for the girl, and be safely away. He looked over his shoulder and saw them coming—huge canine teeth bared, long foreclaws tearing up the ground. Downwind, he could smell their rank, rotting-meat odor.

He cleared the top of the hill, his breath coming in ragged gasps. His heart skipped as he saw that the horses had wandered across the stream and were twenty yards farther away than before. Plunging down the hill, he hoped the difference would not prove fatal.

He could hear the trolls behind him as he entered the stream at a full run. The water was shallow here, but still it slowed him down.

Splashing through the stream, he caught his foot on a stone and fell. He threw his arms forward and broke his fall with his hands, keeping his head above water. Shock ran up through his arms as he tried to regain his feet. He stumbled again and turned as the trolls approached the water's edge. They howled at the sight of their tormentor stumbling in the water and paused for a moment. Pug felt blind terror as he struggled with numb fingers to put a stone in his sling. He fumbled and dropped the sling, and the stream carried it away. Pug felt a scream building in his throat.

As the trolls entered the water, a flash of light exploded behind Pug's eyes. A searing pain ripped across his forehead as letters of grey seemed to appear in his mind. They were familiar to Pug, from a scroll that Kulgan had shown him several times. Without thinking, he mouthed the incantation, each word vanishing from his mind's eye as he spoke it.

When he reached the last word, the pain stopped, and a loud roar sounded from before him. He opened his eyes and saw the two trolls writhing in the water, their eyes wide with agony as they thrashed about helplessly, screaming and groaning.

Dragging himself out of the water, Pug watched while the creatures struggled. They were making choking and sputtering noises now as they flopped about. After a moment one shook and stopped moving, lying facedown in the water. The second took a few minutes longer to die, but like its companion, it also drowned, unable to keep its head above the shallow water.

Feeling light-headed and weak, Pug recrossed the stream. His mind was numb, and everything seemed hazy and disjointed. He stopped after he had taken a few steps, remembering the horses. He looked about and could see nothing of the animals. They must have run off when they caught wind of the trolls and would be on the way to safe pasture.

Pug resumed his walk to where the Princess had been. He topped the hillock and looked around. She was nowhere in sight, so he headed for the overturned basket of food. He was having trouble thinking, and he was ravenous. He knew he should be doing or thinking about something, but all he could sort out of the kaleidoscope of his thoughts was food.

Dropping to his knees, he picked up a wedge of cheese and stuffed it in his mouth. A half-spilled bottle of wine lay nearby, and he washed the cheese down with it. The rich cheese and piquant white wine revived him, and he felt his mind clearing. He ripped a large piece of bread from a loaf and chewed on it while trying to put his thoughts in order. As Pug recalled events, one thing stood out. Somehow he had managed to cast a magic spell. What's more, he had done so without the aid of a book, scroll, or device. He was not sure, but that seemed somehow strange. His thoughts turned hazy again. More than anything he wanted to lie down and sleep, but as he chewed his food, a thought pushed through the crazy quilt of his impressions. The Princess!

He jumped to his feet, and his head swam. Steadying himself, he grabbed up some bread and the wine and set off in the direction he had last seen her running. He pushed himself along, his feet scuffing as he tried to walk. After a few minutes he found his thinking improving and the exhaustion lifting. He started to call the Princess's name, then heard muted sobbing coming from a clump of bushes. Pushing his way through, he found Carline huddled behind the shrubs, her balled fists pulled up into her stomach. Her eyes were wide with terror, and her gown was soiled and torn. Startled when Pug stepped into view, she jumped to her feet and flew into his arms, burying her head in his chest. Great racking sobs shook her body as she clutched the fabric of his shirt. Standing with his arms still outstretched, wine and bread occupying his hands, Pug was totally confused over what to do. He awkwardly placed his arm around the terrified girl and said, "It's all right. They're gone. You're safe."

She hung on to him for a moment, then, when her tears subsided, she stepped away. With a sniffle she said, "I thought they had killed you and were coming back for me."

Pug found this situation more perplexing than any he had ever known. Just when he had come through the most harrowing experience of his young life, he was faced with one that sent his mind reeling with a different sort of confusion. Without thinking, he held the Princess in his arms, and now he was suddenly aware of the contact, and her soft, warm appeal. A protective, masculine feeling welled up inside him, and he started to step toward her.

As if sensing his mood change, Carline retreated. For all her courtly ways and education, she was still a girl of fifteen and was disturbed by the rush of emotions she had experienced when he had held her. She took refuge in the one thing she knew well, her role as Princess of the castle. Trying to sound commanding, she said, "I am glad to see you are unhurt, boy." Pug winced visibly at that. She struggled to regain her aristocratic bearing, but her red nose and tearstained face undermined her attempt. "Find my horse, and we shall return to the keep."

Pug felt as if his nerves were raw. Keeping tight control over his voice, he said, "I'm sorry, Your Highness, but the horses have run off. I'm afraid we'll have to walk."

Carline felt abused and mistreated. It was not Pug's fault any of the afternoon's events had taken place, but her often-indulged temper seized on the handiest available object. "Walk! I can't walk all the way to the keep," she snapped, looking at Pug as if he were supposed to do something about this matter at once and without question.

Pug felt all the anger, confusion, hurt, and frustration of the day surge up within him. "Then you can bloody well sit here until they notice you're missing and send someone to fetch you." He was now shouting. "I figure that will be about two hours after sunset."

Carline stepped back, her face ashen, looking as if she'd been slapped. Her lower lip trembled, and she seemed on the verge of tears again. "I will not be spoken to in that manner, boy."

Pug's eyes grew large, and he stepped toward her, gesturing with the wine bottle. "I nearly got myself killed trying to keep you alive," he shouted. "Do I hear one word of thanks? No! All I hear is a whining complaint that you can't walk back to the castle. We of the keep may be lowborn, but at least we have enough manners to thank someone when it's deserved." As he spoke, he could feel the anger flooding out of him. "You can stay here if you like, but I'm going. . . ." He suddenly realized that he was standing with the bottle raised high overhead, in a ridiculous pose. The Princess's eyes were on the loaf of bread, and he realized that he was holding it at his belt, thumb hooked in a loop, which only added to the awkward appearance. He sputtered for a moment, then felt his anger evaporate and lowered the bottle. The Princess looked at him, her large eyes peeking over her fists, which she held before her face. Pug started to say something, thinking she was afraid of him, when he saw she was laughing. It was a musical sound, warm and unmocking. "I'm sorry, Pug," she said, "but you look so silly standing there like that. You look like one of those awful statues they erect in Krondor, with bottle held high instead of a sword."

Pug shook his head. "I'm the one who's sorry, Your Highness. I had no right to yell at you that way. Please forgive me."

Her expression abruptly changed to one of concern. "No, Pug. You had every right to say what you did. I really do owe you my life, and I've acted horribly." She stepped closer to him and placed a hand on his arm. "Thank you."

Pug was overcome by the sight of her face. Any resolutions to rid himself of his boyhood fantasies about her were now carried away on the sea breeze. The marvelous fact of his using magic was replaced by more urgent and basic considerations. He started to reach for her; then the reality of her station intruded, and he presented the bottle to her. "Wine?"

She laughed, sensing his sudden shift in thought. They were both wrung out and a little giddy from the ordeal, but she still held on to her wits and understood the effect she was having on him. With a nod she took the bottle and sipped. Recovering a shred of poise, Pug said, "We'd better hurry. We might make the keep by nightfall."

She nodded, keeping her eyes upon him, and smiled. Pug was feeling uncomfortable under her gaze and turned toward the way to the keep. "Well, then. We'd best be off."

She fell into step beside him. After a moment she asked, "May I have some bread too, Pug?"

PUG HAD RUN the distance between the bluffs and the keep many times before, but the Princess was unused to walking such distances, and her soft riding boots were ill suited to such an undertaking. When they came into view of the castle, she had one arm draped over Pug's shoulder and was limping badly.

A shout went up from the gate tower, and guards came running toward them. After them came the Lady Marna, the girl's governess, her red dress pulled up before her as she sprinted toward the Princess. Although twice the size of court ladies—and a few of the guards as well—she outdistanced them all. She was coming on like a she-bear whose cub was being attacked. Her great bosom heaved with the effort as she reached the slight girl and grasped her in a hug that threatened to engulf Carline completely. Soon the ladies of the court were gathered around the Princess, overwhelming her with questions. Before the din subsided, Lady Marna turned and fell on Pug like the sow bear she resembled. "How *dare* you allow the Princess to come to such a state!

Limping in, dress all torn and dirty. I'll see you whipped from one end of the keep to the other. Before I have done with you, you'll wish you'd never seen the light of day." Backing away before the onslaught, Pug was overwhelmed by confusion, unable to get a word in. Sensing that somehow Pug was responsible for the Princess's condition, one of the guards stepped up and seized him by the arm.

"Leave him alone!"

Silence descended as Carline forced her way between the governess and Pug. Small fists struck at the guard as he let go of Pug and fell back with a look of astonishment on his face. "He saved my life! He almost got killed saving me." Tears were running down her face. "He's done nothing wrong. And I won't have any of you bullying him." The crowd closed in around them, regarding Pug with newfound respect. Hushed voices sounded from all sides, and one of the guards ran to carry the news to the castle. The Princess placed her arm around Pug's shoulder once more and started toward the gate. The crowd parted, and the two weary travelers could see the torches and lanterns being lit on the wall.

By the time they had reached the courtyard gate, the Princess had consented to let two of her ladies help her, much to Pug's relief. He could not have believed that such a slight girl could become such a burden. The Duke hurried out to her, having been told of Carline's return. He embraced his daughter, then started to speak with her. Pug lost sight of them as curious, questioning onlookers surrounded him. He tried to push his way toward the magician's tower, but the press of people held him back.

"Is there no work to be done?" a voice roared.

Heads turned to see Swordmaster Fannon, followed closely by Tomas. All the keep folk quickly retired, leaving Pug standing before Fannon, Tomas, and those of the Duke's court with rank enough to ignore Fannon's remark. Pug could see the Princess talking to her father, Lyam, Arutha, and Squire Roland. Fannon said, "What happened, boy?"

Pug tried to speak, but stopped when he saw the Duke and his sons approaching. Kulgan came hurrying behind the Duke, having been alerted by the general commotion in the courtyard. All bowed to the Duke when he approached, and Pug saw Carline break free of Roland's solicitations and follow her father, to stand at Pug's side. Lady Marna threw a besieged look heavenward, and Roland followed the girl, an open expression of surprise upon his face. When the Princess took Pug's hand in her own, Roland's expression changed to one of black-humored jealousy.

The Duke said, "My daughter has said some very remarkable things about you, boy. I would like to hear your account." Pug felt suddenly self-conscious and gently disengaged his hand from Carline's. He recounted the events of the day, with Carline enthusiastically adding embellishments. Between the two of them, the Duke gained a nearly accurate account of things. When Pug finished, Lord Borric asked, "How is it the trolls drowned in the stream, Pug?"

Pug looked uncomfortable. "I cast a spell upon them, and they were unable to reach the shore," he said softly. He was still confused by this accomplishment and had not given much thought to it, as the Princess had pushed all other thoughts aside. He could see surprise registered on Kulgan's face. Pug began to say something, but was interrupted by the Duke's next remark.

"Pug, I can't begin to repay the service you've done my family. But I shall find a suitable reward for your courage." In a burst of enthusiasm Carline threw her arms around Pug's neck, hugging him fiercely. Pug stood in embarrassment, looking frantically about, as if trying to communicate that this familiarity was none of his doing.

Lady Marna looked ready to faint, and the Duke pointedly coughed, motioning with his head for his daughter to retire. As she left with the Lady Marna, Kulgan and Fannon simply let their amusement show, as did Lyam and Arutha. Roland shot Pug an angry, envious look, then turned and headed off toward his own quarters. Lord Borric said to Kulgan, "Take this boy to his room. He looks exhausted. I'll order food sent to him. Have him come to the great hall after tomorrow's morning meal." He turned to Pug. "Again, I thank you." The Duke motioned for his sons to follow and walked away. Fannon gripped Tomas by the elbow, for the sandy-haired boy had started to speak with his friend. The old Swordmaster motioned with his head that the boy should come with him, leaving Pug in peace. Tomas nodded, though he was burning with a thousand questions.

When they had all left, Kulgan placed his arm around the boy's shoulder. "Come, Pug. You're tired, and there is much to speak of."

Pug lay back on his pallet, the remains of his meal lying on a platter next to him. He couldn't remember ever having been this tired before. Kulgan paced back and forth across the room. "It's absolutely incredible." He waved a hand in the air, his red robe surging over his heavy frame like water flowing over a boulder. "You close your eyes, and the image of a scroll you saw weeks before appears. You incant the spell, as if you were holding the scroll in your hand before you, and the trolls fall. Absolutely incredible." Sitting down on the stool near the window, he continued. "Pug, nothing like this has ever been done before. Do you know what you've done?"

Pug started from the edge of a warm, soft sleep and looked at the magician. "Only what I said I did, Kulgan."

"Yes, but do you have any idea what it means?"

"No."

"Neither do I." The magician seemed to collapse inside as his excitement left, replaced by complete uncertainty. "I don't have the slightest idea what it all means. Magicians don't toss spells off the top of their heads. Clerics can, but they have a different focus and different magic. Do you remember what I taught you about focuses, Pug?"

Pug winced, not being in the mood to recite a lesson, but forced himself to sit up. "Anyone who employs magic must have a focus for the power he uses. Priests have power to focus their magic through prayer; their incantations are a form of prayer. Magicians use their bodies, or devices, or books and scrolls."

"Correct," said Kulgan, "but you have just violated that truism." He took out his long pipe and absently stuffed tabac into the bowl. "The spell you incanted cannot use the caster's body as a focus. It has been developed to inflict great pain upon another. It can be a very terrible weapon. But it can be cast only by reading from a scroll that it is written upon, *at the time it's cast.* Why is this?"

Pug forced leaden eyelids open. "The scroll itself is magic."

"True. Some magic is intrinsic to the magician, such as taking on the shape of an animal or smelling weather. But casting spells outside the body, upon something else, needs an external focus. Trying to incant the spell you used from memory should have produced terrible pain in *you,* not the trolls, if it would have worked at all! *That* is why magicians developed scrolls, books, and other devices, to focus that sort of magic in a way that will not harm the caster. And until today, I would have sworn that no one alive could have made that spell work without the scroll in hand."

Leaning against the windowsill, Kulgan puffed on his pipe for a moment, gazing out into space. "It's as if you have discovered a completely new form of magic," he said softly. Hearing no response, Kulgan looked down at the boy, who was deeply asleep. Shaking his head in wonder, the magician pulled a cover over the exhausted boy. He put out the lantern that hung on the wall and let himself out. As he walked up the stairs to his own room, he shook his head. "Absolutely incredible."

PUG WAITED AS the Duke held court in the great hall. Everyone in the keep and town who could contrive a way to gain entrance to the audience was there. Richly dressed Craftmasters, merchants, and minor nobles were in attendance. They stood regarding the boy with expressions ranging from wonder to disbelief. The rumor of his deed had spread through the town and had grown in the telling.

Pug wore new clothing, which had been in his room when he awoke. In his newfound splendor he felt self-conscious and awkward. The tunic was a bright yellow affair of the costliest silk, and the hose were a soft pastel blue. Pug tried to wiggle his toes in the new boots, the first he had ever worn. Walking in them seemed strange and uncomfortable. At his side a jeweled dagger hung from a black leather belt with a golden buckle in the form of a gull in flight. Pug suspected the clothing had once belonged to one of the Duke's sons, put aside when outgrown, but still looking new and beautiful.

The Duke was finishing the morning's business: a request from one of the shipwrights for guards to accompany a lumber expedition to the great forest. Borric was dressed, as usual in black, but his sons and daughter wore their finest court regalia. Lyam was listening closely to the business before his father. Roland stood behind him, as was the custom. Arutha was in rare good humor, laughing behind an upraised hand at some quip Father Tully had just made. Carline sat quietly, her face set in a warm smile, looking directly at Pug, which was adding to his discomfort—and Roland's irritation.

The Duke gave his permission for a company of guards to accompany the craftsmen into the forest. The Craftmaster gave thanks and bowed, then returned to the crowd, leaving Pug alone before the Duke. The boy stepped forward as Kulgan had told him to do and bowed properly, albeit a little stiffly, before the Lord of Crydee. Borric smiled at the boy and motioned to Father Tully. The priest removed a document from the sleeve of his voluminous robe and handed it to a herald. The herald stepped forward and unrolled the scroll.

In a loud voice he read: "To all within our demesne: Whereas the youth Pug, of the castle of Crydee, has shown exemplary courage in the act of risking life and limb in defense of the royal person of the Princess Carline, and; Whereas the youth, Pug of Crydee, is considered to hold us forever in his debt; It is my wish that he be known to all in the realm as our beloved and loyal servant, and it is furthermore wished that he be given a place in the court of Crydee, with the rank of Squire, with all rights and privileges pertaining thereunto. Furthermore let it be known that the title for the estate of Forest Deep is conferred upon him and his progeny as long as they shall live, to have and to hold, with servants and properties thereupon. Title to this estate shall be held by the crown until the day of his majority. Set this day by my hand and seal Borric con-Doin, third Duke of Crydee; Prince of the Kingdom; Lord of Crydee, Carse, and Tulan; Warden of the West; Knight-General of the King's Armies; heir presumptive to the throne of Rillanon."

Pug felt his knees go slack but caught himself before he fell. The room erupted in cheers. People were pressing around him, offering their congratulations and slapping him on the back. He was a Squire and a land-holder with franklins, a house, and stock. He was rich. Or at least he would be in three years when he reached his majority. While he was considered a man of the Kingdom at fourteen, grants of land and titles couldn't be conferred until he reached eighteen. The crowd backed away as the Duke approached, his family and Roland behind. Both Princes smiled at Pug, and the Princess seemed positively aglow. Roland gave Pug a rueful smile, as if in disbelief.

"I'm honored, Your Grace," Pug stammered. "I don't know what to say."

"Then say nothing, Pug. It makes you seem wise when everyone is babbling. Come, and we'll have a talk." The Duke motioned for a chair to be placed near his own, as he put an arm around the boy's shoulders and walked him through the crowd. Sitting down, he said, "You may all leave us now. I would speak with the Squire." The crowd pressing around muttered in disappointment, but began to drift out of the hall. "Except you two," the Duke added, pointing toward Kulgan and Tully.

Carline stood by her father's chair, a hesitant Roland at her side. "You as well, my child," said the Duke.

Carline began to protest, but was cut off by her father's stern admonition: "You may pester him later,

Carline." The two Princes stood at the door, obviously amused at her outrage; Roland tried to offer his arm to the Princess, but she pulled away and swept by her grinning brothers. Lyam clapped Roland on the shoulder as the embarrassed Squire joined them. Roland glared at Pug, who felt the anger like a blow.

When the doors clanged closed and the hall was empty, the Duke said, "Pay no heed to Roland, Pug. My daughter has him firmly under her spell; he counts himself in love with her and wishes someday to petition for her hand." With a lingering look at the closed door, he added almost absently, "But he'll have to show me he's more than the rakehell he's growing into now if he ever hopes for my consent."

The Duke dismissed the topic with a wave of his hand. "Now, to other matters. Pug, I have an additional gift for you, but first I want to explain something to you.

"My family is among the oldest in the Kingdom. I myself am descended from a King, for my grandfather, the first Duke of Crydee, was third son to the King. Being of royal blood, we are much concerned with matters of duty and honor. You are now both a member of my court and apprentice of Kulgan. In matters of duty you are responsible to him. In matters of honor you are responsible to me. This room is hung with the trophies and banners of our triumphs. Whether we have been resisting the Dark Brotherhood in their ceaseless effort to destroy us, or fighting off pirates, we have ever fought bravely. Ours is a proud heritage that has never known the stain of dishonor. No member of our court has ever brought shame to this hall, and I will expect the same of you."

Pug nodded, tales of glory and honor remembered from his youth spinning in his mind. The Duke smiled. "Now to the business of your other gift. Father Tully has a document that I asked him to draw up last night. I am going to ask him to keep it, until such time as he deems fit to give it to you. I will say no more on the subject, except that when he gives it to you, I hope you will remember this day and consider long what it says."

"I will, Your Grace." Pug was sure the Duke was saying something very important, but with all the events of the last half hour, it did not register very well.

"I will expect you for supper, Pug. As a member of the court, you will not be eating meals in the kitchen anymore." The Duke smiled at him. "We'll make a young gentleman out of you, boy. And someday when you travel to the King's city of Rillanon, no one will fault the manners of those who come from the court of Crydee."

5

Shipwreck

The breeze was cool.

The last days of summer had passed, and soon the rains of autumn would come: A few weeks later the first snows of winter would follow. Pug sat in his room, studying a book of ancient exercises designed to ready the mind for spell casting. He had fallen back into his old routine once the excitement of his elevation to the Duke's court had worn off.

His marvelous feat with the trolls continued to be the object of speculation by Kulgan and Father Tully. Pug found he still couldn't do many of the things expected of an apprentice, but other feats were beginning to come to him. Certain scrolls were easier to use now, and once, in secret, he had tried to duplicate his feat.

He had memorized a spell from a book, one designed to levitate objects. He had felt the familiar blocks in his mind when he tried to incant it from memory. He had failed to move the object, a candleholder, but it trembled for a few seconds and he felt a brief sensation, as if he had touched the holder with a part of his mind. Satisfied that some sort of progress was being made, he lost much of his former gloom and renewed his studies with vigor.

Kulgan still let him find his own pace. They had had many long discussions on the nature of magic, but mostly Pug worked in solitude.

Shouting came from the courtyard below. Pug walked to his window. Seeing a familiar figure, he leaned out and cried, "Ho! Tomas! What is afoot?" Tomas looked up.

"Ho! Pug! A ship has foundered in the night. The wreck has beached beneath Sailor's Grief. Come and see."

"I'll be right down."

Pug ran to the door, pulling on a cloak, for while the day was clear, it would be cold near the water. Racing down the stairs, he cut through the kitchen, nearly knocking over Alfan, the pastry cook. As he bolted out the door, he heard the stout baker yell, "Squire or not, I'll box your ears if you don't watch where you're going, boy!" The kitchen staff had not changed their attitude toward the boy, whom they considered one of their own, beyond feeling proud of his achievement.

Pug shouted back with laughter in his voice, "My apologies, Mastercook!"

Alfan gave him a good-natured wave as Pug vanished through the outside door and around the corner to where Tomas was waiting. Tomas turned toward the gate as soon as he saw his friend.

Pug grabbed his arm. "Wait. Has anyone from the court been told?"

"I don't know. Word just came from the fishing village a moment ago," Tomas said impatiently. "Come on, or the villagers will pick the wreck clean." It was commonly held that salvage could be legally carried away before any of the Duke's court arrived. As a result, the villagers and townsfolk were less than timely in informing the authorities of such occurrences. There was also a risk of bloodshed, should the beached ship still be manned by sailors determined to keep their master's cargo intact so that they would get their fair sailing bonus. Violent confrontation, and even death, had been the result of such dispute. Only the presence of men-at-arms could guarantee no commoner would come to harm from lingering mariners.

"Oh, no," said Pug. "If there is any trouble down there and the Duke finds out I didn't tell someone else, I'll be in for it."

"Look, Pug. Do you think with all these people rushing about, the Duke will be long in hearing of it?" Tomas ran his hand through his hair. "Someone is probably in the great hall right now, telling him the news. Master Fannon is away on patrol, and Kulgan won't be back awhile yet." Kulgan was due back later that day from his cottage in the forest, where he and Meecham had spent the last week. "It may be our only chance to see a shipwreck." A look of sudden inspiration came over his face. "Pug, I have it! You're a member of the court now. Come along, and when we get there, you declare for the Duke." A calculating expression crossed his face. "And if we find a rich bauble or two, who's to know?"

"I would know." Pug thought a moment. "I can't properly declare for the Duke, then take something for myself . . ." He fixed Tomas with a disapproving expression. ". . . or let one of his men-at-arms take something either." As Tomas's face showed his embarrassment, Pug said, "But we can still see the wreck! Come on!"

Pug was suddenly taken with the idea of using his

new office, and if he could get there before too much was carried away or someone was hurt, the Duke would be pleased with him. "All right," he said, "I'll saddle a horse and we can ride down there before everything is stolen." Pug turned and ran for the stable. Tomas caught up with him as he opened the large wooden doors. "But, Pug, I have never been on a horse in my life. I don't know how."

"It's simple," Pug said, taking a bridle and saddle from the tack room. He spied the large grey he had ridden the day he and the Princess had their adventure. "I'll ride and you sit behind me. Just keep your arms around my waist, and you won't fall off."

Tomas looked doubtful. "I'm to depend on you?" He shook his head. "After all, who has looked after you all these years?"

Pug threw him a wicked smile. "Your mother. Now fetch a sword from the armory in case there's trouble. You may get to play soldier yet."

Tomas looked pleased at the prospect and ran out the door. A few minutes later the large grey with the two boys mounted on her back lumbered out the main gate, heading down the road toward Sailor's Grief.

THE SURF WAS pounding as the boys came in sight of the wreckage. Only a few villagers were approaching the site, and they scattered as soon as a horse and rider appeared, for it could only be a noble from the court to declare the wreck's salvage for the Duke. By the time Pug reined in, no one was about.

Pug said, "Come on. We've got a few minutes to look around before anyone else gets here."

Dismounting, the boys left the mare to graze in a little stand of grass only fifty yards from the rocks. Running through the sand, the boys laughed, with Tomas raising the sword aloft, trying to sound fierce as he yelled old war cries learned from the sagas. Not that he had any delusions about his ability to use it, but it might make someone think twice about attacking them—at least long enough for castle guards to arrive.

As they neared the wreck, Tomas whistled a low note. "This ship didn't just run on the rocks, Pug. It looks like it was driven by a storm."

Pug said, "There certainly isn't much left, is there?"

Tomas scratched behind his right ear. "No, just a section of the bow. I don't understand. There wasn't any storm last night, just a strong wind. How could the ship be broken up so badly?"

"I don't know." Suddenly something registered on Pug. "Look at the bow. See how it's painted."

The bow rested on the rocks, held there until the tide rose. From the deck line down, the hull was painted a bright green, and it shone with reflected sunlight, as if it had been glazed over. Instead of a figurehead, intricate designs were painted in bright yellow, down to the waterline, which was a dull black. A large blue-and-white eye had been painted several feet behind the prow, and all the above-deck railing that they could see was painted white.

Pug grabbed Tomas's arm. "Look!" He pointed to the water behind the prow, and Tomas could see a shattered white mast extending a few feet above the surging foam.

Tomas took a step closer. "It's no Kingdom ship, for certain." He turned to Pug. "Maybe they were from Queg?"

"No," answered Pug. "You've seen as many Quegan ships as I have. This is nothing from Queg or the Free Cities. I don't think a ship like this has ever passed these waters before. Let's look around."

Tomas seemed suddenly timid. "Careful, Pug.

There is something strange here, and I have an ill feeling. Someone may still be about."

Both boys looked around for a minute, before Pug concluded, "I think not; whatever snapped that mast and drove the ship ashore with enough force to wreck it this badly must have killed any who tried to ride her in."

Venturing closer, the boys found small articles lying about, tossed among the rocks by the waves. They saw broken crockery and boards, pieces of torn red sailcloth, and lengths of rope. Pug stopped and picked up a strange-looking dagger fashioned from some unfamiliar material. It was a dull grey and was lighter than steel, but still quite sharp.

Tomas tried to pull himself to the railing, but couldn't find a proper footing on the slippery rocks. Pug moved along the hull until he found himself in danger of having his boots washed by the tide; they could board the hulk if they waded into the sea, but Pug was unwilling to ruin his good clothing. He walked back to where Tomas stood studying the wreck.

Tomas pointed behind Pug. "If we climb up to that ledge, we could lower ourselves down to the deck."

Pug saw the ledge, a jutting single piece of stone that started twenty feet back on their left, extending upward and out to overhang the bow. It looked like an easy climb, and Pug agreed. They pulled themselves up and inched along the ledge, backs flat to the base of the bluffs. The path was narrow, but by stepping carefully, they ran little risk of falling. They reached a point above the hull; Tomas pointed. "Look. Bodies!"

Lying on the deck were two men, both dressed in bright blue armor of unfamiliar design. One had his head crushed by a fallen spar, but the other, lying facedown, didn't show any injuries, beyond his stillness. Strapped across that man's back was an alien-looking broadsword, with strange serrated edges. His head was covered by an equally alien-looking blue helmet, potlike, with an outward flaring edge on the sides and back. Tomas shouted over the sound of the surf, "I'm going to let myself down. After I get on the deck, hand me the sword, and then lower yourself so I can grab you."

Tomas handed Pug the sword, then turned around slowly. He knelt with his face against the cliff wall. Sliding backward, he let himself down until he was almost hanging free. With a shove he dropped the remaining four feet, landing safely. Pug reversed the sword and handed it down to Tomas, then followed his friend's lead, and in a moment they both stood on the deck. The foredeck slanted alarmingly down toward the water, and they could feel the ship move beneath their feet.

"The tide's rising," Tomas shouted. "It'll lift what's left of the ship and smash it on the rocks. Everything will be lost."

"Look around," Pug shouted back. "Anything that looks worth saving we can try to throw up on the ledge."

Tomas nodded, and the boys started to search the deck. Pug put as much space as he could between the bodies and himself when he passed them. All across the deck, debris created a confused spectacle for the eye. Trying to discern what might prove valuable and what might not was difficult. At the rear of the deck was a shattered rail, on either side of a ladder to what was left of the main deck below: about six feet of planking remaining above the water. Pug was sure that only a few feet more could be underwater, or else the ship would be higher on the rocks. The rear of the ship must have already been carried away on the tide.

Pug lay down on the deck and hung his head over

the edge. He saw a door to the right of the ladder. Yelling for Tomas to join him, he made his way carefully down the ladder. The lower deck was sagging, the undersupports having been caved in. He grasped the handrail of the ladder for support. A moment later Tomas stood beside him, stepped around Pug, and moved to the door. It hung half-open, and he squeezed through with Pug a step behind. The cabin was dark, for there was only a single port on the bulkhead next to the door. In the gloom they could see many rich-looking pieces of fabric and the shattered remnants of a table. What looked like a cot or low bed lay upside down in a corner. Several small chests could be seen, with their contents spread around the room as if tossed about by some giant hand.

Tomas tried to search through the mess, but nothing was recognizable as important or valuable. He found one small bowl of unusual design glazed with bright colored figures on the sides, and he put it inside his tunic.

Pug stood quietly, for something in the cabin commanded his attention. A strange, urgent feeling had overtaken him as soon as he had stepped in.

The wreck lurched, throwing Tomas off balance. He caught himself on a chest, dropping the sword. "The ship's lifting. We'd better go."

Pug didn't answer, his attention focused on the strange sensations. Tomas grabbed his arm. "Come on. The ship'll break up in a minute."

Pug shook his hand off. "A moment. There is something . . ." His voice trailed off. Abruptly he crossed the disordered room and pulled open a drawer in a latched chest. It was empty. He yanked open another, then a third. In it was the object of his search. He drew out a rolled parchment with a black ribbon and black seal on it and thrust it into his shirt.

"Come on," he shouted as he passed Tomas. They raced up the ladder and scrambled over the deck. The tide had raised the ship high enough for them to pull themselves up to the ledge with ease, and they turned to sit.

The ship was now floating on the tide, rocking forward and back, while the waves sent a wet spray into the boys' faces. They watched as the bow slid off the rocks, timbers breaking with a loud and deep tearing sound, like a dying moan. The bow lifted high, and the boys were splashed by waves striking the cliffs below their ledge.

Out to sea the hulk floated, slowly leaning over to its port side, until the outward surging tide came to a halt.

Ponderously, it started back toward the rocks. Tomas grabbed at Pug's arm, signaling him to follow. They got up and made their way back to the beach. When they reached the place where the rock overhung the sand, they jumped down.

A loud grinding sound made them turn to see the hull driven onto the rocks. Timbers shattered, and separated with a shriek. The hull heaved to starboard, and debris started sliding off the deck into the sea.

Suddenly Tomas reached over and caught Pug's arm. "Look." He pointed at the wreck sliding backward on the tide.

Pug couldn't make out what he was pointing at. "What is it?"

"I thought for a moment there was only one body on deck."

Pug looked at him. Tomas's face was set in an expression of worry. Abruptly it changed to anger. "Damn!"

"What?"

"When I fell in the cabin, I dropped the sword. Fannon will have my ears."

A sound like an explosion of thunder marked the final destruction of the wreck as the tide smashed it against the cliff face. Now the shards of the once fine, if alien, ship would be swept out to sea, to drift back in along the coast for miles to the south over the next few days.

A low groan ending in a sharp cry made the boys turn. Standing behind them was the missing man from the ship, the strange broadsword held loosely in his left hand and dragging in the sand. His right arm was held tightly against his side; blood could be seen running from under his blue breastplate, and from under his helmet. He took a staggering step forward. His face was ashen, and his eyes wide with pain and confusion. He shouted something incomprehensible at the boys. They stepped back slowly, raising their hands to show they were unarmed.

He took another step toward them, and his knees sagged. He staggered erect and closed his eyes for a moment. He was short and stocky, with powerfully muscled arms and legs. Below the breastplate he wore a short skirt of blue cloth. On his forearms were bracers, and on his legs, greaves that looked like leather, above thonged sandals. He put his hand to his face and shook his head. His eyes opened, and he regarded the boys again. Once more he spoke in his alien tongue. When the boys said nothing, he appeared to grow angry and yelled another series of strange words, from the tone seemingly questions.

Pug gauged the distance necessary to run past the man, who blocked the narrow strip of beach. He decided it wasn't worth the risk of finding out if the man was in a condition to use that wicked-looking sword. As if sensing the boy's thoughts, the soldier staggered a few feet to his right, cutting off any escape. He closed his eyes again, and what little color there was in his face drained away. His gaze began to wander, and the sword slipped from limp fingers. Pug started to take a step toward him, for it was now obvious that he could do them no harm.

As he neared the man, shouts sounded up the beach. Pug and Tomas saw Prince Arutha riding before a troop of horsemen. The wounded soldier turned his head painfully at the sound of approaching horses, and his eyes widened. A look of pure horror crossed his face, and he tried to flee. He took three staggering steps toward the water and fell forward into the sand.

PUG STOOD NEAR the door of the Duke's council chamber. Several feet away a concerned group sat at Duke Borric's round council table. Besides the Duke and his sons, Father Tully, Kulgan, who had returned only an hour before, Swordmaster Fannon, and Horsemaster Algon sat in assembly. The tone was serious, for the arrival of the alien ship was viewed as potentially dangerous to the Kingdom.

Pug threw a quick glance at Tomas, standing on the opposite side of the door. Tomas had never been in the presence of nobility, other than serving in the dining hall, and being in the Duke's council chamber was making him nervous. Master Fannon spoke, and Pug returned his attention to the table.

"Reviewing what we know," said the old Swordmaster, "it is obvious that these people are completely alien to us." He picked up the bowl Tomas had taken from the ship. "This bowl is fashioned in a way unknown to our Masterpotter. At first he thought it was simply a fired and glazed clay, but upon closer inspection it proved otherwise. It is fashioned from some sort of hide, parchment-thin strips being wound around a mold—perhaps wood—then laminated with resins of some type. It is much stronger than anything we know."

To demonstrate, he struck the bowl hard against the table. Instead of shattering, as a clay bowl would have, it made a dull sound. "Now, even more perplexing are these weapons and armor." He pointed to the blue breastplate, helmet, sword, and dagger. "They appear to be fashioned in a similar manner." He lifted the dagger and let it drop. It made the same dull sound as the bowl. "For all its lightness, it is nearly as strong as our best steel."

Borric nodded. "Tully, you've been around longer than any of us. Have you heard of any ship constructed like that?"

"No." Tully absently stroked his beardless chin. "Not from the Bitter Sea, the Kingdom Sea, or even from Great Kesh have I heard of such a ship. I might send word to the Temple of Ishap in Krondor. They have records that go further back than any others. Perhaps they have some knowledge of these people."

The Duke nodded. "Please do. Also we must send word to the elves and dwarves. They have abided here longer than we by ages, and we would do well to seek their wisdom."

Tully indicated agreement. "Queen Aglaranna might have knowledge of these people if they are travelers from across the Endless Sea. Perhaps they have visited these shores before."

"Preposterous," snorted Horsemaster Algon. "There are no nations across the Endless Sea. Otherwise it wouldn't be endless."

Kulgan took on an indulgent expression. "There are theories that other lands exist across the Endless Sea. It is only that we have no ships capable of making such a long journey."

"Theories," was all Algon said.

"Whoever these strangers are," said Arutha, "we had best make sure we can find out as much as possible about them."

Algon and Lyam gave him a questioning look, while Kulgan and Tully looked on without expression. Borric and Fannon nodded as Arutha continued. "From the boys' description, the ship was obviously a warship. The heavy prow with bowsprit is designed for ramming, and the high foredeck is a perfect place for bowmen, as the low middle deck is suitable for boarding other vessels when they have been grappled. I would imagine the rear deck was also high. If more of the hull had survived, I would guess we would have found rowers' benches as well."

"A war galley?" asked Algon.

Fannon looked impatient. "Of course, you simpleton." There was a friendly rivalry between the two masters, which at times degenerated to some unfriendly bickering. "Take a look at our guest's weapon." He indicated the broadsword. "How would you like to ride at a determined man wheeling that toy? He'd cut your horse right out from under you. That armor is light, and efficiently constructed for all its gaudy coloring. I would guess that he was infantry. As powerfully built as he is, he probably could run half a day and still fight." He stroked his mustache absently. "These people have some warriors among them."

Algon nodded slowly. Arutha sat back in his chair, making a tent of his hands, fingertips flexing. "What I can't understand," said the Duke's younger son, "is why he tried to run. We had no weapons drawn and were not charging. There was no reason for him to run."

Borric looked at the old priest. "Will we ever know?"

Tully looked concerned, his brow furrowed. "He had a long piece of wood embedded in his right side, under the breastplate, as well as a bad blow to the head. That helmet saved his skull. He has a high fever and has lost a great deal of blood. He may not survive. I may have to resort to a mind contact, if he regains enough consciousness to establish it." Pug knew of the mind contact; Tully had explained it to him before. It was a method only a few clerics could employ, and it was extremely dangerous for both the subject and the caster. The old priest must feel a strong need to gain information from the injured man to risk it.

Borric turned his attention to Kulgan. "What of the scroll the boys found?"

Kulgan waved a hand absently. "I have given a preliminary, and brief, inspection. It has magical properties without a doubt. That is why Pug felt some compulsion to inspect the cabin and that chest, I think. Anyone as sensitive to magic as he is would feel it." He looked directly at the Duke. "I am, however, unwilling to break the seal until I have made a more involved study of it, to better determine its purpose. Breaking enchanted seals can be dangerous if not handled properly. If the seal was tampered with, the scroll might destroy itself, or worse, those trying to break it. It wouldn't be the first such trap I've seen for a scroll of great power."

The Duke drummed his fingers on the table for a moment. "All right. We will adjourn this meeting. As soon as something new has been learned, either from the scroll or from the wounded man, we will reconvene." He turned to Tully. "See how the man is, and if he should wake, use your arts to glean whatever you can." He stood, and the others rose also. "Lyam, send word to the Elf Queen and the dwarves at Stone

Mountain and the Grey Towers of what has happened. Ask for their counsel."

Pug opened the door. The Duke went through and the others followed. Pug and Tomas were the last to leave, and as they walked down the hall, Tomas leaned over toward Pug.

"We really started something."

Pug shook his head. "We were simply the first to find the man. If not us, then someone else."

Tomas looked relieved to be out of the chamber and the Duke's scrutiny. "If this turns out badly, I hope they remember that."

Kulgan went up the stairs to his tower room as Tully moved off toward his own quarters, where the wounded man was being tended by Tully's acolytes. The Duke and his sons turned through a door to their private quarters, leaving the boys alone in the hallway.

Pug and Tomas cut through a storage room, and into the kitchen. Megar stood supervising the kitchen workers, several of whom waved greetings to the boys. When he saw his son and fosterling, he smiled and said, "Well, what have you two gotten yourselves into, now?" Megar was a loose-jointed man, with sandy hair and an open countenance. He resembled Tomas, as a rough sketch resembled a finished drawing. He was a fair-looking man of middle years, but lacked the fine features that set Tomas apart.

Grinning, Megar said, "Everyone is hushed up about that man in Tully's quarters, and messengers are dashing from here to there, one place to another. I haven't seen such a to-do since the Prince of Krondor visited seven years ago!"

Tomas grabbed an apple from a platter and jumped up to sit on a table. Between bites he recounted to his father what had taken place.

Pug leaned on the counter while listening. Tomas

told the story with a minimum of embellishment. When he was done, Megar shook his head. "Well, well. Aliens, is it? I hope they're not marauding pirates. We have had peaceful enough times lately. Ten years since the time the Brotherhood of the Dark Path"—he gestured spitting—"curse their murderous souls, stirred up that trouble with the goblins. Can't say as I'd welcome that sort of mess again, sending all those stores to the outlying villages. Having to cook based on what will spoil first and what will last longest. I couldn't make a decent meal for a month."

Pug smiled. Megar had the ability to take even the most difficult possibilities and break them down to basics: how much inconvenience they were likely to cause the scullery staff.

Tomas jumped down from the counter. "I had best return to the soldiers' commons and wait for Master Fannon. I'll see you soon." He ran from the kitchen.

Megar said, "Is it serious, Pug?"

Pug shook his head. "I really can't say. I don't know. I know that Tully and Kulgan are worried, and the Duke thinks enough of the problem to want to talk to the elves and dwarves. It could be."

Megar looked out the door that Tomas had used. "It would be a bad time for war and killing." Pug could see the poorly hidden worry in Megar's face and could think of nothing to say to a father of a son who had just become a soldier.

Pug pushed himself away from the counter. "I'd better be off, as well, Megar." He waved good-bye to the others in the kitchen and walked out of the kitchen and into the courtyard. He had little temper for study, being alarmed by the serious tone of the meeting in the Duke's chambers. No one had come out and said as much, but it was obvious they were considering the possibility that the alien ship was the vanguard of an invasion fleet.

Pug wandered around to the side of the keep and climbed the three steps to the Princess's small flower garden. He sat on a stone bench, the hedges and rows of rosebushes masking most of the courtyard from sight. He could still see the top of the high walks, with the guards patrolling the parapets. He wondered if it was his imagination, or were the guards looking especially watchful today?

The sound of a delicate cough made him turn. Standing on the other side of the garden was Princess Carline, with Squire Roland and two of her younger ladies-in-waiting. The girls hid their smiles, for Pug was still something of a celebrity in the keep. Carline shooed them off, saying, "I would like to speak with Squire Pug in private." Roland hesitated, then bowed stiffly. Pug was irritated by the dark look Roland gave him as he left with the young ladies.

The two young ladies looked over their shoulder at Pug and Carline, giggling, which seemed only to add to Roland's irritation.

Pug stood as Carline approached and made an awkward bow. She said, in short tones, "Oh, sit down. I find that rubbish tiring and get all I need from Roland."

Pug sat. The girl took her place next to him, and they were both silent for a moment. Finally she said, "I haven't seen you for more than a week. Have you been busy?

Pug felt uncomfortable, still confused by the girl and her mercurial moods. She had been only warm to him since the day, three weeks ago, when he had saved her from the trolls, stirring up a storm of gossip among the staff of the castle. She remained short-tempered with others, however, especially Squire Roland.

"I have been busy with my studies."

"Oh, pooh. You spend too much time in that awful tower."

Pug didn't consider the tower room the least bit awful—except for being a bit drafty. It was his own, and he felt comfortable there.

"We could go riding, Your Highness, if you would like."

The girl smiled. "I would like that. But I'm afraid Lady Marna won't allow it."

Pug was surprised. He thought that after the way he had protected the Princess, even the girl's surrogate mother would allow that he was proper company. "Why not?"

Carline sighed. "She says that when you were a commoner, you would keep your place. Now that you are a courtier, she suspects you of having aspirations." A slight smile played across her lips.

"Aspirations?" Pug said, not understanding.

Carline said shyly, "She thinks that you have ambitions to rise to higher station. She thinks you seek to influence me in certain ways."

Pug stared at Carline. Abruptly comprehension dawned on him, and he said, "Oh," then, *"Oh!* Your Highness." He stood up. "I never would do such a thing. I mean, I would never think to . . . I mean . . ."

Carline abruptly stood and threw Pug an exasperated look. "Boys! You're all idiots." Lifting the hem of her long green gown, she stormed off.

Pug sat down, more perplexed than before by the girl. It was almost as if . . . He let the thought trail away. The more it seemed possible that she could care for him, the more anxious the prospect made him. Carline was quite a bit more than the fairy-tale Princess he had imagined a short time back. With the stamp of one little foot, she could raise a storm in a saltcellar, one that could shake the keep. A girl of complex mind was the Princess, with a contradictory nature tossed into the bargain.

Further musing was interrupted by Tomas, dashing by. Catching a glimpse of his friend, he leapt up the three steps and halted breathlessly before him. "The Duke wants us. The man from the ship has died."

THEY HASTILY ASSEMBLED in the Duke's council chamber, except Kulgan, who had not answered when a messenger knocked at his door. It was supposed he was too deeply engrossed in the problem of the magic scroll.

Father Tully looked pale and drawn. Pug was shocked by his appearance. Only a little more than an hour had passed, yet the old cleric looked as if he had spent several sleepless nights. His eyes were red-rimmed and deep-set in dark circles. His face was ashen, and a light sheen of perspiration showed across his brow.

Borric poured the priest a goblet of wine from a decanter on a sideboard and handed it to him. Tully hesitated, for he was an abstemious man, then drank deeply. The others resumed their former positions around the table.

Borric looked at Tully and said, simply, "Well?"

"The soldier from the beach regained consciousness for only a few minutes, a final rally before the end. During that time I had the opportunity to enter into a mind contact with him. I stayed with him through his last feverish dreams, trying to learn as much about him as I could. I nearly didn't remove the contact in time."

Pug paled. During the mind contact, the priest's mind and the subject become as one. If Tully had not broken contact with the man when he died, the priest could have died or been rendered mad, for the two men shared feelings, fears, and sensations as well as thought. He now understood Tully's exhausted state: the old priest had spent a great deal of energy maintaining the link with an uncooperative subject and had been party to the dying man's pain and terror.

Tully took another drink of wine, then continued. "If this man's dying dreams were not the product of fevered imaginings, then I fear his appearance heralds a grave situation." Tully took another sip of wine and pushed the goblet aside. "The man's name was Xomich. He was a simple soldier of a nation, Honshoni, in something called the Empire of Tsuranuanni."

Borric said, "I have never heard of this nation, nor of that Empire."

Tully nodded and said, "I would have been surprised if you had. That man's ship came from no sea of Midkemia." Pug and Tomas looked at each other, and Pug felt a chilling sensation, as, apparently, did Tomas, whose face had turned pale.

Tully went on. "We can only speculate on how the feat was managed, but I am certain that this ship comes from another world, removed from our own in time and space." Before questions could be asked, he said, "Let me explain."

"This man was sick with fever, and his mind wandered." Tully's face flickered with remembered pain. "He was part of an honor guard for someone he thought of only as 'Great One.' There were conflicting images, and I can't be sure, but it seems that the journey they were on was considered strange, both for the presence of this Great One and for the nature of the mission. The only concrete thought I gained was that this Great One had no need to travel by ship. Beyond that, I have little but quick and disjointed impressions. There was a city he knew as Yankora, then a terrible storm, and a sudden blinding brilliance, which may have been lightning striking the ship, but I think not. There was a thought of his captain and comrades being washed overboard. Then a crash on the rocks." He paused for a moment. "I am not sure if those images are in order, for I think it likely that the crew was lost before the blinding light."

"Why?" asked Borric.

"I'm ahead of myself," said Tully. "First I'd like to explain why I think this man is from another world.

"This Xomich grew to manhood in a land ruled by great armies. They are a warrior race, whose ships control the seas. But what seas? Never, to my knowledge, has there been mention of contact with these people. And there are other visions that are even more convincing. Great cities, far larger than those in the heart of Kesh, the largest known to us. Armies on parade during high holiday, marching past a review stand; city garrisons larger than the King's Army of the West."

Algon said, "Still, there is nothing to say they are not from"—he paused, as if the admission were difficult—"across the Endless Sea." That prospect seemed to trouble him less than the notion of some place not of this world.

Tully looked irritated at the interruption. "There is more, much more. I followed him through his dreams, many of his homeland. He remembers creatures unlike any I have heard of or seen, things with six legs that pull wagons like oxen, and other creatures, some that look like insects or reptiles, but speak like men. His land was hot, and his memory of the sun was of one larger than ours and more green in color. This man was not of our world." The last was said flatly, removing from all in the room any lingering doubts.

Tully would never make a pronouncement like that unless he was certain.

The room was silent as each person reflected on what had been said. The boys watched and shared the feeling. It was as if no one were willing to speak, as if to do so would seal the priest's information forever in fact, while to stay silent might let it pass like a bad dream. Borric stood and paced over to the window. It looked out upon a blank rear wall of the castle, but he stared as if seeking something there, something that would provide an answer for the questions that spun in his mind. He turned quickly and said, "How did they get here, Tully?"

The priest shrugged. "Perhaps Kulgan can offer a theory as to the means. What I construct as being the most likely series of events is this: the ship foundered in the storm; the captain of the ship and most of its crew were lost. As a last resort this Great One, whoever he is, invoked a spell to remove the ship from the storm, or change the weather, or some other mighty feat. As a result, the ship was cast from its own world into this, appearing off the coast at Sailor's Grief. With the ship moving at great speed on its own world, it may have appeared here with the same movement, and with the westerly blowing strong, and little or no crew, the ship was driven straight onto the rocks. Or it simply may have appeared upon the rocks, smashed at the instant it came into being here."

Fannon shook his head. "From another world. How can that be possible?"

The old priest raised his hands in a gesture of mystification. "One can only speculate. The Ishapians have old scrolls in their temples. Some are reputed to be copies of older works, which in turn are copies of still older scrolls. They claim the originals date back, in unbroken line, to the time of the Chaos Wars. Among them is mention of 'other planes' and 'other dimensions,' and of concepts lost to us. One thing is clear, however. They speak of lands and peoples unknown and suggest that once mankind traveled to other worlds, or to Midkemia from other worlds. These notions have been the center of religious debate for centuries, and no one could say with certainty what truth there was in any of them." He paused, then said, "Until now. If I had not seen what was in Xomich's mind, I would not have accepted such a theory to explain this day's occurrences. But now . . ."

Borric crossed to his chair to stand behind it, his hands gripping each side of the high back. "It seems impossible."

"That the ship and man were here is fact, Father," said Lyam.

Arutha followed his brother's comment with another. "And we must decide what the chances are that this feat may be duplicated."

Borric said to Tully, "You were right when you said this may herald a grave situation. Should a great Empire be turning its attention toward Crydee and the Kingdom . . ."

Tully shook his head. "Borric, have you so long been removed from my tutelage that you miss the point entirely?" He held up a bony hand as the Duke started to protest. "Forgive me, my lord. I am old and tired and forget my manners. But the truth is still the truth. A mighty nation they are, or rather an empire of nations, and if they have the means to reach us, it could prove dire, but most important is the possibility that this Great One is a magician or priest of high art. For if he is not one alone, if there are more within this Empire, and if they did indeed try to reach this world with magic, then grave times are truly in store for us."

When everyone at the table still appeared not to

comprehend what he was alluding to, Tully continued, like a patient teacher lecturing a group of promising but occasionally slow students. "The ship's appearance may be the product of chance and, if so, is only a cause for curiosity. But if it was by design that it came here, then we may be in peril, for to move a ship to another world is an order of magic beyond my imagining. If these people, the Tsurani as they call themselves, know we are here, and if they possess the means to reach us, then not only must we fear armies that rival Great Kesh at the height of its power, when its reach extended to even this remote corner of the world, we must also face magic far greater than any we have known."

Borric nodded, for the conclusion was obvious, once pointed out. "We must have Kulgan's counsel on this at once."

"One thing, Arutha," said Tully. The Prince looked up from his chair, for he had been lost in thought. "I know why Xomich tried to run from you and your men. He thought you were creatures he knew in his own world, centaurlike creatures, called Thūn, feared by the Tsurani."

"Why would he think that?" asked Lyam, looking puzzled.

"He had never seen a horse, or any creature remotely like it. I expect these people have none."

The Duke sat down again. Drumming his fingers on the table, he said, "If what Father Tully says is true, then we must make some decisions, and quickly. If this is but an accident that has brought these people to our shores, then there may be little to fear. If, however, there is some design to their coming, then we should expect a serious threat. Here we are the fewest in number of all the Kingdom's garrisons, and it would be a hard thing should they come here in force."

The others murmured agreement, and the Duke

said, "We would do well to try to understand that what has been said here is still only speculation, though I am inclined to agree with Tully on mo   points. We should have Kulgan's thoughts upon the matter of these people." He turned to Pug. "Lad, see if your master is free to join us."

Pug nodded and opened the door, then raced through the keep. He ran to the tower steps and took them two at a time. He raised his hand to knock and felt a strange sensation, as if he were near a lightning strike, causing the hair on his arms and scalp to stand up. A sudden sense of wrongness swept over him, and he pounded on the door. "Kulgan! Kulgan! Are you all right?" he shouted, but no answer was forthcoming. He tried the door latch and found it locked. He placed his shoulder against the door and tried to force it, but it held fast. The feeling of strangeness had passed, but fear rose in him at Kulgan's silence. He looked about for something to force the door and, finding nothing, ran back down the stairs.

He hurried into the long hall. Here guards in Crydee livery stood at their post. He shouted at the two nearest, "You two, come with me. My master is in trouble." Without hesitation they followed the boy up the stairs, their boots pounding on the stone steps.

When they reached the magician's door, Pug said, "Break it down!" They quickly put aside spear and shield and leaned their shoulders against the door. Once, twice, three times they heaved, and with a protesting groan the timbers cracked around the lock plate. One last shove and the door flew open. The guards stopped themselves from falling through the door and stepped back, amazement and confusion on their faces. Pug shouldered between them and looked into the room.

On the floor lay Kulgan, unconscious. His blue

robes were disheveled, and one arm was thrown across his face, as if in protection. Two feet from him, where his study table should have stood, hung a shimmering void. Pug stared at the place in the air. A large sphere of grey that was not quite grey shimmered with traces of a broken spectrum. He could not see through it, but there was nothing solid there. Coming out of the grey space was a pair of human arms, reaching toward the magician. When they touched the material of his robe, they stopped and fingered the cloth. As if a decision had been made, they traveled over his body, until they identified Kulgan's arm. The hands took hold of him and tried to lift his arm into the void. Pug stood in horror, for whoever or whatever was on the other side of the void was trying to pull the stout magician up and through. Another pair of hands reached through and picked up the magician's arm next to where the first held him, and Kulgan was being pulled toward the void.

Pug turned and grabbed one of the spears from against the wall where the shocked guards had placed them. Before either of the men-at-arms could act, he leveled it at the grey spot and threw.

The spear flew across the ten feet that separated them from Kulgan and disappeared into the void. A brief second after, the arms dropped Kulgan and withdrew. Suddenly the grey void blinked out of existence, with a clap of air rushing in to fill it. Pug ran to Kulgan's side and knelt by his master.

The magician was breathing, but his face was white and beaded with sweat. His skin felt cold and clammy. Pug ran to Kulgan's sleeping pallet and pulled off a blanket. As he was covering the magician, he shouted at the guards, "Get Father Tully."

•   •   •

Pug and Tomas sat up that night, unable to sleep. Tully had tended to the magician, giving a favorable prognosis. Kulgan was in shock but would recover in a day or two.

Duke Borric had questioned Pug and the guards on what they had witnessed, and now the castle was in an uproar. All the guards had been turned out, and patrols to the outlying areas of the Duchy had been doubled. The Duke still did not know what the connection between the appearance of the ship and the strange manifestation in the magician's quarters was, but he was taking no chances with the safety of his realm. All along the walls of the castle, torches burned, and guards had been sent to Longpoint lighthouse and the town below.

Tomas sat next to Pug on a bench in Princess Carline's garden, one of the few quiet places in the castle. Tomas looked thoughtfully at Pug. "I expect that these Tsurani people are coming."

Pug ran a hand through his hair. "We don't know that."

Tomas sounded tired. "I just have a feeling."

Pug nodded. "We'll know tomorrow when Kulgan can tell us what happened."

Tomas looked out toward the wall. "I've never seen it so strange around here. Not even when the Dark Brotherhood and the goblins attacked back when we were little, remember?"

Pug nodded, silent for a moment, then said, "We knew what we were facing then. The dark elves have been attacking castles on and off as far back as anyone can remember. And goblins . . . well, they're goblins."

They sat in silence for a long time; then the sound of boots on the pavement announced someone coming. Swordmaster Fannon, in chain mail and tabard, halted before them. "What? Up so late? You should both be abed." The old fighter turned to survey the castle walls. "There are many who find themselves unable to sleep this night." He turned his attention back to the boys. "Tomas, a soldier needs to learn the knack of taking sleep whenever he can find it, for there are many long days when there is none. And you, Squire Pug, should be asleep as well. Now, why don't you try to rest yourselves?"

The boys nodded, bade the Swordmaster good night, and left. The grey-haired commander of the Duke's guard watched them go and stood quietly in the little garden for a time, alone with his own disquieting thoughts.

PUG WAS AWAKENED by the sound of footsteps passing his door. He quickly pulled on trousers and tunic and hurried up the steps to Kulgan's room. Passing the hastily replaced door, he found the Duke and Father Tully standing over Kulgan's sleeping pallet. Pug heard his master's voice, sounding feeble, as he complained about being kept abed. "I tell you, I'm fine," Kulgan insisted. "Just let me walk about a bit, and I'll be back to normal in no time."

Tully, still sounding weary, said, "Back on your back, you mean. You sustained a nasty jolt, Kulgan. Whatever it was that knocked you unconscious packed no small wallop. You were lucky, it could have been much worse."

Kulgan noticed Pug, who stood quietly at the door, not wishing to disturb anyone. "Ha, Pug," he said, his voice regaining some of its usual volume. "Come in, come in. I understand I have you to thank for not taking an unexpected journey with unknown companions."

Pug smiled, for Kulgan seemed his old, jovial self,

in spite of his wan appearance. "I really did nothing, sir. I just felt that something was not right, and acted."

"Acted quickly and well," said the Duke with a smile. "The boy is again responsible for the well-being of one of my household. At this rate I may have to grant him the title Defender of the Ducal Household."

Pug smiled, pleased with the Duke's praise. Borric turned to the magician. "Well, seeing as you are full of fire, I think we should have a talk about yesterday. Are you well enough?"

The question brought an irritated look from Kulgan. "Of course I'm well enough. That's what I've been trying to tell you for the last ten minutes." Kulgan started to rise from the bed, but as dizziness overtook him, Tully put a restraining hand on his shoulder, guiding him back to the large pile of pillows he had been resting on.

"You can talk here quite well enough, thank you. Now, stay in bed."

Kulgan made no protest. He shortly felt better and said, "Fine, but hand me my pipe, will you, please?"

Pug fetched Kulgan's pipe and pouch of tabac and, as the magician tamped down the bowl, a long burning taper from the fire pot. Kulgan lit his pipe and, when it was burning to his satisfaction, lay back with a contented look on his face. "Now," he said, "where do we begin?"

The Duke quickly filled him in on what Tully had revealed, with the priest adding a few details the Duke overlooked. When they were done, Kulgan nodded. "Your assumption about the origin of these people is likely. I suspected the possibility when I saw the artifacts brought from the ship, and the events in this room yesterday bear me out." He paused for a moment, organizing his thoughts. "The scroll was a personal letter from a magician of these people, the Tsurani, to his wife, but it was also more. The seal was magically endowed to force the reader to incant a spell contained at the end of the message. It is a remarkable spell enabling anyone, whether or not they can normally read, to read the scroll."

The Duke said, "This is a strange thing."

Tully said, "It's astonishing."

"The concepts involved are completely new to me," agreed Kulgan. "Anyway, I had neutralized that spell so I could read the letter without fear of magical traps, common to private messages written by magicians. The language was of course strange, and I employed a spell from another scroll to translate it. Even understanding the language through that spell, I don't fully understand everything discussed.

"A magician named Fanatha was traveling by ship to a city on his homeworld. Several days out to sea, they were struck by a severe storm. The ship lost its mast, and many of the crew were washed overboard. The magician took a brief time to pen the scroll—it was written in a hasty hand—and cast the spells upon it. It seems this man could have left the ship at any time and returned to his home or some other place of safety, but was enjoined from doing so by his concern for the ship and its cargo. I am not clear on this point, but the tone of the letter suggested that risking his life for the others on the ship was somehow unusual. Another puzzling thing was a mention of his duty to someone he called the 'Warlord.' I may be reaching for straws, but the tone leads me to think this was a matter of honor or a promise, not some personal duty. In any event he penned the note, sealed it, and was then going to undertake to move the ship magically."

Tully shook his head in disbelief. "Incredible."

"And as we understand magic, impossible," Kulgan added excitedly.

Pug noticed that the magician's professional interest was not shared by the Duke, who looked openly troubled. The boy remembered Tully's comments on what magic of that magnitude meant if these people were to invade the Kingdom. The magician continued, "These people possess powers about which we can only speculate. The magician was very clear on a number of points—his ability to compress so many ideas into so short a message shows an unusually organized mind.

"He took great pains to reassure his wife he would do everything in his power to return. He referred to opening a rift to the 'new world,' because—and I don't fully understand this—a bridge was already established, and some device he possessed lacked . . . some capacity or another to move the ship on his own world. From all indications, it was a most desperate gamble. He placed a second spell on the scroll—and this is what caught me in the end. I thought by neutralizing the first spell I had countered the second also, but I was in error. The second spell was designed to activate as soon as someone had finished reading the scroll aloud, another unheard-of piece of magical art. The spell caused another of these rifts to open, so the message would be transported to a place called 'the Assembly' and from there to his wife. I was nearly caught in the rift with the message."

Pug stepped forward. Without thinking, he blurted, "Then those hands might have been his friends trying to find him."

Kulgan looked at his apprentice and nodded. "A possibility. In any event, we can derive much from this episode. These Tsurani have the ability to control magic that we can only hint at in our speculation. We know a little about the occurrences of rifts, and nothing of their nature."

The Duke looked surprised. "Please explain."

Kulgan drew deep on his pipe, then said, "Magic, by its nature, is unstable. Occasionally a spell will become warped—why, we don't know—to such a degree, it . . . tears at the very fabric of the world. For a brief time a rift occurs, and a passage is formed, going . . . somewhere. Little else is known about such occurrences, except that they involve tremendous releases of energy."

Tully said, "There are theories, but no one understands why every so often a spell, or magic device, suddenly explodes in this fashion and why this instability in reality is created. There have been several occurrences like this, but we have only secondhand observations to go on. Those who witnessed the creation of these rifts died or vanished."

Kulgan picked up the narrative again. "It's considered axiomatic that they were destroyed along with anything within several feet of the rift." He looked thoughtful for a moment. "By rights I should have been killed when that rift appeared in my study."

The Duke interrupted. "From your description, these rifts, as you call them, are dangerous."

Kulgan nodded. "Unpredictable, as well. They are one of the most uncontrollable forces ever discovered. If these people know how to manufacture them and control them as well, to act as a gate between worlds, and can pass through them safely, then they have arts of the most powerful sort."

Tully said, "We've suspected something of the nature of rifts before, but this is the first time we've had anything remotely like hard evidence."

Kulgan said, "Bah! Strange people and unknown objects have appeared suddenly from time to time over the years, Tully. This would certainly explain where they came from."

Tully appeared unwilling to concede the point. "Theory only, Kulgan; not proof. The people have all been dead, and the devices . . . no one understands the two or three that were not burned and twisted beyond recognition."

Kulgan smiled. "Really? What about the man who appeared twenty years ago in Salador?" To the Duke he said, "This man spoke no language known and was dressed in the strangest fashion."

Tully looked down his nose at Kulgan. "He was also hopelessly mad and never could speak a word that could be understood. The temples invested much time on him—"

Borric paled. "Gods! A nation of warriors, with armies many times the size of our own, who have access to our world at will. Let us hope they have not turned their eyes toward the Kingdom."

Kulgan nodded and blew a puff of smoke. "As yet, we have not heard of any other appearances of these people, and we may not have to fear them, but I have a feeling . . ." He left the thought unfinished for a moment. He turned a little to one side, easing some minor discomfort, then said, "It may be nothing, but a reference to a bridge in the message troubles me. It smacks of a permanent way between the worlds already in existence. I hope I'm wrong." The sound of feet pounding up the stairs made them turn. A guard hurried in and came to attention before the Duke, handing him a small paper.

The Duke dismissed the man and opened the folded paper. He read it quickly, then handed it to Tully. "I sent fast riders to the elves and the dwarves, with pigeons to carry replies. The Elf Queen sends word that she is already riding to Crydee and will be here in two days' time."

Tully shook his head. "As long as I have lived, I have never heard of the Lady Aglaranna leaving Elvandar. This sets my bones cold."

Kulgan said, "Things must be approaching a serious turn for her to come here. I hope I am wrong, but think that we are not the only ones to have news of these Tsurani."

Silence descended over the room, and Pug was struck by a feeling of hopelessness. He shook it off, but its echoes followed him for days.

6

Elfcounsel

Pug *leaned out* the window.

Despite the driving rain that had come in early morning, the courtyard was in an uproar. Besides the necessary preparations for any important visit, there was the added novelty of these visitors being elves. Even the infrequent elf messenger from Queen Aglaranna was the object of much curiosity when one appeared at the castle, for rarely did the elves venture south of the river Crydee. The elves lived apart from the society of men, and their ways were thought strange and magical. They had lived in these lands long before the coming of men to the West, and there was an unvoiced agreement that, in spite of any claims made by the Kingdom, they were a free people.

A cough caused Pug to turn and see Kulgan sitting over a large tome. The magician indicated with a glance that the boy should return to his studies. Pug closed the window shutters and sat on his pallet. Kulgan said, "There will be ample time for you to gawk at elves, boy, in a few hours. Then there will be little time for studies. You must learn to make the best use of what time you have."

Fantus scrambled over to place his head in the boy's lap. Pug scratched absently behind an eye ridge as he picked up a book and started to read. Kulgan had given Pug the task of formulating shared qualities of spells as described by different magicians, in the hope it would deepen his understanding of the nature of magic.

Kulgan was of the opinion that Pug's spells with the trolls had been the result of the tremendous stress of the moment. He hoped the study of other magicians' research might help the boy break through the barriers that held him back in his studies. The book work also proved fascinating to Pug, and his reading had improved greatly.

Pug glanced at his master, who was reading while puffing great clouds of smoke from his long pipe. Kulgan showed no signs of the weakness of the day before and had insisted the boy use these hours to study, rather than sit idly by waiting for the arrival of the Elf Queen and her court.

A few minutes later, Pug's eyes began to sting from the pungent smoke, and he turned back to the window and pushed open the shutters. "Kulgan?"

"Yes, Pug?"

"It would be much nicer working with you if we could somehow keep the fire going for warmth but move the smoke outside." Between the smoking fire pot and the magician's pipe, the room was thick with a blue-white haze.

The magician laughed loudly. "Right you are." He closed his eyes for a moment, his hands flew in a furious motion, and he softly mouthed a series of incantations. Soon he was holding a large sphere of white and grey smoke, which he took to the window and tossed outside, leaving the room fresh and clear.

Pug shook his head, laughing. "Thank you, Kulgan. But I had a more mundane solution in mind. What do you think of making a chimney for the fire pot?"

"Not possible, Pug," Kulgan said, sitting down. He pointed to the wall. "If one had been installed when the tower was built, fine. But to try to remove the stones from the tower, from here past my room, and up to the roof would be difficult, not to mention costly."

"I wasn't thinking of a chimney in the wall, Kulgan. You know how the forge in the smithy has a stone hood taking the heat and smoke through the roof?" The magician nodded. "Well, if I could have a metal one fashioned by the smith, and a metal chimney coming from the hood to carry the smoke away, it would work the same way, wouldn't it?"

Kulgan pondered this for a moment. "I don't see why it wouldn't. But where would you put this chimney?"

"There." Pug pointed to two stones above and to the left of the window. They had been ill fitted when the tower was built, and now there was a large crack between them that allowed the wind to come howling into the room. "This stone could be taken out," he said, indicating the leftmost one. "I checked it and it's loose. The chimney could come from above the fire pot, bend here"—he pointed to a spot in the air above the pot and level with the stone—"and come out here. If we covered the space around it, it would keep the wind out."

Kulgan looked impressed. "It's a novel idea, Pug. It might work. I'll speak to the smith in the morning and get his opinion on the matter. I wonder that no one thought of it before."

Feeling pleased with himself for having thought of the chimney, Pug resumed his studies. He reread a passage that had caught his eye before, puzzling over an ambiguity. Finally he looked up at the magician and said, "Kulgan."

"Yes, Pug?" he answered, looking up from his book.

"Here it is again. Magician Lewton uses the same cantrip here as Marsus did, to baffle the effects of the spell upon the caster, directing it to an external target." Placing the large tome down so as not to lose his place, he picked up another. "But here Dorcas writes that the use of this cantrip blunts the spell, increasing the chance that it will not work. How can there be so much disagreement over the nature of this single construction?"

Kulgan narrowed his gaze a moment as he regarded his student. Then he sat back, taking a long pull on his pipe, sending forth a cloud of blue smoke. "It shows what I've said before, lad. Despite any vanity we magicians might feel about our craft, there's really very little order or science involved. Magic is a collection of folk arts and skills passed along from master to apprentice since the beginning of time. Trial and error, trial and error is the way. There has never been an attempt to create a system for magic, with laws and rules and axioms that are well understood and widely accepted." He looked thoughtfully at Pug. "Each of us is like a carpenter, making a table, but each of us choosing different woods, different types of saws, some using pegs and dowel, others using nails, another dovetailing joints, some staining, others not . . . in the end there's a table, but the means for making it are not the same in each case.

"What we have here is most likely an insight about the limits of each of these venerable sages you study, rather than any sort of prescription for magic. For Lewton and Marsus, the cantrip aided the construction of the spell; for Dorcas, it hindered."

"I understand your example, Kulgan, but I'll never understand how these magicians all could do the *same* thing, but in so many different ways. I understand that each of them wanted to achieve his end and found a different means, but there is something missing in the manner they did it."

Kulgan looked intrigued. "What is missing, Pug?"

The boy looked thoughtful. "I . . . I don't know. It's as if I expect to find something that will tell me, 'This is the way it must be done, the only way,' or something like that. Does that make any sense?"

Kulgan nodded. "I think I know you well enough to understand. You have a very well-ordered mind, Pug. You understand logic far better than most, even those much older than yourself. You see things as a system, rather than as a haphazard collection of events. Perhaps that is part of your trouble."

Pug's expression showed his interest in what the magician was saying. Kulgan continued. "Much of what I am trying to teach is based on a system of logic, cause and effect, but much is not. It is like trying to teach someone to play the lute. You can show them the fingering of the strings, but that knowledge alone will not make a great troubadour. It is the art, not the scholarship, that troubles you."

"I think I understand, Kulgan." He sounded dispirited.

Kulgan stood up. "Don't dwell on it; you are still young, and I have hope for you yet." His tone was light, and Pug felt the humor in it.

"Then I am not a complete loss?" he said with a smile.

"Indeed not." Kulgan looked thoughtfully at his

pupil. "In fact, I have the feeling that someday you may use that logical mind of yours for the betterment of magic."

Pug was a little startled. He did not think of himself as one to accomplish great things.

Shouts came through the window, and Pug hurried to look out. A troop of guards was running toward the front gate. Pug turned to Kulgan. "The elves must be coming! The guard is out."

Kulgan said, "Very well. We are done with study for this day. There will be no holding you until you get a look at the elves. Run along."

Pug raced out the door and down the stairs. He took them two at a time, jumping to the bottom of the tower landing over the last four and hitting the floor at a full run. He dashed through the kitchen and out the door. As he rounded the keep to the front courtyard, he found Tomas standing atop a hay wagon. Pug climbed up next to him, to be better able to see the arrival over the heads of the curious keep folk gathered around.

Tomas said, "I thought you weren't coming, thought you'd be locked away with your books all day."

Pug said, "I wouldn't miss this. Elves!"

Tomas playfully dug his elbow into Pug's side. "Haven't you had your fill of excitement for this week?"

Pug threw him a black look. "If you're so indifferent, why are you standing in the rain on this wagon?"

Tomas didn't answer. Instead he pointed. "Look!"

Pug turned to see the guard company snap to attention as riders in green cloaks entered through the gate. They rode to the main doors of the keep, where the Duke waited. Pug and Tomas watched in awe, for they rode the most perfect white horses the boys had ever seen, using no saddle or bridle. The horses seemed untouched by wetness, and their coats glowed faintly; whether by some magic, or a trick of the grey afternoon light, Pug couldn't tell. The leader rode on an especially grand animal, full seventeen hands in height, with a long flowing mane and a tail like a plume. The riders reared the mounts in salute, and an audible intake of breath could be heard from those in the crowd.

"Elf steeds," said Tomas, in hushed tones. The horses were the legendary mounts of the elves. Martin Longbow had once told the boys they lived in hidden, deep glades near Elvandar. It was said they possessed intelligence and a magic nature, and no human could sit on their backs. It was also said that only one with royal elvish blood could command them to carry riders.

Grooms rushed forward to take the horses, but a musical voice said, "There is no need." It came from the first rider, the one mounted on the greatest steed. She jumped nimbly down, without aid, landing lightly on her feet, and threw back her hood, revealing a mane of thick reddish hair. Even in the gloom of the afternoon rain it appeared to be shot through with golden highlights. She was tall, nearly a match for Borric. She mounted the steps as the Duke came forward to meet her.

Borric held out his hands and took hers in greeting. "Welcome, my lady; you do me and my house a great honor."

The Elf Queen said, "You are most gracious, Lord Borric." Her voice was rich and surprisingly clear, able to carry over the crowd so that all in the courtyard could hear. Pug felt Tomas's hand clutching his shoulder. He turned to see a rapt expression on Tomas's face. "She's beautiful," said the taller boy.

Pug returned his attention to the welcome. He was forced to agree that the Queen of the elves was indeed beautiful, if not in entirely human terms. Her eyes were large and a pale blue, nearly luminous in the gloom. Her face was finely chiseled, with high cheekbones and a strong but not masculine jaw. Her smile was full, and her teeth shone white between almost-red lips. She wore a simple circlet of gold around her brow, which held back her hair, revealing the lobeless, upswept ears that were the hallmark of her race.

The others in her company dismounted, all dressed in rich clothing. Each tunic was bright with contrasting leggings below. One wore a tunic of deep russet, another pale yellow with a surcoat of bright green. Some wore purple sashes, and others crimson hose. Despite the bright colors, these were elegant and finely made garments, with nothing loud or gaudy about them. There were eleven riders with the Queen, all similar in appearance, tall, youthful, and lithe in movement.

The Queen turned from the Duke and said something in her musical language. The elf steeds reared in salute, then ran through the gate, past the surprised onlookers. The Duke ushered his guests inside, and soon the crowd drifted away. Tomas and Pug sat quietly in the rain.

Tomas said, "If I live to be a hundred, I don't think that I'll ever see her like."

Pug was surprised, for his friend rarely showed such feelings. He had a brief impulse to chide Tomas over his boyish infatuation, but something about his companion's expression made that seem inappropriate. "Come on," he said, "we're getting drenched."

Tomas followed Pug from the wagon. Pug said, "You had better change into some dry clothing, and see if you can borrow a dry tabard."

Tomas said, "Why?"

With an evil grin, Pug said, "Oh? Didn't I tell you? The Duke wants you to dine with the court. He wants you to tell the Elf Queen what you saw on the ship."

Tomas looked as if he were going to break down and run. "Me? Dine in the great hall?" His face went white. "Talk? To the Queen?"

Pug laughed with glee. "It's easy. You open your mouth and words come out."

Tomas swung a roundhouse at Pug, who ducked under the blow, grabbing his friend from behind when he spun completely around. Pug had strength in his arms even if he lacked Tomas's size, and he easily picked his larger friend off the ground. Tomas struggled, and soon they were laughing uncontrollably. "Pug, put me down."

"Not until you calm down."

"I'm all right."

Pug put him down. "What brought that on?"

"Your smug manner, and not telling me until the last minute."

"All right. So I'm sorry I waited to tell you. Now what's the rest of it?"

Tomas looked uncomfortable, more than was reasonable from the rain. "I don't know how to eat with quality folk. I'm afraid I'll do something stupid."

"It's easy. Just watch me and do what I do. Hold the fork in your left hand and cut with the knife. Don't drink from the bowls of water; they're to wash with, and use them a lot, because your hands will get greasy from the rib bones. And make sure you toss the bones over your shoulder to the dogs, and not on the floor in front of the Duke's table. And don't wipe your mouth on your sleeves, use the tablecloth, that's what it's for."

They walked toward the soldiers' commons, with Pug giving his friend instruction on the finer points of court manners. Tomas was impressed at the wealth of Pug's knowledge.

· · ·

TOMAS VACILLATED BETWEEN looking sick and pained. Each time someone regarded him, he felt as if he had been found guilty of the most grievous breach of etiquette and looked sick. Whenever his gaze wandered to the head table and he caught sight of the Elf Queen, his stomach tied up in knots and he looked pained.

Pug had arranged for Tomas to sit next to him at one of the more removed tables from the Duke's. Pug's usual place was at Lord Borric's table, next to the Princess. He was glad for this chance to be away from her, for she still showed displeasure with him. Usually she chatted with him about the thousand little bits of gossip the ladies of the court found so interesting, but last night she had pointedly ignored him, lavishing all her attention on a surprised and obviously pleased Roland. Pug found his own reaction puzzling, relief mixed with a large dose of irritation. While he felt relieved to be free of her wrath, he found Roland's fawning upon her a bothersome itch he couldn't scratch.

Pug had been troubled by Roland's hostility toward him of late, poorly hidden behind stiff manners. He had never been as close to Roland as Tomas had, but they had never before had cause to be angry with one another. Roland had always been one of the crowd of boys Pug's age. He had never hidden behind his rank when he had cause to be at odds with the common boys, always standing ready to settle the matter in whatever way proved necessary. And already being an experienced fighter when he arrived in Crydee, his differences soon were settled peacefully as often as not. Now there was this dark tension between Pug and Roland, and Pug found himself wishing he was Tomas's equal in fighting; Tomas was the only boy Roland was unable to best with fists, their one encounter ending quickly with Roland receiving a sound thumping. For as certain as the sun was rising in the morning, Pug knew a confrontation with the hotheaded young Squire was quickly approaching. He dreaded it, but knew once it came, he'd feel relief.

Pug glanced at Tomas, finding his friend lost in his own discomfort. Pug returned his attention to Carline. He felt overwhelmed by the Princess, but her allure was tempered by a strange discomfort he felt whenever she was near. As beautiful as he found her— her black locks and blue eyes igniting some very uncomfortable flames of imagination—the images were always somehow hollow, colorless at heart, lacking the amber-and-rose glow such daydreams had possessed when Carline had been a distant, unapproachable, and unknown figure. Observing her closely for even as short a time as he had recently made such idealized musing impossible. She was proving herself to be just too complicated to fit into simple daydreams. On the whole he found the question of the Princess troublesome, but seeing her with Roland made him forget his internal conflicts over her, as a less intellectual, more basic emotion came to the fore. He was becoming jealous.

Pug sighed, shaking his head as he thought about his own misery at this moment, ignoring Tomas's. At least, thought Pug, I'm not alone. To Roland's obvious discomfort, Carline was deeply involved at the moment in conversation with Prince Calin of Elvandar, son of Aglaranna. The Prince seemed to be the same age as Arutha, or Lyam, but then so did his mother, who appeared to be in her early twenties. All the elves, except the Queen's seniormost adviser, Tathar, were quite young looking, and Tathar looked no older than the Duke.

When the meal was over, most of the Duke's court retired. The Duke rose and offered his arm to

Aglaranna and led those who had been ordered to attend them to his council chamber.

For the third time in two days, the boys found themselves in the Duke's council chamber. Pug was more relaxed about being there than before, thanks in part to the large meal, but Tomas seemed more disturbed than ever. If the taller boy had spent the hour before dinner staring at the Elf Queen, in these close quarters he seemed to be looking everywhere but in her direction. Pug thought Aglaranna noticed Tomas's behavior and smiled slightly, but he couldn't be sure.

The two elves who came with the Queen, Calin and Tathar, went at once to the side table that held the bowl and the artifacts taken from the Tsurani soldier. They examined them closely, fascinated by every detail.

The Duke called the meeting to order, and the two elves came to chairs on either side of the Queen. Pug and Tomas stood by the door as usual.

The Duke said, "We have told you what has occurred as well as we know, and now you have seen proof with your own eyes. If you think it would be helpful, the boys can recount the events on the ship."

The Queen inclined her head, but it was Tathar who spoke. "I would like to hear the story firsthand, Your Grace."

Borric motioned for the boys to approach. They stepped forward, and Tathar said, "Which of you found this outworlder?"

Tomas threw Pug a look that indicated the shorter boy should do the talking. Pug said, "We both did, sir," not knowing the proper address for the elf. Tathar seemed content with the general honorific. Pug recounted the events of that day, leaving out nothing he could remember. When he had done, Tathar asked a series of questions, each jogging Pug's memory, bringing out small details he had forgotten.

When he was done, Pug stepped back, and Tathar repeated the process with Tomas. Tomas began haltingly, obviously discomfited, and the Elf Queen bestowed a reassuring smile on him. That only served to make him more unsettled, and he was soon dismissed.

Tathar's questions provided more details about the ship, small things forgotten by the boys: fire buckets filled with sand tossed about the deck, empty spearracks, substantiating Arutha's surmise that it had been, indeed, a warship.

Tathar leaned back. "We have never heard of such a ship. It is in many ways like other ships, but not in all ways. We are convinced."

As if by silent signal, Calin spoke. "Since the death of my Father-King, I serve as Warleader of Elvandar. It is my duty to supervise the scouts and patrols that guard our glades. For some time we have been aware that there were strange occurrences in the great forest, south of the river Crydee. Several times our runners have found tracks made by men, in isolated parts of the forest. They have been found as near as the borders of Elvandar, and as far as the North Pass near Stone Mountain.

"Our scouts have tried for weeks to find these men, but only tracks could be seen. There were none of the usual things that would be expected of a scouting or raiding party. These people were taking great care to disguise their presence. Had they not passed so close to Elvandar, they might have remained undetected, but no one may intrude near our home and go unnoticed.

"Several days ago, one of our scouts sighted a band of strangers passing the river, near the edge of our forests heading in the direction of the North Pass. He followed for a half day's march, then lost them."

Fannon raised his eyebrows. "An elven tracker lost them?"

Calin inclined his head slightly. "Not by his lack of skill. They simply entered a thick glade and never appeared on the other side. He followed their tracks up to the point where they vanished."

Lyam said, "I think we know now where they went." He looked uncommonly somber, resembling his father more than usual.

Calin continued. "Four days before your message arrived, I led a patrol that sighted a band near the place of last sighting. They were short and stocky men, without beards. Some were fair and others dark. There were ten of them, and they moved through the forest with little ease; the slightest sound put them on guard. But with all their caution, they still had no idea they were being tracked.

"They all wore armor of bright colors, reds and blues, some green, others yellow, save one in black robes. They carried swords like the one on the table and others without the serration, round shields, and strange bows, short and curved in an odd doubled-back way."

Algon sat forward. "They're recurved bows, like the ones used by Keshian dog-soldiers."

Calin spread his hands. "Kesh has long been gone from these lands, and when we knew the Empire, they used simple bows of yew or ash."

Algon interrupted in excited tones. "They have a way, secret to them, of fashioning such bows from wood and animal horn. They are small, but possess great power, though not as much as the longbow. Their range is surprisingly—"

Borric cleared his throat pointedly, being unwilling to let the Horsemaster indulge himself in his preoccupation with weaponry. "If His Highness will please continue?"

Algon sat back, blushing furiously, and Calin said,

"I tracked them for two days. They stopped and made cold camp at night and took great care not to leave signs of their passing. All food scraps and body wastes were gathered together in a sack and carried by one of their band. They moved carefully, but were easy for us to follow.

"When they came to the edge of the forest, near the mouth of North Pass, they made marks upon a parchment as they had several times during their trek. Then the one in black activated some strange device, and they vanished." There was a stir from the Duke's company. Kulgan especially looked disturbed.

Calin paused. "The thing that was most strange, however, was their language, for their speech was unlike any we know. They spoke in hushed tones, but we could hear them, and their words were without meaning."

The Queen then spoke. "Hearing this, I became alarmed, for these outworlders are clearly mapping the West, ranging freely through the great forest, the hills of Stone Mountain, and now the coasts of the Kingdom. Even as we prepared to send you word, the reports of these outworlders became more frequent. Several more bands were seen in the area of the North Pass."

Arutha sat forward, resting his arms on the table. "If they cross the North Pass, they will discover the way to Yabon, and the Free Cities. The snows will have started to fall in the mountains, and they may discover we are effectively isolated from aid during the winter."

For a moment alarm flickered on the Duke's face, betraying his stoic demeanor. He regained his composure and said, "There is still the South Pass, and they may not have mapped that far. If they were in that area, the dwarves would most likely have seen signs of them, as the villages of the Grey Towers are more widely scattered than those of Stone Mountain."

"Lord Borric," said Aglaranna, "I would never have ventured from Elvandar if I had not thought the situation critical. From what you have told us of the outworld Empire, if they are as powerful as you say, then I fear for all the free peoples of the West. While the elves have little love for the Kingdom as such, we respect those of the Crydee, for you have ever been honorable men and have never sought to extend your realm into our lands. We would ally with you should these outworlders come for conquest."

Borric sat quietly for a moment. "I thank the Lady of Elvandar for the aid of the elven folk should war come. We are also in your debt for your counsel, for now we can act. Had we not known of these happenings in the great forests, we would likely have given the aliens more time for whatever trouble they are preparing." He paused again, as if considering his next words. "And I am convinced that these Tsurani plan us ill. Scouting an alien and strange land I could see, trying to determine the nature and temper of the people who live there, but extensive mapping by warriors can only be a prelude to invasion."

Kulgan sounded fatigued as he said, "They most likely will come with a mighty host."

Tully shook his head. "Perhaps not." All eyes turned to him as he said, "I am not so certain. Much of what I read in Xomich's mind was confused, but there is something about this Empire of Tsuranuanni that makes it unlike any nation we know of; there is something very alien about their sense of duty and alliances. I can't tell you how I know, but I suspect they may choose to test us first, with but a small part of their might. It's as if their attentions are elsewhere, and we're an afterthought." He shook his head in admitted confusion. "I have this sense, nothing more."

The Duke sat upright, a commanding tone coming into his voice. "We will act. I will send messages to Duke Brucal of Yabon, and again to Stone Mountain and the Grey Towers."

Aglaranna said, "It would be good to hear what the dwarven folk know."

Borric said, "I had hoped for word by now, but our messengers have not returned, nor have the pigeons they carry."

Lyam said, "Hawks, perhaps. The pigeons are not always reliable, or perhaps the messengers never reached the dwarves."

Borric turned to Calin. "It has been forty years since the siege of Carse, and we have had little traffic with the dwarves since. Who commands the dwarven clans now?"

The Elf Prince said, "As then. Stone Mountain is under the banner of Harthorn, of Hogar's line, at village Delmoria. The Grey Towers rally to the banner of Dolgan, of Tholin's line, at village Caldara."

"Both are known to me, though I was but a boy when they raised the Dark Brothers' siege at Carse," said Borric. "They will prove fierce allies if trouble comes."

Arutha said, "What of the Free Cities, and the Prince in Krondor?"

Borric sat back. "I must think on that, for there are problems in the East, or so I have word. I will give thought to the matter this night." He stood. "I thank you all for this counsel. Return to your quarters and avail yourselves of rest and refreshments. I will ask you to consider plans for dealing with the invaders, should they come, and we will meet again tomorrow."

As the Elf Queen rose, he offered her his arm,

then escorted her through the doors that Tomas and Pug held open. The boys were the last to exit. Fannon took Tomas in tow, leading him to the soldiers' commons, while Kulgan stood outside the hall with Tully and the two elven advisers.

The magician turned to his apprentice. "Pug, Prince Calin expressed an interest in your small library of magic books. Would you please show them to him?"

Pug said he would and led the Prince up the stairs to his door and opened it for him. Calin stepped through, and Pug followed. Fantus was asleep and woke with a start. He threw the elf a distrustful look.

Calin slowly crossed over to the drake and spoke a few soft words in a language that Pug didn't understand. Fantus lost his nervousness and stretched forth his neck to allow the Prince to scratch his head.

After a moment the drake looked expectantly to Pug. Pug said, "Yes, dinner is over. The kitchen will be full of scraps." Fantus moved to the window with a wolfish grin and used his snout to push it open. With a snap of his wings he was out, gliding toward the kitchen.

Pug offered Calin a stool, but the Prince said, "Thank you, but your chairs and stools are of little comfort to my kind. I will just sit on the floor, with your leave. You have a most unusual pet, Squire Pug." He gave Pug a small smile. Pug was a little uncomfortable hosting the Elf Prince in his poor room, but the elf's manner was such that the boy started to relax.

"Fantus is less a pet than a permanent guest. He has a mind of his own. It is not unusual for him to disappear for weeks at a time, now and again, but mostly he stays here. He must eat outside the kitchen now that Meecham has gone."

Calin inquired who Meecham was. Pug explained, adding, "Kulgan has sent him over the mountains to

Bordon, with some of the Duke's guards, before the North Pass is snowed in. He didn't say why he was going, Highness."

Calin looked at one of the boy's books. "I prefer to be called Calin, Pug."

Pug nodded, pleased. "Calin, what do you think the Duke has in mind?"

The elf gave him an enigmatic smile. "The Duke will reveal his own plans, I think. My guess is that Meecham is preparing the way should the Duke choose to journey east. You will most probably know on the morrow." He held up the book he had glanced at. "Did you find this interesting?"

Pug leaned over and read the title. "Dorcas's *Treatise on the Animation of Objects?* Yes, though it seemed a little unclear."

"A fair judgment. Dorcas was an unclear man, or at least I found him so."

Pug started. "But Dorcas died thirty years ago."

Calin smiled broadly, showing even white teeth. His pale eyes shone in the lantern light. "Then you know little of elven lore?"

"Little," Pug agreed. "You are the first elf I have ever spoken with, though I may have seen another elf once, when I was very little. I'm not sure." Calin tossed aside the book. "I know only what Martin Longbow has told me, that you can somehow speak with animals, and some spirits. That you live in Elvandar and the surrounding elven forests, and that you stay among your own kind mostly."

The elf laughed, a soft, melodic sound. "Nearly all true. Knowing friend Longbow, I wager some of the tales were colorful, for while he is not a deceiving man, he has an elf's humor." Pug's expression showed he did not understand. "We live a very long time by your standards. We learn to appreciate the humor in the

world, often finding amusement in places where men
find little. Or you can call it simply a different way of
looking at life. Martin has learned this from us, I
think."

Pug nodded. "Mocking eyes."

Calin raised an eyebrow in question. Pug explained, "Many people here find Martin difficult to be
with. Different, somehow. I once heard a soldier say he
had mocking eyes."

Calin sighed. "Life has been difficult for Martin.
He was left on his own at an early age. The Monks of
Silban are good, kindly men, but ill equipped to raise a
boy. Martin lived in the woods like a wild thing when
he could flee his tutors. I found him one day, fighting
with two of our children—we are not very much different from men when very young. Over the years he has
grown to be one of the few humans who is free to come
to Elvandar at will. He is a valued friend. But I think he
bears a special burden of loneliness, not being fully in
the world of elves nor of men, but partially in both."

Pug saw Martin in a new light and resolved to
attempt to know the Huntmaster better. Returning
to the original topic, he said, "Is what he said true?"

Calin nodded. "In some respects. We can speak to
animals only as men do, in tones to make them easy,
though we are better at it than most humans, for we
read the moods of wild things more readily. Martin has
some of this knack. We do not, however, speak with
spirits. There are creatures we know whom humans
consider spirits—dryads, sprites, pixies—but they are
natural beings who live near our magic."

Pug's interest was piqued. "Your magic?"

"Ours is a magic that is part of our being, strongest in Elvandar. It is a heritage ages old, allowing us to
live at peace within our forests. There we work as others do, hunting, tending our gardens, celebrating our

joys, teaching our young. Time passes slowly in El-vandar, for it is an ageless place. That is why I can remember speaking with Dorcas, for in spite of my youthful appearance, I am over a hundred years old."

"A hundred . . ." Pug shook his head. "Poor Tomas, he was distressed to hear you were the Queen's son. Now he will be desolate."

Calin inclined his head, a half-smile playing across his face. "The lad who was with us in the council hall?"

Pug nodded. Calin said, "It is not the first time my Mother-Queen has had such an effect upon a human, though older men can mask the effect with more ease."

"You don't mind?" asked Pug, feeling protective toward his friend.

"No, Pug, of course not. All in Elvandar love the Queen, and it is acknowledged her beauty is unsurpassed. I find it not surprising your friend is smitten. Since my Father-King passed, more than one bold noble of your race has come to press his suit for Aglaranna's hand. Now her mourning is at an end, and she may take another should she wish. That it would be one of your race is unlikely, for while a few such marriages have been made, they are very rare, and tend to be sad things at the end for our kind. She will live many more human life spans, the gods willing."

Calin looked around the room, then added, "It is likely our friend Tomas will outgrow his feelings for the great lady of the elves. Much as your Princess will change her feelings toward you, I would think."

Pug felt embarrassed. He had been curious as to what Carline and the Elf Prince had spoken about during dinner, but had been uncomfortable asking. "I noticed you spoke with her at great length."

"I had expected to meet a hero of seven feet in height, with lightning dancing around his shoulders. It seems you slew a score of trolls with a cast of your hand."

Pug blushed. "It was only two, and mostly by accident."

Calin's eyebrows shot up. "Even two is an accomplishment. I had thought the girl guilty of a flight of fancy. I would like to hear the story."

Pug told him what had happened. When he was done, Calin said, "It is an unusual tale, Pug. I know little of human magic, but I do know enough to think that what you did was as strange as Kulgan said. Elf magic is far different from human, but we understand ours better than you understand your own. Never have I heard of such an occurrence, but I can share this with you. Occasionally, at times of great need, an inner call can be made, bringing forth powers that lay dormant, deep within."

Pug said, "I have thought as much, though it would be nice to understand a little better what happened."

"That may come in time."

Pug looked at his guest and sighed deeply. "I wish I could understand Carline, as well."

Calin shrugged and smiled. "Who can understand another's mind? I think for some time to come you will be the object of her attention. Then, it may be, another will distract her, perhaps young Squire Roland. He seems held in thrall by her."

Pug snorted. "Roland! That . . . bother."

Calin smiled appreciatively. "Then you are fond of the Princess?"

Pug looked upward, as if seeking guidance from some higher source. "I do like her," he admitted with a heavy sigh. "But I don't know if I care for her that special way. Sometimes I think I do—especially when I see Roland fawning over her—but other times I don't.

She makes it *very* hard for me to think clearly, and I always seem to say the wrong things to her."

"Unlike Squire Roland," prompted Calin.

Pug nodded. "He's court born and bred. He knows all the right things to say." Pug leaned back on his elbows and sighed wistfully. "I guess I'm just bothered by him out of envy as much as anything. He makes me feel like an ill-mannered clod with great lumps of stone for hands and tree stumps for feet."

Calin nodded understandingly. "I don't count myself an expert in all the ways of your people, Pug, but I've spent enough time with humans to know that you choose how you feel; Roland makes you feel clumsy only because you let him.

"I would hazard a guess young Roland might feel much the same way when your positions are reversed. The faults we see in others never seem as dreadful as those we see in ourselves. Roland might envy your direct speech and honest manner.

"In any event, what you or Roland do will have little effect on the Princess so long as she's determined to have her own way. She has romanticized you in much the same manner your friend has our Queen. Short of you becoming a hopeless boor, she will not be shaken from this attitude until she is ready. I think she has you in mind as her future consort."

Pug gaped for a moment, then said, "Consort?"

Calin smiled. "The young are often overly concerned with matters to be settled in later years. I suspect her determination in the matter is as much a result of your reluctance as from a true appreciation of your worth. She, like many children, simply wants what she can't have." In a friendly tone he added, "Time will decide the issue."

Pug leaned forward, a worried expression on his face. "Oh, my, I have made a hash of things. Half the keep boys think themselves in love with the Princess. If they only knew how terrifying the real thing can be." He closed his eyes, squeezing them tightly shut a moment. "My head aches. I thought she and Roland . . ."

Calin said, "He may be but a tool to provoke your interest. Sadly, that seems to have resulted in bad feelings between you."

Pug nodded slowly. "I think so. Roland is a good enough sort on the whole; we've been friends for the most part. But since I was elevated in rank, he's been openly hostile. I try to ignore it, but it gets under my skin after a while. Maybe I should try to talk to him."

"That would prove wise, I think. But don't be surprised if he is not receptive to your words. He is most certainly caught up in her spell."

Pug was getting a headache from the topic, and the mention of spells made him ask, "Would you tell me more about elven magic?"

"Our magic is ancient. It is part of what we are and in what we create. Elven boots can make even a human silent when walking, and elven bows are better able to strike the mark, for that is the nature of our magic. It is vested in ourselves, our forests, our creations. It can sometimes be managed, subtly by those who fully understand it . . . Spellweavers, such as Tathar. But this is not easily done, for out magic resists manipulation. It is more like air than anything, always surrounding us, yet unseen. But like air, which can be felt when the wind blows, it has substance. Our forests are called enchanted by men, for so long have we dwelled there, our magic has created the mystery of Elvandar. All who dwell there are at peace. No one may enter Elvandar uninvited, save by mighty arts, and even the distant boundaries of the elven forests cause unease in those who enter with evil intent. It has not always been so; in ages past we shared our lot with others, the moredhel, those you call the Brotherhood of the Dark Path. Since the great break, when we drove them from our forests, Elvandar has been changing, becoming more our place, our home, our essence."

Pug said, "Are the Brothers of the Dark Path truly cousin to the elves?"

Calin's eyes grew hooded. He paused for a moment, then said, "We speak little of such things, for there is much we wish were not true. I can tell you this: there is a bond between the moredhel, whom you call the Brotherhood, and my people, though ancient and long strained. We wish it were not so, but they are true cousins to us. Once in a great while one comes back to us, what we call Returning." He looked as if the topic were making him very uncomfortable.

Pug said, "I'm sorry if "

Calin waved away the apology. "Curiosity is nothing to apologize for in a student, Pug. I just would rather not say more on this subject."

They spoke late into the night, of many things. Pug was fascinated by the Elf Prince and was flattered so many things he said seemed to be of interest to Calin.

At last Calin said, "I should retire. Though I need little rest, I do need some. And I think you do as well."

Pug rose and said, "Thank you for telling me so much." Then he smiled, half in embarrassment. "And for talking to me about the Princess."

"You needed to talk."

Pug led Calin to the long hall, where a servant showed him to his quarters. Pug returned to his room and lay down for sleep, rejoined by a damp Fantus, who snorted in indignation at having to fly through the rain. Fantus was soon asleep. Pug, however, lay staring at the flickering light from his fire pot that danced on the ceiling, unable to call up sleep. He tried to put the tales of strange warriors out of his mind, but images of brightly clad fighters stalking through the forests of the westlands made sleep impossible.

THERE WAS A somber mood throughout Castle Crydee the next morning. The servants' gossip had spread the news about the Tsurani, though the details were lacking. Everyone went about his duties with one ear open for a tidbit of speculation on what the Duke was going to do. Everyone was agreed to one thing: Borric conDoin, Duke of Crydee, was not a man to sit idly by waiting. Something would be done, and soon.

Pug sat atop a bale of hay, watching Tomas practice with a sword, swinging at a pell post, hacking backhand, then forehand, over and over. His blows were halfhearted, and finally he threw his sword down with disgust. "I'm not accomplishing a thing." He walked over and sat next to Pug. "I wonder what they're talking about."

Pug shrugged. "They" were the Duke's council; today the boys had not been asked to attend, and the last four hours had passed slowly.

Abruptly the courtyard became busy as servants began to rush toward the front gate. "Come on," said Tomas. Pug jumped off the bale and followed his friend.

They rounded the keep in time to see the guards turning out as they had the day before. It was colder than yesterday, but there was no rain. The boys climbed on the same wagon, and Tomas shivered. "I think the snows will come early this year. Maybe tomorrow."

"If they do, it will be the earliest snowfall in memory. You should have worn your cloak. Now you're all sweaty from the drill, and the air is chilling you."

Tomas looked pained. "Gods, you sound like my mother."

Pug mimicked an exasperated manner. In a tone that was high-pitched and nasal, he said, "And don't come running to me when you're all blue with chill, and coughing and sneezing, looking for comfort, for you'll find none here, Tomas Megarson."

Tomas grinned. "Now you sound exactly like her."

They turned at the sound of the great doors opening. The Duke and Elf Queen led the other guests from the central keep, the Duke holding the Queen's hand in a parting gesture of friendship. Then the Queen placed her hand to her mouth and sang out a musical series of words, not loud, but carrying over the noise of the crowd. The servants who were standing in the court became silent, and soon the sound of hoofbeats could be heard outside the castle.

Twelve white horses ran through the gates and reared up in greeting to the Elf Queen. The elves quickly mounted, each springing up on an elf steed's back without assistance. They raised their hands in salute to the Duke, then turned and raced out the gate.

For a few minutes after they were gone, the crowd stood around, as if loath to admit that they had seen their last of the elves, probably their last in this lifetime. Slowly they began to drift back to work.

Tomas looked far away, and Pug turned toward him. "What is it?"

Tomas said softly, "I wish I could see Elvandar, someday."

Pug understood. "Maybe you will." Then he added, in lighter tones, "But I doubt it. For I will be a magician, and you will be a soldier, and the Queen will reign in Elvandar long after we are dead."

Tomas playfully jumped atop his friend, wrestling

him down in the straw. "Oh! Is that so. Well, I will too go to Elvandar someday." He pinned Pug under him, sitting atop his chest. "And when I do, I'll be a great hero, with victories over the Tsurani by the score. She'll welcome me as an honored guest. What do you think of that?"

Pug laughed, trying to push his friend off. "And I'll be the greatest magician in the land."

They both laughed. A voice broke through their play. "Pug! There you are."

Tomas got off, and Pug sat up. Approaching them was the stocky figure of Gardell the smith. He was a barrel-chested man, with little hair but a thick black beard. His arms were grimy with smoke, and his apron was burned through with many small holes. He came to the side of the wagon and placed fists on hips. "I've been looking all over for you. I have that hood Kulgan asked me to fashion for your fire pot."

Pug scrambled out of the wagon, with Tomas close behind. They walked after Gardell toward the smithy behind the central keep. The burly smith said, "Damned clever idea, that hood. I've worked the forge for nearly thirty years and never thought of using a hood for a fire pot. Had to make one as soon as Kulgan told me of the plan."

They entered the smithy, a large shed with a large and small forge and several different-sized anvils. All manner of things lay about waiting for repair: armor, stirrup irons, and kitchen utensils. Gardell walked to the larger forge and picked up the hood. It was about three feet to a side, about three feet high, and formed a cone with a hole at the top. Lengths of round metal pipe lay nearby, fashioned especially thin.

Gardell held out his creation for them to study. "I made it fairly thin, using a lot of tin for lightness, for were it too heavy, it would collapse." With his toe he pointed to several lengths of metal rods. "We'll knock some little holes in the floor and use these for support. It may take a bit of time to get it right, but I think this thing of yours is going to work."

Pug smiled broadly. He found great pleasure in seeing an idea of his taking concrete form. It was a novel and gratifying sensation. "When can we install it?"

"Now if you like. I would like to see it work, I must confess."

Pug gathered up some of the pipe, and Tomas the rest, as well as the rods. Juggling the awkward load, they set out toward the magician's tower, with the chuckling smith following.

KULGAN WAS DEEP in thought as he started to mount the stairs to his room. Suddenly a shout from above sounded: "Watch out!" Kulgan glanced up in time to see a block of stone come tumbling down the stairs, bounding over the steps as if in some fit of drunken craziness. He leapt aside as it struck against the wall where he had stood and came to rest at the bottom of the stairs. Mortar dust filled the air, and Kulgan sneezed.

Tomas and Pug came running down the stairs, expressions of worry on their faces. When they saw no one was hurt, they both looked relieved.

Kulgan leveled a baleful gaze upon the pair and said, "What is all this?"

Pug appeared sheepish, while Tomas tried to blend in with the wall. Pug spoke first. "We were trying to carry the stone down to the yard, and it sort of slipped."

"Sort of slipped? It looked more like a mad dash for freedom. Now, why were you carrying the stone, and where did it come from?"

"It's the loose one from my wall," answered Pug. "We took it out so that Gardell could put the last pipe in place." When Kulgan still appeared uncomprehending, Pug said, "It's for my fire pot hood, remember?"

"Ah," said Kulgan, "yes. Now I do." A servant arrived to investigate the noise, and Kulgan asked him to fetch a couple of workmen from the yard to carry the block away. He left, and Kulgan said to the boys, "I think it would be better to let someone a little larger tote that stone out. Now let us see this marvel."

They climbed the stairs to the boy's room and found Gardell installing the last length of pipe. The smith turned when they entered and said, "Well, what do you think?"

The pot had been moved a little closer to the wall, and the hood sat on four metal rods of equal length over it. All of the smoke was trapped by the hood and carried away through the light metal pipe. Unfortunately, the hole where the stone was missing was considerably larger than the pipe, so most of the smoke was blown back into the room by the wind.

"Kulgan, what do you think?" said Pug.

"Well, boy. It looks rather impressive, but I can't see much improvement in the atmosphere here."

Gardell gave the hood a solid whack with his hand, causing it to ring out with a tinny sound. His thick calluses kept his hand from being burned by the hot metal. "She'll do, soon as I plug up that hole, magician. I'll fetch some bull hide that I use for making shields for the horsemen and cut a hole in a piece, slip it around the pipe, and nail it to the wall. A few slaps of tanning agent on it, and the heat will dry it out all stiff and hard. It will take the heat and keep the rain and wind out of the room, as well as the smoke." The smith looked pleased with his handiwork. "Well, I'll fetch the hide. Back in a moment."

Pug looked as if he would burst from pride, seeing his invention before him, and Tomas reflected Pug's glory. Kulgan chuckled softly to himself for a moment. Suddenly Pug turned to the magician, remembering where he had spent the day. "What is the news from the council?"

"The Duke sends messages to all the nobles of the West, explaining what has occurred in great detail, and asking that the Armies of the West be made ready. I am afraid Tully's scribes have some rigorous days ahead of them, since the Duke wants them all finished as soon as possible. Tully's in a state, for he has been commanded to stay and act as Lyam's adviser, along with Fannon and Algon, during the Duke's absence."

"Lyam's adviser? Absence?" asked Pug, uncomprehendingly.

"Yes, the Duke, Arutha, and I are going to journey to the Free Cities, and on to Krondor, to speak with Prince Erland. I am going to send a dream message to a colleague of mine tonight, if I can. Belgan lives north of Bordon. He will send word to Meecham, who should be there by now, to find us a ship. The Duke feels it best that he should carry the word in person."

Pug and Tomas looked excited. Kulgan knew they both wanted to come along. To visit Krondor would be the greatest adventure of their young lives. Kulgan stroked his grey beard. "It will be difficult to continue your lessons, but Tully can brush you up on a trick or two."

Pug looked as if he were going to burst. "Please, Kulgan, may I come too?"

Kulgan feigned surprise. "You come? I never thought of that." He paused for a moment while the suspense built. "Well . . ." Pug's eyes pleaded. ". . . I guess it would be all right." Pug let out a yelp and jumped in the air.

Tomas struggled to hide his disappointment. He forced a thin smile and tried to look happy for Pug.

Kulgan walked to the door. Pug noticed Tomas's dejected expression. "Kulgan?" Pug said. The magician turned, a faint smile on his lips.

"Yes, Pug?"

"Tomas, too?"

Tomas shook his head, for he was neither a member of the court nor the magician's charge, but his eyes looked at Kulgan imploringly.

Kulgan smiled broadly. "I guess we're better off keeping you together, so we need look for trouble in only one place. Tomas, too. I'll arrange things with Fannon."

Tomas shouted, and the two boys slapped each other on the back.

Pug said, "When do we leave?"

Kulgan laughed. "In five days' time. Or sooner, if the Duke hears from the dwarves. Runners are being sent to the North Pass to see if it is clear. If not, we ride by the South Pass."

Kulgan departed, leaving the two boys dancing arm in arm and whooping with excitement.

7

Understanding

Pug *hurried across* the courtyard.

Princess Carline had sent him a note asking him to meet her in her flower garden. It was the first word from the girl since she had stormed away from their last meeting, and Pug was anxious. He did not want to be on bad terms with Carline, regardless of any conflicts he might be feeling. After his brief discussion with Calin, two days earlier, he had sought out Father Tully and talked with him at length.

The old priest had been willing to take time out to speak with the boy, in spite of the demands the Duke was placing upon his staff. It had been a good talk for Pug, leaving him with a surer sense of himself. The final message from the old cleric had been: Stop worrying about what the Princess feels and thinks, and start discovering what Pug feels and thinks.

He had taken the cleric's advice and was now sure of what he would say should Carline start referring to any sort of "understanding" between them. For the first time in weeks he felt something like a sense of direction—even if he was not sure what destination he would eventually reach, holding to such a course.

Reaching the Princess's garden, he rounded a corner, then stopped, for instead of Carline, Squire Roland stood by the steps. With a slight smile, Roland nodded. "Good day, Pug."

"Good day, Roland." Pug looked around.

"Expecting someone?" said Roland, forcing a note of lightness that did little to hide a belligerent tone. He casually rested his left hand on the pommel of his sword. Apart from his sword, he was dressed as usual, in colorful breeches and tunic of green and gold, with tall riding boots.

"Well, actually, I was expecting to see the Princess," Pug said, with a small note of defiance in his manner.

Roland feigned surprise. "Really? Lady Glynis mentioned something about a note, but I had come to understand things were strained between the two of you . . ."

While Pug had tried to sympathize with Roland's situation over the last few days, his offhanded, superior attitude and his chronic antagonism conspired to irritate Pug. Letting his exasperation get the better of him, he snapped, "As *one squire to another,* Roland, let me put it this way: how things stand between Carline and myself is *none of your business!*"

Roland's face took on an expression of open anger. He stepped forward, looking down at the shorter boy. "Be damned it's none of my business! I don't know what you're playing at, Pug, but if you do anything to hurt her, I'll—"

"Me hurt her!" Pug interrupted. He was shocked by the intensity of Roland's anger and infuriated by the threat. "She's the one playing us one against the other—"

Abruptly Pug felt the ground tilt under him, rising up to strike him from behind. Lights exploded before his eyes and a bell-like clanging sounded in his ears. It was a long moment before he realized Roland had just hit him. Pug shook his head and his eyes refocused. He saw the older, larger squire standing over him, both hands balled into fists. Through tightly clenched teeth, Roland spat his words. "If you ever say ill of her again, I'll beat you senseless."

Pug's anger fired within him, rising each second. He got carefully to his feet, his eyes upon Roland, who stood ready to fight. Feeling the bitter taste of anger in his mouth, Pug said, "You've had two years and more to win her, Roland. Leave it alone."

Roland's face grew livid and he charged, bowling Pug off his feet. They went down in a tangle, Roland striking Pug harmlessly on the shoulders and arms. Rolling and grappling, neither could inflict much damage. Pug got his arm around Roland's neck and hung on as the older squire thrashed in a frenzy. Suddenly Roland wedged a knee against Pug's chest and shoved him away. Pug rolled and came to his feet. Roland was up an instant later, and they squared off. Roland's expression had changed from rage to cold, calculating anger as he measured the distance between them. He advanced carefully, his left arm bent and extended, his right fist held ready before his face. Pug had no experience with this form of fighting, called fist-boxing, though he had seen it practiced for money in traveling shows. Roland had demonstrated on several occasions that he had more than a passing acquaintance with the sport.

Pug sought to take the advantage and swung a wild, roundhouse blow at Roland's head. Roland dodged back as Pug swung completely around; then the squire jumped forward, his left hand snapping out, catching Pug on the cheek, rocking his head back with a stinging blow. Pug stumbled away, and Roland's right hand missed Pug's chin by a fraction.

Pug held up his hands to ward off another blow and shook his head, clearing it of the dancing lights that obscured his vision, barely managing to duck beneath Roland's next blow. Under Roland's guard, Pug lunged, catching the other boy in the stomach with his shoulder, knocking him down again. Pug fell on top of him and struggled to pin the larger boy's arms to his side. Roland struck out, catching Pug's temple with an elbow, and the dazed magician's apprentice fell away, momentarily confused.

As he rose to his feet again, pain exploded in Pug's face, and the world tilted once more. Disoriented, unable to defend himself, Pug felt Roland's blows as distant events, somehow muted and not fully recognized by his reeling senses. A faint note of alarm sounded in part of Pug's mind. Without warning, processes began to occur under the level of pain-dimmed consciousness. Basic, more animal instincts took hold, and in a disjointed, hardly understood awareness, a new force emerged. As in the encounter with the trolls, blinding letters of light and flame appeared in his mind's eye, and he silently incanted.

Pug's being became primitive. In his remaining consciousness he was a primal creature fighting for survival with murderous intent. All he could envision was choking the very life from his adversary.

Suddenly an alarm rang within Pug's mind. A deep sense of wrongness, of evil, struck him. Months of training came to the fore, and it was as if he could hear Kulgan's voice crying, "This is not how the power is to be used!" Ripping aside the mental shroud that covered him, Pug opened his eyes.

Through blurred vision and sparkling lights, Pug saw Roland kneeling a mere yard before him, eyes enlarged, vainly struggling with the invisible fingers around his neck. Pug felt no sense of contact with what he saw, and with returning clarity of mind knew at once what had occurred. Leaning forward, he seized Roland's wrists. "Stop it, Roland! Stop it! It isn't real. There are no hands but your own at your throat." Roland, blind with panic, seemed unable to hear Pug's shouts. Mustering what remaining strength he possessed, Pug yanked Roland's hands away, then struck him a stinging slap to the face. Roland's eyes teared and suddenly he breathed in, a gasping, ragged sound.

Still panting, Pug said, "It's an illusion. You were choking yourself."

Roland gasped and pushed himself back from Pug, fear evident on his face. He struggled weakly to pull his sword. Pug leaned forward and firmly gripped Roland's wrist. Barely able to speak, he shook his head and said, "There's no reason."

Roland looked into Pug's eyes, and the fear in his own began to subside. Something inside the older squire seemed to break, and there was only a fatigued, drained young man sitting on the ground. Breathing heavily, Roland sat back, tears forming in his eyes, and asked, "Why?"

Pug's own fatigue made him lean back, supporting himself on his hands. He studied the handsome young face before him, twisted by doubt. "Because you're held under a spell more compelling than any I could fashion." He looked Roland in the eyes. "You truly love her, don't you?"

The last vestige of Roland's anger slowly evaporated and his eyes showed some slight fear remaining, but also Pug saw deep pain and anguish as a tear fell to his cheek. His shoulders slumped and he nodded, his breath ragged as he tried to speak. For a moment he was on the verge of crying, but he fought off his pain and regained his poise. Taking a deep breath, Roland wiped away the tears and took another deep breath. He looked directly at Pug, then guardedly asked, "And you?"

Pug sprawled on the ground, feeling some strength returning. "I . . . I'm not sure. She makes me doubt myself. I don't know. Sometimes I think of no one else, and other times I wish I were as far from her as I could be."

Roland indicated understanding, the last residue of fear draining away. "Where she's concerned, I don't have a whit of wit."

Pug giggled. Roland looked at him, then also began to laugh. "I don't know why," said Pug, "but for some reason, I find what you said terribly funny." Roland nodded and began to laugh too. Soon they were both sitting with tears running down their faces as the emotional vacuum left by the fleeing anger was replaced by giddiness.

Roland recovered slightly, holding back the laughter, when Pug looked at him and said, "A whit of wit!" which sent both of them off on another jag of laughter.

"Well!" a voice said sharply. They turned and found Carline, flanked by two ladies-in-waiting, surveying the scene before her. Instantly both boys became silent. Casting a disapproving look upon the pair as they sprawled upon the ground, she said, "Since you two seem so taken with each other, I'll not intrude."

Pug and Roland exchanged looks and suddenly erupted into uproarious laughter. Roland fell over backward, while Pug sat, legs stretched before him, laughing into his cupped hands. Carline flushed angrily and her eyes widened. With cold fury in her voice she said "Excuse me!" and turned, sweeping by her ladies. As she left, they could hear her loudly exclaim, "Boys!"

Pug and Roland sat for a minute until the near-hysterical fit passed; then Roland rose and extended his hand to Pug. Pug took it and Roland helped him to his feet. "Sorry, Pug. I had no right to be angry with you." His voice softened. "I can't sleep nights thinking of her. I wait for the few moments we're together each day. But since you saved her, all I ever hear is your name." Touching his sore neck, Roland said, "I got so angry, I thought I'd kill you. Damn near got myself killed instead."

Pug looked at the corner where the Princess had disappeared, nodding agreement. "I'm sorry, too, Roland. I'm not very good at controlling magic yet, and when I lose my temper, it seems all sorts of terrible things can happen. Like with the trolls." Pug wanted Roland to understand he was still Pug, even though he was now a magician's apprentice. "I would never do something like that on purpose—especially to a friend."

Roland studied Pug's face a moment and grinned, half-wryly, half-apologetically. "I understand. I acted badly. You were right: she's only setting us one against the other. I am the fool. It's you she cares for."

Pug seemed to wilt. "Believe me, Roland, I'm not so sure I'm to be envied."

Roland's grin widened. "She is a strong-willed girl, that's clear." Caught halfway between an open display of self-pity and mock-bravado, Roland selected mock-bravado.

Pug shook his head. "What's to be done, Roland?"

Roland looked surprised, then laughed loudly. "Don't look to me for advice, Pug. I dance to her tune more than any. But 'there are as many changes in a young girl's heart as in the fickle winds,' as the old saying goes. I'll not blame you for Carline's actions." He winked at Pug conspiratorially. "Still, you won't mind if I keep an eye out for a change in the weather?"

Pug laughed in spite of his exhaustion. "I thought you seemed a little too gracious in your concessions." A thoughtful look came over his face. "You know, it would be simpler—not better, but simpler—if she'd ignore me forever, Roland. I don't know what to think about all this. I've got my apprenticeship to complete. Someday I'll have estates to manage. Then there's this business with the Tsurani. It's all come so quickly, I don't know what to do."

Roland regarded Pug with some sympathy. He put his hand upon the younger boy's shoulder. "I forget this business of being apprentice and noble is all rather new to you. Still, I can't say I've given too much time to such weighty considerations myself, even though my lot was decided before I was born. This worrying about the future is a dry sort of work. I think it would be benefited by a mug of strong ale."

Feeling his aches and bruises, Pug nodded agreement. "Would that we could. But Megar will be of a different mind, I'm afraid."

Roland placed his finger alongside his nose. "We shan't let the Mastercook smell us out, then. Come on, I know a place where the boards of the ale shed are loose. We can quaff a cup or two in private."

Roland began to walk away, but Pug halted him by saying, "Roland, I am sorry we came to blows."

Roland stopped, studied Pug a moment, and grinned. "And I." He extended his hand. "A peace."

Pug gripped it. "A peace."

They turned the corner, leaving the Princess's garden behind, then stopped. Before them was a scene of unalloyed misery. Tomas was walking the length of the court, from the soldiers' commons to the side gate, in full armor—old chain mail over gambeson, full helm, and heavy metal greaves over knee boots. On one arm he bore a heater shield, and in the other hand he held a heavy spear, twelve feet long and iron-tipped, which bore down cruelly upon his right shoulder. It also gave him a comic appearance, as it caused him to lean a little to the right and wobble slightly as he struggled to keep it balanced while he marched.

The sergeant of the Duke's Guard stood counting out cadence for him. Pug knew the sergeant, a tall, friendly man named Gardan. He was Keshian by ancestry, evident in his dark skin. His white teeth split his dark, nappy beard in a grin at the sight of Pug and Roland. He stood nearly as broad in the shoulders as Meecham, with the same loose-gaited movement of a hunter or fighter. Though his black hair was lightly dusted with grey, his face was young-looking and unlined, despite thirty years' service. With a wink at Pug and Roland, he barked, "Halt!" and Tomas stopped in his tracks.

As Pug and Roland closed the distance between them, Gardan snapped, "Right turn!" Tomas obeyed. "Members of the court approaching. Present arms!" Tomas extended his right arm, and his spear dipped in salute. He let the tip drop slightly too low, and nearly broke from attention to pull it back.

Pug and Roland came up to stand next to Gardan, and the large soldier gave them a casual salute and a warm smile. "Good day, Squires." He turned to Tomas for a moment. "Shoulder arms! March post . . . march!" Tomas set off, marching the "post" assigned to him, in this case the length of the yard before the soldiers' commons.

With a laugh, Roland said, "What is this? Special drills?"

Gardan stood with one hand on his sword, the other pointed at Tomas. "Swordmaster Fannon felt it might prove beneficial to our young warrior if someone was here to see his drilling didn't become sloppy from exhaustion or some other petty inconvenience." Dropping his voice a bit, he added, "He's a tough lad; he'll be fine, if a little footsore."

"Why the special drilling?" asked Roland. Pug shook his head as Gardan told them.

"Our young hero lost two swords. The first was understandable, for the matter of the ship was vital, and in the excitement of the moment such an oversight could be forgiven. But the second was found lying on the wet ground near the pell the afternoon the Elf Queen and her party left, and young Tomas was nowhere in sight." Pug knew Tomas had forgotten all about returning to his drilling when Gardell had come with the hood for his fire pot.

Tomas reached the end of his appointed route, did an about-face, and began his return. Gardan regarded the two bruised and dirty boys and said, "What have you two young gentlemen been up to?"

Roland cleared his throat in a theatrical fashion and said, "Ah . . . I was giving Pug a fist-boxing lesson."

Gardan reached out and took Pug's chin in his hand, turning the boy's face for inspection. Evaluating the damage, he said, "Roland, remind me never to ask you to instruct my men in swordplay—we couldn't withstand the casualty rate." Releasing his hold upon Pug's face, he said, "You'll have a beautiful eye in the morning, Squire."

Changing the topic, Pug said, "How are your sons, Gardan?"

"Well enough, Pug. They learn their craft and dream of making themselves rich, save for the youngest, Faxon, who is still intent on becoming a soldier next Choosing. The rest are becoming expert cartwrights under my brother Jeheil's tutelage." He smiled sadly. "With only Faxon at home the house is very empty, though my wife seems glad for the peace." Then he grinned, an infectious smile that rarely could be viewed and not answered. "Still, it won't be too long before the elder boys marry, and then there'll be grandchildren under foot and plenty of merry noise again, from time to time."

As Tomas drew near, Pug asked, "May I speak with the condemned?"

Gardan laughed, stroking his short beard. "I guess I might look the other way for a moment, but be brief, Squire." Pug left Gardan talking with Roland and fell into step beside Tomas as he passed on his way to the opposite end of the court. "How goes it?" Pug asked.

Out of the side of his mouth, Tomas said, "Oh, just fine. Two more hours of this and I'll be ready for burial."

"Can't you rest?"

"On the half hour I get five minutes to stand at attention." He reached the terminus of his post and did a reasonably sharp about-face, then resumed walking back toward Gardan and Roland. "After the fire-pot cover was finished, I came back to the pell and found the sword missing. I thought my heart would stop. I looked everywhere. I almost thrashed Rulf, thinking he had hidden it to spite me. When I returned to the commons, Fannon was sitting on my bunk, oiling down the blade. I thought the other soldiers would hurt themselves holding in the laughter when he said, 'If you judge yourself skilled enough with the sword, perhaps you'd care to spend your time learning the proper way to walk post with a poll arm.' All day walking punishment," he added woefully. "I'll die."

They passed Roland and Gardan, and Pug struggled to feel sympathy. Like the others, he found the situation comical. Hiding his amusement, he lowered his voice to a conspiratorial tone and said, "I'd better get along. Should the Swordmaster come along, he might tack on an extra day's marching."

Tomas groaned at the thought. "Gods preserve me. Get away, Pug."

Pug whispered, "When you're done, join us in the ale shed if you're able." Pug left Tomas's side and rejoined Gardan and Roland. To the sergeant he said, "Thank you, Gardan."

"You are welcome, Pug. Our young knight-in-the-making will be fine, though he feels set upon now. He also chafes at having an audience."

Roland nodded. "Well, I expect he'll not be losing a sword again soon."

Gardan laughed. "Too true. Master Fannon could forgive the first, but not the second. He thought it wise to see Tomas didn't make a habit of it. Your friend is the finest student the Swordmaster has known since Prince Arutha, but don't tell Tomas that. Fannon's always hardest on those with the most potential. Well, good day to you both, Squires. And, boys,"—they paused—"I won't mention the 'fist-boxing lesson.'"

They thanked the sergeant for his discretion and walked toward the ale shed, with the measured cadence of Gardan's voice filling the court.

PUG WAS WELL into his second mug of ale and Roland finishing his fourth when Tomas appeared through the loose boards. Dirty and sweating, he was rid of his armor and weapons. With a great display of fatigue, he said, "The world must be coming to an end; Fannon excused me from punishment early."

"Why?" asked Pug.

Roland lazily reached over to a storage shelf, next to where he sat upon a sack of grain soon to be used for making ale, and got a cup from a stack. He tossed it to Tomas, who caught it, then filled it from the hogshead of ale that Roland rested his feet upon.

Taking a deep drink, Tomas wiped his mouth with the back of his hand and said, "Something's afoot. Fannon swooped down, told me to put away my toys, and nearly dragged Gardan off, he was in such a hurry."

Pug said, "Maybe the Duke is getting ready to ride east?"

Tomas said, "Maybe." He studied his two friends, taking note of their freshly bruised countenances. "All right. What happened?"

Pug regarded Roland, indicating he should explain the sad state of their appearance. Roland gave Tomas a lopsided grin and said, "We had a practice bout in preparation for the Duke's fist-boxing tourney."

Pug nearly choked on his ale, then laughed. Tomas shook his head. "If you two don't look a pair. Fighting over the Princess?"

Pug and Roland exchanged glances; then as one they leaped at Tomas and bore him to the floor under their combined weight. Roland pinned Tomas to the floor, then, while Pug held him in place, took a half-filled cup of ale and held it high. With mock solemnity Roland said, "I hearby anoint thee, Tomas, First Seer of Crydee!" So saying, he poured the contents of the cup over the struggling boy's face.

Pug belched, then said, "As do I." He poured what remained in his cup over his friend.

Tomas spat ale, laughing as he said, "Right! I was right!" Struggling against the weight upon him, he said,

"Now get off! Or need I remind you, Roland, of who gave you your last bloody nose?"

Roland moved off very slowly, intoxicated dignity forcing him to move with glacial precision. "Quite right." Turning toward Pug, who had also rolled off Tomas, he said, "Still, it must be made clear that at the time, the *only reason* Tomas managed to bloody my nose is that during our fight he had an unfair advantage."

Pug looked at Roland through bleary eyes and said, "What unfair advantage?"

Roland put his finger to his lips indicating secrecy, then said, "He was winning."

Roland collapsed back upon the grain sack and Pug and Tomas dissolved into laughter. Pug found the remark so funny, he couldn't stop, and hearing Tomas's laughter only caused his own to redouble. At last he sat up, gasping, with his sides hurting.

Catching his breath, Pug said, "I missed that set-to. I was doing something else, but I don't remember what."

"You were down in the village learning to mend nets, if I remember rightly, when Roland first came here from Tulan."

With a crooked grin Roland said, "I got into an argument with someone or another—do you remember who?" Tomas shook his head no. "Anyway, I got into an argument, and Tomas came over and tried to break it up. I couldn't believe this skinny boy—" Tomas began to voice an objection, but Roland cut him off, holding a finger upright and wiggling it. "Yes, you were. Very skinny. I couldn't believe this skinny boy— skinny *common* boy—would *presume* to tell me—a newly appointed member of the Duke's court *and a gentleman,* I must add—the way to behave. So I did the only thing a proper gentleman could do under the circumstances."

"What?" asked Pug.

"I hit him in the mouth." The three laughed again.

Tomas shook his head at the recollection, while Roland said, "Then he proceeded to give me the worst beating I had since the last time my father caught me out at something.

"That's when I got serious about fist-boxing."

With an air of mock gravity, Tomas said, "Well, we were younger then."

Pug refilled the cups. Moving his jaw in discomfort, he said, "Well, right now I feel about a hundred years old."

Tomas studied them both a moment. "Seriously, what was the fight about?"

With a mixture of humor and regret, Roland said, "Our liege lord's daughter, a girl of ineffable charm . . ."

"What's ineffable?" Tomas asked.

Roland looked at him with intoxicated disdain. "Indescribable, dolt!"

Tomas shook his head. "I don't think the Princess is an indescribable dolt —" He ducked as Roland's cup sailed through the space occupied by his head an instant before. Pug fell over backward laughing again.

Tomas grinned as Roland, in a display of great ceremony, fetched down another cup from the shelf. "As I was saying," he began, filling the cup from the hogshead, "our lady, a girl of ineffable charms—if somewhat questionable judgment—has taken it into her head—for reasons only the gods may fully comprehend—to favor our young magician here with her attentions. *Why*—when she could spend time with me— I can't imagine." He paused to belch. "In any event, we were discussing the proper manner in which to accept such largess."

Tomas looked at Pug, a huge grin on his face. "You have my sympathy, Pug. You most certainly have your hands full."

Pug felt himself flush. Then with a wicked leer, he said, "Do I? And what about a certain young apprentice soldier, well-known hereabouts, who has been seen sneaking into the larder with a certain kitchen girl?" He leaned back and with a look of mock concern etched upon his face added, "I'd hate to think what would happen to him should Neala find out. . . ."

Tomas's mouth fell open. "You wouldn't . . . you couldn't!"

Roland lay back, holding his sides. "Never have I seen such a fair impersonation of a freshly landed fish!" He sat up, crossed his eyes, and opened and shut his mouth rapidly. All three degenerated into helpless mirth again.

Another round was poured, and Roland held up his cup. "Gentlemen, a toast!"

Pug and Tomas held up their cups.

Roland's voice turned serious, and he said, "No matter what differences we have had in the past, you are two fellows I gladly count friends." He held his cup higher and said, "To friendship!"

The three drained their cups and refilled them. Roland said, "Your hand upon it."

The three boys joined hands, and Roland said, "No matter where we go, no matter how many years pass, never again shall we be without friends."

Pug was stuck by the sudden solemnity of the pledge and said, "Friends!"

Tomas echoed Pug's words, and the three shook hands in a gesture of affirmation.

Again the cups were drained, and the afternoon

sun quickly fled beyond the horizon as the three boys lost time in the rosy glow of camaraderie and ale.

PUG CAME AWAKE, groggy and disoriented. The faint glow from his nearly extinguished fire pot cast the room into halftones of rose and black. A faint but persistent knocking sounded on his door. He slowly stood, then nearly fell, still intoxicated from his drinking bout. He had stayed with Tomas and Roland in the storage room all evening and into the night, missing supper entirely. "Putting a considerable dent" in the castle's ale supply, as Roland had described it. They hadn't partaken of any great amount, but as their capacity was slight, it seemed a heroic undertaking.

Pug drew on his trousers and wobbled over to the door. His eyelids felt gritty, and his mouth was cotton dry. Wondering who could be demanding entrance in the middle of the night, he threw aside the door.

A blur of motion passed him, and he turned to find Carline standing in the room, a heavy cloak wrapped around her. "Close the door!" she hissed. "Someone might pass the base of the tower and see light upon the stairway."

Pug obeyed, still disoriented. The only thing that penetrated his numb mind was the thought that it was unlikely the faint light from the coals would cast much brightness down the stairwell. He shook his head, gathering his wits about him, and crossed to the fire pot. He lit a taper from the coals and lit his lantern. The room sprang into cheery brightness.

Pug's thinking began to pick up a little as Carline looked about the room, taking stock of the disorderly pile of books and scrolls next to the pallet. She peered into every corner of the room, then said, "Where is that dragon thing you keep about?"

Pug's eyes focused a little, and marshaling his

balky tongue, he said, "Fantus? He's off somewhere, doing whatever it is firedrakes do."

Removing her cloak, she said, "Good. He frightens me." She sat on Pug's unmade pallet and looked sternly at him. "I want to speak with you." Pug's eyes went wide, and he stared, for Carline was wearing only a light cotton sleeping gown. While covering her from neck to ankles, it was thin and clung to her figure with alarming tenacity. Pug suddenly realized he was dressed only in trousers and hurriedly grabbed up his tunic from where he had dropped it onto the floor and pulled it over his head. As he struggled with the shirt, the last shreds of alcoholic fog evaporated. "Gods!" he said, in a pained whisper. "Should your father learn of this, he'd have my head."

"Not if you've wits enough to keep your voice lowered," she answered with a petulant look.

Pug crossed to the stool near his pallet, freed of his drunken wobble by newly arrived terror. She studied his rumpled appearance and with a note of disapproval in her voice said, "You've been drinking." When he didn't deny it, she added, "When you and Roland didn't appear at supper, I wondered where you'd gotten yourselves off to. It's a good thing Father also skipped the meal with the court, otherwise he'd have sent someone to find you."

Pug's discomfort was growing at an alarming rate as every tale of what horrible fate awaits lowborn lovers of noblewomen rushed back into his memory. That Carline was an uninvited guest and that nothing untoward had occurred were niceties he didn't think the Duke would find particularly mitigating. Gulping down panic, Pug said, "Carline, you can't stay here. You'll get us both into more trouble than I can imagine."

Her expression became determined. "I'm not leaving until I tell you what I came to say."

Pug knew it was futile to argue. He had seen that look too many times in the past. With a resigned sigh, he said, "All right, then, what is it?"

Carline's eyes widened at his tone. "Well, if that's how you're going to be, I won't tell you!"

Pug suppressed a groan and sat back with his eyes closed. Slowly shaking his head, he said, "Very well. I'm sorry. Please, what do you want me to do?"

She patted the pallet next to her. "Come, sit here."

He complied, trying to ignore the feeling that his fate—an abruptly short life—was being decided by this capricious girl. He landed rather than sat beside her. She giggled at the groan he made. "You got drunk! What's it like?"

"At this moment, not terribly entertaining. I feel like a used kitchen rag."

She tried to look sympathetic, but her blue eyes sparkled with mirth. With a theatrical pout, she said, "You boys get to do all the interesting things, like sword work and archery. Being a proper lady can be such a bore. Father would have a fit if I should ever drink more than a cup of watered wine with supper."

With rising desperation in his voice, Pug said, "Nothing compared to the fit he will have if you're found here. Carline, why did you come here?"

She ignored the question. "What were you and Roland doing this afternoon, fighting?" He nodded. "Over me?" she asked, a glimmer in her eyes.

Pug sighed. "Yes, over you." Her pleased look at the reply nettled him, and irritation crept into his voice. "Carline, you've used him rather badly."

"He's a spineless idiot!" she snapped back. "If I asked him to jump off the wall, he'd do it."

"Carline," Pug nearly whined, "why have—"

His question was cut off as she leaned forward and covered his mouth with her own. The kiss was one-sided, for Pug was too stunned to respond. She quickly sat back, leaving him agape, and she said, "Well?"

Lacking any original response, Pug said, "What?"

Her eyes flashed. "The kiss, you simpleton."

"Oh!" said Pug, still in shock. "It was . . . nice."

She rose and looked down on him, her eyes widening with mixed anger and embarrassment. She crossed her arms and stood tapping her foot, making a sound like summer hail striking the window shutters. Her tone was low and harsh. "Nice! Is that all you have to say?"

Pug watched her, a variety of conflicting emotions surging inside. At this moment panic was contesting with a nearly painful awareness of how lovely she looked in the dim lantern light, her features alive and animated, her dark hair loose around her face, and the thin shift pulled tight across her bosom by her crossed arms. His own confusion made his pose seem unintentionally casual, which further fueled her petulance. "You're the first man—not counting Father and my brothers—I've ever kissed, and all you can say is 'nice.' "

Pug was unable to recover. Still awash with tumultuous emotions, he blurted, "Very nice."

She placed her hands upon her hips—which pulled her nightdress in disturbing new directions and stood looking down on him with an expression of open disbelief. In controlled tones she said, "I come here and throw myself at you. I risk getting myself banished to a convent for life!" Pug noticed she failed to mention his possible fate. "Every other boy—and not a slight number of the older nobles—in the West fall over themselves to get my attention. And all you do is treat me like some common kitchen drudge, a passing amusement for the young lord."

Pug's wits returned, less of their own accord than from the realization that Carline was arguing her case a little more emphatically than was warranted. Suddenly struck with the insight that there was a fair bit of dramatics mixed in with her genuine irritation, he said, "Carline, wait. Give me a moment."

"A moment! I've given you weeks. I thought . . . well, I thought we had an understanding."

Pug tried to look sympathetic, as his mind raced. "Sit down, please. Let me try to explain."

She hesitated, then returned to sit next to him. Somewhat clumsily he took her hands in his own. Instantly he was struck by the nearness of the girl, her warmth, the smell of her hair and skin. The feelings of desire he had felt on the bluffs returned with stunning impact, and he had to fight to keep his mind upon what he wished to say.

Forcing his thoughts away from the hot surge he experienced, he said, "Carline, I do care for you. A great deal. Sometimes I even think I love you as much as Roland does, but most of the time I only get confused when you're around. That's the problem: there's so much confusion inside of me. I don't understand what it is I feel most of the time."

Her eyes narrowed, for this obviously wasn't the answer she expected. Her tone was sharp as she said, "I don't know what you mean. I've never known a boy so caught up in understanding things."

Pug managed to force a smile. "Magicians are trained to seek explanations. Understanding things is very important to us." He saw a flicker of comprehension in her eyes at this and pressed on. "I have two offices now, both new to me. I may not become a magician, in spite of Kulgan's attempts to make me one, for I have trouble with a lot of my work. I don't really avoid you, you see, but with this trouble I have, I must spend as much time with my studies as I can."

Seeing his explanation was gaining little sympathy, he changed tactics. "In any event, I have little time to consider my other office. I may end up another noble of your father's court, running my estates—small though they might be—caring for my tenants, answering calls to arms, and the rest. But I can't even think of that until I resolve this other matter, my studies of magic. I must keep trying until I'm satisfied I made the wrong choice. Or until Kulgan dismisses me," he added quietly.

He stopped and studied her face. Her large blue eyes watched him intently. "Magicians are of little consequence in the Kingdom. I mean, should I become a master magician . . . Well, could you see yourself married to a magician, whatever his rank?"

She looked slightly alarmed. Quickly she leaned over and kissed him again, rupturing his already frayed composure. "Poor Pug," she said, pulling away a little. Her soft voice rang sweetly to his ears. "You don't have to be. A magician, I mean. You have land and title, and I know Father could arrange others when the time was right."

"It's not a question of what I want, don't you see? It's a question of what I am. Part of the problem may be I haven't truly given myself over to my work. Kulgan took me for his apprentice as much from pity as need, you know. And in spite of what he and Tully have said, I've never been really convinced I was especially talented. But perhaps I need to dedicate myself, commit myself to becoming a magician." He took a breath. "How can I do that if I'm concerning myself with my estates and offices? Or gaining new ones?" He paused. "Or you?"

Carline bit her lower lip slightly, and Pug fought down the urge to take her in his arms and tell her everything would be all right. He had no doubt that once he did that, matters would quickly be beyond his control. No girl in his limited experience, even the prettier ones in the town, aroused such strong feelings in him.

Lowering her lashes a little as she looked down, she softly said, "I'll do whatever you say, Pug." Pug felt relief for a moment, then the full impact of what she had just said hit him. Oh, gods! he thought. No magician's trick could keep him focused in the face of youthful passion. He frantically sought some way to drive desire from him and then thought of her father. Instantly an image of a scowling Duke of Crydee standing before the hangman's gibbet banished most of his lust.

Taking a deep breath, Pug said, "In my own way, I do love you, Carline." Her face came aglow, and forfending disaster, he plunged on. "But I think I should try to find out about myself before I try to make up my mind about the rest." His concentration was sorely tested as the girl seemed to ignore his remarks, being busy kissing his face.

Then she stopped and sat back. Her happy expression faded into one of thoughtfulness as her natural intelligence overrode her childish need to get everything she wanted. Comprehension came into her eyes as he said, "If I chose now, Carline, I might always doubt the choice. Would you want to face the possibility I would come to resent you for the choice I made?"

She said nothing for a while, then quietly said, "No. I don't think I could stand that, Pug."

He breathed a sigh of relief as he felt tension drain

away. Suddenly the room seemed cold, and both of them shivered. Carline gripped his hands tight, with surprising strength. She mustered a smile and said, with forced calm, "I understand, Pug." She took a long breath, then softly added, "That's why I think I love you. You could never be false with anyone. Least of all with yourself."

"Or you, Carline." Her eyes grew moist, but she maintained her smile. "This isn't easy," Pug said, assaulted by feelings for the girl. "Please, please, believe me, this is not easy."

Suddenly the tension broke, and Carline laughed softly, sweet music to Pug. Caught halfway between tears and laughter, she said, "Poor Pug. I've upset you."

Pug's face showed his relief at her understanding. He felt buoyant with his affection for the girl. Shaking his head slowly, with a smile of released tension that gave him a somewhat silly expression, he said, "You've no idea, Carline. No idea." He reached out and touched her face tenderly. "We have time. I'm not going anywhere."

From under lowered lashes, blue eyes regarded him with worry. "You'll be leaving with Father soon."

"I mean when I return. I'll be here for years." Gently he kissed her cheek. Forcing a lighter tone, he said, "I can't inherit for three more years, that's the law. And I doubt your father would part with you for as many years yet." Attempting a wry smile, he added, "In three years you might not be able to stand the sight of me."

She came softly into his arms, holding him tightly, her face resting on his shoulder. "Never, Pug. I could never care for another." Pug could only marvel at the feel of her. Her body trembled as she said, "I don't have words, Pug. You're the only one who tried to . . . understand me. You see more than anyone else."

Gently he pulled back a little and raised up her face
with his hand. Again he kissed her, tasting salty tears
upon her lips. She suddenly responded, holding him
tighter and kissing him with passion. He could feel the
heat of her body through the thin fabric of her gown,
and heard soft sighing sounds in his ear as he felt himself drifting back into mindless passion, his own body
beginning to respond. Steeling his resolve, he gently
disengaged himself from Carline's embrace. Slowly he
forced himself away from her and, with regret in his
voice, said, "I think you should return to your rooms,
Carline."

Carline looked up at Pug, her cheeks flushed and
her lips slightly parted. Her breathing was husky, and
Pug fought a mighty struggle to control himself and the
situation. More firmly, he said, "You had best return to
your rooms, *now.*"

They rose slowly from the sleeping pallet, each
intensely aware of the other. Pug held her hand a moment longer, then released it. He bent and retrieved her
cloak, holding it for her as she slipped into it. Guiding
her to the door, he pulled it open and peered down the
steps of the tower. With no hint of anyone nearby, he
opened the door fully. She stepped through, then
turned. Softly she said, "I know you think me a sometimes silly and vain girl, and there are times when I am,
Pug. But I do love you."

Before he could say a word, she vanished down
the stairs, the faint rustling of her cloak echoing in the
darkness. Pug quietly closed the door and then put out
the lamp. He lay upon his pallet, staring up into the
darkness. He could still smell her fresh scent in the air
around him, and the remembered touch of her soft
body under his hands made them tingle. Now that she
was gone and the need for self-control gone with her,
he let longing rush through himself. He could see her

face alive with desire for him. Covering his eyes with his forearm, he groaned softly to himself and said, "I'm going to hate myself tomorrow."

PUG AWOKE TO pounding on the door. His first thought as he scrambled toward the door was of the Duke having learned of Carline's visit. He's here to hang me! was all he could think. It was still dark outside, so Pug opened the door expecting the worst. Instead of the girl's angry father leading a company of castle guards, a castle porter stood outside the door.

"Sorry to wake you, Squire, but Master Kulgan wishes you to join him at once," he said, pointing up toward Kulgan's room. "At once," he repeated, mistaking Pug's expression of relief for one of sleepy confusion. Pug nodded and shut the door.

He took stock. He was still dressed, having fallen asleep again without undressing. He stood quietly as his pounding heart stilled. His eyes felt as if they were packed with sand, and his stomach was upset, leaving a foul taste in his mouth. He went to his small table and splashed cold water on his face, muttering that he would never have another cup of ale again.

Pug reached Kulgan's room and found the magician standing over a pile of personal belongings and books. Sitting on a stool by the magician's sleeping pallet was Father Tully. The priest watched the magician adding to the steadily growing pile and said, "Kulgan, you can't take all those books along. You would need two pack mules for them, and where you would keep them aboard ship where they would do you any good is beyond me."

Kulgan looked at two books he held, like a mother regarding her young. "But I must take them along to further the boy's education."

"Pah! So you'll have something to mull over

around the campfires and aboard ship, more likely. Spare me excuses. You will be riding hard to clear the South Pass before it is snowed in. And who can read in a ship crossing the Bitter Sea in winter? The boy will only be away from his studies a month or two. He'll have over eight years more study after that. Give him a rest."

Pug was perplexed by the conversation and tried to ask a question, but was ignored by the two old companions as they bickered. After several more remonstrations from Tully, Kulgan surrendered. "I suppose you're right," he said, tossing the books onto his pallet. He saw Pug waiting by the door and said, "What? Still here?"

Pug said, "You haven't told me why you sent for me yet, Kulgan."

"Oh?" Kulgan said, eyes blinking wide like those of a barn owl caught in a bright light. "I haven't?" Pug nodded. "Well, then. The Duke orders us ready to ride at first light. The dwarves have not answered, but he will not wait. The North Pass is almost certain to be closed, and he fears snow in the South Pass." Kulgan said as an aside, "Which he should. My weather nose tells me snow is nearly here. We are in for an early and hard winter."

Tully shook his head as he stood up. "This from the man who predicted drought seven years ago, when we had the worst flooding in memory. Magicians! Charlatans, all of you." He walked slowly to the door, then stopped to look at Kulgan, his mock irritation replaced by genuine concern. "Though you are right this time, Kulgan. My bones ache deeply. Winter is upon us."

Tully left and Pug asked, "We're leaving?"

With exasperation, Kulgan said, "Yes! I just said

so, didn't I? Get your things together and quickly. Dawn's less than an hour away."

Pug turned to leave, when Kulgan said, "Oh, a moment, Pug."

The magician crossed to the door and glanced through it, ensuring Tully was down the stairs and out of earshot. Kulgan turned to Pug and said, "I have no fault to find with your behavior . . . but should you in the future find yourself with another late-night caller, I suggest you not subject yourself to further . . . testing. I'm not so sure you would do as well a second time."

Pug blanched. "You heard?"

Kulgan pointed to a spot where the floor and wall met. "That fire-pot thing of yours exits the wall a foot below there, and it seems a marvelous conduit for sound." Absently he said, "I'll have to look to see how it conducts sound so well when we return." Returning to the boy, he said, "In any event, I was working late and didn't mean to eavesdrop, but I heard every word." Pug flushed. Kulgan said, "I don't mean to embarrass you, Pug. You acted rightly and showed surprising wisdom." Putting his hand upon Pug's shoulder, he said, "I'm not one to advise you in such matters, I fear, as I've had scant experience with women, of any age, let alone such young and headstrong ones." Looking Pug in the eyes, he said, "But this much I do know, it is almost impossible in the heat of the moment to understand long-term consequences. I am proud you were able to do this."

Pug smiled self-consciously. "It was easy enough, Kulgan, I just kept my mind focused on something."

"What?"

"Capital punishment."

Kulgan laughed, a sharp barking sound, then said, "Very well, but the potential for disaster would be as high for the Princess, too, Pug. A city-bred noble-woman of the eastern court may indulge herself in as many lovers of any rank that she can enjoy while main-taining discretion, but the only daughter of a frontier duke who is so closely related to the king has no such luxury. She must be above suspicion in all things. Even suspicion could harm Carline. One who cares for her would take that into consideration. Do you under-stand?"

Pug nodded, fully relieved now that he had re-sisted temptation the night before.

"Good, I know you'll be careful in the future." Kulgan smiled. "And don't mind old Tully. He's just cross because the Duke ordered him to stay behind. He still thinks he's as young as his acolytes. Now run along and get ready. Dawn's less than an hour away."

Pug nodded and hurried off, leaving Kulgan to regard the piles of books before him. With regret he picked the nearest one up and placed it on a nearby shelf. After a moment he grabbed another and stuffed it into a sack. "Just one won't cause any harm," he said to the invisible specter of Tully shaking his head in disap-proval. He put the rest of the books back on the shelf, save the last volume, which he shoved into the sack. "All right, then," he said defiantly, "two!"

8

Journey

A light wet snow was falling.

Pug shivered under his greatcloak, sitting astride his horse. He had been in the saddle for the last ten minutes, waiting as the rest of the Duke's company made ready.

The courtyard filled with hurrying, shouting men, lashing supplies onto the balky mules of the baggage train. Dawn was just commencing, giving the courtyard a little color instead of the blacks and grey that had greeted Pug when he came from the tower. Porters had already carried his baggage down and were securing it among the other items being brought along.

A panicked "Whoa!" erupted behind Pug, and he turned to see Tomas pulling frantically at the reins of a spirited bay, his head tossing high. Like Pug's own sleek, light war-horse, he was a far cry from the old draft animal they had ridden to the site of the shipwreck. "Don't pull so hard," Pug shouted. "You'll saw at his mouth and make him mad. Pull back gently and release a couple of times."

Tomas did, and the horse quieted down, moving alongside Pug's own. Tomas sat as if the saddle had nails sticking through it. His face was a study in concentration as he tried to guess what the horse would do next.

"If you hadn't been walking post yesterday, you could have gone riding, getting in some practice. Now I'll have to teach you as we go."

Tomas looked thankful for the promise of aid. Pug smiled. "By the time we reach Bordon, you'll be riding like the King's Lancers."

"And walking like a ruptured spinster." Tomas shifted in the saddle. "Already I feel like I've been sitting on a stone block for hours. After just a little way from the saddling post."

Pug jumped down from his horse and looked over Tomas's saddle, making Tomas move his leg so he could examine under the saddle flap, then asked, "Who saddled this horse for you?"

"Rulf. Why?"

"I thought so. He's paying you back for threatening him about that sword, or because we're friends. He doesn't dare threaten me anymore, now that I'm a Squire, but he thinks nothing of knotting your stirrup leathers. A couple of hours riding like this, and you'd be standing at meals for a month, if you didn't get pitched on your head and killed. Here, get down and I'll show you."

Tomas dismounted, halfway between a leap and a fall. Pug showed him the knots. "They would have rubbed the inside of your thighs raw by the end of the day. And they're not long enough." Pug took out the knots and adjusted the leathers to the proper length. "It's going to feel very strange for a while, but you've got to keep your heels down. I'll remind you until you're sick of hearing it, but it'll keep you out of trouble when you do it without thought. And *don't* try to grip with your knees; that's wrong, and it'll make your legs so sore, you'll hardly be able to walk by tomorrow." He went on with a few basic instructions and inspected the cinch, which was loose. He tried tightening it, and the horse sucked air. Pug struck the gelding a blow in the side, and the animal exhaled sharply. Pug quickly pulled the cinch strap and said, "Sometime today, you most likely would have found yourself listing to one side, a most discomforting position."

"That Rulf!" Tomas turned toward the stable. "I'll thrash him within an inch of death!"

Pug grabbed his friend's arm. "Wait. We don't have time for brawling."

Tomas stood with fists clenched, then relaxed with a relieved sigh. "I'm in no condition for fighting, anyway." He turned to see Pug inspecting the horse.

Pug shook his head, then winced. "Me too." He finished inspecting the saddle and bridle, and the horse shied. Pug gentled the horse. "Rulf's also given you a temperamental mount. This fellow would have probably thrown you before noon, and be halfway back to the stable before you hit the ground. With sore legs and shortened stirrup leathers, you never would have stood a chance. I'll trade with you." Tomas looked relieved and struggled into the saddle of the other horse. Pug readjusted the stirrups for both riders. "We can swap our travel rolls when we take our noon meal." Pug then soothed the high-strung war-horse and climbed nimbly into the saddle. Feeling surer hands at the reins, and a firm leg on either side, the gelding quieted.

"Ho! Martin," shouted Tomas as the Duke's Huntmaster walked into view. "Are you traveling with us?"

A wry grin split the face of the hunter, who was wearing his heavy green cloak over his forester's leathers. "For a short while, Tomas. I'm to lead some trackers around the boundaries of Crydee. I'll be heading due eastward when we come to the south branch of the river. Two of my trackers were on their way an hour ago, breaking trail for the Duke."

"What do you think of this Tsurani business, Martin?" Pug asked.

The still-youthful Huntmaster's face clouded. "If elves are given to worry, there is something to worry over." He turned toward the front of the assembling line. "Excuse me, I must instruct my men." He left the boys sitting alone.

Pug asked Tomas, "How's your head this morning?"

Tomas made a face. "About two sizes smaller than when I awoke." His face brightened a bit. "Still, the excitement seems to have stopped the banging inside. I feel almost good."

Pug gazed at the keep. Memories of his encounter last night kept tugging at his mind, and suddenly he regretted the need to travel with the Duke.

Tomas noticed his friend's pensive mood and said, "Why so glum? Aren't you excited about going?"

"It's nothing. Just thinking."

Tomas studied Pug for a moment. "I think I understand." With a deep sigh, he sat back in the saddle, and his horse stamped and nickered. "I, for one, am glad to be leaving. I think Neala has tumbled to that little matter we spoke of yesterday."

Pug laughed. "That will teach you to be mindful of who you escort into pantries."

Tomas smiled sheepishly.

The doors to the keep opened, and the Duke and Arutha came out, accompanied by Kulgan, Tully, Lyam, and Roland. Carline followed, with Lady Marna behind. The Duke and his companions made their way

to the head of the column, but Carline hurried down to
where Pug and Tomas sat. As she passed, guardsmen
saluted her, but she paid them no heed. She reached
Pug's side, and when he bowed politely, she said, "Oh,
get off that stupid horse."

Pug climbed down, and Carline threw her arms
around his neck, holding him closely for a moment.
"Take care and stay well," she said. "Don't let anything
happen to you." She pulled away, then kissed him
briefly. "And come home." Holding back tears, she
hurried to the head of the line, where her father and
brother waited to say good-bye.

Tomas let out a theatrical whoop and laughed,
while Pug remounted; the soldiers nearby attempted to
restrain their own amusement. "It seems the Princess
has made plans for you, m'lord," Tomas gibed. He
ducked as Pug stirred to give him a backhanded cuff.
The motion caused his horse to start forward, and suddenly Tomas was fighting to bring his horse back into
line. The horse seemed determined to go in any direction except the one Tomas wished; now it was Pug's
turn to laugh. He finally moved his own horse alongside Tomas's and herded the fractious mare back into
line. She flattened her ears and turned to nip at Pug's
horse, and the short boy said, "We both have accounts
to settle with Rulf; he gave us two horses that don't like
each other, too. We'll trade your mount off with one of
the soldiers."

With relief Tomas half dismounted, half fell to the
ground, and Pug directed the exchange with a soldier
down the line. The exchange was made, and as Tomas
returned to his place, Roland came down to where they
stood and offered them both his hand. "You two watch
yourselves, now. There's plenty of trouble waiting out
there without your looking for it."

They acknowledged they would, and Roland said to Pug, "I'll keep an eye on things for you."

Pug noticed his wry smile, glanced back to where Carline stood with her father, and said, "No doubt," then added, "Roland, whatever happens, good luck to you, too."

Roland said, "Thank you. I'll take that as it's meant." To Tomas he said, "And things are certainly going to be dull without you around."

Tomas said, "Given what's going on, dull would be welcome."

Roland said, "As long as it's not too dull, right? Take good care! You're a bothersome pair, but I'd hate to lose you."

Tomas laughed as Roland walked off with a friendly wave. Watching the Squire go up to the Duke's party, and seeing Carline standing next to her father, Pug turned to Tomas. "That decides it. I am glad to be going. I need a rest."

Sergeant Gardan came riding back with orders to move the column, and they set off. The Duke and Arutha rode in the van, with Kulgan and Gardan behind. Martin Longbow and his trackers set off at a run beside the Duke's horse. Twenty pair of mounted guards followed, with Tomas and Pug nestled between them and the baggage train at the rear with its five pair of guards. Slowly at first, then with increasing speed, they moved through the gates of the castle and down the south road.

THEY HAD BEEN riding for three days, the last two through dense woodlands. Martin Longbow and his men had turned east that morning as they crossed the southern branch of the river Crydee, called river Boundary. It marked the border between Crydee and the Barony of Carse, one of Lord Borric's vassal provinces.

The sudden snows of early winter had come and draped the autumn landscape in white. Many of the denizens of the forest had been caught unaware by the sudden winter, rabbits whose coats were still more brown than white, and ducks and geese who scampered across half-frozen ponds, resting as they migrated south. The snow fell in flurries of heavy wet flakes, melting slightly during the day, to refreeze at night, making a thin crust of ice. As the horses' and mules' hooves cracked through the ice, the crunching of leaves underneath could be heard in the still winter air.

In the afternoon Kulgan observed a flight of firedrakes circling in the distance, barely visible through the trees. The colorful beasts, red, gold, green, and blue in color, raced over the treetops and dipped out of sight, then reappeared as they spiraled upward, with cries and small bursts of flame. Kulgan reined in as the train passed and waited for Pug and Tomas to overtake him. When they were alongside, he pointed out the display, saying, "It has the appearance of a mating flight. See, the more aggressively the males act, the more responsive the females. Oh, I wish we had time to study this more closely."

Pug followed the creatures with his eyes as they rode through a clearing, then, somewhat startled, said, "Kulgan, isn't that Fantus there, hovering near the edge?"

Kulgan's eyes widened. "By the gods! I think it is."

Pug asked, "Shall I call him?"

The magician chuckled. "Given the attention he's receiving from those females, I think it would do little good." They lost sight of the congregation of drakes as they rode after the Duke's train. Kulgan said, "Unlike most creatures, drakes mate at first snow. The females will lay eggs in nests, then sleep the winter, warming them with their bodies. In the spring the young hatch and are cared for by their mothers. Fantus will most likely spend the next few days . . . ahem, fathering a clutch of young. Then he'll be back at the keep, annoying Megar and the kitchen staff for the rest of the winter."

Tomas and Pug laughed. Tomas's father made a great show of considering the playful drake a plague from the gods visited upon his well-ordered kitchen, but on several occasions both boys had spied Megar lavishing some of the choicest dinner scraps upon the beast. In the fifteen months since Pug had become Kulgan's apprentice, Fantus had become a winged, scaled house pet to most of the Duke's staff, though a few, like the Princess, found Fantus's dragonlike appearance disquieting.

They continued to move east by south, as quickly as the terrain would permit. The Duke was concerned about reaching the South Pass before the snows made it impassable, cutting them off from the east until spring. Kulgan's weather sense had allowed they had a fair chance of making it before any big storms struck. Soon they came to the edge of the deepest part of the great southern forests, the Green Heart.

Deep within the glades, at prearranged locations, two troops of guards from the keep at Carse were waiting for them with fresh horses. Duke Borric had sent pigeons south with instructions for Baron Bellamy, who sent a reply the same way that horses would be waiting. The remounts and guards would be hurrying to the meeting places from the Jonril garrison, maintained by Bellamy and Tolburt of Tulan near the edge of the great forests. By changing mounts, the Duke would save three, perhaps four days of travel to Bordon.

Longbow's trackers had left clear blazes for the Duke to follow, and they were due to reach the first meeting place later that day.

Pug turned to Tomas. The taller boy was sitting his horse somewhat better, though he still flapped his arms like a chicken trying to fly when they were forced to a fast trot. Gardan came riding back down the line, to where the boys rode before the baggage guards. "Be wary," he shouted. "From here to the Grey Towers is the darkest part of the Green Heart. Even the elves pass through here quickly and in numbers." The sergeant of the Duke's Guard turned his horse and galloped back to the head of the line.

They traveled the balance of the day, every eye searching the forest for signs of trouble. Tomas and Pug made light conversation, with Tomas remarking on the chance of a good fight. Both boys' banter sounded hollow to the soldiers around them, who sat silent and vigilant. They reached the place of meeting just before sundown. It was a clearing of considerable size, with several tree stumps grown over with ground cover that peeked through the snow, showing that the trees had been harvested long ago.

The fresh horses stood in a picket, each tied to a long line, while six guards stood careful watch around them. When the Duke's party had ridden up, they had weapons ready. They lowered their weapons when they saw the familiar banner of Crydee. These were men of Carse, who wore the scarlet tabard of Baron Bellamy quartered by a gold cross, a golden griffin rampant over their hearts. The shield of each man bore the same device.

The sergeant of the six guards saluted. "Well met, my lord."

Borric acknowledged the salute. "The horses?" he asked simply.

"They are fit, lord, and restless from waiting. As are the men."

Borric dismounted; another soldier of Carse took his horse's reins.

"Trouble?"

"None, my lord, but this place is suited for other than honest men. All last night we stood watches by twos and felt the crawl of eyes upon us." The sergeant was a scarred veteran, who had fought goblins and bandits in his day. He was not the type to give in to flights of imagination, and the Duke acknowledged this. "Double the watch this night. You will escort the horses back to your garrison tomorrow. I would rather have them rested a day, but this is a poor place."

Prince Arutha came forward. "I have also felt eyes upon us for the last few hours, Father."

Borric turned to the sergeant. "It may be that we have been shadowed by a band of brigands, seeking to judge our mission. I will send two men back with you, for fifty men or forty-eight is of little difference, but eight is a far better number than six." If the sergeant felt any relief at this, he did not show it, simply saying, "I thank my lord."

Borric dismissed the man and with Arutha walked toward the center of the camp, where a large fire was burning. The soldiers were erecting rude shelters against the night wind, as they had each night of the journey. Borric saw two mules with the horses and noted that bales of hay had been brought along. Arutha followed his gaze. "Bellamy is a prudent man; he serves Your Grace well."

Kulgan, Gardan, and the boys approached the two nobles, who stood warming themselves before the fire. Darkness was descending quickly; even at noon there was little light in the snow-shrouded forest. Borric looked around and shivered from more than the cold.

"This is an ill-omened place. We will do well to be away as soon as possible."

They ate a quick meal and turned in. Pug and Tomas lay close, starting at every strange sound until fatigue lulled them to sleep.

THE DUKE'S COMPANY passed deep into the forest, through glades so thick that often the trackers had had to change their course, doubling back to find another way for the horses, marking the trail as they went. Much of this forest was dark and twisted, with choking underbrush that impeded travel.

Pug said to Tomas, "I doubt the sun ever shines here." He spoke in soft tones. Tomas slowly nodded, his eyes watching the trees. Since leaving the men from Carse three days ago, they had felt more tension each passing day. The noises of the forest had lessened as they moved deeper into the trees, until they now rode in silence. It was as if the animals and birds themselves shunned this part of the forest. Pug knew it was only because there were few animals that hadn't migrated south or gone into hibernation, but that knowledge didn't lessen his and Tomas's dread.

Tomas slowed down. "I feel something terrible is about to happen."

Pug said, "You've been saying that for two days now." After a minute he added, "I hope we don't have to fight. I don't know how to use this sword, in spite of what you've tried to show me."

"Here," said Tomas, holding something out. Pug took it and found a small pouch inside of which was a collection of small, smooth rocks and a sling. "I thought you might feel better with a sling. I brought one, too."

They rode for another hour, then stopped to rest the horses and eat a cold meal. It was midmorning, and

Gardan inspected each horse, ensuring it was fit. No soldier was given a chance to overlook the slightest possible injury or illness. Should a horse falter, its rider would have to double up with another, and those two would have to return as best they could, for the Duke could not wait for such a delay. This far from any safe haven, it was something no one wished to think about or discuss aloud.

They were due to meet the second detachment of horses at midafternoon. The breakneck pace of the first four days had given way to a careful walk, for to rush through the trees would be dangerous. At the rate they were progressing, they would be on time. Still, the Duke was chafing at the slow pace.

On and on they rode, at times having to stop while guards drew swords and cut at the brush before them, their sword blows echoing through the stillness of the forest as they followed the narrow path left by the trackers.

Pug was lost in thoughts of Carline when, later, a shout erupted from the front of the column, out of sight of the boys. Suddenly the horsemen near Pug and Tomas were charging forward, oblivious to the thicket around them, dodging low-hanging branches by instinct.

Pug and Tomas spurred their horses after the others, and soon their senses recorded a blur of brown and white, as snow-spotted trees seemed to fly past. They stayed low, close to the necks of their mounts, avoiding most tree branches, while they struggled to stay aboard. Pug looked over his shoulder and saw Tomas falling behind. Branches and twigs caught at Pug's cloak as he crashed through the forest into a clearing. The sounds of battle assaulted his ears, and the boy saw fighting in progress. The remount horses were trying to pull up their stakes, while fighting exploded around them. Pug could only vaguely make out the form of combatants, dark shrouded shapes slashing upward with swords at the horsemen.

A figure broke away and came running toward him, avoiding the blow of a guard a few yards ahead of Pug. The strange warrior grinned wickedly at Pug, seeing only the boy before him. Raising his sword for a blow, the fighter screamed and clawed at his face as blood ran between his fingers. Tomas had reined in behind Pug and with a yell let fly with another stone. "I thought you'd get yourself into trouble," he shouted. He spurred his horse forward and rode over the fallen figure. Pug sat rooted for a moment, then spurred his own horse. Pulling out his sling, he let fly at a couple of targets, but couldn't be sure if the stones struck.

Suddenly Pug was in a place of calm in the fighting. On all sides he could see figures in dark grey cloaks and leather armor pouring out from the forest. They looked like elves, save their hair was darker, and they shouted in a language unpleasant to Pug's ears. Arrows flew from the trees, emptying saddles of Crydee horsemen.

Lying about were bodies of both attackers and soldiers. Pug saw the lifeless bodies of a dozen men of Carse, as well as Longbow's two lead trackers, tied to stakes in lifelike poses around the campfire. Scarlet bloodstains spotted the white snow beside them. The ruse had worked, for the Duke had ridden straight into the clearing, and now the trap was sprung.

Lord Borric's voice rang out over the fray. "To me! To me! We are surrounded."

Pug looked about for Tomas as he frantically kicked his mount toward the Duke and his gathering men. Arrows filled the air, and the screams of the dying echoed in the glade. Borric shouted, "This way!" and the survivors followed him. They crashed into the forest, riding over attacking bowmen. Shouts followed them while they galloped away from the ambush, keeping low over the necks of their mounts, avoiding arrows and low-hanging branches.

Pug frantically pulled his horse aside, avoiding a large tree. He looked about, but could not see Tomas. Fixing his gaze upon the back of another horseman, Pug determined to concentrate on one thing only, not losing sight of the man's back. Strange loud cries could be heard from behind, and other voices answered from one side. Pug's mouth was dry and his hands sweating in the heavy gloves he wore.

They sped through the forest, shouts and cries echoing around them. Pug lost track of the distance covered, but he thought it surely a mile or more. Still the voices shouted in the forest, calling to others the course of the Duke's flight.

Suddenly Pug was crashing through the thick underbrush, forcing his lathered, panting horse up a small but steep rise. All around him was a gloom of grey and greens, broken only by patches of white. Atop the rise the Duke waited, his sword drawn, as others pulled up around him. Arutha sat by his father, his face covered with perspiration in spite of the cold. Panting horses and exhausted guards gathered around. Pug was relieved to see Tomas beside Kulgan and Gardan.

When the last rider approached, Lord Borric said, "How many?"

Gardan surveyed the survivors and said, "We've lost eighteen men, have six wounded, and all the mules and baggage were taken."

Borric nodded. "Rest the horses a moment. They'll come."

Arutha said, "Are we to stand, Father?"

Borric shook his head. "There are too many of them. At least a hundred struck the clearing." He spat.

"We rode into that ambush like a rabbit into a snare." He glanced about. "We've lost nearly half our company."

Pug asked a soldier sitting beside him, "Who were they?"

The soldier looked at Pug. "The Brotherhood of the Dark Path, Squire, may Ka-hooli visit every one of the bastards with piles," he answered, invoking the vengeance god. The soldier indicated a circle around them with his hand. "Small bands of them travel through the Green Heart, though they mostly live in the mountains east of here, and way up in the Northlands. That was more than I'd have bargained was around, curse the luck."

Voices shouted from behind, and the Duke said, "They come. Ride!"

The survivors wheeled and rode off, again racing through the trees ahead of their pursuers. Time became suspended for Pug as he negotiated the dangerous course through the dense forest. Twice men nearby screamed, whether from striking branches or from arrows Pug didn't know.

Again they came to a clearing, and the Duke signaled a halt. Gardan said, "Your grace, the horses can't endure much more of this."

Borric struck his saddle horn in frustration, his face dark with anger. "Damn them! And where are we?"

Pug looked about. He had no idea of where they stood in relationship to the original site of attack, and from the looks on the faces around him, no one else did either.

Arutha said, "We must strike eastward, Father, and make for the mountains."

Borric nodded. "But which way lies east?" The

tall trees and overcast sky with its defused sunlight conspired to deny them any point of reference.

Kulgan said, "One moment, your grace," and closed his eyes. Again shouts of pursuit echoed through the trees, as Kulgan opened his eyes and pointed. "That way. There lies the east." Without question or comment, the Duke spurred his horse in the indicated direction, motioning for the others to follow. Pug felt a strong urge to be near someone familiar and tried to rejoin Tomas, but couldn't make his way through the press of riders. He swallowed hard and admitted to himself he was badly scared. The grim faces of the nearby soldiers told him he was not alone in that feeling.

More time passed as they raced through the dark corridors of the Green Heart. Every advance along the escape route was accompanied by the echoing cries of Dark Brothers as they alerted others of the fugitives' route. Occasionally Pug would spy a shape loping along in the distance, quickly lost in the darkness of the trees as it ran a parallel course. The accompanying runners did not seek to hinder them, but always they were near.

Once more the Duke ordered a halt. Turning to Gardan, he said, "Skirmishers! Find out how close they follow. We must have rest." Gardan indicated three men, who quickly leapt from their horses and ran back along the route of their retreat. A single clash of steel and a strangled cry heralded their encounter with the closest Dark Brother tracker.

"Damn them!" said the Duke. "They're herding us in a circle, seeking to bring us back into their main strength. Already we're moving more north than east."

Pug took the opportunity to move next to Tomas. The horses were panting and shivering as perspiration steamed off them in the cold. Tomas managed a feeble smile, but said nothing.

Men moved quickly among the horses, checking for injury. In a few minutes the skirmishers returned at a run. Panting, one said, "Lord, they are close behind, fifty, sixty at least."

"How long?"

The man stood with perspiration pouring down his face as he answered, "Five minutes, my lord." With grim humor he said, "The two we killed will make them pause, but no more time than that."

Borric said to the company, "We rest a moment, then we ride."

Arutha said, "A moment or an hour, what does it matter? The horses are done. We should stand before more Brothers come to the call."

Borric shook his head. "I must get through to Erland. He must know of the coming of the Tsurani."

An arrow, quickly followed by a second, flew from the nearby trees, and another rider fell. Borric shouted, "Ride!"

They cantered the exhausted horses deeper into the woods, then slowed to a walk, while they kept watch for the coming attack. The Duke used hand signals to deploy the line of soldiers so they might swing to either flank and charge on command. Horses blew foam as their nostrils distended, and Pug knew they were close to dropping.

"Why don't they attack?" whispered Tomas.

"I don't know," answered Pug. "They just harry us from the sides and behind."

The Duke raised his hand and the column halted. No sounds of pursuit could be heard. He turned and spoke in a low tone. "They may have lost us. Pass the word to inspect your mounts——" An arrow sped past his head, missing him by inches. "Forward!" he shouted, and they began a ragged trot along the path they had been following.

Gardan shouted, "My lord, it seems they wish us to keep moving."

In a harsh whisper Borric swore, then asked, "Kulgan, which way lies east?"

The magician closed his eyes again, and Pug knew he was tiring himself with this particular spell. Not difficult if one was standing calmly, it had to be fatiguing him under these conditions. Kulgan's eyes opened and he pointed to the right. The column was heading northward.

Arutha said, "Again they slowly turn us, Father, back into their main strength."

Raising his voice, Borric said, "Only fools or children would keep to this route. On my command, wheel to the right and charge." He waited as every man readied weapons and made silent prayers to their gods that the horses could withstand one more gallop. Then the Duke shouted, "Now!" As a body, the column wheeled to the right, and riders spurred their flagging mounts. Arrows came pouring from the trees, and men and horses screamed.

Pug ducked under a branch, desperately holding on to the reins while he fumbled with sword and shield. He felt the shield slipping and, as he struggled with it, sensed his horse slowing. He couldn't exercise the needed control over the animal and manage the weapons at the same time.

Pug reined in, risking a momentary stop to put his equipment right. A noise made him look to the right. Standing less than five yards away was a bowman of the Brotherhood of the Dark Path. Pug stayed rooted for a moment, as did the bowman. Pug was struck by his resemblance to the Elf Prince, Calin. There was little to distinguish the two races, nearly the same in height and build, save hair and eyes. The creature's bowstring had

snapped, and he stood with dark eyes fixed upon Pug
while calmly setting about restringing his bow.

Pug's astonishment at finding the Dark Brother
standing so close to him momentarily caused him to
forget the reason he had halted. He sat numbly watching the bowman repairing his weapon, entranced by the
dark elf's coolly efficient manner.

Then he was pulling an arrow from his quiver in a
fluid motion and fitting the shaft to the bowstring.
Sudden alarm made Pug act. His staggering horse answered his frantic kicks and was off again. He didn't see
the bowman's arrow, but heard and felt it speed past his
ear, then he was back to a gallop, the bowman lost
behind as Pug overtook the Duke's company.

Noise from ahead made Pug urge his horse on,
though the poor animal was giving every indication it
was moving as fast as possible. Pug wove through the
forest, the gloom making it difficult to negotiate.

Abruptly he was behind a rider wearing the
Duke's colors and then passing the man as Pug's horse
proved fresher for carrying a lighter rider. The terrain
became more hilly, and Pug wondered if they were entering the foothills of the Grey Towers.

A horse's scream caused Pug to glance behind. He
saw the soldier he had passed thrown as his mount
collapsed, foaming blood spurting from the animal's
nose. Pug and another rider halted, and the soldier
turned back, riding over to where the first man stood.
He extended his hand to offer the fallen man a double
ride. The fallen soldier just shook his head, as he struck
the standing horse on the rump, sending it ahead again.
Pug knew the second man's horse could barely carry
one rider, never two. The fallen rider pulled his sword
and put down the injured horse, then turned to wait
for the pursuing Dark Brothers. Pug found his eyes
tearing as he contemplated the man's courage. The

other soldier shouted something over his shoulder that was lost to the boy, then suddenly he was riding by. He shouted, "Move, Squire!"

Pug put heels to the sides of his horse, and the animal picked up a staggering trot.

The fleeing column continued on its stumbling, exhausted flight, Pug moving up through the company of riders to a place near the Duke. After a few minutes Lord Borric signaled for them to slow. They entered another clearing. Borric surveyed his company. A look of helpless rage crossed his face, to be replaced by surprise. He held his hand aloft, and the riders stopped their milling about. Shouts sounded in the forest, but from some distance away.

Arutha, eyes wide with wonder, said, "Have we lost them?"

Slowly the Duke nodded, his attention focused on the distant shouts. "For the moment. When we broke through the archers, we must have slipped behind their pursuit. They'll discover that fact shortly and double back. We have ten, fifteen minutes at best." He looked over his ragged company. "If only we could find a place to hide."

Kulgan moved his staggering horse alongside the Duke. "My lord, I might have a solution, though it is risky and might prove fatal."

Borric said, "No more fatal than waiting for them to come for us. What is your plan?"

"I have an amulet, which can control weather. I had planned to save it against possible storms at sea, for its use is limited. I may be able to mask our whereabouts with it. Let every man gather his horse at the far end of the clearing, near that outcropping of rock. Have them silence the animals."

Borric ordered it done, and the animals were moved to the opposite end of the clearing. Reassuring hands gentled exhausted and excited horses, quieting the mounts after their long flight.

They had gathered at the highest end of a narrow clearing, their backs to an outcropping of granite that rose overhead like a grey fist. On three sides the ground sloped away gently. Kulgan began to walk along the perimeter of the compact company.

He chanted in a low voice, waving the amulet in an intricate pattern. Slowly the grey afternoon light faded, and a mist began to gather around him. At first only light wisps appeared nearby, then other, more substantial patches of moisture formed, becoming light fog.

Soon the air between the Duke's company and the tree line grew hazy. Kulgan moved more quickly and the fog deepened, filling the clearing with whiteness, moving outward from the magician into the trees on all sides. Within a few minutes it was impossible to see beyond a few yards.

On and on paced Kulgan, sending thicker blankets of haze to obscure the already grey light in the trees. The clearing slowly became darker as the gloomy fog deepened with every incantation made by the magician.

Then Kulgan stopped and turned to the Duke, whispering, "All must remain quiet. Should the dark elves wander blindly into the fog, the sloping terrain will, I hope, guide them past on one side or the other as they come around the rocks. But let no man move. Any sound will defeat us."

Each man nodded, understanding the danger coming fast. They would stand in the center of this deep fog in the hope the Dark Brothers would walk past, putting the Duke and his men once more behind them. It was an all-or-nothing gambit, for should they win free, there was a good chance they would be far removed from this spot when the Brotherhood once more backtracked.

Pug looked at Tomas and whispered, "It's a good thing it's rocky here, else we'd leave some pretty tracks."

Tomas nodded, too frightened to speak. A nearby guard motioned for Pug to be silent, and the young Squire nodded.

Gardan and several guards, with the Duke and Arutha, took up position near the front of the company, weapons ready should the ploy fail. Shouts grew louder as the Dark Brotherhood returned along their trail. Kulgan stood near the Duke, enchanting quietly, gathering more mist around him, then sending it forth. Pug knew the mist would be expanding rapidly, shrouding a continuously larger area as long as Kulgan continued to incant. Every extra minute would encompass more of the Green Heart in fog, making it increasingly more difficult for the attackers to find them.

Pug felt wetness on his cheek and looked up. Snow was beginning to fall. With apprehension he looked to the mist, to see if the newly arriving snow was affecting it. He watched a tense minute, then silently sighed with relief, for if anything, the snow was adding to the masking effects of the fog.

A soft footfall could be heard nearby. Pug froze, as did every man near him. A voice rang out in the Brotherhood's strange language.

Pug felt an itch between his shoulders, but refused to move, fighting to ignore the nagging sensation on his back. He glanced sideways at Tomas. Tomas stood stock-still, his hand on his horse's muzzle, looking like a statue in the haze. Like every other remaining horse, Tomas's mount knew the hand upon his face was a command for quiet.

Another voice rang out in the mist, and Pug

nearly jumped. It sounded as if the caller were standing directly in front of him. Again the answering call came, sounding farther away.

Gardan stood directly before Pug, who saw the sergeant's back twitch. Gardan slowly knelt, silently laying his sword and shield on the ground. He rose up, still moving slowly, pulling his belt knife. Then suddenly he stepped into the mist, his movements as quick and fluid as a cat disappearing into the night. There was a faint sound, and Gardan reappeared.

Before him struggled the form of a Dark Brother, one of Gardan's huge black hands clamped tightly over the creature's mouth. The other arm was choking its throat. Pug could see the sergeant couldn't risk letting go for the brief instant needed to plunge the knife in its back. Gardan gritted his teeth in pain as the creature raked the sergeant's arm with clawlike nails. Its eyes bulged as it fought to breathe. Gardan stood rooted to the spot, holding the Dark Brother off the ground by main force as it struggled to get free. The creature's face turned red, then purple, as Gardan choked the life from it. Blood from the creature's raking nails flowed freely down Gardan's arm; but the powerful soldier barely moved at all. Then the Dark Brother went limp, and Gardan gave it a final, throat-crushing jerk of his arm and let the creature slide silently to the ground.

Gardan's eyes were wide with exertion, and he panted quietly as he regained his breath. Slowly he turned, knelt, and replaced his knife. Recovering his sword and shield, he stood, resuming his watch in the mist.

Pug felt nothing but awe and admiration for the sergeant, but like the others he could only silently watch. Time passed, and the voices grew more faint as they sounded their angry inquiries to one another, seeking the fugitives' hiding place. The voices moved off, and then, like a long sigh of relief heaved by all in the clearing, it was silent. The Duke whispered, "They are past us. Lead the horses. We go east."

PUG LOOKED ABOUT in the gloom. Ahead, Duke Borric and Prince Arutha led the way. Gardan stayed beside Kulgan, who was still exhausted from his magical undertaking. Tomas walked silently beside his friend. Of the fifty guardsmen who had set out with the Duke from Crydee, thirteen remained. Only six horses had survived the day. As they had faltered, the others had been quickly put down by silent, tight-lipped riders.

They trudged upward, climbing higher into the foothills. The sun had set, but the Duke ordered them onward, fearful of the return of their pursuers. The men stepped cautiously forward, tentative in the rough terrain at night. The darkness was punctuated by softly uttered oaths as men lost their footing on the icy rocks time and again.

Pug plodded along, his body numb with fatigue and cold. The day had seemed an eternity, and he could not remember when he had last stopped or eaten. Once he had been handed a waterskin by a soldier, but the lone drink was a dim memory. He grabbed a handful of snow and put it in his mouth, but the melting iciness gave him little relief. The snow was falling more heavily, or at least it seemed so to Pug; he couldn't see it fall, but it struck his face with more frequency and force. It was bitterly cold, and he shivered inside his cloak.

Like a booming call, the Duke's whisper sounded in the murk. "Stop. I doubt they are wandering about in the dark. We'll rest here."

Arutha's whisper could be heard from somewhere ahead: "The falling snow should cover our tracks by morning."

Pug dropped to his knees and pulled his cloak about himself. Tomas's voice sounded nearby. "Pug?"

Softly he answered, "Here."

Tomas dropped heavily beside him. "I think . . . ," he said between panting breaths, "I'll never . . . move again."

Pug could only nod. The Duke's voice came from a short distance away. "No fires."

Gardan answered, "It's a bitter night for a cold camp, Your Grace."

Borric said, "Agreed, but if those sons of hell are nearby, a fire would bring them howling down upon us. Huddle together for warmth, so no one will freeze. Post guards and tell the others to sleep. When dawn breaks, I want to put as much distance between ourselves and them as possible." Pug felt bodies begin to press around him and didn't mind the discomfort for the warmth. Soon he drifted off into a fitful doze, starting awake often during the night. Then suddenly it was dawn.

THREE MORE HORSES died during the night, their frozen bodies lying uncovered in the snow. Pug came to his feet, feeling light-headed and stiff. He shivered uncontrollably as he stamped his feet, trying to stir some life into his chilled, aching body. Tomas stirred, then awoke with a start, looking to see what was occurring. He climbed awkwardly to his feet, then joined Pug in stamping feet and swinging arms. "I've never been so cold in my life," he said through chattering teeth.

Pug looked around. They were in a hollow between large outcroppings of granite, still bare and grey in patches, which rose up behind them thirty feet into the air, joining a ridge above. The ground sloped away along the path of their march, and Pug noticed the

trees were thinner here. "Come along," he said to Tomas as he began to scramble up the rocks.

"Damn!" sounded from behind, and Pug and Tomas looked back to see Gardan kneeling over the still
form of a guard. The sergeant looked at the Duke and
said, "Died in the night, Your Grace." He shook his
head as he added, "He took a wound and never spoke
of it."

Pug counted; besides himself, Tomas, Kulgan, the
Duke, and his son, there were now just twelve soldiers.
Tomas looked up at Pug, who had climbed ahead, and
said, "Where are we going?"

Pug noticed he whispered. He inclined his head
upward and said, "To see what's over there."

Tomas nodded, and they continued their climb.
Stiff fingers protested against the need to grip hard
rock, but soon Pug found himself warm again as exertion heated his body. He reached up and gripped the
edge of the ridge above. He pulled himself up and over
and waited for Tomas.

Tomas came over the ridge, panting for breath,
looked past Pug, and said, "Oh, glory!"

Rising up majestically before them were the tall
peaks of the Grey Towers. The sun rose behind, casting
rose and golden highlights on the north faces of the
mountains, while the western faces were still veiled in
indigo darkness. The sky was clear, the snowfall over.
Everywhere they looked, the scenery was draped in
white.

Pug waved toward Gardan. The sergeant walked
up to the base of the rocks, climbed a short way, and
said, "What is it?" Pug said, "The Grey Towers! No
more than five miles away."

Gardan waved for the boys to return, and they
scrambled down, falling the last few feet to land with a
thump. With their destination in sight, they felt re-

vived. They came to where Gardan stood in conference with the Duke, Arutha, and Kulgan. Borric spoke softly, his words carrying clearly in the crisp morning air. "Take whatever is left on the dead animals and divide it among the men. Bring the remaining horses, but no one rides. No use covering the animals, for we'll make broad tracks anyway."

Gardan saluted and began circulating among the soldiers. They stood about in pairs or singly, eyes watching for signs of possible pursuit.

Borric said to Kulgan, "Have you an idea where the South Pass lies?"

"I will try to use my magic sight, my lord." Kulgan concentrated, and Pug watched closely, for seeing with the mind's eye was another of the feats that had eluded him in his studies. It was akin to using the crystal, but less pictorial, more an impression of where something was in relation to the spellcaster. After a few minutes of silence, Kulgan said, "I cannot tell, Sire. If I had been there before, then perhaps, but I get no impression of where the pass may lie."

Borric nodded. "I wish Longbow were here. He knows the landmarks of the area." He turned to the east, as if seeing the Grey Towers through the intervening ridge. "One mountain looks much like another to me."

Arutha said, "Father, to the north?"

Borric smiled a little at Arutha's logic. "Yes. If the pass lies northward, we still might chance across it before it is impassable. Once across the mountains, the weather will prove milder in the east—at least that is the rule this time of year. We should be able to walk to Bordon. If we are already north of the pass, then we will eventually reach the dwarves. They will shelter us and perhaps know another route to the east." He inspected his exhausted company. "With three horses and snow melted for drinking water, we should last another week." He looked around, studying the sky. "If the weather holds."

Kulgan said, "We should be free of bad weather in two, perhaps three days. Farther into the future I cannot judge." A distant shout echoed over the trees, from deep within the forest below. Instantly everyone was still. Borric looked to Gardan. "Sergeant, how far away do you judge them?"

Gardan listened. "It is hard to say, my lord. One mile, two, maybe more. Sound carries oddly in the forest, more so when it is this cold." Borric nodded. "Gather the men. We leave now."

PUG'S FINGERTIPS BLED through his torn gloves. At every opportunity during the day, the Duke had kept the men traveling over rock, to prevent Dark Brotherhood trackers from following. Every hour guards had been sent back to cut false trails over their own, pulling blankets taken from the dead horses behind, obscuring the tracks as best they could.

They stood at the edge of a clearing, a circle of bare rock surrounded on all sides by scattered pines and aspens. The trees had grown progressively thinner as they moved up into the mountains, staying on the rougher, higher terrain rather than risk being followed. Since dawn they had moved northeast, following a ridge of rugged hills toward the Grey Towers, but to Pug's dismay the mountains seemed no closer.

The sun stood high overhead, but Pug felt little of its warmth, for a cold wind blew down from the heights of the Grey Towers. Pug heard Kulgan's voice some distance behind. "As long as the wind is from the northeast, we'll have no snow, as any moisture will have fallen on the peaks. Should the wind shift and come from the west, or northwest, from off the Endless Sea, we'll have more snow."

Pug panted as he scrambled along the rocks, balancing on the slippery surface. "Kulgan, must we have lessons, too?"

Several men laughed, and momentarily the grim tension of the last two days lessened. They reached a large flat, before another upward rise, and the Duke ordered a halt. "Build a fire and slaughter an animal. We'll wait here for the last rear guard."

Gardan quickly sent men to gather wood in the trees, and one was given two of the horses to lead away. The high-strung mounts were footsore, tired, and unfed, and in spite of their training, Gardan wanted them removed from the smell of blood.

The chosen horse screamed, then was suddenly silent, and when the fires were ready, the soldiers placed spits over the flames. Soon the aroma of roasting meat filled the air. In spite of his anticipated distaste, Pug found his mouth watering at the smell. In a while he was handed a stick, with a large piece of roasted liver on it, which he wolfed down. Nearby, Tomas was doing equal justice to a portion of sizzling haunch.

When they were done eating, the still-hot meat left over was wrapped with strips from horse blankets and torn tabards, then divided among the men.

Pug and Tomas sat by Kulgan as men broke camp, putting out fires, covering signs of passing, and readying for the resumption of the march.

Gardan came to the Duke. "My lord, the rear guard is overdue."

Borric nodded. "I know. They should have returned a half hour ago." He peered down the hillside, toward the huge forest, mist shrouded in the distance. "We'll wait five more minutes, then we will go."

They waited in silence, but the guards didn't return. Finally Gardan gave the order. "All right, lads. Off we go."

The men formed up behind the Duke and Kulgan, and the boys fell in at the rear. Pug counted. There were only ten soldiers left.

TWO DAYS LATER the howling winds came, icy knives ripping at exposed flesh. Cloaks were gathered around each figure tramping slowly northward, leaning into the wind. Rags had been torn and tied around boots in a feeble attempt to hold off frostbite. Pug tried vainly to keep his eyelashes free of ice, but the harsh wind made his eyes tear, and the drops quickly froze, blurring his vision.

Pug heard Kulgan's voice above the wind. "My lord, a storm comes. We must find shelter or perish." The Duke nodded and waved two men ahead to seek shelter. The two set off at a stumbling run, moving only slightly faster than the others, but valiantly putting their remaining meager strength into the task.

Clouds began to roll in from the northwest, and the skies darkened. "How much time, Kulgan?" shouted the Duke over the shrieking wind.

The magician waved his hand above his head, as the wind blew his hair and beard back from his face, exposing his high forehead. "An hour at most." The Duke nodded again and exhorted his men to move along.

A sad sound, a neighing cry, pierced the wind, and a soldier called out that the last horse was down. Borric stopped and with a curse ordered it slaughtered as quickly as possible. Soldiers butchered the animal, steaming hunks of meat being cut away, to chill in the snow where they were cast before they could be wrapped. When they were done, the meat was divided among the men.

"If we can find shelter, we will build a fire and cook the meat," the Duke shouted.

Silently Pug added that if they couldn't find shelter, they'd have little use for the meat. They resumed their march.

A short time later the two guards returned with the news of a cave less than a quarter mile distant. The Duke ordered them to show the way.

Snow began to fall, whipped by the driving wind. The sky was now dark, limiting visibility to only a few hundred feet. Pug felt light-headed and had to struggle to pull his feet from the resisting snow. Both hands were numb, and he wondered if he was frostbitten.

Tomas looked slightly better, being somewhat hardier by nature, but he also was too exhausted to speak. He just plodded along beside his friend.

Suddenly Pug was lying face down in the snow feeling surprisingly warm and sleepy. Tomas knelt beside the fallen magician's apprentice. He shook Pug, and the nearly unconscious boy groaned.

"Get up," Tomas shouted. "It's only a little way farther."

Pug struggled upright, aided by Tomas and one of the soldiers. When he was standing, Tomas indicated to the soldier he could take care of his friend. The soldier nodded, but stayed near. Tomas loosened one of the many strips of blanket tied around him for warmth, knotted one end to Pug's belt, and half guided, half pulled the smaller boy along.

The boys followed the guard who had helped them around an outcropping of rock and found themselves at the mouth of a cave. They staggered forward a few steps into the sheltering darkness, then fell to the stone floor. In contrast to the biting wind outside, the cave seemed warm, and they lapsed into an exhausted sleep.

· · ·

PUG AWOKE TO the smell of cooking horse meat. He roused himself and saw it was dark outside, beyond the fire. Piles of branches and deadwood were heaped nearby, and men were carefully feeding the fire. Others stood by, roasting pieces of meat. Pug flexed his fingers and found them painfully sore, but as he peeled off his tattered gloves, he saw no signs of frostbite. He nudged Tomas awake, and the other boy raised himself up on his elbows, blinking at the firelight.

Gardan stood on the other side of the fire, speaking with a guard. The Duke sat nearby, in quiet conversation with his son and Kulgan. Beyond Gardan and the guard, Pug could see only blackness. He couldn't remember what time of day it had been when they found the cave, but he and Tomas must have slept for hours.

Kulgan saw them stirring and came over. "How do you feel?" he asked, a look of concern on his face. The boys indicated they felt all right, considering the circumstances. Pug and Tomas doffed their boots at Kulgan's orders, and he was pleased to report they had suffered no frostbite, though one of the soldiers, he said, hadn't been as lucky.

"How long were we asleep?" asked Pug.

"Throughout last night and all this day," said the magician with a sigh.

Then Pug noticed signs that a lot of work had been done. Besides the brush being cut, he and Tomas had been covered by some of the blankets. A pair of snared rabbits hung near the cave mouth with a row of freshly filled waterskins stacked near the fire. "You could have woken us," Pug said, a note of worry in his voice.

Kulgan shook his head. "The Duke wouldn't have moved until the storm had passed, and that was only a

few hours ago. In any event, you and Tomas weren't
the only tired ones here. I doubt even the hearty sergeant there could have gone more than another few
miles with only one night's rest. The Duke will see how
things stand tomorrow. I expect we shall leave then, if
the weather holds."

Kulgan stood and, with a small gesture indicating
the boys should return to sleep if possible, went to
stand beside the Duke. Pug was surprised that, for
someone who had slept the day around, he was again
tired, though he thought he would fill his stomach before seeking more sleep. Tomas nodded at his unspoken
question, and the two scooted over by the fire. One of
the soldiers was busy cooking meat and handed them
hot portions.

The boys wolfed down the food and after they
were done sat back against one wall of the large cave.
Pug started to speak to Tomas but was distracted when
he caught sight of the guard by the cave's mouth. A
queer look passed over the man's face as he stood talking to Sergeant Gardan, then his knees buckled.
Gardan reached out to catch him, lowering him to the
floor. The big sergeant's eyes widened as he saw the
arrow protruding from the man's side.

Time seemed suspended for an instant, then
Gardan shouted, "Attack!"

A howling cry sounded from outside the cave's
mouth, and a figure came bounding into the light,
jumping over the low brush, then again bounding over
the fire, knocking down the soldier cooking meat. It
landed a short way from the boys and spun to face
those it had leapt past. It was wrapped in a coat and
trousers of animal furs. On one arm it bore a battle-
scarred buckler-size shield, and in the other a curved
sword was held high.

Pug stayed motionless as the creature regarded the

company in the cave, a snarl on inhuman lips, eyes glowing with reflected firelight and fangs bared. Tomas's training asserted itself, and the sword he had clung to over the long march was out of its scabbard in an instant. With a show the creature swung downward at Pug, who rolled sideways, avoiding the blow. The blade rang out as it struck the ground, and Tomas made an off-balance lunge, awkwardly taking the creature low in the chest. It fell to its knees and gurgled as blood filled its lungs, then fell forward.

Other attackers were leaping into the cave and were quickly engaged by the men from Crydee. Curses and oaths sounded, and swords rang out in the close confines of the cave. Guards and attackers stood face-to-face, unable to move more than a few feet. Several of the Duke's men dropped swords and pulled daggers from their belts, better for close fighting.

Pug grabbed his sword and looked for an attacker, but found none. In the dancing light of the fire, he could see the attackers were outnumbered by the remaining guards, and as two or three men of Crydee grappled with each attacker, it was quickly down and killed.

Suddenly the cave was quiet, save for the heavy breathing of the soldiers. Pug looked and saw only one man down, the one who had taken the arrow. A few others sported light wounds. Kulgan hurried among the men, checking the wounds, then said to the Duke, "My lord, we have no other serious injuries."

Pug looked at the dead creatures. Six of them lay sprawled upon the cave floor. They were smaller than men, but not by much. Above thick browridges, their sloping foreheads were topped by thick black hair. Their blue-green tinged skins were smooth, save for one who had something like a youth's beard upon his cheeks. Their eyes, open in death, were huge and round, with black irises on yellow. All died with snarls upon their hideous faces, showing long teeth that came close to being fangs.

Pug crossed to Gardan, peering into the gloom of the night for signs of more of the creatures. "What are they, Sergeant?"

"Goblins, Pug. Though I can't fathom what they are doing this far from their normal range."

The Duke came to stand next to him and said, "Only a half dozen, Gardan. I have never heard of goblins attacking armed men except when the advantage was theirs. This was suicide."

"My lord, look here," came Kulgan's call, as he knelt over the body of a goblin. He had pulled away the dirty fur jacket worn by the creature and pointed to a poorly bandaged long, jagged wound on its chest. "This was not made by us. It is three, four days old and healing badly."

Guards inspected the other bodies and reported three others also bore recent wounds, not caused by this fight. One had a broken arm and had fought without a shield.

Gardan said, "Sire, they wear no armor. Only the weapons in their hands." He pointed to a dead goblin with a bow slung over its back, and an empty quiver at its belt. "They had but the one arrow they used to wound Daniel."

Arutha glanced at the carnage. "This was madness. Hopeless madness."

Kulgan said, "Yes, Highness; madness. They were battle weary, freezing, and starved. The smell of cooking meat must have driven them mad. From their appearance I'd say they've not eaten in some time. They preferred to gamble all on one last, frantic assault than to watch us eat while they froze to death."

Borric looked at the goblins again, then ordered

his men to take the bodies outside the cave. To no one in particular, he said, "But who have they been fighting?"

Pug said, "The Brotherhood?"

Borric shook his head. "They are the Brotherhood's creatures, or when not allied against us, they leave one another alone. No, it was someone else."

Tomas looked around as he joined those by the entrance. He wasn't as comfortable speaking to the Duke as Pug, but finally he said, "My lord, the dwarves?"

Borric nodded. "If there's been a dwarven raid on a nearby goblin village, it would explain why they were unarmored and unprovisioned. They would have grabbed the nearest weapons and fought their way free, fleeing at first chance. Yes, perhaps it was the dwarves."

The guards who had carried the bodies off into the snow ran back into the cave. "Your Grace," one of them said, "we hear movement in the trees."

Borric turned to the others. "Get ready!"

Every man in the cave quickly readied his weapons. Soon all could hear the tread of feet crunching through the icy snow. It grew louder as they waited, getting closer. Pug stood tensely, holding his sword, pushing down a churning feeling inside.

Suddenly the sounds of footfalls stopped, as those outside halted. Then the sound of a single pair of boots could be heard coming closer. Appearing out of the dark came a figure directly toward the cave. Pug craned his neck to see past the soldiers, and the Duke said, "Who passes this night?"

A short figure, no more than five feet tall, pulled back the hood of his cloak, revealing a metal helm sitting over a shock of thick brown hair. Two sparkling green eyes reflected the firelight. Heavy brows of brown-red hair came together at a point above a large hooked nose. The figure stood regarding the party, then signaled behind. More figures appeared from out of the night, and Pug pressed forward to get a better view, Tomas at his side. At the rear they could see several of the arrivals leading mules.

The Duke and soldiers visibly relaxed, and Tomas said, "They're dwarves!"

Several of the guards laughed, as did the closest dwarf. The dwarf fixed Tomas with a wry gaze, saying, "What were you expecting, boy? Some pretty dryad come to fetch you away?"

The lead dwarf walked into the firelight. He stopped before the Duke and said, "From your tabard, I see you to be men of Crydee." He struck himself upon the chest and said, formally, "I hight Dolgan, chief of village Caldara, and Warleader of the Grey Towers dwarven people." Pulling a pipe out of his cloak, from under a long beard that fell below his belt, he filled his pipe as he looked at the others in the cave. Then in less formal language he said, "Now, what in the name of the gods brings such a sorry-looking party of tall folk to this cold and forlorn place?"

9

Mac Mordain Cadal

The dwarves stood guard.

Pug and the others from Crydee sat around the campfire as they hungrily ate the meal prepared by Dolgan's men. A pot of stew bubbled near the fire. Hot loaves of trail bread, thick hard crust broken to reveal dark sweet dough thick with honey, were quickly being devoured. Smoked fish, from the dwarves' pack animals, provided a welcome change from the diet of horse meat of the last few days.

Pug looked from where he sat beside Tomas, who was hard at work consuming his third portion of bread and stew. Pug watched as the dwarves worked efficiently about the camp. Most were outside the cave's mouth, for they seemed less inconvenienced by the cold than the humans. Two tended the injured man, who would live, while two others served the hot meal to the Duke's men, and another filled ale cups from a large skin filled with the bubbling brown liquid.

There were forty dwarves with Dolgan. The

dwarven chief was flanked by his sons, Weylin, the older, and Udell. Both showed a striking resemblance to their father, though Udell tended to darkness, having black hair rather than red-brown. Both seemed quiet compared to their father, who gestured expansively with a pipe in one hand and a cup of ale in the other as he spoke with the Duke.

The dwarves had been on some sort of patrol along the edge of the forest, though Pug gained the impression a patrol this far from their villages was unusual. They had come across the tracks of the goblins who had attacked a few minutes before and were following closely behind, otherwise they would have missed the Duke's party as the night's storm obliterated all tracks of the men from Crydee's passage.

"I remember you, Lord Borric," said Dolgan, sipping at his ale cup, "though you were scarcely more than a baby when I was last at Crydee. I dined with your father. He set a fine table."

"And should you come again to Crydee, Dolgan, I hope you'll find my table equally satisfactory." They had spoken of the Duke's mission, and Dolgan had remained mostly silent during the preparation of the meal, lost in thought. Suddenly he regarded his pipe, which had gone out. He sighed forlornly, putting it away, until he noticed Kulgan had pulled out his own and was producing respectable clouds of smoke. Brightening visibly, he said, "Would you be having the requirement of an extra pipe upon you, master magician?" He spoke with the deep, rolling burr the dwarves made when speaking the King's Tongue.

Kulgan fetched out his tabac pouch and handed it across to the dwarf. "Providentially," said Kulgan, "my pipe and pouch are two items always kept upon my person at all times. I can withstand the loss of my other goods—though the loss of my two books troubles me deeply—but to endure any circumstance without the comfort of my pipe is unthinkable."

"Aye," agreed the dwarf as he lit up his own, "you have the right of it there. Except for autumn's ale—and my loving wife's company or a good fight, of course— there's little to match the pipe for pure pleasure." He drew forth a long pull and blew out a large cloud of smoke to emphasize his point. A thoughtful look crossed his rugged face, and he said, "Now to the matter of the news you carry. They are strange tidings, but explain away some mysteries we have been tussling with for some time now."

Borric said, "What mysteries?"

Dolgan pointed out of the cave mouth. "As we told you, we've had to patrol the area hereabouts. This is a new thing, for in years past the lands along the borders of our mines and farms have been free from trouble." He smiled. "Occasionally a band of especially bold bandits or moredhel—the Dark Brothers you call them—or a more than usually stupid tribe of goblins troubles us for a time. But for the most part things remain pretty peaceful.

"But of late, everything's gone agley. About a month ago, or a bit more, we began to see signs of large movements of moredhel and goblins from their villages to the north of ours. We sent some lads to investigate. They found entire villages abandoned, both goblin and moredhel. Some were sacked, but others stood empty without sign of trouble.

"Needless to say, the displacement of those miscreants caused an increase in problems for us. Our villages are in the higher meadows and plateaus, so they dare not attack, but they do raid our herds in the lower valleys as they pass—which is why we now mount patrols down the mountainside. With the winter upon us, our herds are in our lowest meadows, and we must keep vigilant.

"Most likely your messengers didn't reach our villages because of the large number of moredhel and goblins fleeing the mountains down into the forests. Now at least we've some gleaning of what's causing this migration."

The Duke nodded. "The Tsurani."

Dolgan was thoughtful for a moment, while Arutha said, "Then they're up there in strength."

Borric gave his son a questioning look, while Dolgan chuckled and said, "That's a bright lad you've got, Lord Borric." He nodded thoughtfully, then said, "Aye, Prince. They're up there, and in strength. Despite their other grievous faults, the moredhel are not without skill in warcraft." He fell silent again, lost in thought for a few minutes. Then, tapping out the dottle of his pipe, he said, "The dwarven folk are not counted the finest warriors in the West for naught, but we lack the numbers to dispose of our more troublesome neighbors. To dislodge such a host as have been passing would require a great force of men, well armed and provisioned."

Kulgan said, "I would give anything to know how they reached these mountains."

"I would rather know how many there are," said the Duke.

Dolgan refilled his pipe and, after it was lit, stared thoughtfully into the fire. Weylin and Udell nodded at each other, and Weylin said, "Lord Borric, there may be as many as five thousand."

Before the startled Duke could respond, Dolgan came out of his reverie. Swearing an oath, he said, "Closer to ten thousand!" He turned to look at the Duke, whose expression showed he clearly didn't understand what was being said. Dolgan added, "We've given every reason for this migration save invasion. Plague, internal warfare between bands, pests in their crops causing famine, but an invading army of aliens was not one of them.

"From the number of towns empty, we guess a few thousand goblins and moredhel have descended into the Green Heart. Some of those villages are a clutch of huts my two boys could overcome unaided. But others are walled hill forts, with a hundred, two hundred warriors to man the palisade. They've swept away a dozen such in little over a month. How many men do you judge you'd need to accomplish such a deed, Lord Borric?"

For the first time in his memory, Pug saw fear clearly etched upon the Duke's face. Borric leaned forward, his arm resting across his knee, as he said, "I've fifteen hundred men in Crydee, counting those in the frontier garrisons along the boundary. I can call another eight hundred or a thousand each from the garrisons at Carse and Tulan, though to do so would strip them fully. The levies from the villages and towns number at best a thousand, and most would be old veterans from the siege at Carse or young boys without skills."

Arutha looked as grim as his father as he said, "Forty-five hundred at the outside, a full third unproved, against an army of ten thousand."

Udell looked at his father, then at Lord Borric. "My father makes no boast of our skills, nor of the moredhel's, Your Grace. Whether there be five thousand or ten thousand, they'll be hard, experienced fighters to drive out the enemies of our blood so quickly."

"Then I'm thinking," said Dolgan, "you'd best send word to your older son and your vassal barons, telling them to stay safely behind the walls of your castles, and hie yourself to Krondor. It will take all the Armies of the West to withstand these newcomers this spring."

Tomas suddenly said, "Is it really that bad?" then looked embarrassed for interrupting the council. "I'm sorry, my lord."

Borric waved away the apology. "It may be we are weaving many threads of fear together into a larger tapestry than exists, but a good soldier prepares for the worst, Tomas. Dolgan is right. I must enlist the Prince's aid." He looked at Dolgan. "But to call the Armies of the West to arms, I must reach Krondor."

Dolgan said, "The South Pass is closed, and your human ships' masters have too much sense to brave the Straits of Darkness in winter. But there is another way, though it is a difficult path. There are mines throughout these mountains, ancient tunnels under the Grey Towers. Many were carved by my people as we dug for iron and gold. Some are natural, fashioned when the mountains were born. And still others were here when my people first came to these mountains, dug by only the gods know whom. There is one mine that passes completely under the mountains, coming out on the other side of the range, only a day's march from the road to Bordon. It will take two days to pass through, and there may be dangers."

The dwarven brothers looked at their father, and Weylin said, "Father, the Mac Mordain Cadal?"

Dolgan nodded his head. "Aye, the abandoned mine of my grandfather, and his father before him." He said to the Duke, "We have dug many miles of tunnels under the mountain, and some connect with the ancient passages I have spoken of. There are dark and queer tales about Mac Mordain Cadal, for it is connected with these old passages. Not a few dwarves have ventured deep into the old mines, seeking legendary riches, and most have returned. But a few have vanished. Once upon a path, a dwarf can never lose his way back, so they were not lost in their searching. Something must have befallen them. I tell you this so there will be no misunderstandings, but if we keep to the passages dug by my ancestors, we should have small risk."

" 'We,' friend dwarf?" said the Duke.

Dolgan grinned. "Should I simply place your feet upon the path, you'd be hopelessly lost within an hour. No, I'd care not for traveling to Rillanon to explain to your King how I'd managed to lose one of his better Dukes. I will guide you willingly, Lord Borric, for a small price." He winked at Pug and Tomas as he spoke the last. "Say, a pouch of tabac and a fine dinner at Crydee."

The Duke's mood lightened a little. With a smile he said, "Done, and our thanks, Dolgan."

The dwarf turned to his sons. "Udell, you take half the company and one of the mules, and the Duke's men too ill or wounded to continue. Make for the castle at Crydee. There's an ink horn and quill, wrapped in parchment, somewhere in our baggage; find it for his lordship, so he may instruct his men. Weylin, take the others of our kin back to Caldara, then send word to the other villages before the winter blizzards strike. Come spring, the dwarves of the Grey Towers go to war."

Dolgan looked at Borric. "No one has ever conquered our highland villages, not in the longest memory of the dwarven folk. But it would prove an irritation for someone to try. The dwarves will stand with the Kingdom, Your Lordship. You have long been a friend to us, trading fairly and giving aid when asked. And we have never run from battle when we were called."

Arutha said, "And what of Stone Mountain?"

Dolgan laughed. "I thank His Highness for the jog to my memory. Old Harthorn and his clans would be sorely troubled should a good fight come and they were not invited. I'll send runners to Stone Mountain as well."

Pug and Tomas watched while the Duke wrote messages to Lyam and Fannon, then full stomachs and fatigue began to lull them, despite their long sleep. The dwarves gave them the loan of heavy cloaks, which they wrapped about pine boughs to make comfortable mattresses. Occasionally Pug would turn in the night, coming out of his deep sleep, and hear voices speaking low. More than once he heard the name Mac Mordain Cadal.

DOLGAN LED THE Duke's party along the rocky foothills of the Grey Towers. They had left at first light, the dwarven chieftain's sons departing for their own destinations with their men. Dolgan walked before the Duke and his son, followed by the puffing Kulgan and the boys. Five soldiers of Crydee, those still able to continue, under the supervision of Sergeant Gardan followed behind, leading two mules. Walking behind the struggling magician, Pug said, "Kulgan, ask for a rest. You're all done in."

The magician said, "No, boy, I'll be all right. Once into the mines, the pace will slow, and we should be there soon."

Tomas regarded the stocky figure of Dolgan, marching along at the head of the party, short legs striding along, setting a rugged pace. "Doesn't he ever tire?"

Kulgan shook his head. "The dwarven folk are renowned for their strong constitutions. At the Battle of Carse Keep, when the castle was nearly taken by the

Dark Brotherhood, the dwarves of Stone Mountain and the Grey Towers were on the march to aid the besieged. A messenger carried the news of the castle's imminent fall, and the dwarves ran for a day and a night and half a day again to fall on the Brotherhood from behind without any lessening of their fighting ability. The Brotherhood was broken, never again organizing under a single leader." He panted a bit. "There was no idle boasting in Dolgan's appraisal of the aid forthcoming from the dwarves, for they are undoubtedly the finest fighters in the West. While they have few numbers compared to men, only the Hadati hillmen come close to their equal as mountain fighters."

Pug and Tomas looked with newfound respect upon the dwarf as he strode along. While the pace was brisk, the meal of the night before and another this morning had restored the flagging energies of the boys, and they were not pushed to keep up.

They came to the mine entrance, overgrown with brush. The soldiers cleared it away, revealing a wide, low tunnel. Dolgan turned to the company. "You might have to duck a bit here and there, but many a mule has been led through here by dwarven miners. There should be ample room."

Pug smiled. The dwarves proved taller than tales had led him to expect, averaging about four and a half to five feet tall. Except for being short-legged and broad-shouldered, they looked much like other people. It was going to be a tight fit for the Duke and Gardan, but Pug was only a few inches taller than the dwarf, so he'd manage.

Gardan ordered torches lit, and when the party was ready, Dolgan led them into the mine. As they entered the gloom of the tunnel, the dwarf said, "Keep alert, for only the gods know what is living in these tunnels. We should not be troubled, but it is best to be cautious."

Pug entered and, as the gloom enveloped him, looked over his shoulder. He saw Gardan outlined against the receding light. For a brief instant he thought of Carline, and Roland, then wondered how she could seem so far removed so quickly, or how indifferent he was to his rival's attentions. He shook his head, and his gaze returned to the dark tunnel ahead.

THE TUNNELS WERE damp. Every once in a while they would pass a tunnel branching off to one side or the other. Pug peered down each as he passed, but they were quickly swallowed up in gloom. The torches sent flickering shadows dancing on the walls, expanding and contracting as they moved closer or farther from each other, or as the ceiling rose or fell. At several places they had to pull the mules' heads down, but for most of their passage there was ample room.

Pug heard Tomas, who walked in front of him, mutter, "I'd not want to stray down here; I've lost all sense of direction." Pug said nothing, for the mines had an oppressive feeling to him.

After some time they came to a large cavern with several tunnels leading out. The column halted, and the Duke ordered watches to be posted. Torches were wedged in the rocks and the mules watered. Pug and Tomas stood with the last watch, and Pug thought a hundred times that shapes moved just outside the fire's glow. Soon guards came to replace them, and the boys joined the others, who were eating. They were given dried meat and biscuits to eat. Tomas asked Dolgan, "What place is this?"

The dwarf puffed on his pipe. "It is a glory hole, laddie. When my people mined this area, we fashioned many such places. When great runs of iron, gold, silver, and other metals would come together, many tunnels would be joined. And as the metals were taken out, these caverns would be formed. There are natural ones down here as large, but the look of them is different. They have great spires of stone rising from the floor, and others hanging from the ceiling, unlike this one. You'll see one as we pass through."

Tomas looked above him. "How high does it go?"

Dolgan looked up. "I can't rightly say. Perhaps a hundred feet, perhaps two or three times as much. These mountains are rich with metals still, but when my grandfather's grandfather first mined here, the metal was rich beyond imagining. There are hundreds of tunnels throughout these mountains, with many levels upward and downward from here. Through that tunnel there"—he pointed to another on the same level as the floor of the glory hole—"lies a tunnel that will join with another tunnel, then yet another. Follow that one, and you'll end up in the Mac Bronin Alroth, another abandoned mine. Beyond that you could make your way to the Mac Owyn Dur, where several of my people would be inquiring how you managed entrance into their gold mine." He laughed. "Though I doubt you could find the way, unless you were dwarven born."

He puffed at his pipe, and the balance of the guards came over to eat. Dolgan said, "Well, we had best be on our way."

Tomas looked startled. "I thought we were stopping for the night."

"The sun is yet high in the sky, laddie. There's half the day left before we sleep."

"But I thought . . ."

"I know. It is easy to lose track of time down here, unless you have the knack of it."

They gathered together their gear and started off

again. After more walking they entered a series of twisting, turning passages that seemed to slant down. Dolgan explained that the entrance on the east side of the mountains was several hundred feet lower than on the west, and they would be moving downward most of the journey.

Later they passed through another of the glory holes, smaller than the last, but still impressive for the number of tunnels leading from it. Dolgan picked one with no hesitation and led them through.

Soon they could hear the sound of water, coming from ahead. Dolgan said, over his shoulder, "You'll soon see a sight that no man living and few dwarves have ever seen."

As they walked, the sound of rushing water became louder. They entered another cavern, this one natural and larger than the first by several times. The tunnel they had been walking in became a ledge, twenty feet wide, that ran along the right side of the cavern. They all peered over the edge and could see nothing but darkness stretching away below.

The path rounded a curve in the wall, and when they passed around it, they were greeted with a sight that made them all gasp. Across the cavern, a mighty waterfall spilled over a huge outcropping of stone. From fully three hundred feet above where they stood, it poured into the cavern, crashing down the stone face of the opposite wall to disappear into the darkness below. It filled the cavern with reverberations that made it impossible to hear it striking bottom, confounding any attempt to judge the fall's height. Throughout the cascade luminous colors danced, aglow with an inner light. Reds, golds, greens, blues, and yellows played among the white foam, falling along the wall, blazing with brief flashes of intense luminosity where the water struck the wall, painting a fairy picture in the darkness.

Dolgan shouted over the roar, "Ages ago the river Wynn-Ula ran from the Grey Towers to the Bitter Sea. A great quake opened a fissure under the river, and now it falls into a mighty underground lake below. As it runs through the rocks, it picks up the minerals that give it its glowing colors." They stood quietly for a while, marveling at the sight of the falls of Mac Mordain Cadal.

The Duke signaled for the march to resume, and they moved on. Besides the spectacle of the falls, they had been refreshed by spray and cool wind off them, for the caverns were dank and musty. Onward they went, deeper into the mines, past numberless tunnels and passages. After a time, Gardan asked the boys how they fared. Pug and Tomas both answered that they were fine, though tired.

Later they came to yet another cavern, and Dolgan said it was time to rest the night. More torches were lit, and the Duke said, "I hope we have enough brands to last the journey. They burn quickly."

Dolgan said, "Give me a few men, and I will fetch some old timbers for a fire. There are many lying about if you know where to find them without bringing the ceiling down upon your head."

Gardan and two other men followed the dwarf into a side tunnel, while the others unloaded the mules and staked them out. They were given water from the waterskins and a small portion of grain carried for the times when they could not graze.

Borric sat next to Kulgan. "I have had an ill feeling for the last few hours. Is it my imagining, or does something about this place bode evil?"

Kulgan nodded as Arutha joined them. "I have felt something also, but it comes and goes. It is nothing I can put a name to."

Arutha hunkered down and used his dagger to

draw aimlessly in the dirt. "This place would give anyone a case of the jumping fits and starts. Perhaps we all
feel the same thing: dread at being where men do not
belong."

The Duke said, "I hope that is all it is. This would
be a poor place to fight"—he paused—"or flee from."
The boys stood watch, but could overhear the conversation, as could the other men, for no one else was speaking in the cavern and the sound carried well. Pug said
in a hushed voice, "I will also be glad to be done with
this mine."

Tomas grinned in the torchlight, his face set in an
evil leer. "Afraid of the dark, little boy?"

Pug snorted. "No more than you, should you but
admit it. Do you think you could find your way out?"

Tomas lost his smile. Further conversation was interrupted by the return of Dolgan and the others. They
carried a good supply of broken timbers, used to shore
up the passages in days gone by. A fire was quickly
made from the old, dry wood, and soon the cavern was
brightly lit.

The boys were relieved of guard duty and ate. As
soon as they were done eating, they spread their cloaks.
Pug found the hard dirt floor uncomfortable, but he
was very tired, and sleep soon overtook him.

THEY LED THE mules deeper into the mines, the animal's hooves clattering on the stone, the sound echoing
down the dark tunnels. They had walked the entire
day, taking only a short rest to eat at noon. Now they
were approaching the cavern where Dolgan said they
were to spend their second night. Pug felt a strange
sensation, as if remembering a cold chill. It had
touched him several times over the last hour, and he
was worried. Each time he had turned to look behind

him. This time Gardan said, "I feel it too, boy, as if something is near."

They entered another large glory hole, and Dolgan stood with his hand upraised. All movement ceased as the dwarf listened for something. Pug and Tomas strained to hear as well, but no sounds came to them. Finally the dwarf said, "For a time I thought I heard . . . but then I guess not. We will camp here." They had carried spare timber with them and used it to make a fire.

When Pug and Tomas left their watch, they found a subdued party around the fire. Dolgan was saying, "This part of Mac Mordain Cadal is closest to the deeper, ancient tunnels. The next cavern we come to will have several that lead directly to the old mines. Once past that cavern, we will have a speedy passage to the surface. We should be out of the mine by midday tomorrow."

Borric looked around. "This place may suit your nature, dwarf, but I will be glad to have it behind."

Dolgan laughed, the rich, hearty sound echoing off the cavern walls. "It is not that the place suits my nature, Lord Borric, but rather that my nature suits the place. I can travel easily under the mountains, and my folk have ever been miners. But as to choice, I would rather spend my time in the high pastures of Caldara tending my herd, or sit in the long hall with my brethren, drinking ale and singing ballads."

Pug asked, "Do you spend much time singing ballads?"

Dolgan fixed him with a friendly smile, his eyes shining in the firelight. "Aye. For winters are long and hard in the mountains. Once the herds are safely in winter pasture, there is little to do, so we sing our songs and drink autumn ale, and wait for spring. It is a good life."

Pug nodded. "I would like to see your village sometime, Dolgan."

Dolgan puffed on his ever-present pipe. "Perhaps you will someday, laddie."

They turned in for the night, and Pug drifted off to sleep. Once in the dead of night, when the fire had burned low, he awoke, feeling the chilling sensation that had plagued him earlier. He sat up, cold sweat dripping down his body, and looked around. He could see the guards who were on duty, standing near their torches. Around him he saw the forms of sleeping bodies. The feeling grew stronger for a moment, as if something dreadful was approaching, and he was about to wake Tomas when it passed, leaving him tired and wrung out. He lay back down and soon was lost in dreamless sleep.

HE AWOKE COLD and stiff. The guards were readying the mules, and soon they would all leave. Pug roused Tomas, who protested at being pulled from his dream. "I was in the kitchen at home, and Mother was preparing a large platter of sausages and corn cakes dripping with honey," he said sleepily.

Pug threw a biscuit at him. "This will have to do until Bordon. Then we shall eat."

They gathered together their meager provisions, loaded them on the mules, and set off. As they made their way along, Pug began to experience the icy feeling of the night before. Several times it came and went. Hours passed, and they came to the last great cave. Here Dolgan stopped them while he looked into the gloom. Pug could hear him saying, "For a moment I thought . . ."

Suddenly the hairs on Pug's neck stood up, and the feeling of icy terror swept over him, more horrible than before. "Dolgan, Lord Borric!" he cried. "Something terrible is happening!"

Dolgan stood stock-still, listening. A faint moan echoed from down another tunnel.

Kulgan shouted, "I feel something also."

Suddenly the sound repeated, closer, a chilling moan that echoed off the vaulted ceiling, making its origins uncertain.

"By the gods!" shouted the dwarf. "'Tis a wraith! Hurry! Form a circle, or it will be upon us and we'll be lost."

Gardan pushed the boys forward, and the guards moved the mules to the center of the cavern. They quickly staked the two mules down and formed a circle around the frantic animals. Weapons were drawn. Gardan placed himself before the two boys, forcing them back near the mules. Both had swords out, but held them uncertainly. Tomas could feel his heart pound, and Pug was bathed in cold sweat. The terror that gripped him had not increased since Dolgan had put a name to it, but it had not lessened either.

They heard the sharp hiss of intaken breath and looked to the right. Before the soldier who had made the sound, a figure loomed out of the darkness: a shifting man-shape, darker blackness against the black, with two glowing, red-coal lights where eyes should be.

Dolgan shouted, "Keep close, and guard your neighbor. You can't kill it, but they like not the feel of cold iron. Don't let it touch you, for it'll draw your life from your body. It is how they feed."

It approached them slowly, as if having no need to hurry. It stopped for a moment, as if inspecting the defense before it.

The wraith let out another low, long moan, sounding like all the terror and hopelessness of the world given voice. Suddenly one of the guards struck downward, slashing at the wraith. A shrill moan erupted from the creature when the sword hit, and cold blue fire danced along the blade for a moment. The creature shrank away, then with sudden speed struck out at the guard. An armlike shadow extended from its body, and the guard shrieked as he crumpled to the ground.

The mules broke, pulling up stakes, terrified by the presence of the wraith. Guards were knocked to the ground, and confusion reigned. Pug lost sight of the wraith for a moment, being more concerned with flying hooves. As the mules kicked, Pug found himself dodging through the melee. He heard Kulgan's voice behind him and saw the magician standing next to Prince Arutha. "Stand close, all of you," the magician commanded. Obeying, Pug closed to Kulgan with the others as the scream of another guard echoed through the gallery. Within a moment a great cloud of white smoke began to appear around them, issuing from Kulgan's body. "We must leave the mules," said the magician. "The undead will not enter the smoke, but I cannot keep it together long or walk far. We must escape now!"

Dolgan pointed to a tunnel, on the other side of the cavern from where they had entered. "That's the way we must go." Keeping close together, the group started toward the tunnel while a terrified bray sounded. Bodies lay on the floor: the two mules as well as the fallen guards. Dropped torches flickered, giving the scene a nightmarish quality, as the black shape closed upon the party. Reaching the edge of the smoke, it recoiled from its touch. It ranged about the edge, unable or unwilling to enter the white smoke.

Pug looked past the creature, and the pit of his stomach churned.

Clearly standing in the light of a torch held in his

hand was Tomas, behind the creature. Tomas looked helplessly past the wraith at Pug and the escaping party. "Tomas!" ripped from Pug's throat, followed by a sob.

The party halted for a brief second, and Dolgan said, "We can't stop. We'd all perish for the sake of the boy. We must press on." A firm hand clutched at Pug's shoulder as he started forward to aid his friend. He looked back and saw that it was Gardan holding him. "We must leave him, Pug," he said, a grim expression on his ebony face. "Tomas is a soldier. He understands." Pug was pulled along helplessly. He saw the wraith follow along for a moment, then stop and turn toward Tomas.

Whether alerted by Pug's cries or by some evil sense, the undead creature started toward Tomas, slowly stalking him. The boy hesitated, then spun and ran to another tunnel. The wraith shrieked and started after him. Pug saw the glow of Tomas's torch disappear down the tunnel, then flicker into blackness.

TOMAS SAW THE pained expression on Pug's face as Gardan pulled his friend away. When the mules had broken, he had dodged away from the others and now found himself separated from them. He looked for a way to circle around the wraith, but it was too close to the passage his companions were taking. As Kulgan and the others escaped up the tunnel, Tomas saw the wraith turn toward him. It started to approach, and he hesitated a moment, then ran toward a different tunnel.

Shadows and light danced madly on the walls as Tomas fled down the passage, his footfalls echoing in the gloom. His torch was held tightly in his left hand, the sword clutched in his right. He looked over his shoulder and saw the two glowing red eyes pursuing him, though they seemed not to be gaining. With grim determination he thought, if it catches me, it will catch the fastest runner in all of Crydee. He lengthened his strides into a long, easy lope, saving strength and wind. He knew that if he had to turn and face the creature, he would surely die. The initial fear lessened, and now he felt a cold clarity holding his mind, the cunning reason of a prey knowing it is hopeless to fight. All his energy was turned toward fleeing. He would try to lose the creature any way possible.

He ducked into a side corridor and hurried along it, checking to see if the wraith would follow. The glowing red eyes appeared at the entrance to the tunnel he had turned into, following him. The distance between them seemed to have increased. The thought that many might have died at the thing's hand because they were too frightened to run crossed his mind. The wraith's strength lay in the numbing terror it caused.

Another corridor and another turn. Still the wraith followed. Ahead lay a large cavern, and Tomas found himself entering the same hall in which the wraith had attacked the party. He had circled around and entered through another tunnel. Racing across the floor, he saw the bodies of mules and guards lying in his path. He paused long enough to grab a fresh torch, for his was nearly spent, and transferred the flame.

He looked backward to see the undead creature closing on him and started off again. Hope briefly flickered in his breast, for if he could pick the proper corridor, he might catch up to the others. Dolgan had said that from this cavern it was a straight journey to the surface. He picked what he thought was the proper one, though he was disoriented and couldn't be sure.

The wraith let out a howl of rage at its prey's eluding it again, and followed. Tomas felt terror bordering on elation as his long legs stretched out, eating up the distance ahead of him. He gained his second wind and set a steady pace for himself. Never had he run so well, but then never had he possessed such a reason.

After what seemed an endless time of running, he found himself coming to a series of side tunnels, set closely together. He felt hope die, for this was not the straight path the dwarf had mentioned. Picking one at random, he turned into a passage and found more tunnels close by. Cutting through several more, he turned as quickly as possible, weaving his way through a maze of passages. Ducking around a wall formed between two such tunnels, he stopped briefly and caught his breath. He listened for a moment and heard only the sound of his pounding heart. He had been too busy to look behind and was unsure of the wraith's whereabouts.

Suddenly a shriek of rage echoed faintly down the corridors, sounding far off. Tomas sank to the floor of the tunnel and felt his body go limp. Another shriek echoed more faintly, and Tomas felt certain that the wraith had lost his trail and was moving off in another direction.

A sense of relief flooded through him, nearly causing him to laugh giddily. It was closely followed by the sudden realization of his situation. He sat up and took stock. If he could find his way back to the dead animals, he would at least have food and water. But as he stood up, he realized that he had no notion which way the cavern lay. Cursing himself for not counting the turns as he had made them, he tried to remember the general pattern he had followed. He had turned mostly to the right, he reminded himself, so if he retraced his steps mostly to the left, he should be able to find one of the many tunnels that led to the glory hole. Looking cautiously around the first corner, Tomas set off, searching his way through the maze of passages.

. . .

AFTER AN UNKNOWN time had passed, Tomas stopped and looked around in the second large cavern he had come to since he had fled the wraith. Like the first, this cavern was devoid of mules and men—and the hoped-for food and water. Tomas opened his pouch and took out the small biscuit he had hoarded to nibble while walking. It gave him little relief from his hunger.

When he was done, he set off again, trying to find some clue to the way out. He knew he had only a short time before his torch died, but he refused to simply sit and wait for a nameless death in the dark.

After some time Tomas could hear the sound of water echoing through the tunnel. Hurrying forward, his thirst spurring him on, he entered a large cavern, the biggest yet, as far as he could tell. Far away he could hear the faint roar of the Mac Mordain Cadal falls, but in which direction he couldn't be sure. Somewhere high in the darkness lay the path that they had taken two days earlier. Tomas felt his heart sink, he had moved deeper into the earth than he had thought.

The tunnel widened to a landing of some sort and disappeared beneath what appeared to be a large lake, constantly lapping against the sides of the cavern, filling it with muted echoes. Quickly he fell to his knees and drank. The water tasted rich with minerals, but was clear and fresh.

Sitting back on his haunches, he looked about. The landing was packed earth and sand and appeared to be fashioned rather than natural. Tomas guessed the dwarves might have used boats to cross the underground lake, but could only wonder what lay on the other side. Then the thought hit him that perhaps someone other than the dwarves had used boats to cross the lake, and he felt fear again.

To his left he spied a pile of wood, nestled against a junction of the landing and the cavern wall. Crossing to it, he pulled out several pieces and started a small fire. The wood was mostly timber pieces, used to shore up the tunnels, but mixed in were several branches and twigs. They must have been brought down by the falls from above, where the river enters the mountain, he thought. Underneath the pile he found some fibrous weeds growing. Wondering at the plants' ability to grow without sunlight, the boy was nevertheless thankful, for after cutting them with his sword, he was able to fashion some rude torches with the weeds wrapped around some driftwood. He tied them in a bundle, using his sword belt, forcing him to give up his scabbard. At least, he thought, I'll have a little more light. Some extra time to see where he was going was comforting.

He threw some bigger timber pieces on his small fire, and soon it was roaring into brightness. Abruptly the cavern seemed to light up, and Tomas spun around. The entire cavern was glowing with sparkling light, as some sort of mineral, or crystal, caught the light and reflected it to be caught and reflected again. It was a glittering, sparkling rainbow of colors cascading over walls and ceiling, giving the entire cavern a fairylike quality as far as the eye could follow.

Tomas stood in awe for a minute, drinking in the sight, for he knew he would never be able to explain in words what he was seeing. The thought struck him that he might be the only human ever to have witnessed the display.

It was hard to tear his eyes from the glory of the vision, but Tomas forced himself. He used the extra illumination to examine the area he was in. There was nothing beyond the landing, but he did spy another tunnel off to the left, leaving the cavern at the far end of the sand.

He gathered together his torches and walked along

the landing. As he reached the tunnel, his fire died down, the dry timber being quickly consumed. Another glorious vision assaulted his senses, for the gem-like walls and ceiling continued to glimmer and glow. Again he stood silently watching the display. Slowly the sparkling dimmed, until the cavern was again dark, except for his torch and the quickly dying fire's red glow.

He had to stretch to reach the other tunnel, but made it without dropping his sword or torches, or getting his boots wet. Turning away from the cavern, he resumed his journey.

He made his way for hours, the torch burning lower. He lit one of the new ones and found that it gave a satisfactory light. He was still frightened, but felt good about keeping his head under these conditions and was sure Swordmaster Fannon would approve of his actions.

After walking for a while, he came to an intersection. He found the bones of a creature in the dust, its fate unknowable. He spotted the tracks of some other small creature leading away, but they were faint with age. With no other notion than the need for a clear path, Tomas followed them. Soon they also vanished in the dust.

He had no means to reckon time, but thought that it must be well into night by now. There was a timeless feeling to these passages, and he felt lost beyond recovery. Fighting down what he recognized as budding panic, he continued to walk. He kept his mind on pleasant memories of home, and dreams of the future. He would find a way out, and he would become a great hero in the coming war. And most cherished dream of all, he would journey to Elvandar and see the beautiful lady of the elves again.

He followed the tunnel downward. This area seemed different from the other caverns and tunnels, its manner of fashioning unlike the others. He thought that Dolgan could tell if this was so, and who had done the work.

He entered another cavern and looked around. Some of the tunnels that entered the cavern were barely tall enough for a man to walk through upright. Others were broad enough for a company of men to walk through ten abreast, with long spears upon their shoulders. He hoped this meant the dwarves had fashioned the smaller tunnels and he could follow one upward, back to the surface.

Looking around, he spied a likely ledge to rest upon, within jumping distance. He crossed to it and tossed up his sword and the bundle of torches. He then gently tossed up his torch, so as not to put it out, and pulled himself up. It was large enough to sleep upon without rolling off. Four feet up the wall was a small hole, about three feet in diameter. Looking down it, Tomas could see that it opened up quickly to a size large enough to stand in and stretched away into blackness.

Satisfied that nothing lurked immediately above him, and that anything coming from below would awaken him, Tomas pulled his cloak around him, rested his head on his hand, and put out the torch. He was frightened, but the exhaustion of the day lulled him quickly to sleep. He lay in fitful dreams of red glowing eyes chasing him down endless black corridors, terror washing over him. He ran until he came to a green place where he could rest, feeling safe, under the gaze of a beautiful woman with red-gold hair and pale blue eyes.

He started awake to some nameless call. He had no idea of how long he had slept, but he felt as if it had been long enough for his body to run again, if need be. He felt in the dark for his torch and took flint and steel from out of his pouch. He struck sparks into the wadding of the torch and started a glow. Quickly bringing the torch close, he blew the spark into flame. Looking about, he found the cavern unchanged. A faint echoing of his own movements was all he heard.

He realized he could have a chance of survival only if he kept moving and found a way up. He stood and was about to climb down from the ledge when a faint noise sounded from the hole above.

He peered down it but could see nothing. Again there came a faint sound, and Tomas strained to hear what it was. It was almost like the tread of footfalls, but he could not be sure. He nearly shouted, but held off, for there was no assurance it was his friends returned to find him. His imagination provided many other possibilities, all of them unpleasant.

He thought for a moment, then decided. Whatever was making the noise might lead him out of the mines, even if only by providing a trail to follow. With no other option appearing more attractive, he pulled himself up through the small hole, entering the new tunnel.

10

Rescue

It was a dispirited group that emerged from the mine.

The survivors sank to the ground, near exhaustion. Pug had fought tears for hours after Tomas had fled, and now he lay on the wet ground staring upward at the grey sky, feeling numb. Kulgan had fared worst of all, being completely drained of energy by the spell used to repel the wraith. He had been carried on the shoulders of the others most of the way, and they showed the price of their burden. All fell into an exhausted sleep, except Dolgan, who lit a fire and stood watch.

Pug awoke to the sound of voices and a clear, starry night. The smell of food cooking greeted him. When Gardan and the three remaining guards awakened, Dolgan had left them to watch over the others and had snared a brace of rabbits. These were roasting over a fire. The others awoke, except Kulgan, who snored deeply.

Arutha and the Duke saw the boy wake, and the Prince came to where he sat. The younger son of the Duke, ignoring the snow, sat on the ground next to Pug, who had his cloak wrapped around him. "How do you feel, Pug?" Arutha asked, concern showing in his eyes.

This was the first time Pug had seen Arutha's gentler nature. Pug tried to speak and found tears coming to his eyes. Tomas had been his friend as long as he could remember, more a brother than a friend. As he tried to speak, great racking sobs broke from his throat, and he felt hot, salty tears run down into his mouth.

Arutha placed his arm around Pug, letting the boy cry on his shoulder. When the initial flood of grief had passed, the Prince said, "There is nothing shameful in mourning the loss of a friend, Pug. My father and I share your pain."

Dolgan came to stand behind the Prince. "I also, Pug, for he was a likable lad. We all share your loss." The dwarf seemed to consider something and spoke to the Duke.

Kulgan had just awakened, sitting up like a bear waking from winter's sleep. He regained his bearings and, seeing Arutha with Pug, quickly forgot his own aching joints and joined them.

There was little they could say, but Pug found comfort in their closeness. He finally regained his composure and pulled away from the Prince. "Thank you, Your Highness," he said, sniffing. "I will be all right."

They joined Dolgan, Gardan, and the Duke near the fire. Borric was shaking his head at something the dwarf had said. "I thank you for your bravery, Dolgan, but I can't allow it."

Dolgan puffed on his pipe, a friendly smile splitting his beard. "And how do you intend to stop me, Your Grace? Surely not by force?"

Borric shook his head. "No, of course not. But to go would be the sheerest folly."

Kulgan and Arutha exchanged questioning looks. Pug paid little attention, being lost in a cold, numb world. In spite of having just awakened, he felt ready for sleep again, welcoming its warm, soft relief.

Borric told them, "This mad dwarf means to return to the mines."

Before Kulgan and Arutha could voice a protest, Dolgan said, "I know it is only a slim hope, but if the boy has eluded the foul spirit, he'll be wandering lost and alone. There are tunnels down there that have never known the tread of a dwarf's foot, let alone a boy's. Once down a passage, I have no trouble making my way back, but Tomas has no such natural sense. If I can find his trail, I can find him. If he is to have any chance of escaping the mines, he'll be needing my guidance. I'll bring home the boy if he lives, on this you have the word of Dolgan Tagarson, chief of village Caldara. I could not rest in my long hall this winter if I did not try."

Pug was roused from his lethargy by the dwarf's words. "Do you think you can find him, Dolgan?"

"If any can, I can," he said. He leaned close to Pug. "Do not get your hopes too high, for it is unlikely that Tomas eluded the wraith. I would do you a disservice if I said otherwise, boy." Seeing the tears brimming in Pug's eyes again, he quickly added, "But if there is a way, I shall find it."

Pug nodded, seeking a middle path between desolation and renewed hope. He understood the admonition, but still could not give up the faint flicker of comfort Dolgan's undertaking would provide.

Dolgan crossed over to where his shield and ax lay and picked them up. "When the dawn comes, quickly follow the trail down the hills through the woodlands.

While not the Green Heart, this place has menace
aplenty for so small a band. If you lose your way, head
due east. You'll find your way to the road to Bordon.
From there it is a matter of three days' walk. May the
gods protect you."

Borric nodded, and Kulgan walked over to where
the dwarf made ready to leave. He handed Dolgan a
pouch. "I can get more tabac in the town, friend dwarf.
Please take this."

Dolgan took it and smiled at Kulgan. "Thank
you, magician. I am in your debt."

Borric came to stand before the dwarf and place a
hand on his shoulder. "It is we who are in your debt,
Dolgan. If you come to Crydee, we will have that meal
you were promised. That, and more. May good fortune
go with you."

"Thank you, Your Lordship. I'll look forward to
it." Without another word, Dolgan walked into the
blackness of Mac Mordain Cadal.

DOLGAN STOPPED BY the dead mules, pausing only
long enough to pick up food, water, and a lantern. The
dwarf needed no light to make his way underground—
his people had long ago adapted other senses for the
darkness. But, he thought, it will increase the chances
of finding Tomas if the boy can see the light, no matter
the risk of attracting unwelcome attention. Assuming
he is still alive, he added grimly.

Entering the tunnel where he had last seen Tomas,
Dolgan searched about for signs of the boy's passing.
The dust was thin, but here and there he could make
out a slight disturbance, perhaps a footprint. Following,
the dwarf came to even dustier passages, where the
boy's footfalls were clearly marked. Hurrying, he followed them.

Dolgan came back to the same cavern, after a few minutes, and cursed.

He felt little hope of finding the boy's tracks again among all the disturbance caused by the fight with the wraith. Pausing briefly, he set out to examine each tunnel leading out of the cavern for signs. After an hour he found a single footprint heading away from the cavern, through a tunnel to the right of where he had entered the first time. Moving up it, he found several more prints, set wide apart, and decided the boy must have been running. Hurrying on, he saw more tracks, as the passage became dustier.

Dolgan came to the cavern on the lake and nearly lost the trail again, until he saw the tunnel near the edge of the landing. He slogged through the water, pulling himself up into the passage, and saw Tomas's tracks. His faint lantern light was insufficient to illuminate the crystals in the cavern. But even if it had, he would not have paused to admire the sight, so intent was he on finding the boy.

Downward he followed, never resting. He knew that Tomas had long before outdistanced the wraith. There were signs that most of his journey was at a slower pace: footprints in the dust showed he had been walking, and the cold campfire showed he had stopped. But there were other terrors besides the wraith down here, just as dreadful.

Dolgan again lost the trail in the last cavern, finding it only when he spied the ledge above where the tracks ended. He had difficulty climbing to it, but when he did, he saw the blackened spot where the boy had snuffed out his torch. Here Tomas must have rested. Dolgan looked around the empty cavern. The air did not move this deep below the mountains. Even the dwarf, who was used to such things, found this an unnerving place. He looked down at the black mark on the ledge. But how long did Tomas stay, and where did he go?

Dolgan saw the hole in the wall and, since no tracks led away from the ledge, decided that was the way Tomas must have gone. He climbed through and followed the passage until it came to a larger one, heading downward, into the bowels of the mountain.

Dolgan followed what seemed to be a group of tracks, as if a band of men had come this way. Tomas's tracks were mixed in, and he was worried, for the boy could have been along this way before or after the others, or could have been with them. If the boy was held prisoner by someone, then Dolgan knew every moment was critical.

The tunnel wound downward and soon changed into a hall fashioned from great stone blocks fitted closely together and polished smooth. In all his years he had never seen its like. The passage leveled out, and Dolgan walked along quietly. The tracks had vanished, for the stone was hard and free of dust. High overhead, Dolgan could make out the first of several crystal chandeliers hung from the ceiling by chains. They could be lowered by means of a pulley, so the candles might be lit. The sound of his boots echoed hollowly off the high ceiling.

At the far end of the passage he spied large doors, fashioned from wood, with bands of iron and a great lock. They were ajar, and light could be seen coming through.

Without a sound, Dolgan crept close to the doors and peered in. He gaped at what he saw, his shield and ax coming up instinctively.

Sitting on a pile of gold coins, and gems the size of a man's fist, was Tomas, eating what looked to be a fish. Opposite him crouched a figure that caused Dolgan to doubt his eyes.

A head the size of a small wagon rested on the floor. Shield-size scales of a deep golden color covered it, and the long, supple neck led back to a huge body extending into the gloom of the giant hall. Enormous wings were folded across its back, their drooping tips touching the floor. Two pointed ears sat atop its head, separated by a delicate-looking crest, flecked with silver. Its long muzzle was set in a wolflike grin, showing fangs as long as broadswords, and a long forked tongue flicked out for a moment.

Dolgan fought down the overwhelming and rare urge to run, for Tomas was sitting, and to all appearances sharing a meal, with the dwarven folk's most feared hereditary enemy: a great dragon. He stepped forward, and his boots clacked on the stone floor.

Tomas turned at the sound, and the dragon's great head came up. Giant ruby eyes regarded the small intruder. Tomas jumped to his feet, an expression of joy upon his face. "Dolgan!" He scrambled down from the pile of wealth and rushed to the dwarf.

The dragon's voice rumbled through the great hall, echoing like thunder through a valley. "Welcome, dwarf. Thy friend hath told me that thou wouldst not forsake him."

Tomas stood before the dwarf, asking a dozen questions, while Dolgan's senses reeled. Behind the boy, the Prince of all dragons sat quietly observing the exchange, and the dwarf was having trouble maintaining the equanimity that was normally his. Making little sense of Tomas's questions, Dolgan gently pushed him to one side to better see the dragon. "I came alone," he said softly to the boy. "The others were loath to leave the search to me, but they had to press on, so vital was the mission."

Tomas said, "I understand."

"What manner of wizardry is this?" asked Dolgan softly.

The dragon chuckled, and the room rumbled with the sound. "Come into my home, dwarf, and I will tell thee." The great dragon's head returned to the floor, his eyes still resting above Dolgan's head. The dwarf approached slowly, shield and ax unconsciously at the ready. The dragon laughed, a deep, echoing sound, like water cascading down a canyon. "Stay thy hand, small warrior, I'll not harm thee or thy friend."

Dolgan let his shield down and hung his ax on his belt. He looked around and saw that they were standing in a vast hall, fashioned out of the living rock of the mountain. On all its walls could be seen large tapestries and banners, faded and torn; something about their look set Dolgan's teeth on edge, for they were as alien as they were ancient—no creature he knew of, human, elf, or goblin fashioned those pennants. More of the giant crystal chandeliers hung from timbers across the ceiling. At the far end of the hall, a throne could be seen on a dais, and long tables with chairs for many diners stood before it. Upon the tables were flagons of crystal and plates of gold. And all was covered with the dust of ages.

Elsewhere in the hall lay piles of wealth: gold, gems, crowns, silver, rich armor, bolts of rare cloth, and carved chests of precious woods, fitted with inlaid enamels of great craft.

Dolgan sat upon a lifetime's riches of gold, absently moving it around to make as comfortable a seat as was possible. Tomas sat next to him as the dwarf pulled out his pipe. He didn't show it, but he felt the need to calm himself, and his pipe always soothed his nerves. He lit a taper from his lantern and struck it to his pipe. The dragon watched him, then said, "Canst thou now breathe fire and smoke, dwarf? Art thou the new dragon? Hath ever a dragon been so small?"

Dolgan shook his head. "'Tis but my pipe." He explained the use of tabac.

The dragon said, "This is a strange thing, but thine are a strange folk, in truth."

Dolgan cocked a brow at this but said nothing. "Tomas, how did you come to this place?"

Tomas seemed unmindful of the dragon, and Dolgan found this reassuring. If the great beast had wished to harm them, he could have done so with little effort. Dragons were undisputedly the mightiest creatures on Midkemia. And this was the mightiest dragon Dolgan had heard of, half again the size of those he had fought in his youth.

Tomas finished the fish he had been eating and said, "I wandered for a long time and came to a place where I could sleep."

"Aye, I found it."

"I awoke at the sound of something and found tracks that led here."

"Those I saw also. I was afraid you had been taken."

"I wasn't. It was a party of goblins and a few Dark Brothers, coming to this place. They were very concerned about what was ahead and didn't pay attention to what was behind, so I could follow fairly close."

"That was a dangerous thing to do."

"I know, but I was desperate for a way out. I thought they might lead me to the surface, and I could wait while they went on ahead, then slip out. If I could get out of the mines, I could have headed north toward your village."

"A bold plan, Tomas," said Dolgan, an approving look in his eyes.

"They came to this place, and I followed."

"What happened to them?"

The dragon spoke. "I sent them far away, dwarf, for they were not company I would choose."

"Sent them away? How?"

The dragon raised his head a little, and Dolgan could see that his scales were faded and dull in places. The red eyes were filmed over slightly, and suddenly Dolgan knew the dragon was blind.

"The dragons have long had magic, though it is unlike any other. It is by my arts that I can see thee, dwarf, for the light hath long been denied me. I took the foul creatures and sent them far to the north. They do not know how they came to that place, nor remember this place."

Dolgan puffed on his pipe, thinking of what he was hearing. "In the tales of my people, there are legends of dragon magicians, though you are the first I have seen."

The dragon lowered his head to the floor slowly, as if tired. "For I am one of the last of the golden dragons, dwarf, and none of the lesser dragons have the art of sorcery. I have sworn never to take a life, but I would not have their kind invade my resting place."

Tomas spoke up. "Rhuagh has been kind to me, Dolgan. He let me stay until you found me, for he knew that someone was coming."

Dolgan looked at the dragon, wondering at his foretelling.

Tomas continued, "He gave me some smoked fish to eat, and a place to rest."

"Smoked fish?"

The dragon said, "The kobolds, those thou knowest as gnomes, worship me as a god and bring me offerings, fish caught in the deep lake and smoked, and treasure gleaned from deeper halls."

"Aye," said Dolgan, "gnomes have never been known for being overly bright."

The dragon chuckled. "True. The kobolds are shy and harm only those who trouble them in their deep tunnels. They are a simple folk, and it pleaseth them to have a god. As I am not able to hunt, it is an agreeable arrangement."

Dolgan considered his next question. "I mean no disrespect, Rhuagh, but it has ever been my experience with dragons that you have little love for others not your own kind. Why have you aided the boy?"

The dragon closed his eyes for a moment, then opened them again to stare blankly toward the dwarf. "Know this, dwarf, that such was not always the way of it. Thy people are old, but mine are the oldest of all, save one. We were here before the elves and the moredhel. We served those whose names may not be spoken, and were a happy people."

"The Dragon Lords?"

"So your legends call them. They were our masters, and we were their servants, as were the elves and the moredhel. When they left this land, on a journey beyond imagining, we became the most powerful of the free people, in a time before the dwarves or men came to these lands. Ours was a dominion over the skies and all things, for we were mighty beyond any other.

"Ages ago, men and dwarves came to our mountains, and for a time we lived in peace. But ways change, and soon strife came. The elves drove the moredhel from the forest now called Elvandar, and men and dwarves warred with dragons.

"We were strong, but humans are like the trees of the forest, their numbers uncountable. Slowly my people fled to the south, and I am the last in these mountains. I have lived here for ages, for I would not forsake my home.

"By magic I could turn away those who sought this treasure, and kill those whose arts foiled my clouding of their minds. I sickened of the killing and vowed to take no more lives, even those as hateful as the moredhel. That is why I sent them far, and why I aided the boy, for he is undeserving of harm."

Dolgan studied the dragon. "I thank you, Rhuagh."

"Thy thanks are welcome, Dolgan of the Grey Towers. I am glad of thy coming also. It is only a little longer that I could shelter the boy, for I summoned Tomas to my side by magic arts, so he might sit my deathwatch."

"What?" exclaimed Tomas.

"It is given to dragons to know the hour of their death, Tomas, and mine is close. I am old, even by the measure of my people, and have led a full life. I am content for it to be so. It is our way."

Dolgan looked troubled. "Still, I find it strange to sit here hearing you speak of this."

"Why, dwarf? Is it not true with thine own people that when one dieth, it is accounted how well he lived, rather than how long?"

"You have the truth of that."

"Then why should it matter if the death hour is known or not? It is still the same. I have had all that one of my kind could hope for: health, mates, young, riches, and rest. These are all I have ever wanted, and I have had them."

"'Tis a wise thing to know what is wanted, and wiser still to know when 'tis achieved," said Dolgan.

"True. And still wiser to know when it is unachievable, for then striving is folly. It is the way of my people to sit the deathwatch, but there are none of my kind near enough to call. I would ask thee to wait for my passing before thy leaving. Wilt thou?"

Dolgan looked at Tomas, who bobbed his head in agreement. "Aye, dragon, we will, though it is not a thing to gladden our hearts."

The dragon closed his eyes; Tomas and Dolgan could see they were beginning to swell shut. "Thanks to thee, Dolgan, and to thee, Tomas."

The dragon lay there and spoke to them of his life, flying the skies of Midkemia, of far lands where tigers lived in cities, and mountains where eagles could speak. Tales of wonder and awe were told, long into the night.

When his voice began to falter, Rhuagh said, "Once a man came to this place, a magician of mighty arts. He could not be turned from this place by my magic, nor could I slay him. For three days we battled, his arts against mine, and when done, he had bested me. I thought he would slay me and carry off my riches, but instead he stayed, for his only thought was to learn my magic, so that it would not be lost when I passed."

Tomas sat in wonder, for as little as he knew about magic from Pug, he thought this a marvelous thing. In his mind's eye he could see the titanic struggle and the great powers working.

"With him he had a strange creature, much like a goblin, though upright, and with features of finer aspect. For three years he stayed with me, while his servant came and went. He learned all I could teach, for I could deny him not. But he taught as well, and his wisdom gave me great comfort. It was because of him that I learned to respect life, no matter how mean of character, and vowed to spare any that came to me. He also had suffered at the hands of others, as I had in the wars with men, for much that I cherished was lost. This man had the art of healing the wounds of the heart and mind, and when he left, I felt the victor, not the vanquished." He paused and swallowed, and Tomas could see that speech was coming to him with more difficulty. "If a dragon could not have attended my deathwatch, I would as soon have him sit here, for he was the first of thy kind, boy, that I would count a friend."

"Who was he, Rhuagh?" Tomas asked.

"He was called Macros."

Dolgan looked thoughtful. "I've heard his name, a magician of most puissant arts. He is nearly a myth, having lived somewhere to the east."

"A myth he is not, Dolgan," said Rhuagh, thickly. "Still, it may be that he is dead, for he dwelt with me ages ago." The dragon paused. "My time is now close, so I must finish. I would ask a boon of thee, dwarf." He moved his head slightly and said, "In yon box is a gift from the mage, to be used at this time. It is a rod fashioned of magic. Macros left it so that when I die no bones will be left for scavengers to pick over. Wilt thou bring it here?"

Dolgan went to the indicated chest. He opened it to discover a black metal rod lying upon a blue velvet cloth. He picked up the rod and found it surprisingly heavy for its size. He carried it over to the dragon.

The dragon spoke, his words nearly unintelligible, for his tongue was swollen. "In a moment, touch the rod to me, Dolgan, for then will I end."

"Aye," said Dolgan, "though it will give me scant pleasure to see your end, dragon."

"Before that I have one last thing to tell. In a box next to the other is a gift for thee, dwarf. Thou mayest take whatever else here pleaseth thee, for I will have no use for any of it. But of all in this hall, that in the box is what I wish thee to have." He tried to move his head toward Tomas, but could not. "Tomas, thanks to thee, for spending my last with me. In the box with the dwarf's gift is one for you. Take whatever else pleaseth thee, also, for thy heart is good." He drew a deep breath, and Tomas could hear it rattle in his throat. "Now, Dolgan."

Dolgan extended the rod and lightly touched the dragon on the head with it. At first nothing happened. Rhuagh said softly, "It was Macros's last gift."

Suddenly a soft golden light began to form around the dragon. A faint humming could be heard, as if the walls of the hall reverberated with fey music. The sound increased as the light grew brighter and began to pulse with energy. Tomas and Dolgan watched as the discolored patches faded from Rhuagh's scales. His hide shone with golden sparkle, and the film started to lift from his eyes. He slowly raised his head, and they knew he could again see the hall around him. His crest stood erect, and his wings lifted, showing the rich silver sheen underneath. The yellowed teeth became brilliant white, and his faded black claws shone like polished ebony as he stood upright, lifting his head high.

Dolgan said softly, "'Tis the grandest sight I've ever beheld."

Slowly the light grew in intensity as Rhuagh returned to the image of his youthful power. He pulled himself to his full, impressive height, his crest dancing with silver lights. The dragon threw back his head, a youthful, vigorous motion, and with a shout of joy sent a powerful blast of flame up to the high vaulted ceiling. With a roar like a hundred trumpets he shouted, "I thank thee, Macros. It is a princely gift indeed."

Then the strangely harmonic thrumming changed in tone, becoming more insistent, louder. For a brief instant both Dolgan and Tomas thought a voice could be heard among the pulsing tones, a deep, hollow echo saying, "You are welcome, friend."

Tomas felt wetness on his face, and touched it. Tears of joy from the dragon's sheer beauty were running down his cheeks. The dragon's great golden wings unfolded, as if he were about to launch himself in flight. The shimmering light became so bright, Tomas and Dolgan could barely stand to look, though they could not pull their eyes from the spectacle. The sound in the room grew to a pitch so loud, dust fell from the ceiling upon their heads, and they could feel the floor shake. The dragon launched himself upward, wings extended, then vanished in a blinding flash of cold white light. Suddenly the room was as it had been and the sound was gone.

The emptiness in the cavern felt oppressive after the dragon vanished, and Tomas looked at the dwarf. "Let's leave, Dolgan. I have little wish to stay."

Dolgan looked thoughtful. "Aye, Tomas, I also have little desire to stay. Still, there is the matter of the dragon's gifts." He crossed over to the box the dragon had identified and opened it.

Dolgan's eyes became round as he reached in and pulled out a dwarven hammer. He held it out before himself and looked upon it with reverence. The head was made from a silver metal that shone in the lantern light with bluish highlights. Across the side were carved dwarven symbols. The haft was carved oak, with scrollwork running the length. It was polished, and the deep rich grain showed through the finish. Dolgan said, faintly, "'Tis the Hammer of Tholin. Long removed from my people. Its return will cause rejoicing in every dwarven long hall throughout the West. It is the symbol of our last king, lost ages ago."

Tomas came over to watch and saw something else in the box. He reached past Dolgan and pulled out a large bundle of white cloth. He unrolled it and found that the cloth was a tabard of white, with a golden dragon emblazoned on the front. Inside were a shield with the same device and a golden helm. Most marvelous of all was a golden sword with a white hilt. Its scabbard was fashioned from a smooth white material like ivory, but stronger, like metal. Beneath the bundle lay a coat of golden chain mail, which he removed with an "Oh!" of wonder.

Dolgan watched him and said, "Take them, boy. The dragon said it was your gift."

"They are much too fine for me, Dolgan. They belong to a prince or a king."

"I'm thinking the previous owner has scant use for them, laddie. They were freely given, and you may do what you will, but I think that there is something special to them, or else they wouldn't have been placed in the box with the hammer. Tholin's hammer is a weapon of power, forged in the ancient hearths of the Mac Cadman Alair, the oldest mine in these mountains. In it rests magic unsurpassed in the history of the dwarves. It is likely the gilded armor and sword are also such. It may be there is a purpose in their coming to you."

Tomas thought for a moment, then quickly pulled off his great cloak. His tunic was no gambeson, but the golden mail went over it easily enough, being fashioned for someone of larger stature. He pulled the tabard over it and put the helm upon his head. Picking up the sword and shield, he stood before Dolgan. "Do I look foolish?"

The dwarf regarded him closely. "They are a bit large, but you'll grow into them, no doubt." He thought he saw something in the way the boy stood and held the sword in one hand and the shield in the other. "No, Tomas, you do not look foolish. Perhaps not at ease, but not foolish. They are grand, and you will come to wear them as they were meant to be worn, I think."

Tomas nodded, picked up his cloak, and turned toward the door, putting up his sword. The armor was surprisingly light, much lighter than what he had worn at Crydee. The boy said, "I don't feel like taking anything else, Dolgan. I suppose that sounds strange."

Dolgan walked over to him. "No, boy, for I also wish nothing of the dragon's riches." With a backward glance at the hall, he added, "Though there will be nights to come when I will wonder at the wisdom of that. I may return someday, but I doubt it. Now let us find a way home." They set off and soon were in tunnels Dolgan knew well, taking them to the surface.

DOLGAN GRIPPED TOMAS'S arm in silent warning. The boy knew enough not to speak. He also felt the same alarm he had experienced just before the wraith had attacked the day before. But this time it was almost physically felt. The undead creature was near. Putting down the lantern, Tomas shuttered it. His eyes widened in sudden astonishment, for instead of the expected blackness, he saw faintly the figure of the dwarf moving slowly forward. Without thought he said, "Dolgan—"

The dwarf turned, and suddenly a black form loomed up at his back. "Behind you!" shouted Tomas.

Dolgan spun to confront the wraith, instinctively bringing up his shield and Tholin's hammer. The undead creature struck at the dwarf, and only Dolgan's battle-trained reflexes and dwarven ability to sense movement in the inky darkness saved him, for he took the contact on his iron-bosked shield. The creature howled in rage at the contact with iron. Then Dolgan lashed out with the legendary weapon of his ancestors, and the creature screamed as the hammer struck its form. Blue-green light sprang about the head of the hammer, and the creature retreated, wailing in agony.

"Stay behind me," shouted Dolgan. "If iron irritates it, then Tholin's hammer pains it. I may be able to drive it off."

Tomas began to obey the dwarf, then found his right hand crossing to pull the golden sword free of the scabbard on his left hip. Suddenly the ill-fitting armor seemed to settle more comfortably around his shoulders, and the shield balanced upon his arm as if he had carried it for years. Without volition of his own, Tomas moved behind Dolgan, then stepped past, bringing the golden sword to the ready.

The creature seemed to hesitate, then moved toward Tomas. Tomas raised his sword, readying to strike. With a sound of utter terror, the wraith turned and fled. Dolgan glanced at Tomas, and something he saw made him hesitate as Tomas seemed to come to an awareness of himself and put up his sword.

Dolgan returned to the lantern and said, "Why did you do that, lad?"

Tomas said, "I . . . don't know." Feeling suddenly self-conscious at having disobeyed the dwarf's instructions, he said, "But it worked. The thing left."

"Aye, it worked," agreed Dolgan, removing the shutter from the lantern. In the light he studied the boy.

Tomas said, "I think your ancestor's hammer was too much for it."

Dolgan said nothing, but he knew that wasn't the case. The creature had fled in fear from the sight of Tomas in his armor of white and gold. Then another thought struck the dwarf. "Boy, how did you know to warn me the creature was behind me?"

"I saw it."

Dolgan turned to look at Tomas with open astonishment. "You *saw* it? How? You had shuttered the lantern."

"I don't know how. I just did."

Dolgan closed the shutter on the lantern again

and stood up. Moving a few feet away, he said, "Where am I now, lad?"

Without hesitation Tomas came to stand before him, placing a hand upon his shoulder. "Here."

"What—?" said the dwarf.

Tomas touched the helm, then the shield. "You said they were special."

"Aye, lad. But I didn't think they were *that* special."

"Should I take them off?" asked the worried boy.

"No, no." Leaving the lantern upon the floor, Dolgan said, "We can move more quickly if I don't have to worry about what you can and can't see." He forced a note of cheeriness into his voice. "And despite there being no two finer warriors in the land, it's best if we don't announce our presence with that light. The dragon's telling of the moredhel being down in our mines gives me no comfort. If one band was brave enough to risk my people's wrath, there may be others. Yon wraith may be terrified of your golden sword and my ancient hammer, but twenty or so moredhel might not be so easily impressed."

Tomas could find nothing to say, so they started moving off into the darkness.

THREE TIMES THEY stopped and hid while hurrying groups of goblins and Dark Brothers passed near by. From their dark vantage point they could see that many of those who passed harbored wounds or were aided by their kinsmen as they limped along. After the last group was gone, Dolgan turned to Tomas and said, "Never in history have the goblins and moredhel dared to enter our mines in such numbers. Too much do they fear my people to risk it."

Tomas said, "They look pretty beat up, Dolgan,

and they have females and young with them, and carry great bundles, too. They are fleeing something."

The dwarf nodded. "They are all moving from the direction of the northern valley in the Grey Towers, heading toward the Green Heart. Something still drives them south."

"The Tsurani?"

Dolgan nodded. "My thought also. Come. We had best return to Caldara as quickly as we can." They set off and soon were in tunnels Dolgan knew well, taking them to the surface and home.

THEY WERE BOTH exhausted when they reached Caldara five days later. The snows in the mountains were heavy, and the going was slow. As they approached the village, they were sighted by guards, and soon the entire village turned out to greet them.

They were taken to the village long hall, and Tomas was given a room. He was so tired that he fell asleep at once, and even the stout dwarf was fatigued. The dwarves agreed to call the village elders together the next day in council and discuss the latest news to reach the valley.

Tomas awoke feeling ravenous. He stretched as he stood up and was surprised to find no stiffness. He had fallen asleep in the golden mail and should have wakened to protesting joints and muscles. Instead he felt rested and well. He opened the door and stepped into a hall. He saw no one until he came to the central room of the long hall. There were several dwarves seated along the great table, with Dolgan at the head. Tomas saw one was Weylin, Dolgan's son. Dolgan motioned the boy to a chair and introduced him to the company.

The dwarves all greeted Tomas, who made polite responses. Mostly he stared at the great feast of food on the table.

Dolgan laughed and said, "Help yourself, laddie; there is little cause for you to be hungry with the board full." Tomas heaped a plate with beef, cheese, and bread and took a flagon of ale, though he had little head for it and it was early in the day. He quickly consumed what was on the platter and helped himself to another portion, looking to see if anyone disapproved. Most of the dwarves were involved in a complicated discussion of an unknown nature to Tomas, having to do with the allocation of winter stores to various villages in the area.

Dolgan called a halt to the discussion and said, "Now that Tomas is with us, I think we had best speak of these Tsurani."

Tomas's ears pricked up at that, and he turned his attention fully to what was being said. Dolgan continued, "Since I left on patrol, we have had runners from Elvandar and Stone Mountain. There have been many sightings of these aliens near the North Pass. They have made camp in the hills south of Stone Mountain."

One of the dwarves said, "That is Stone Mountain's business, unless they call us to arms."

Dolgan said, "True, Orwin, but there is also the news they have been seen moving in and out of the valley just south of the pass. They have intruded on lands traditionally ours, and that is the business of the Grey Towers."

The dwarf addressed as Orwin nodded. "Indeed it is, but there is naught we can do until spring."

Dolgan put his feet up on the table, lighting a pipe. "And that is true also. But we can be thankful the Tsurani can do naught until spring, as well."

Tomas put down a joint of beef he was holding. "Has the blizzard struck?"

Dolgan looked at him. "Aye, laddie, the passes are all solid with snow, for the first winter blizzard came upon us last night. There will be nothing that can move out there, least of all an army."

Tomas looked at Dolgan. "Then . . ."

"Aye. You'll guest with us this winter, for not even our hardiest runner could make his way out of these mountains to Crydee."

Tomas sat back, for in spite of the comforts of the dwarven long hall, he wished for more familiar surroundings. Still, there was nothing that could be done. He resigned himself to that and returned his attention to his meal.

11

Sorcerer's Isle

The weary group trudged into Bordon.

Around them rode a company of Natalese Rangers, dressed in their traditional grey tunics, trousers, and cloaks. They had been on patrol, had encountered the travelers a mile out of town, and were now escorting them. Borric was irritated that the rangers had not offered to let the exhausted travelers ride double, but he hid it well. They had little reason to recognize this group of ragamuffins as the Duke of Crydee and his party, and even if he should have arrived in state, there was little warmth between the Free Cities of Natal and the Kingdom.

Pug looked at Bordon with wonder. It was a small city by Kingdom standards, little more than a seaport town, but far larger than Crydee. Everywhere he looked, people were hurrying about on unknown tasks, busy and preoccupied. Little attention was paid the travelers except for an occasional glance from a shopkeeper or a woman at market. Never had the boy seen so many people, horses, mules, and wagons all in one place. It was a confusion of colors and sounds, overwhelming his senses. Barking dogs ran behind the rangers' horses, nimbly avoiding kicks by the irritated mounts. A few street boys shouted obscenities at the party, all obviously outlanders from their look, and most likely prisoners from the escort. Pug was vaguely troubled by this rudeness, but his attention was quickly distracted by the newness of the city.

Bordon, like the other cities in the area, had no standing army, but instead supported a garrison of Natalese Rangers, descendants of the legendary Imperial Keshian Guides and counted among the best horse soldiers and trackers in the west. They could provide ample warning of approaching trouble and allow the local militia time to turn out. Nominally independent, the rangers were free to dispose of outlaws and renegades on the spot, but after hearing the Duke's story, and at mention of the name Martin Longbow—whom they knew well—the leader of the patrol decided this matter should be turned over to the local prefects.

They were taken to the office of the local prefect, located in a small building near the city square. The rangers appeared pleased to be shed of the prisoners and return to their patrol as they gave over custody to the prefect.

The prefect was a short, swarthy man given to brightly colored sashes about his ample girth and large golden rings upon his fingers. He smoothed his dark, oiled beard as the ranger captain explained his company's meeting with the Duke's party. As the rangers rode off, the prefect greeted Borric coolly. When the Duke made it clear they were expected by Talbott Kilrane, the largest ships' broker in the city and Borric's trading agent in the Free Cities, the prefect's manner changed abruptly. They were taken from the office to the prefect's private quarters and offered hot, dark coffee. The prefect sent one of his servants with a message to the house of Kilrane and waited quietly, only occasionally making noncommittal small talk with the Duke.

Kulgan leaned over to Pug and said, "Our host is the sort who sees which way the wind blows before making up his mind; he waits word from the merchant before deciding if we're prisoners or guests." The magician chuckled. "You'll find as you grow older that minor functionaries are the same the world over."

An angry storm in the person of Meecham appeared suddenly in the door of the prefect's home a short time later, one of Kilrane's senior clerks at his elbow. The clerk quickly made it clear that this was indeed the Duke of Crydee and, yes, he was expected by Talbott Kilrane. The prefect was abjectly apologetic and hopeful the Duke would forgive the inconvenience, but under the present conditions, in these troubled times, he could understand? His manner was fawning and his smile unctuous.

Borric indicated that, yes, he did understand, all too well. Without any further delay, they left the prefect and went outside, where a group of grooms waited with horses. Quickly they mounted up, and Meecham and the clerk led them through the town, toward a hillside community of large, imposing houses.

The house of Talbott Kilrane stood topmost upon the highest hill overlooking the city. From the road Pug could see ships standing at anchor. Dozens of them were sitting with masts removed, obviously out of service during the harsh weather. A few coast-huggers bound for Ylith in the north or the other Free Cities were making their way cautiously in and out of the harbor, but for the most part the harbor was quiet.

They reached the house and entered an open gate

in a low wall, where servants ran to take their horses. As they dismounted, their host came through the large entrance to the house.

"Welcome, Lord Borric, welcome," he said, a warm smile splitting his gaunt face. Talbott Kilrane looked like a vulture reincarnated into human form, with a balding head, sharp features, and small, dark eyes. His expensive robes did little to hide his gauntness, but there was an ease to his manner, and a concern in his eyes, that softened the unattractive aspect.

In spite of the man's appearance, Pug found him likable. He shooed servants off, to make ready rooms and hot meals for the party. He would not listen as the Duke tried to explain the mission. Raising a hand, he said, "Later, Your Grace. We can speak at length, after you have had rest and food. I will expect you for dinner tonight, but for now there are hot baths and clean beds for your party. I will have warm meals delivered to your quarters. Good food, rest, and clean clothes, and you'll feel like a new man. Then we can speak."

He clapped his hands, and a housecarl came to show them their rooms. The Duke and his son were given separate quarters, while Pug and Kulgan shared another. Gardan was shown to Meecham's room, and the Duke's soldiers were taken to the servants' quarters.

Kulgan told Pug to take the first bath while the magician spoke with his servant for a while. Meecham and Kulgan went off to the franklin's room, and Pug stripped off his dirty clothes. In the center of the room was a large metal tub, filled with scented water, hot and steaming. He stepped into it and pulled his foot out quickly. After three days of walking through snow, the water felt as if it were boiling. Gently he placed his foot back in and, when he had become used to the heat, slowly entered the water.

He sat back in the tub, the sloping back providing

support. The inside of the tub was enameled, and Pug found the slick, smooth feeling strange after the wooden tubs of home. He lathered himself over with a sweet soap and washed the dirt from his hair, then stood in the tub and poured a bucket of cold water over his head to rinse off.

He dried himself and put on the clean nightshirt that had been left for him. In spite of the early hour he fell into the warm bed. His last thought was of the sandy-haired boy with the ready grin. As Pug slipped into sleep, he wondered if Dolgan had found his friend.

He awoke once during the day, hearing a nameless tune being hummed, while water was being splashed about with great zeal as Kulgan soaped his large body. Pug closed his eyes and was quickly asleep again.

He was hard asleep when Kulgan roused him for dinner. His tunic and trousers had been cleaned and a small rent in the shirt mended. His boots were polished and shone with a black gleam. As he stood inspecting himself in a mirror, he noticed for the first time a soft black shadow on his cheeks. He leaned closer and saw the early signs of a beard.

Kulgan watched him and said, "Well, Pug. Shall I have them fetch you a razor so you can keep your chin bare like Prince Arutha? Or do you wish to cultivate a magnificent beard?" He exaggeratedly brushed his own grey beard.

Pug smiled for the first time since leaving Mac Mordain Cadal. "I think I can leave off worrying about it for a time."

Kulgan laughed, glad to see the boy's spirits returning. The magician had been troubled at the depth of Pug's mourning for Tomas and was relieved to see the boy's resilient nature assert itself. Kulgan held the door open. "Shall we?"

Pug inclined his head, imitating a courtly bow,

and said, "Certes, master magician. After you?" and broke into a laugh.

They made their way to the dining room, a large and well-lit hall, though nothing as large as in the castle of Crydee. The Duke and Prince Arutha were already seated, and Kulgan and Pug quickly took their places at the table.

Borric was just finishing his account of the events at Crydee and in the great forest when Pug and Kulgan sat. "So," he said, "I chose to carry this news myself, so important I believe it to be."

The merchant leaned back in his chair as servants brought a wide variety of dishes for the diners. "Lord Borric," said Talbott, "when your man Meecham first approached me, his request on your behalf was somewhat vague, due, I believe, to the manner in which the information was transmitted." He referred to the magic employed by Kulgan to contact Belgan, who had in turn sent the message to Meecham. "I never expected your desire to reach Krondor would prove as vital to my own people as I now see it to be." He paused, then continued, "I am, of course, alarmed by the news you bear. I was willing to act as a broker to find you a ship, but now I will undertake to send you in one of my own vessels." He picked up a small bell that sat near his hand and rang. In a moment a servant was standing at his shoulder. "Send word to Captain Abram to ready the *Storm Queen.* He leaves on tomorrow's afternoon tide for Krondor. I will send more detailed instructions later."

The servant bowed and left. The Duke said, "I thank you, Master Kilrane. I had hoped that you would understand, but I did not expect to find a ship so quickly."

The merchant looked directly at Borric. "Duke Borric, let me be frank. There is little love lost between the Free Cities and the Kingdom. And, to be franker still, less love for the name conDoin. It was your grandfather who laid waste to Walinor and siege to Natal. He was stopped only ten miles north of this very city, and that memory still rankles many of us. We are Keshian by ancestry, but freemen by birth, and have little affection for conquerors." Kilrane continued as the Duke sat stiffly in his chair, "Still, we are forced to admit that your father later, and yourself now, have been good neighbors, treating fairly with the Free Cities, even generously at times. I believe you to be a man of honor and realize these Tsurani people are likely all you say they are. You are not the sort of man given to exaggeration, I think."

The Duke relaxed a little at this. Talbott took a sip of wine, then resumed his conversation. "We would be foolish not to recognize that our best interests lie with those of the Kingdom, for alone we are helpless. When you have departed, I will summon a meeting of the Council of Guilds and Merchants and will argue for support of the Kingdom in this." He smiled, and all at the table could see that here was a man as confident in his influence and authority as the Duke was in his. "I think I will have little difficulty in making the council see the wisdom of this. A brief mention of that Tsurani war galley and a little conjecture on how our ships would fare against a fleet of such ships should convince them."

Borric laughed and slapped his hand upon the table. "Master merchant, I can see your wealth was not acquired by a lucky cast of fate's knucklebones. Your shrewd mind is a match for my own Father Tully's. As is your wisdom. I give you my thanks."

The Duke and the merchant continued to talk late into the night, but Pug was still tired and returned to his bed. When Kulgan came in hours later, he found the boy lying restfully, a peaceful expression on his face.

THE *STORM QUEEN* ran before the wind, her topgallants and sky sails slamming her through the raging sea. The swirling, stinging icy rain made the night so black that the tops of her tall masts were lost in hazy darkness to those who stood on her decks.

On the quarterdeck, figures huddled under great fur-lined oilcloth cloaks, trying to stay warm and dry in the bitterly cold wetness. Twice during the last two weeks they had run through high seas, but this was by far the worst weather they had encountered. A cry went up from the rigging, and word was carried to the captain that two men had fallen from the yards. Duke Borric shouted to Captain Abram, "Can nothing be done?"

"Nay, my lord. They are dead men, and to search would be folly, even if possible, which it is not," the captain shouted back, his voice carrying over the storm's roar.

A full watch was above in the treacherous rigging, knocking away the ice that was forming on the spars, threatening to crack them with additional weight, disabling the ship. Captain Abram held the rail with one hand, watching for signs of trouble, his whole body in tune with his ship. Next to him stood the Duke and Kulgan, less sure of their footing on the pitching deck. A loud groaning, cracking sound came from below, and the captain swore.

Moments later a sailor appeared before them. "Captain, we've cracked a timber and she's taking water."

The captain waved to one of his mates who stood on the main deck. "Take a crew below and shore up the damage, then report."

The mate quickly picked four men to accompany him below. Kulgan seemed to go into a trance for a minute before he said, "Captain, this storm will blow another three days."

The captain cursed the luck the gods had sent him and said to the Duke, "I can't run her before the storm for three days taking water. I must find a place to heave to and repair the hull."

The Duke nodded, shouting over the storm, "Are you turning for Queg?"

The captain shook his head, dislodging snow and water dripping from his black beard. "I cannot turn her into the wind for Queg. We will have to lie off Sorcerer's Isle."

Kulgan shook his head, though the gesture was not noticed by the others. The magician asked, "Is there nowhere else we can put in?"

The captain looked at the magician and the Duke. "Not as close. We would risk the loss of a mast. Then, if we didn't founder and sink, we'd lose six days rather than three. The seas run higher, and I fear I may lose more men." He shouted orders aloft and to the steersman, and they took a more southerly course, heading for Sorcerer's Isle.

Kulgan went below with the Duke. The rocking, surging motion of the ship made the ladder and narrow passageway difficult to negotiate, and the stout magician was tossed from one side to the other as they made their way to their cabins. The Duke went into his cabin, shared with his son, and Kulgan entered his own. Gardan, Meecham, and Pug were trying to rest on their respective bunks during the buffeting. The boy was having a difficult time, for he had been sick the first two days. He had gained sea legs of a sort, but still couldn't bring himself to eat the salty pork and hardtack they were forced to consume. Because of the rough seas, the ship's cook had been unable to perform his usual duties.

The ship's timbers groaned in protest at the pounding the waves were giving, and from ahead they could hear the sound of hammers as the work crew struggled to repair the breached hull.

Pug rolled over and looked at Kulgan. "What about the storm?"

Meecham came up on one elbow and looked at his master. Gardan did likewise. Kulgan said, "It will blow three days longer. We will put in to the lee of an island and hold there until it slackens."

"What island?" asked Pug.

"Sorcerer's Isle."

Meecham shot up out of his bunk, hitting his head on the low ceiling. Cursing and rubbing his head, while Gardan stifled a laugh, he exclaimed, "The island of Macros the Black?"

Kulgan nodded, while using one hand to steady himself as the ship nosed over a high crest and forward into a deep trough. "The same. I have little liking for the idea, but the captain fears for the ship." As if to punctuate the point, the hull creaked and groaned alarmingly for a moment.

"Who is Macros?" asked Pug.

Kulgan looked thoughtful for a moment, as much from listening to the work crew in the hold as from the boy's question, then said, "Macros is a great sorcerer, Pug. Perhaps the greatest the world has ever known."

"Aye," added Meecham, "and the spawn of some demon from the deepest circle of hell. His arts are the blackest, and even the bloody Priests of Lims-Kragma fear to set foot on his island."

Gardan laughed. "I have yet to see a wizard who

could cow the death goddess's priests. He must be a powerful mage."

"Those are only stories, Pug," Kulgan said. "What we do know about him is that when the persecution of magicians reached its height in the Kingdom, Macros fled to this island. No one has since traveled to or from it."

Pug sat up on his bunk, interested in what he was hearing, oblivious to the terrible noise of the storm. He watched as Kulgan's face was bathed in moving half lights and shadows by the crazily swinging lantern that danced with every lurch of the ship.

"Macros is very old," Kulgan continued. "By what arts he keeps alive, only he knows, but he has lived there over three hundred years."

Gardan scoffed, "Or several men by the same name have lived there."

Kulgan nodded. "Perhaps. In any event, there is nothing truly known about him, except terrible tales told by sailors. I suspect that even if Macros does practice the darker side of magic, his reputation is greatly inflated, perhaps as a means of securing privacy."

A loud cracking noise, as if another timber in the hull had split, quieted them. The cabin rolled with the storm, and Meecham spoke all their minds: "And I'm hoping we'll all be able to stand upon Sorcerer's Isle."

THE SHIP LIMPED into the southern bay of the island. They would have to wait until the storm subsided before they could put divers over the side to inspect the damage to the hull.

Kulgan, Pug, Gardan, and Meecham came out on deck. The weather was slightly kinder with the cliffs cutting the fury of the storm. Pug walked to where the captain and Kulgan were standing. He followed their gaze up to the top of the cliffs.

High above the bay sat a castle, its tall towers outlined against the sky by the grey light of day. It was a strange place, with spires and turrets pointing upward like some clawed hand. The castle was dark save for one window in a high tower that shone with blue, pulsating light, as if lightning had been captured and put to work by the inhabitant.

Pug heard Meecham say, "There, upon the bluff. Macros."

THREE DAYS LATER the divers broke the surface and yelled to the captain their appraisal of the damage. Pug was on the main deck with Meecham, Gardan, and Kulgan. Prince Arutha and his father stood near the captain, awaiting the verdict on the ship's condition. Above, the seabirds wheeled, looking for the scraps and garbage heralded by a ship in these waters. The storms of winter did little to supplement the meager feeding of the birds, and a ship was a welcome source of fare.

Arutha came down to the main deck where the others waited. "It will take all of this day and half tomorrow to repair the damage, but the captain thinks it will hold fair until we reach Krondor. We should have little trouble from here."

Meecham and Gardan threw each other meaningful glances. Not wanting to let the opportunity pass, Kulgan said, "Will we be able to put ashore, Your Highness?"

Arutha rubbed his clean-shaven chin with a gloved hand. "Aye, though not one sailor will put out a boat to carry us."

"Us?" asked the magician.

Arutha smiled his crooked smile. "I have had my fill of cabins, Kulgan. I feel the need to stretch my legs on firm ground. Besides, without supervision, you'd spend the day wandering about places where you've no business." Pug looked up toward the castle, his glance noted by the magician.

"We'll keep clear of that castle and the road up from the beach, to be sure. The tales of this island only speak of ill coming to those who seek to enter the sorcerer's halls."

Arutha signaled a seaman. A boat was readied, and the four men and the boy got aboard. The boat was hauled over the side and lowered by a crew sweating despite the cold wind that still blew after the storm. By the glances they kept throwing toward the crest of the bluffs, Pug knew they were not sweating because of work or weather.

As if reading his thoughts, Arutha said, "There may be a more superstitious breed on Midkemia than sailors, but who they are I could not tell you."

When the boat was in the water, Meecham and Gardan cast off the lines that hung suspended from the davits. The two men awkwardly took oars and began to row toward the beach. It was a broken, stuttering rhythm at first, but with disapproving looks from the Prince, along with several comments about how men could spend their lives in a sea town and not know how to row, they finally got the boat moving in good order.

They put in at a sandy stretch of beach, a little cove that broke the bluffs of the bay. Upward toward the castle ran a path, which joined another leading away across the island.

Pug leaped out of the boat and helped pull it ashore. When it was fast aground, the others got out and stretched their legs.

Pug felt as if they were being watched, but each time he looked around, there was nothing in sight but the rocks, and the few seabirds that lived the winter in clefts of the cliff face.

Kulgan and the Prince studied the two paths up

from the beach. The magician looked at the other path, away from the sorcerer's castle, and said, "There should be little harm in exploring the other trail. Shall we?"

Days of boredom and confinement outweighed whatever anxiety they felt. With a brusque nod, Arutha led the way up the trail.

Pug followed last, behind Meecham. The big-shouldered franklin was armed with a broadsword, upon which his hand rested. Pug kept his sling handy, for he still didn't feel comfortable with a sword, though Gardan was giving him lessons when possible. The boy fingered the sling absently, his eyes taking in the scene before them.

Along the trail they startled several colonies of turnstones and plovers, which took flight when the party came near. The birds squawked their protests and hovered near their roosts until the hikers passed, then returned to the scant comfort of the hillside.

They crested the first of a series of hills, and the path away from the castle could be seen to dip behind another crest. Kulgan said, "It must lead somewhere. Shall we continue?" Arutha nodded, and the others said nothing. They continued their journey until they came to a small valley, little more than a dell, between two ranges of low hills. On the floor of the valley sat some buildings.

Arutha said softly, "What do you think, Kulgan? Are they inhabited?"

Kulgan studied them for a moment, then turned to Meecham, who stepped forward. The franklin inspected the vista below, his gaze traveling from the floor of the vale to the hills around. "I think not. There is no sign of smoke from cook fires, nor sound of people working."

Arutha resumed his march down toward the floor of the valley, and the others followed. Meecham turned to watch Pug for a moment, then noticed the boy was unarmed except for his sling. The franklin pulled a long hunting knife from his belt and handed it to the boy without comment. Pug bobbed his head once in acknowledgment and took the knife in silence.

They reached a plateau above the buildings, and Pug could see an alien-looking house, the central building circled by a large court and several outbuildings. The entire property was surrounded by a low wall, no more than four feet tall.

They worked their way down the hillside to a gate in the wall. There were several barren fruit trees in the courtyard, and a garden area overgrown with weeds. Near the front of the central building a fountain stood, topped with a statue of three dolphins. They approached the fountain and saw that the interior of the low pool surrounding the statue was covered in blue tiles, faded and discolored with age. Kulgan examined the construction of the fountain. "This is fashioned in a clever manner. I believe that water should issue from the mouths of the dolphins."

Arutha agreed. "I have seen the King's fountains in Rillanon, and they are similar, though lacking the grace of this."

There was little snow on the ground, for it seemed the sheltered valley and the entire island received little even in the most severe winters. But it was still cold. Pug wandered a little way off and studied the house. It had a single story, with windows every ten feet along the wall. There was but one opening for a double door in the wall he stood facing, though the doors were long off their hinges.

"Whoever lived here expected no trouble."

Pug turned to see Gardan standing behind him, staring at the house as well. "There is no tower for lookout," continued the Sergeant. "And the low wall seems more likely to keep livestock out of the gardens than for defense."

Meecham joined them, hearing Gardan's last remark. "Aye, there is little concern for defense here. This is the lowest spot on the island, save for that small stream you could see behind the house when we came down the hill." He turned to stare up at the castle, the highest spires of which could still be seen from the valley. "There is where you build for trouble. This place," he said, indicating the low buildings with a sweep of his hand, "was fashioned by those who knew little of strife."

Pug nodded as he moved away. Gardan and Meecham headed in a different direction, toward an abandoned stable.

Pug moved around to the back of the house and found several smaller buildings. He clutched his knife in his right hand and entered the closest. It was open to the sky, for the roof had collapsed. Red roof tiles, shattered and faded, lay about the floor, in what seemed to be a storeroom, with large wooden shelves along three walls. Pug investigated the other rooms in the building, finding them to be of similar configuration. The entire building was some sort of storage area.

He moved to the next building and found a large kitchen. A stone stove stood against one wall, big enough for several kettles to cook upon it simultaneously, while a spit hung over a back opening above the fire was large enough for a beef side or whole lamb. A mammoth butcher's block stood in the center of the room, scarred from countless blows of cleaver and knife.

Pug examined a strange-looking bronze pot in the corner, overlaid with dust and cobwebs. He turned it over and found a wooden spoon. As he looked up, he thought he saw a glimpse of someone outside the door of the cookhouse.

"Meecham? Gardan?" he asked, as he slowly approached the door. When he stepped outside, there was no one in sight, but he did catch another glimpse of movement at the rear door of the main house.

He hurried toward that door, assuming his companions had already entered the building. As he entered the main house, he caught a hint of movement down a side corridor. He stopped for a moment to survey this strange house.

The door before him stood open, a sliding door fallen from railings that had once held it in place. Through the door he could see a large central courtyard, open to the sky above. The house was actually a hollow square, with pillars holding up the interior of the partial roof. Another fountain and a small garden occupied the very center of the courtyard. Like the one outside, the fountain was in disrepair, and this garden was also choked with weeds.

Pug turned toward the hall down which he had seen movement. He passed through a low side door into a shadowy corridor. In places the roof had lost several tiles, so that occasionally light shone down from above, making it easy for the boy to find his way. He passed two empty rooms; he suspected they might be sleeping quarters.

He turned a corner to find himself before the door of an odd-looking room and entered. The walls were tile mosaics, of sea creatures sporting in the foam with scantily dressed men and women. The style of art was new to Pug. The few tapestries and fewer paintings on display in the Duke's halls were all very lifelike, with muted colors and detailed execution in the finish.

These mosaics were suggestive of people and animals without capturing details.

In the floor was a large depression, like a pool, with steps leading down before him. Out of the wall opposite obtruded a brass fish head, hanging over the pool. The nature of the room was beyond Pug.

As if someone had read his thoughts, a voice from behind said, "It is a tepidarium."

Pug turned and saw a man standing behind him. He was of average height, with a high forehead and deep-set black eyes. There were streaks of grey at the temples of his dark hair, but his beard was black as night. He wore a brown robe of simple material, a whipcord belt around the waist. In his left hand he held a sturdy oak staff. Pug came on guard, holding the long hunting knife before him.

"Nay, lad. Put up your scramasax, I mean you no harm." He smiled in a way that made Pug relax.

Pug lowered his knife and said, "What did you call this room?"

"A tepidarium," he said, entering the room. "Here warm water was piped into the pool, and bathers would remove their clothing and place them on those shelves." He pointed to some shelves against the rear wall.

"Servants would clean and dry the clothing of dinner guests while they bathed here."

Pug thought the idea of dinner guests bathing at someone's home in a group a novel one, but he said nothing. The man continued, "Through that door"— he pointed to a door next to the pool—"was another pool with very hot water, in a room called a calidarium. Beyond was another pool with cold water in a room called a frigidarium. There was a fourth room called the unctorium, where servants would rub down the bathers with scented oils. And they scraped their skins with wooden sticks. They didn't use soap then."

Pug was confused by all the different bathing rooms. "That sounds like a lot of time spent getting clean. This is all very odd."

The man leaned on his staff. "So it must seem to you, Pug. Still, I expect those that built this house would consider your keep halls strange as well."

Pug started. "How did you know my name?"

The man smiled again. "I heard the tall soldier call you by name as you approached the building. I was watching you, keeping out of sight until I was sure you were not pirates come to seek ancient loot. Few pirates come so young, so I thought it would be safe to talk to you."

Pug studied the man. There was something about him that suggested hidden meanings in his words. "Why would you speak with me?"

The man sat on the edge of the empty pool. The hem of his robe was pulled back, revealing cross-gartered sandals of sturdy construction. "I am alone mostly, and the chance to speak with strangers is a rare thing. So I thought to see if you would visit with me awhile, for a few moments at least, until you return to your ship."

Pug sat down also, but kept a comfortable distance between himself and the stranger. "Do you live here?"

The man looked around the room. "No, though I once did, long ago." There was a contemplative note in his voice, as if the admission were calling up long-buried memories.

"Who are you?"

The man smiled again, and Pug felt his nervousness vanish. There was something reassuring about his manner, and Pug could see that he intended no harm.

"Mostly I am called the traveler, for many lands have I seen. Here I am sometimes known as the hermit, for so I live. You may call me what you like. It is all the same."

Pug looked at him closely. "Have you no proper name?"

"Many, so many that I have forgotten a few. At the time of my birth I was given a name, as you were, but among those of my tribe it is a name known only to the father and the mage-priest."

Pug considered this. "It is all very strange, much like this house. Who are your people?"

The man called the traveler laughed, a good-natured chuckle. "You have a curious mind, Pug, full of questions. That is good." He paused for a moment, then said, "Where are you and your companions from? The ship in the bay flies the Natalese banner of Bordon, but your accent and dress are of the Kingdom."

Pug said, "We are of Crydee," and gave the man a brief description of the journey. The man asked a few simple questions, and without being aware of it, Pug found that soon he had given a full accounting of the events that had brought them to the island, and the plans for the rest of the journey.

When he had finished, the traveler said, "That is a wondrous story indeed. I should think there will be many more wonders before this strange meeting of worlds is finished."

Pug questioned him with a look. "I don't understand."

The traveler shook his head. "I don't expect you to, Pug. Let us say that things are occurring that can be understood only by examination after the fact, with a distance of time separating the participants from the participating."

Pug scratched his knee. "You sound like Kulgan, trying to explain how magic works."

The traveler nodded. "An apt comparison. Though sometimes the only way to understand the workings of magic is to work magic."

Pug brightened. "Are you also a magician?"

The traveler stroked his long black beard. "Some have thought me one, but I doubt that Kulgan and I share the same understanding of such things."

Pug's expression showed he considered this an unsatisfactory explanation even if he didn't say so. The traveler leaned forward. "I can effect a spell or two, if that answers your question, young Pug."

Pug heard his name shouted from the courtyard. "Come," said the traveler. "Your friends call. We had best go and reassure them that you are all right."

They left the bathing room and crossed the open court of the inner garden. A large anteroom separated the garden from the front of the house, and they passed through to the outside. When the others saw Pug in the company of the traveler, they looked around quickly, their weapons drawn. Kulgan and the Prince crossed the court to stand before them. The traveler put up his hands in the universal sign that he was unarmed.

The Prince was the first to speak. "Who is your companion, Pug?"

Pug introduced the traveler. "He means no harm. He hid until he could see that we were not pirates." He handed the knife to Meecham.

If the explanation was unsatisfactory, Arutha gave no sign. "What is your business here?"

The traveler spread his hands, with the staff in the crook of his left arm. "I abide here, Prince of Crydee. I should think that the question better serves me."

The Prince stiffened at being addressed so, but

after a tense moment relaxed. "If that is so, then you are correct, for we are the intruders. We came seeking relief from the solitary confines of the ship. Nothing more."

The traveler nodded. "Then you are welcome at Villa Beata."

Kulgan said, "What is Villa Beata?"

The traveler made a sweeping motion with his right hand. "This home is Villa Beata. In the language of the builders, it means 'blessed home,' and so it was for many years. As you can see, it has known better days."

Everyone was relaxing with the traveler, for they also felt a reassurance in his easy manner and friendly smile. Kulgan said, "What of those who built this strange place?"

"Dead . . . or gone. They thought this the Insula Beata, or Blessed Isle, when they first came here. They fled a terrible war, which changed the history of their world." His dark eyes misted over, as if the pain of remembering was great. "A great king died . . . or is thought to have died, for some say he may return. It was a terrible and sad time. Here they sought to live in peace."

"What happened to them?" asked Pug.

The traveler shrugged. "Pirates, or goblins? Sickness, or madness? Who can tell? I saw this home as you see it now, and those who lived here were gone."

Arutha said, "You speak of strange things, friend traveler. I know little of such, but it seems that this place has been deserted for ages. How is it you knew those who lived here?"

The traveler smiled. "It is not so long ago as you would imagine, Prince of Crydee. And I am older than I look. It comes from eating well and bathing regularly."

Meecham had been studying the stranger the entire time, for of all those who had come ashore, his was the most suspicious nature. "And what of the Black One? Does he not trouble you?"

The traveler looked over his shoulder at the top of the castle. "Macros the Black? The magician and I have little cause to be at odds. He suffers me the run of the island, as long as I don't interfere with his work."

A suspicion crossed Pug's mind, but he said nothing, as the traveler continued. "Such a powerful and terrible sorcerer has little to fear from a simple hermit, I'm sure you'll agree." He leaned forward and added in conspiratorial tones, "Besides, I think much of his reputation is inflated and overboasted, to keep intruders away. I doubt he is capable of the feats attributed to him."

Arutha said, "Then perhaps we should visit this sorcerer."

The hermit looked at the Prince. "I don't think you would find a welcome at the castle. The sorcerer is oftentimes preoccupied with his work and suffers interruption with poor grace. He may not be the mythical author of all the world's ills that some imagine him to be, but he could still cause more trouble than it is worth to visit him. On the whole he is often poor company." There was a faint, wry hint of humor in his words.

Arutha looked around and said, "I think we have seen all of interest we are likely to. Perhaps we should return to the ship."

When none disagreed, the Prince said, "What of you, friend traveler?"

The stranger spread his hands in a general gesture. "I continue my habit of solitude, Your Highness. I have enjoyed this small visit, and the boy's news of the occurrences of the world outside, but I doubt that you would find me tomorrow if you were to seek me."

It was evident he was unlikely to provide any more information, and Arutha found himself growing irritated with the man's obscure answers. "Then we bid you farewell, traveler. May the gods watch over you."

"And you as well, Prince of Crydee."

As they turned to leave, Pug felt something trip his ankle, and he fell hard against Kulgan. Both went down in a tangle of bodies, and the traveler helped the boy up. Meecham and Gardan assisted the stout mage to his feet. Kulgan put weight upon his foot and started to fall. Arutha and Meecham grabbed him. The traveler said, "It appears your ankle is turned, friend magician. Here." He held out his staff. "My staff is stout oak and will bear your weight as you return to the ship."

Kulgan took the offered staff and put his weight on it. He took an experimental step and found that he could negotiate the path with the aid of the staff. "Thank you, but what of yourself?"

The stranger shrugged. "A simple staff, easily replaced, friend magician. Perhaps I shall have the opportunity of reclaiming it someday."

"I will keep it against that day."

The traveler turned away, saying, "Good. Then until that day, again farewell."

They watched as he walked back into the building, and then turned to face each other, expressions of wonder upon their faces. Arutha was the first to speak. "A strange man, this traveler."

Kulgan nodded. "More strange than you know, Prince. At his leaving I feel the lifting of some enchantment, as if he carries a spell about him, one that makes all near him trusting."

Pug turned to Kulgan. "I wanted to ask him so

many questions, but I didn't seem to be able to make myself."

Meecham said, "Aye, I felt that also."

Gardan said, "There is a thought in my mind. I think we have been speaking to the sorcerer himself."

Pug said, "That is my thought."

Kulgan leaned on the staff and said, "Perhaps. If it is so, then he has his own reasons for masking his identity." They talked about this as they walked slowly up the path from the villa.

As they reached the cove where the boat was beached, Pug felt something brush against his chest. He reached inside his tunic and found a small folded piece of parchment. He withdrew it, startled by his find. He had not picked it up, as well as he could remember. The traveler must have slipped it inside his shirt when he had helped Pug to his feet.

Kulgan looked back as he started for the boat and, seeing Pug's expression, said, "What have you there?"

Pug handed the parchment over, while the others gathered around the magician. Kulgan unfolded the parchment. He read it, and a surprised expression crossed his face. He read it again, aloud. "I welcome those who come with no malice in their hearts. You will know in days to come that our meeting was not by chance. Until we meet again, keep the hermit's staff as a sign of friendship and goodwill. Seek me not until the appointed time, for that too is foreordained. Macros."

Kulgan handed the message back to Pug, who read it. "Then the hermit was Macros!"

Meecham rubbed his beard. "This is something beyond my understanding."

Kulgan looked up to the castle, where the lights still flashed in the single window. "As it is beyond mine, old friend. But whatever it means, I think the sorcerer wishes us well, and I find that a good thing."

They returned to the ship and retired to their cabins. After a night of rest, they found the ship ready to leave on the midday tide. As they raised sail, they were greeted with unseasonably light breezes, blowing them directly for Krondor.

12

Councils

Pug was restless.

He sat looking out a window of the Prince's palace in Krondor. Outside, the snow was falling, as it had been for the last three days. The Duke and Arutha had been meeting with the Prince of Krondor daily. On the first day Pug had told his story about finding the Tsurani ship, then had been dismissed. He remembered that awkward interview.

He had been surprised to find the Prince to be young, in his thirties, if not a vigorous and well man. Pug had been startled during their interview when the Prince's remarks were interrupted by a violent attack of coughing. His pale face, drenched with sweat, showed him to be in worse health than his manner indicated.

He had waved off Pug's suggestion that he should leave and come back when more convenient for him. Erland of Krondor was a reflective person, who listened patiently to Pug's narration, lessening the boy's discomfort at being before the heir apparent to the throne of the Kingdom. His eyes regarded Pug with reassurance and understanding, as if it were a common thing to have awkward boys standing before him. After listening to Pug's narration, he had spent a short time talking with Pug about small things, such as his studies and his fortuitous rise to the nobility, as if these were important matters to his realm.

Pug decided he liked Prince Erland. The second most powerful man in the Kingdom, and the single most powerful man in the West, was warm and friendly and cared for the comfort of his least-important guest.

Pug looked around the room, still not used to the splendor of the palace. Even this small room was richly appointed, with a canopied bed instead of a sleeping pallet. It was the first time Pug had ever slept in one, and he found it difficult to get comfortable on the deep, soft, feather-stuffed mattress. In the corner of the room stood a closet with more clothing in it than he thought he could wear in his lifetime, all of costly weave and fine cut, and all seemingly in his size. Kulgan had said it was a gift from the Prince.

The quiet of his room reminded Pug how little he had seen of Kulgan and the others. Gardan and his soldiers had left that morning with a bundle of dispatches for Prince Lyam from his father, and Meecham was housed with the palace guard. Kulgan was involved in the meetings as often as not, so Pug had a lot of time to himself. He wished he had his books with him, for then at least the time could be put to some good use. Since his arrival in Krondor there had been little for him to do.

More than once Pug had thought of how much Tomas would have loved the newness of this place— seemingly fashioned from glass and magic more than stone—and the people in it. He thought about his lost friend, hoping Dolgan had somehow found him, but not believing he had. The pain of loss was now a dull ache, but still tender. Even after the last month, he would find himself turning, expecting to see Tomas close by.

Not wishing to sit idle any longer, Pug opened the door and looked down the hallway that ran the length of the east wing of the Prince's palace. He hurried down the hall, looking for any familiar face to break the monotony.

A guard passed him by, going the other way, and saluted. Pug still couldn't get used to the idea of being saluted every time a guard passed, but as a member of the Duke's party he was given full honors due his Squire's rank by the household staff.

Reaching a smaller hallway, he decided to explore. One way was the same as another, he thought. The Prince had personally told him he had the run of the palace, but Pug had been shy about overstepping himself. Now boredom drove him to adventuring, or at least as much adventuring as possible under the circumstances.

Pug found a small alcove with a window, providing a different view of the palace grounds. Pug sat upon the window seat. Beyond the palace walls he could see the port of Krondor lying below like a white-shrouded toy village. Smoke was coming from many of the buildings, the only sign of life in the city. The ships in the harbor looked like miniatures, lying at anchor, waiting for more propitious conditions under which to sail.

A small voice behind him brought Pug out of his reverie. "Are you Prince Arutha?"

A girl was standing behind him, about six or seven years old, with big green eyes and dark reddish brown hair done up in silver netting. Her dress was simple but fine looking, of red cloth with white lace at the sleeves.

Her face was pretty, but was set in an expression of deep concentration that gave it a comic gravity.

Pug hesitated for a moment, then said, "No, I'm Pug. I came with the Prince."

The girl made no attempt to hide her disappointment. With a shrug she came over and sat next to Pug. She looked up at him with the same grave expression and said, "I was so hoping that you might be the Prince, for I wanted to catch a glimpse of him before you leave for Salador."

"Salador," Pug said flatly. He had hoped the journey would end with the visit to the Prince. Lately he had been thinking of Carline.

"Yes. Father says you are all to leave at once for Salador, then take a ship for Rillanon to see the King."

"Who's your father?"

"The Prince, silly. Don't you know anything?"

"I guess not." Pug looked at the girl, seeing another Carline in the making. "You must be Princess Anita."

"Of course. And I'm a real princess too. Not the daughter of a duke, but the daughter of a prince. My father would have been King if he had wanted, but he didn't want to. If he had, I would be Queen someday. But I won't be. What do you do?"

The question, coming so suddenly without preamble, caught Pug off guard. The child's prattling wasn't very irksome, and he wasn't following closely, being more intent on the scene through the window.

He hesitated, then said, "I'm apprenticed to the Duke's magician."

The Princess's eyes grew round, and she said, "A real magician?"

"Real enough."

Her little face lit up with delight. "Can he turn

people into toads? Mummy said magicians turn people into toads if they are bad."

"I don't know. I'll ask him when I see him—if I see him again," he added under his breath.

"Oh, would you? I would so very much like to know." She seemed utterly fascinated by the prospect of finding out if the tale was true. "And could you please tell me where I might see Prince Arutha?"

"I don't know. I haven't seen him myself in two days. What do you want to see him for?"

"Mummy says I may marry him someday. I want to see if he is a nice man."

The prospect of this tiny child's being married to the Duke's younger son confounded Pug for a moment. It was not an uncommon practice for nobles to pledge their children in marriage years before their coming of age. In ten years she would be a woman, and the Prince would still be a young man, the Earl of some minor keep in the Kingdom. Still, Pug found the prospect fascinating.

"Do you think you would like living with an earl?" Pug asked, realizing at once it was a stupid question. The Princess confirmed the opinion with a glance that would have done Father Tully credit.

She said, "Silly! How could I possibly know that when I don't even know who Mummy and Father will have me marry?"

The child jumped up. "Well, I must go back. I'm not supposed to be here. If they find me out of my rooms, I'll be punished. I hope you have a nice journey to Salador and Rillanon."

"Thank you."

With a sudden expression of worry, she said, "You won't tell anyone that I was here, will you?"

Pug gave her a conspiratorial smile. "No. Your secret's safe." With a look of relief, she smiled and peeked both ways down the hallway. As she started to leave, Pug said, "He's a nice man."

The Princess stopped. "Who?"

"The Prince. He's a nice man. Given to brooding and moods, but on the whole a nice person."

The Princess frowned for a moment as she digested the information. Then, with a bright smile, she said, "That's good. I'd not want to marry a man who's not nice." With a giggle she turned the corner and was gone.

Pug sat awhile longer, watching the snow fall, musing over the fact of children being concerned about matters of state, and over a child with big, serious green eyes.

THAT NIGHT THE entire party was feted by the Prince. The whole population of nobles at court and most of the rich commoners of Krondor were attending the gala. Over four hundred people sat to dine, and Pug found himself at a table with strangers who, out of respect for the quality of his clothing and the simple fact of his being there in the first place, politely ignored him. The Duke and Prince Arutha were seated at the head table with Prince Erland and his wife, Princess Alicia, along with Duke Dulanic, Chancellor of the Principality and Knight-Marshal of Krondor. Owing to Erland's ill health, the business of running Krondor's military fell to Dulanic and the man he was deep in conversation with, Lord Barry, Erland's Lord-Admiral of the Krondorian fleet. Other royal ministers were seated nearby, while the rest of the guests were at smaller tables. Pug was seated at the one farthest removed from the royal table.

Servants were bustling in and out of the hall, carrying large platters of food and decanters of wine. Jongleurs strolled the hall, singing the newest ballads and ditties. Jugglers and acrobats performed between the tables, mostly ignored by the dinner guests, but giving their best, for the Master of Ceremony would not call them back again should he judge their efforts lacking.

The walls were covered with giant banners and rich tapestries. The banners were of every major household in the Kingdom, from the gold and brown of Crydee in the far west, to the white and green of far Ran, in the east. Behind the royal table hung the banner of the Kingdom, a golden lion rampant holding a sword, with a crown above his head, upon a field of purple, the ancient crest of the conDoin kings. Next to it hung Krondor's banner, an eagle flying above a mountain peak, silver upon the royal purple. Only the Prince, and the King in Rillanon, could wear the royal color. Borric and Arutha wore red mantles over their tunics, signifying they were princes of the realm, related to the royal family. It was the first time Pug had ever seen the two wearing the formal marks of their station.

Everywhere were sights and sounds of gaiety, but even from across the room Pug could tell that the talk at the Prince's table was subdued. Borric and Erland spent most of the dinner with their heads close together, speaking privately.

Pug was startled by a touch on his shoulder and turned to see a doll-like face peering through the large curtains not two feet behind him. Princess Anita put her finger to her lips and beckoned for him to step through. Pug saw the others at the table were looking at the great and near-great in the room and would scarcely notice the departure of a nameless boy. He rose and moved through the curtain, finding himself in a small servants' alcove. Before him was another curtain, leading to the kitchen, Pug supposed, through which peeked the tiny fugitive from bed. Pug moved to where Anita waited, discovering it was, indeed, a long connecting corridor between the kitchen and the great hall. A lengthy table covered with dishware and goblets ran along the wall.

Pug said, "What are you doing here?"

"Shush!" she said in a loud whisper. "I'm not supposed to be here."

Pug smiled at the child. "I don't think you have to worry about being heard, there's too much noise for that."

"I came to see the Prince. Which one is he?"

Pug motioned for her to step into the small alcove, then drew aside the curtain a little. Pointing at the head table, he said, "He's two removed from your father, in the black-and-silver tunic and red mantle."

The child stretched up on tiptoe and said, "I can't see."

Pug held the girl up for a moment. She smiled at him. "I am in your debt."

"Not at all," Pug intoned with mock gravity. They both giggled.

The Princess started as a voice spoke close to the curtain. "I must fly!" She darted through the alcove, passed through the second curtain, and disappeared from sight heading toward the kitchen and her get-away.

The curtain into the banquet hall parted, and a startled servant stared at Pug. Uncertain what to say, the servingman nodded. The boy by rights shouldn't be there, but by his dress he was certainly someone.

Pug looked about and, without much conviction, finally said, "I was looking for the way to my room. I must be going the wrong way."

"The guest wing is through the first door on the left in the dining hall, young sir. Ah . . . this way lies the kitchen. Would you care to have me show you the way?" The servant obviously didn't care to do so, and

Pug was equally lacking any desire for a guide. "No, thank you, I can find it," he said.

Pug rejoined his table, unnoticed by the other guests. The balance of the meal passed without incident, except for an occasional strange glance by a servingman.

PUG PASSED THE time after dinner talking with the son of a merchant. The two young men found each other in the crowded room where the Prince's afterdinner reception was being held. They spent a fitful hour being polite to one another, before the boy's father came and took him in tow. Pug stood around being ignored by the Prince's other dinner guests for a while, then decided he could slip back to his own quarters without affronting anyone—he wouldn't be missed. Besides he hadn't seen the Prince, Lord Borric, or Kulgan since they left the dinner table. Most of the reception seemed under the supervision of a score of household officials and Princess Alicia, a charming woman who had spoken politely with Pug for a moment as he passed through the reception line.

Pug found Kulgan waiting for him in his room when he returned. Kulgan said, without preamble, "We leave at first light, Pug. Prince Erland is sending us on to Rillanon to see the King."

Pug said, "Why is the Prince sending *us?*" His tone was cross, for he was deeply homesick.

Before Kulgan could answer, the door flew open and Prince Arutha came storming in. Pug was surprised by Arutha's expression of unconfined anger.

"Kulgan! There you are," Arutha said, slamming the door. "Do you know what our royal cousin is doing about the Tsurani invasion?"

Before Kulgan could speak, the Prince supplied the answer. "Nothing! He won't lift a finger to send aid to Crydee until Father has seen the King. That will take another two months at least."

Kulgan raised his hand. Instead of an adviser to the Duke, Arutha saw one of his boyhood instructors. Kulgan, like Tully, could still command both sons of the Duke when the need arose. "Quietly, Arutha."

Arutha shook his head as he pulled over a chair. "I am sorry, Kulgan. I should have mastered my temper." He noticed Pug's confusion. "I apologize to you also, Pug. There is much involved here that you don't know of. Perhaps . . ." He looked questioningly at Kulgan.

Kulgan took out his pipe. "You might as well tell him, he's going along for the journey. He'll find out soon enough."

Arutha drummed his fingers on the arm of the chair for a moment, then sitting forward, said, "My father and Erland have been conferring for days on the best way to meet these outworlders should they come. The Prince even agrees it is likely they will come." He paused. "But he will do nothing to call the Armies of the West together until he has been given permission by the King."

"I don't understand," said Pug. "Aren't the Armies of the West the Prince's to command as he sees fit?"

"No longer," said Arutha with a near-grimace. "The King sent word, less than a year ago, that the armies may not be mustered without his permission." Arutha sat back in his chair as Kulgan blew a cloud of smoke. "It is in violation of tradition. Never have the Armies of the West had another commander than the Prince of Krondor, as the Armies of the East are the King's."

Pug was still unclear about the significance of all this. Kulgan said, "The Prince is the King's Lord-Marshal in the West, the only man besides the King who

•

may command Duke Borric and the other Knight-Generals. Should he call, every Duke from Malac's Cross to Crydee would respond, with their garrisons and levies. King Rodric, for his own reasons, has decided that none may gather the armies without his authority."

Arutha said, "Father would come to the Prince's call, regardless, as would the other Dukes."

Kulgan nodded. "That may be what the King fears, for the Armies of the West have long been more the Prince's armies than the King's. If your father called, most would gather, for they revere him nearly as much as they revere Erland. And if the King should say not . . ." He let the sentence slip away.

Arutha nodded. "Strife within the Kingdom."

Kulgan looked at his pipe. "Even to civil war, perhaps."

Pug was troubled by the discussion. He was a keep boy, in spite of his newly acquired title. "Even if it is in defense of the Kingdom?"

Kulgan shook his head slowly. "Even then. For some men, kings also, there is as much importance in the manner in which things are done as the doing." Kulgan paused. "Duke Borric will not speak of it, but there has long been trouble between himself and certain eastern dukes, especially his cousin, Guy du Bas-Tyra. This trouble between the Prince and the King will only add to the strain between West and East."

Pug sat back. He knew that this was somehow more important than what he was understanding, but there were blank places in his picturings of the way things were. How could the King resent the Prince's summoning the armies in defense of the Kingdom? It didn't make sense to him, in spite of Kulgan's explanation. And what sort of trouble in the East was Duke Borric unwilling to speak of?

The magician stood. "We have an early day tomorrow, so we had best get some sleep. It will be a long ride to Salador, then another long passage by ship to Rillanon. By the time we reach the King, the first thaw will have come to Crydee."

PRINCE ERLAND BADE the party a good journey as they sat upon their horses in the courtyard of the palace. He looked pale and deeply troubled as he wished them well.

The little Princess stood at an upstairs window and waved at Pug with a tiny handkerchief. Pug was reminded of another Princess and wondered if Anita would grow to be like Carline or be more even-tempered.

They rode out of the courtyard, where an escort of Royal Krondorian Lancers stood ready to accompany them to Salador. It would be a three weeks' ride over the mountains and past the marshes of Darkmoor, past Malac's Cross—the dividing point between the western and eastern realms—and on to Salador. There they would take ship, and after another two weeks they would reach Rillanon.

The lancers were shrouded in heavy cloaks of grey, but the purple-and-silver tabards of Krondor's Prince could be seen underneath, and their shields bore the device of the royal Krondorian household. The Duke was being honored by an escort of the Prince's own household guard, rather than a detachment from the city garrison.

As they left the city, the snow began to fall once more, and Pug wondered if he would ever see spring in Crydee again. He sat quietly on his horse as it plodded along the road east, trying to sort out the impressions of the last few weeks, then gave up, resigning himself to whatever was to happen.

• • •

THE RIDE TO Salador took four weeks instead of three, for there had been a storm of unusual intensity in the mountains west of Darkmoor. They had been forced to take lodging at an inn outside the village that took its name from the marshes. It had been a small inn, and they had all been forced to crowd together regardless of rank for several days. The food had been simple and the ale indifferent, and by the time the storm passed, they were all glad to leave Darkmoor behind.

Another day had been lost when they chanced upon a village being troubled by bandits. The sight of approaching cavalry had driven the brigands away, but the Duke had ordered a sweep of the area to insure that they didn't return as soon as the soldiers rode off. The villagers had opened their doors to the Duke's party, welcoming them and offering their best food and warmest beds. Poor offerings by the Duke's standards, yet he received their hospitality with graciousness, for he knew it was all they had. Pug enjoyed the simple food and company, the closest yet to home since he had left Crydee.

When they were a half day's ride short of Salador, they encountered a patrol of city guards. The guard captain rode forward. Pulling up his horse, he shouted, "What business brings the Prince's guard to the lands of Salador?" There was little love lost between the two cities, and the Krondorians rode without a heraldic banner. His tone left no doubt that he regarded their presence as an infringement upon his territory.

Duke Borric threw back his cloak, revealing his tabard. "Carry word to your master that Borric, Duke of Crydee, approaches the city and would avail himself of Lord Kerus's hospitality."

The guard captain was taken aback. He stammered, "My apologies, Your Grace. I had no idea . . . there was no banner. . . ."

Arutha said dryly, "We mislaid it in a forest sometime back."

The captain looked confused. "My lord?"

Borric said, "Never mind, Captain. Just send word to your master."

The captain saluted. "At once, Your Grace." He wheeled his horse and signaled for a rider to come forward. He gave him instructions, and the soldier spurred his horse toward the city and soon galloped out of sight.

The captain returned to the Duke. "If Your Grace will permit, my men are at your disposal."

The Duke looked at the travel-weary Krondorians, all of whom seemed to be enjoying the captain's discomfort. "I think thirty men-at-arms are sufficient, Captain. The Salador city guard is renowned for keeping the environs near the city free of brigands."

The captain, not realizing he was being made sport of, seemed to puff up at this. "Thank you, Your Grace."

The Duke said, "You and your men may continue your patrol."

The captain saluted again and returned to his men. He shouted the order to move out, and the guard column moved past the Duke's party. As they passed, the captain ordered a salute, and lances were dipped toward the Duke. Borric returned the salute with a lazy wave of his hand, then when the guards had passed, said, "Enough of this foolishness, let us to Salador."

Arutha laughed and said, "Father, we have need of men like that in the West."

Borric turned and said, "Oh? How so?"

As the horses moved forward, Arutha said, "To polish shields and boots."

The Duke smiled and the Krondorians laughed. The western soldiers held those of the East in low regard. The East had been pacified long before the West had been opened to Kingdom expansion, and there was little trouble in the Eastern Realm requiring real skill in warcraft. The Prince of Krondor's guards were battle-proved veterans, while those of Salador were considered by the guardsmen from the West to do their best soldiering on the parade ground.

Soon they saw signs that they were nearing the city: cultivated farmland, villages, roadside taverns, and wagons laden with trade goods. By sundown they could see the walls of distant Salador.

As they entered the city, a full company of Duke Kerus's own household guards lined the streets to the palace. As in Krondor, there was no castle, for the need for a small, easily defensible keep had passed as the lands around became civilized.

Riding through the city, Pug realized how much of a frontier town Crydee was. In spite of Lord Borric's political power, he was still Lord of a frontier province.

Along the streets, citizens stood gawking at the western Duke from the wild frontier of the Far Coast. Some cheered, for it seemed like a parade, but most stood quietly, disappointed that the Duke and his party looked like other men, rather than blood-drenched barbarians.

When they reached the courtyard of the palace, household servants ran to take their horses. A household guard showed the soldiers from Krondor to the soldiers' commons, where they would rest before returning to the Prince's city. Another, with a captain's badge of rank on his tunic, led Borric's party up the steps of the building.

Pug looked with wonder, for this palace was even larger than the Prince's in Krondor. They walked through several outer rooms, then reached an inner courtyard. Here fountains and trees decorated a garden, beyond which stood the central palace. Pug realized that the building they had passed through was simply one of the buildings surrounding the Duke's living quarters. He wondered what use Lord Kerus could possibly have for so many buildings and such a large staff.

They crossed the garden courtyard and mounted another series of steps toward a reception committee that stood in the door of the central palace. Once this building might have been a citadel, protecting the surrounding town, but Pug couldn't bring himself to imagine it as it might have been ages ago, for numerous renovations over the years had transformed an ancient keep into a glittering thing of glass and marble.

Duke Kerus's chamberlain, an old dried-up stick of a man with a quick eye, knew every noble worth noting—from the borders of Kesh in the south to Tyr-Sog in the north—by sight. His memory for faces and facts had often saved Duke Kerus from embarrassment. By the time Borric had made his way up the broad stairway from the courtyard, the chamberlain had provided Kerus with a few personal facts and a quick evaluation of the right amount of flattery required.

Duke Kerus took Borric's hand. "Ah, Lord Borric, you do me great honor by this unexpected visit. If you had only sent word of your arrival, I would have prepared a more fitting welcome."

They entered the antechamber of the palace, the Dukes in front. Borric said, "I am sorry to put you to any trouble, Lord Kerus, but I am afraid our mission is dependent on speed, and that the formal courtesies will have to be put aside. I bear messages for the King and must put to sea for Rillanon as soon as is possible."

"Of course, Lord Borric, but you will surely be able to stay for a short while, say a week or two?"

"I regret not. I would put to sea tonight if I could."

"That is indeed sorry news. I so hoped that you could guest with us for a time."

The party reached the Duke's audience hall, where the chamberlain gave instructions to a company of household servants, who jumped to the task of readying rooms for the guests. Entering the vast hall, with its high vaulted ceiling, gigantic chandeliers, and great arched glass windows, Pug felt dwarfed. The room was the largest he had ever seen, greater than the hall of the Prince of Krondor.

A huge table was set with fruits and wine, and the travelers fell to with vigor. Pug sat down with little grace, his whole body one mass of aches. He was turning into a skilled horseman simply from long hours in the saddle, but that fact didn't ease his tired muscles.

Lord Kerus pressed the Duke for the cause of his hurried journey, and between mouthfuls of fruit and drinks of wine, Borric filled him in on the events of the last three months. After he was done, Kerus looked distressed. "This is grave news indeed, Lord Borric. Things are unsettled in the Kingdom. I am sure the Prince has told you of some of the trouble that has occurred since last you came to the East."

"Yes, he did. But reluctantly and in only the most cursory manner. Remember, it has been thirteen years since I journeyed to the capital, at Rodric's coronation when I came to renew my vassalage. He seemed a bright enough young man then, able enough to learn to govern. But from what I've heard in Krondor, there seems to have been a change."

Kerus glanced around the room, then waved away his servants. Looking pointedly at Borric's companions, he raised one eyebrow questioningly.

Lord Borric said, "These have my trust and will not betray a confidence."

Kerus nodded. Loudly he said, "If you would like to stretch your legs before retiring, perhaps you'd care to see my garden?"

Borric frowned and was about to speak when Arutha put his hand upon his father's arm, nodding agreement.

Borric said, "That sounds interesting. Despite the cold I could use a short walk."

The Duke motioned for Kulgan, Meecham, and Gardan to remain, but Lord Kerus indicated Pug should join them. Borric looked surprised, but nodded agreement. They left through a small set of doors to the garden, and once outside, Kerus whispered, "It will look less suspicious if the boy comes with us. I can't even trust my own servants anymore. The King has agents everywhere."

Borric seemed infuriated. "The King has placed agents in your *household?*"

"Yes, Lord Borric, there has been a great change in our King. I know Erland has not told you the entire story, but it is one you must know."

The Duke and his companions watched Duke Kerus, who looked uncomfortable. He cleared his throat as he glanced around the snow-covered garden. Between the light from the palace windows and the large moon above, the gardan was a winterscape of white and blue crystals, undisturbed by footprints.

Kerus pointed to a set of tracks in the snow and said, "I made those this afternoon when I came here to think about what I could safely tell you." He glanced around one more time, seeing if anyone could overhear the conversation, then continued. "When Rodric the Third died, everyone expected Erland would take the crown. After the official mourning, the Priests of Ishap called all the possible heirs forward to present their claims. You were expected to be one of them."

Borric nodded. "I know the custom. I was late getting to the city. I would have renounced the claim in any event, so there was no importance in my absence."

Kerus nodded. "History might have been different had you been here, Borric." He lowered his voice. "I risk my neck by saying this, but many, even those of us here in the East, would have urged you to take the crown."

Borric's expression showed he did not like hearing this, but Kerus pressed on. "By the time you got here, all the back-hallway politics had been done—with most lords content to give the crown to Erland—but it was a tense day and a half while the issue was in doubt. Why the elder Rodric didn't name an heir I don't know. But when the priests had chased away all the distant kin with no real claim, three men stood before them, Erland, young Rodric, and Guy du Bas-Tyra. The priests asked for their declarations, and each gave them in turn. Rodric and Erland both had solid claims, while Guy was there as a matter of form, as you would have been had you arrived in time."

Arutha interjected dryly, "The time of mourning ensures no western Lord will be King."

Borric threw a disapproving glance at his son, but Kerus said, "Not entirely. If there had been any doubt to the rights of succession, the priest would have held off the ceremony until your father arrived, Arutha. It has been done before."

He looked at Borric and lowered his voice. "As I said, it was expected Erland would take the crown. But when the crown was presented to him, he refused, conceding the claim to Rodric. No one at that time knew of Erland's ill health, so most lords judged the decision a generous affirmation of Rodric's claim, as the only son of the King. With Guy du Bas-Tyra's backing the boy, the assembled Congress of Lords ratified his succession. Then the real infighting began, until at last your late wife's uncle was named as King's Regent."

Borric nodded. He remembered the battle over who would be named the then boy King's Regent. His despised cousin Guy had nearly won the position, but Borric's timely arrival and his support of Caldric of Rillanon, along with the support of Duke Brucal of Yabon and Prince Erland, had swung the majority of votes in the congress away from Guy.

"For the next five years there was only an occasional border clash with Kesh. Things were quiet. Eight years ago"—Kerus paused to glance around again—"Rodric embarked upon a program of public improvements, as he calls them, upgrading roads and bridges, building dams, and the like. At first they were of little burden, but the taxes have been increased yearly until now the peasants and freemen, even the minor nobles, are being bled white. The King has expanded his programs until now he is rebuilding the entire capital, to make it the greatest city known in the history of man, he says.

"Two years ago a small delegation of nobles came to the King and asked him to abjure this excessive spending and ease the burden upon the people. The King flew into a rage, accused the nobles of being traitors, and had them summarily executed."

Borric's eyes widened. The snow under his boot crunched dryly as he turned suddenly. "We've heard nothing of this in the West!"

"When Erland heard the news, he went immediately to the King and demanded reparation for the families of the nobles who were executed, and a lessening of the taxes. The King—or so it is rumored—was ready to seize his uncle, but was restrained by the few counselors he still trusted. They advised His Majesty that such an act, unheard of in the history of the Kingdom, would surely cause the western lords to rise up against the King."

Borric's expression darkened. "They were right. Had that boy hanged Erland, the Kingdom would have been irretrievably split."

"Since that time the Prince has not set foot in Rillanon, and the business of the Kingdom is handled by aides, for the two men will not speak to one another."

The Duke looked skyward, and his voice became troubled. "This is much worse than I had heard. Erland told me of the taxes and his refusal to impose them in the West. He said that the King was agreed, for he understood the need of maintaining the garrisons of the North and West."

Kerus slowly shook his head no. "The King agreed only when his aides painted pictures of goblin armies pouring down from the Northlands and plundering the cities of his Kingdom."

"Erland spoke of the strain between himself and his nephew, but even in light of the news I carry, said nothing about His Majesty's actions."

Kerus drew a deep breath and started walking once more. "Borric, I spend so much time with the sycophants of the King's court, I forget that you of the West are given to plain speech." Kerus was silent a moment, then said, "Our King is not the man he once was. Sometimes he seems his old self, laughing and open, filled with grand plans for the Kingdom; other times he is . . . someone else, as if a dark spirit has taken possession of his heart.

"Take care, Borric, for only Erland stands closer to the throne than yourself. Our King is well aware of that fact—even if you never think of it—and sees daggers and poison where none exists."

Silence descended over the group, and Pug saw Borric look openly troubled. Kerus continued. "Rodric fears others covet his crown. That may be, but not those the King suspects. There are only four conDoin males besides the King, all of whom are men of honor." Borric inclined his head at the compliment. "But there are perhaps a dozen more who can claim ties to the throne, through the King's mother and her people. All are eastern lords, and many would not flinch from the opportunity to press their claim to the throne before the Congress of Lords."

Borric looked incensed. "You speak of treason."

"Treason in men's hearts, if not in deeds . . . yet."

"Have things come to such a pass in the East, without us of the West knowing?"

Kerus nodded as they reached the far end of the garden. "Erland is an honorable man, and as such would keep unfounded rumors from his subjects, even yourself. As you have said, it is thirteen years since you last were at Rillanon. All warrants and missives from the King still pass through the Prince's court. How would you know?

"I fear it is only a matter of time before one or other of the King's advisers positions himself over the fallen heads of those of us who hold to our beliefs that the nobility are wardens of the nation's welfare."

Borric said, "Then you risk much with your frank speech."

Duke Kerus shrugged, indicating they should begin their return to the palace. "I have not always been a man to speak my mind, Lord Borric, but these are difficult times. Should anyone else have passed through, there would have been only polite conversation. You are unique, for with the Prince estranged from his nephew, you are the only man in the Kingdom with the strength and rank to possibly influence the King. I do not envy your weighty position, my friend.

"When Rodric the Third was king, I was among the most powerful nobles in the East, but I might as well be a landless freebooter for all the influence I now hold in Rodric the Fourth's court." Kerus paused. "Your black-hearted cousin Guy is now closest to the King, and the Duke of Bas-Tyra and I have little love between us. Our reasons for disliking one another are not as personal as yours. But as his star rises, mine falls even more."

Kerus slapped his hands as the cold was beginning to bite. "But one bit of good news. Guy is wintering at his estate near Pointer's Head, so the King is free of his plotting for the present." Kerus gripped Borric's arm. "Use whatever influence you can muster to stem the King's impulsive nature, Lord Borric, for with this invasion you bring word of, we need to stand united. A lengthy war would drain us of what little reserves we possess, and should the Kingdom be put to the test, I do not know whether it would endure."

Borric said nothing, for even his worst fears since leaving the Prince were surpassed by Kerus's remarks. The Duke of Salador said, "One last thing, Borric. With Erland having refused the crown thirteen years ago, and the rumors of his health failing, many of the Congress of Lords will be looking to you for guidance. Where you lead, many will follow, even some of us in the East."

Borric said coldly, "Are you speaking of civil war?"

Kerus waved a hand, a pained expression crossing his face. His eyes seemed moist, as if near tears. "I am ever loyal to the crown, Borric, but if it comes to the right of things, the Kingdom must prevail. No one man is more important than the Kingdom."

Borric said through clenched jaws, "The King *is* the Kingdom."

Kerus said, "You would not be the man you are and say otherwise. I hope you are able to direct the King's energies toward this trouble in the West, for should the Kingdom be imperiled, others will not hold to such lofty beliefs."

Borric's tone softened a little as they walked up the steps leading from the garden. "I know you mean well, Lord Kerus, and there is only love of the realm in your heart. Have faith and pray, for I will do whatever I can to ensure the survival of the Kingdom."

Kerus stood before the door back into the palace. "I fear we will all be in deep water soon, my lord Borric. I pray that this invasion you speak of will not be the wave that drowns us. In whatever way I can aid you, I will." He turned toward the door, which was opened by a servant. Loudly he said, "I will bid you a good night, for I can see you're all tired."

The tension in the room was heavy as Borric, Arutha, and Pug reentered, and the Duke's mood one of dark reflection. Servants came to show the guests to their rooms, and Pug followed a boy near his own age, dressed in the Duke's livery. Pug looked over his shoulder as they left the hall to see the Duke and his son standing together, speaking quietly to Kulgan.

Pug was shown to a small but elegant room and, ignoring the richness of the bed covers, fell across them still fully clothed. The servant boy said, "Do you need aid in undressing, Squire?"

Pug sat up and looked at the boy with such a frank expression of wonder that the servant backed away a step. "If that will be all, Squire?" he asked, obviously uncomfortable.

Pug just laughed. The boy stood uncertainly for an instant, then bowed and hurriedly left the room. Pug pulled off his clothing, wondering at the eastern nobles and servants who had to help them undress. He was too tired to fold his garments, simply letting them fall to the floor in a heap.

After blowing out the bedside candle, Pug lay for a time in the darkness, troubled by the evening's discussion. He knew little of court intrigue, but knew that Kerus must have been deeply worried to speak as he did before strangers, in spite of Borric's reputation as a man of high honor.

Pug thought of all the things that had taken place in the last months and knew that his dreams of the King answering the call of Crydee with banners flying were another boyish fancy shattered upon the hard rock of reality.

13

Rillanon

he ship sailed into the harbor.

The climate of the Kingdom Sea was more clement than that of the Bitter Sea, and the journey from Salador had proven uneventful. They'd had to beat a tack much of the way against a steady northeast wind, so three weeks had passed instead of two.

Pug stood on the foredeck of the ship, his cloak pulled tightly around him. The winter wind's bitterness had given way to a softer cool, as if spring were but a few days in coming.

Rillanon was called the Jewel of the Kingdom, and Pug judged the name richly deserved. Unlike the squat cities of the West, Rillanon stood a mass of tall spires, gracefully arched bridges, and gently twisting roadways, scattered atop rolling hills in delightful confusion. Upon heroic towers, banners and pennons fluttered in the wind, as if the city celebrated the simple fact of its own existence. To Pug, even the ferrymen who worked the barges going to and from the ships at anchor in the harbor were more colorful for being within the enchantment of Rillanon.

The Duke of Salador had ordered a ducal banner sewn for Borric, and it now flew from the top of the ship's mainmast, informing the officials of the royal city that the Duke of Crydee had arrived. Borric's ship was given priority in docking by the city's harbor pilot, and quickly the ship was being secured at the royal quay. The party disembarked and were met by a company of the Royal Household Guard. At the head of the guards was an old, grey-haired, but still erect man, who greeted Borric warmly.

The two men embraced, and the older man, dressed in the royal purple and gold of the guard but with a ducal signet over his heart, said, "Borric, it is good to see you once more. What has it been? Ten . . . eleven years?"

"Caldric, old friend. It has been thirteen." Borric regarded him fondly. He had clear blue eyes and a short salt-and-pepper beard.

The man shook his head and smiled. "It has been much too long." He looked at the others. Spying Pug, he said, "Is this your younger boy?"

Borric laughed. "No, though he would be no shame to me if he were." He pointed out the lanky figure of Arutha. "This is my son. Arutha, come and greet your great-uncle."

Arutha stepped forward, and the two embraced. Duke Caldric, Lord of Rillanon, Knight-General of the King's Royal Household Guard, and Royal Chancellor, pushed Arutha back and regarded him at arm's length. "You were but a boy when I last saw you. I should have known you, for though you have some of your father's looks, you also resemble my dear brother—your mother's father—greatly. You do honor to my family."

Borric said, "Well, old war-horse, how is your city?"

Caldric said, "There is much to speak of, but not here. We shall bring you to the King's palace and quarter you in comfort. We shall have much time to visit. What brings you here to Rillanon?"

"I have pressing business with His Majesty, but it is not something to be spoken of in the streets. Let us go to the palace."

The Duke and his party were given mounts, and the escort cleared away the crowds as they rode through the city. If Krondor and Salador had impressed Pug with their splendor, Rillanon left him speechless.

The island city was built upon many hills, with several small rivers running down to the sea. It seemed to be a city of bridges and canals, as much as towers and spires. Many of the buildings seemed new, and Pug thought that this must be part of the King's plan for rebuilding the city. At several points along the way he saw workers removing old stones from a building, or erecting new walls and roofs. The newer buildings were faced with colorful stonework, many of marble and quartz, giving them a soft white, blue, or pink color. The cobblestones in the streets were clean, and gutters ran free of the clogs and debris Pug had seen in the other cities. Whatever else he might be doing, the boy thought, the King is maintaining a marvelous city.

A river ran before the palace, so that entrance was made over a high bridge that arched across the water into the main courtyard. The palace was a collection of great buildings connected by long halls that sprawled atop a hillside in the center of the city. It was faced with many-colored stone, giving it a rainbow aspect.

As they entered the courtyard, trumpets sounded from the walls, and guards stood to attention. Porters stepped forward to take the mounts, while a collection of palace nobles and officials stood near the palace entrance in welcome.

Approaching, Pug noticed that the greeting given by these men was formal and lacked the personal warmth of Duke Caldric's welcome. As he stood behind Kulgan and Meecham, he could hear Caldric's voice. "My lord Borric, Duke of Crydee, may I present Baron Gray, His Majesty's Steward of the Royal Household." This was a short, plump man in a tight-fitting tunic of red silk, and pale grey hose that bagged at the knees. "Earl Selvec, First Lord of the Royal Navies." A tall, gaunt man with a thin, waxed mustache bowed stiffly. And so on through the entire company. Each made a short statement of pleasure at Lord Borric's arrival, but Pug felt there was little sincerity in their remarks.

They were taken to their quarters. Kulgan had to raise a fuss to have Meecham near him, for Baron Gray had wanted to send him to the distant servants' wing of the palace, but he relented when Caldric asserted himself as Royal Chancellor.

The room that Pug was shown to far surpassed in splendor anything he had yet seen. The floors were polished marble, and the walls were made from the same material but flecked with what looked to be gold. A great mirror hung in a small room to one side of the sleeping quarters, where a large, gilded bathing tub sat. A steward put his few belongings—what they had picked up along the way since their own baggage had been lost in the forest—in a gigantic closet that could have held a dozen times all that Pug owned. After the man had finished, he inquired, "Shall I ready your bath, sir?"

Pug nodded, for three weeks aboard ship had made his clothes feel as if they were sticking to him. When the bath was ready, the steward said, "Lord Caldric will expect the Duke's party for dinner in four hours' time, sir. Shall I return then?"

Pug said yes, impressed with the man's diplomacy. He knew only that Pug had arrived with the Duke, and left it to Pug to decide whether or not he was included in the dinner invitation.

As he slipped into the warm water, Pug let out a long sigh of relief. He had never been one for baths when he had been a keep boy, preferring to wash away dirt in the sea and the streams near the castle. Now he could learn to enjoy them. He mused about what Tomas would have thought of that. He drifted off in a warm haze of memories, one very pleasant, of a dark-haired, lovely princess, and one sad, of a sandy-haired boy.

THE DINNER OF the night before had been an informal occasion, with Duke Caldric hosting Lord Borric's party. Now they stood in the royal throne room waiting to be presented to the King. The hall was vast, a high vaulted affair, with the entire southern wall fashioned of floor-to-ceiling windows overlooking the city. Hundreds of nobles stood around as the Duke's party was led down a central aisle between the onlookers.

Pug had not thought it possible to consider Duke Borric poorly dressed, for he had always worn the finest clothing in Crydee, as had his children. But among the finery in evidence around the room, Borric looked like a raven amid a flock of peacocks. Here a pearl-studded doublet, there a gold-thread-embroidered tunic—each noble seemed to be outdoing the next. Every lady wore the costliest silks and brocades, but only slightly outshone the men.

They halted before the throne, and Caldric announced the Duke. The King smiled, and Pug was struck by a faint resemblance to Arutha, though the

King's manner was more relaxed. He leaned forward on his throne and said, "Welcome to our city, cousin. It is good to see Crydee in this hall after so many years."

Borric stepped forward and knelt before Rodric the Fourth, King of the Kingdom of the Isles. "I am gladdened to see Your Majesty well."

A brief shadow passed over the monarch's face, then he smiled again. "Present to us your companions."

The Duke presented his son, and the King said, "Well, it is true that one of the conDoin line carries the blood of our mother's kin besides ourself." Arutha bowed and backed away. Kulgan was next as one of the Duke's advisers. Meecham, who had no rank in the Duke's court, had stayed in his room. The King said something polite, and Pug was introduced. "Squire Pug of Crydee, Your Majesty, Master of Forest Deep, and member of my court."

The King clapped his hands together and laughed. "The boy who kills trolls. How wonderful. Travelers have carried the tale from the far shores of Crydee, and we would hear it spoken by the author of the brave deed. We must meet later so that you may tell us of this marvel."

Pug bowed awkwardly, feeling a thousand eyes upon him. There had been times before when he had wished the troll story had not been spread, but never so much as now.

He backed away, and the King said, "Tonight we will hold a ball to honor the arrival of our cousin Borric."

He stood, arranging his purple robes around him, and pulled his golden chain of office over his head. A page placed the chain on a purple velvet cushion. The King then lifted his golden crown from his black-tressed head and handed it to another page.

The crowd bowed as he stepped down from his

throne. "Come, cousin," he said to Borric, "let us retire to my private balcony, where we can speak without all the rigors of office. I grow weary of the pomp."

Borric nodded and fell in next to the King, motioning Pug and the others to wait. Duke Caldric announced that the day's audience was at an end, and that those with petitions for the King should return the next day.

Slowly the crowd moved out the two great doors at the end of the hall, while Arutha, Kulgan, and Pug stood by. Caldric approached and said, "I will show you to a room where you may wait. It would be well for you to stay close, should His Majesty call for your attendance."

A steward of the court took them through a small door near the one the King had escorted Borric through. They entered a large, comfortable room with a long table in the center laden with fruit, cheese, bread, and wine. At the table were many chairs, and around the edge of the room were several divans, with plump cushions piled upon them.

Arutha crossed over to large glass doors and peered through them. "I can see Father and the King sitting on the royal balcony."

Kulgan and Pug joined him and looked to where Arutha indicated. The two men were at a table, overlooking the city and the sea beyond. The King was speaking with expansive gestures, and Borric nodded as he listened.

Pug said, "I had not expected that His Majesty would look like you, Your Highness."

Arutha replied with a wry smile, "It is not so surprising when you consider that, as my father was cousin to his father, so my mother was cousin to his mother."

Kulgan put his hand on Pug's shoulder. "Many of the noble families have more than one tie between them, Pug. Cousins who are four and five times removed will marry for reasons of politics and bring the families closer again. I doubt there is one noble family in the East that can't claim some relationship to the crown, though it may be distant and follow along a twisted route."

They returned to the table, and Pug nibbled at a piece of cheese. "The King seems in good humor," he said, cautiously approaching the subject all had on their minds.

Kulgan looked pleased at the circumspect manner of the boy's comment, for after leaving Salador, Borric had cautioned them all regarding Duke Kerus's remarks. He had ended his admonition with the old adage, "In the halls of power, there are no secrets, and even the deaf can hear."

Arutha said, "Our monarch is a man of moods; let us hope he stays in a good one after he hears Father's tidings."

The afternoon slowly passed as they awaited word from the Duke. When the shadows outside had grown long, Borric suddenly appeared at a door. He crossed over to stand before them, a troubled expression on his face. "His Majesty spent most of the afternoon explaining his plans for the rebirth of the Kingdom."

Arutha said, "Did you tell him of the Tsurani?"

The Duke nodded. "He listened and then calmly informed me that he would consider the matter. We will speak again in a day or so was all he said."

Kulgan said, "At least he seemed in good humor."

Borric regarded his old adviser. "I fear too good. I expected some sign of alarm. I do not ride across the Kingdom for minor cause, but he seemed unmoved by what I had to tell him."

Kulgan looked worried. "We are overlong on this

journey as it is. Let us hope that His Majesty will not take long in deciding upon a course of action."

Borric sat heavily in a chair and reached for a glass of wine. "Let us hope."

PUG WALKED THROUGH the door to the King's private quarters, his mouth dry with anticipation. He was to have his interview with King Rodric in a few minutes, and he was unsettled to be alone with the ruler of the Kingdom. Each time he had been close to other powerful nobles, he had hidden in the shadow of the Duke or his son, coming forward to tell briefly what he knew of the Tsurani, then able to disappear quickly back into the background. Now he was to be the only guest of the most powerful man north of the Empire of Great Kesh.

A house steward showed him through the door to the King's private balcony. Several servants stood around the edge of the large open veranda, and the King occupied the lone table, a carved marble affair under a large canopy.

The day was clear. Spring was coming early, as winter had before it, and there was a hint of warmth in the gusting air. Below the balcony, past the hedges and stone walls that marked its edge, Pug could see the city of Rillanon and the sea beyond. The colorful rooftops shone brightly in the midday sun, as the last snows had melted completely over the last four days. Ships sailed in and out of the harbor, and the streets teemed with citizens. The faint cries of merchants and hawkers, shouting over the noise of the streets, floated up to become a soft buzzing where the King took his midday meal.

As Pug approached the table, a servant pulled out a chair. The King turned and said, "Ah! Squire Pug, please take a seat." Pug began a bow, and the King said,

"Enough. I don't stand on formality when I dine with a friend."

Pug hesitated, then said, "Your Majesty honors me," as he sat.

Rodric waved the comment way. "I remember what it is to be a boy in the company of men. When I was but a little older than you, I took the crown. Until then I was only my father's son." His eyes got a distant look for a moment. "The Prince, it's true, but still only a boy. My opinion counted for nothing, and I never seemed to satisfy my father's expectations, in hunting, riding, sailing, or swordplay. I took many a hiding from my tutors, Caldric among them. That all changed when I became King, but I still remember what it was like." He turned toward Pug, and the distant expression vanished as he smiled. "And I do wish us to be friends." He glanced away and again his expression turned distant. "One can't have too many friends, now, can one? And since I'm the King, there are so many who claim to be my friend, but aren't." He was silent a moment, then again came out of his revery. "What do you think of my city?"

Pug said, "I have never seen anything like it, Majesty. It's wonderful."

Rodric looked out across the vista before them. "Yes, it is, isn't it?" He waved a hand, and a servant poured wine into crystal goblets. Pug sipped at his; he still hadn't developed a taste for wine, but found this very good, light and fruity with a hint of spices. Rodric said, "I have tried very hard to make Rillanon a wonderful place for those who live here. I would have the day come when all the cities of the Kingdom are as fine as this, where everywhere the eye travels, there is beauty. It would take a hundred lifetimes to do that, so I can only set the pattern, building an example for those who follow to imitate. But where I find brick, I leave marble. And those who see it will know it for what it is—my legacy."

The King seemed to ramble a bit, and Pug wasn't sure of all that he was saying as he continued to talk about buildings and gardens and removing ugliness from view. Abruptly the King changed topics. "Tell me how you killed the trolls."

Pug told him, and the King seemed to hang on every word. When the boy had finished, the King said, "That is a wonderful tale. It is better than the versions that have reached the court, for while it is not half so heroic, it is twice as impressive for being true. You have a stout heart, Squire Pug."

Pug said, "Thank you, Majesty."

Rodric said, "In your tale you mentioned the Princess Carline."

"Yes, Majesty?"

"I have not seen her since she was a baby in her mother's arms. What sort of woman has she become?"

Pug found the shift in topic surprising, but said, "She has become a beautiful woman, Majesty, much like her mother. She is bright and quick, if given to a little temper."

The King nodded. "Her mother was a beautiful woman. If the daughter is half as lovely, she is lovely indeed. Can she reason?"

Pug looked confused. "Majesty?"

"Has she a good head for reason, logic? Can she argue?"

Pug nodded vigorously. "Yes, Your Majesty. The Princess is very good at that."

The King rubbed his hands together. "Good. I must have Borric send her for a visit. Most of these eastern ladies are vapid, without substance. I was hoping Borric gave the girl an education. I would like to meet a young woman who knew logic and philosophy, and could argue and declaim."

Pug suddenly realized what the King had meant by arguing wasn't what he had thought. He decided it best not to mention the discrepancy.

The King continued. "My ministers dun me to seek a wife and give the Kingdom an heir. I have been busy, and frankly, have found little to interest me in the court ladies—oh, they're fine for a moonlight walk and . . . other things. But as the mother of my heirs? I hardly think so. But I should become serious in my search for a queen. Perhaps the only conDoin daughter would be the logical place to start."

Pug began to mention another conDoin daughter, then stifled the impulse, remembering the tension between the King and Anita's father. Besides, the girl was only seven.

The King shifted topics again. "For four days cousin Borric has regaled me with tales of these aliens, these Tsurani. What do you think of all this business?"

Pug looked startled. He had not thought the King might ask him for an opinion on anything, let alone a matter as important as the security of the Kingdom. He thought for a long moment, trying to frame his answer as best he could, then said, "From everything I have seen and heard, Your Majesty, I think these Tsurani people not only are planning to invade, but are already here."

The King raised an eyebrow. "Oh? I would like to hear your reasoning."

Pug considered his words carefully. "If there have been as many sightings as we are aware of, Majesty, considering the stealth these people are employing, wouldn't it be logical that there are many more occurrences of their coming and going than we know of?"

The King nodded. "A good proposition. Continue."

"Then might it also not be true that once the snows have fallen, we are less likely to find signs of them, as they are holding to remote areas?"

Rodric nodded and Pug continued. "If they are as warlike as the Duke and the others have said them to be, I think they have mapped out the West to find a good place to bring their soldiers in during the winter so they can launch their offensive this spring."

The King slapped the table with his hand. "A good exercise in logic, Pug." Motioning for the servants to bring food, he said, "Now, let us eat."

Food of an amazing variety and amount for just the two of them was produced, and Pug picked small amounts of many things, so as not to appear indifferent to the King's generosity. Rodric asked him a few questions as they dined, and Pug answered as well as he could.

As Pug was finishing his meal, the King put his elbow on the table and stroked his beardless chin. He stared out into space for a long time, and Pug began to feel self-conscious, not knowing the proper courtesy toward a king who is lost in thought. He elected to sit quietly.

After a time Rodric came out of his revery. There was a troubled note in his voice as he looked at Pug and said, "Why do these people come to plague us now? There is so much to be done. I can't have war disrupting my plans." He stood and paced around the balcony for a while, leaving Pug standing, for he had risen when the King had. Rodric turned to Pug. "I must send for Duke Guy. He will advise me. He has a good head for such things."

The King paced, looking at the city for a few minutes more, while Pug stood by his chair. He heard the monarch mutter to himself about the great works that must not be interrupted, then felt a tug on his sleeve. He turned and saw a palace steward standing quietly at his side. With a smile and a gesture toward the door, the steward indicated the interview was at an end. Pug followed the man to the door, wondering at the staff's ability to recognize the moods of the King.

Pug was shown the way back to his room, and he asked the servant to carry word to Lord Borric that Pug wished to see him if he was not busy. He went into his room and sat down to think. A short time later he was brought out of his musing by a knock at the door. He gave permission for the caller to enter, and the same steward who had carried the message to the Duke entered, with the message that Borric would see Pug at once.

Pug followed the man from his room and sent him away, saying he could find the Duke's room without guidance. He walked slowly, thinking of what he was going to tell the Duke. Two things were abundantly clear to the boy: the King was not pleased to hear that the Tsurani were a potential threat to his kingdom, and Lord Borric would be equally displeased to hear that Guy du Bas-Tyra was being called to Rillanon.

As WITH EVERY dinner over the last few days, there was a hushed mood at the table. The five men of Crydee sat eating in the Duke's quarters, with palace servants, all wearing the King's purple-and-gold badge on their dark tunics, hovering nearby.

The Duke was chafing to leave Rillanon for the West. Nearly four months had passed since they left Crydee: the entire winter. Spring was upon them, and if the Tsurani were going to attack, as they all believed, it was only a matter of days now. Arutha's restlessness matched his father's. Even Kulgan showed signs that the waiting was telling upon him. Only Meecham, who revealed nothing of his feelings, seemed content to wait.

Pug also longed for home. He had grown bored in the palace. He wished to be back in his tower with his studies. He also wished to see Carline again, though he didn't speak of this to anyone. Lately he found himself remembering her in a softer light, forgiving those qualities that had once irritated him. He also knew, with mixed feelings of anticipation, that he might discover the fate of Tomas. Dolgan should soon send word to Crydee, if the thaw came early to the mountains.

Borric had endured several more meetings with the King over the last week, each ending unsatisfactorily as far as he was concerned. The last had been hours ago, but he would say nothing about it until the room was emptied of servants.

As the last dishes were being cleared away, and the servants were pouring the King's finest Keshian brandy, a knock came at the door and Duke Caldric entered, waving the servants outside. When the room was cleared, he turned to the Duke.

"Borric, I am sorry to interrupt your dining, but I have news."

Borric stood, as did the others. "Please join us. Here, take a glass."

Caldric took the offered brandy and sat in Pug's chair, while the boy pulled another over. The Duke of Rillanon sipped his brandy and said, "Messengers arrived less than an hour ago from the Duke of Bas-Tyra. Guy expresses alarm over the possibility that the King might be 'unduly' distressed by these 'rumors' of trouble in the West."

Borric stood and threw his glass across the room, shattering it. Amber fluid dripped down the wall as the

Duke of Crydee nearly roared with anger. "What game does Guy play at? What is this talk of rumors and undue distress!"

Caldric raised a hand and Borric calmed a little, sitting again. The old Duke said, "I myself penned the King's call to Guy. Everything you had told, every piece of information and every surmise, was included. I can only think Guy is ensuring that the King reaches no decision until he arrives at the palace."

Borric drummed his fingers on the table and looked at Caldric with anger flashing in his eyes. "What is Bas-Tyra doing? If war comes, it comes to Crydee and Yabon. My people will suffer. My lands will be ravaged."

Caldric shook his head slowly. "I will speak plainly, old friend. Since the estrangement between the King and his uncle, Erland, Guy plays to advance his own banner to primacy in the Kingdom. I think that, should Erland's health fail, Guy sees himself wearing the purple of Krondor."

Through clenched teeth Borric said, "Then hear me clearly, Caldric. I would not put that burden on myself or mine for any but the highest purpose. But if Erland is as ill as I think, in spite of his claims otherwise, it will be Anita who sits the throne in Krondor, not Black Guy. If I have to march the Armies of the West into Krondor and assume the regency myself, that is what shall be, even should Rodric wish it otherwise. Only if the King has issue will another take the western throne."

Caldric looked at Borric calmly. "And will you be branded traitor to the crown?"

Borric slapped the table with his hand. "Curse the day that villain was born. I regret that I must acknowledge him kinsman."

Caldric waited for a minute until Borric calmed

down, then said, "I know you better than you know yourself, Borric. You would not raise the war banner of the West against the King, though you might happily strangle your cousin Guy. It was always a sad thing for me that the Kingdom's two finest generals could hate each other so."

"Aye, and with cause. Every time there is a call to aid the West, it is cousin Guy who opposes. Every time there is intrigue and a title is lost, it is one of Guy's favorites who gains. How can you not see? It was only because you, Brucal of Yabon, and I myself held firm that the congress did not name Guy regent for Rodric's first three years. He stood before every Duke in the Kingdom and called you a tired old man who was not fit to rule in the King's name. How can you forget?"

Caldric did look tired and old as he sat in the chair, one hand shading his eyes, as if the room light were too bright. Softly he said, "I do see, and I haven't forgotten. But he also is my kinsman by marriage, and if I were not here, how much more influence do you think he would have with Rodric? As a boy the King idolized him, seeing in him a dashing hero, a fighter of the first rank, a defender of the Kingdom."

Borric leaned back in his chair. "I am sorry, Caldric," he said, his voice losing its harsh edge. "I know you act for the good of us all. And Guy did play the hero, rolling the Keshian Army back at Deep Taunton, all those years ago. I should not speak of things I have not seen firsthand."

Arutha sat passively through all this, but his eyes showed he felt the same anger as his father. He moved forward in his chair, and the dukes looked at him. Borric said, "You have something to say, my son?"

Arutha spread his hands wide before him. "In all this the thought has bothered me: should the Tsurani come, how would it profit Guy to see the King hesitate?"

Borric drummed his fingers on the table. "That is the puzzle, for in spite of his scheming, Guy would not peril the Kingdom, not to spite me."

"Would it not serve him," said Arutha, "to let the West suffer a little, until the issue was in doubt, then to come at the head of the Armies of the East, the conquering hero, as he was at Deep Taunton?"

Caldric considered this. "Even Guy could not think so little of these aliens, I would hope."

Arutha paced the room. "But consider what he knows. The ramblings of a dying man. Surmise on the nature of a ship that only Pug, here, has seen, and I caught but a glimpse of as it slid into the sea. Conjecture by a priest and a magician, both callings Guy holds in little regard. Some migrating Dark Brothers. He might discount such news."

"But it is all there for the seeing," protested Borric.

Caldric watched the young Prince pace the room. "Perhaps you are right. What may be lacking is the urgency of your words, an urgency lacking in the dry message of ink and parchment. When he arrives, we must convince him."

Borric nearly spat his words. "It is for the King to decide, not Guy!"

Caldric said, "But the King has given much weight to Guy's counsel. If you are to gain command of the Armies of the West, it is Guy who must be convinced."

Borric looked shocked. "I? I do not want the banner of the armies. I only wish for Erland to be free to aid me, should there be need."

Caldric placed both hands upon the table. "Borric, for all your wisdom, you are much the rustic noble.

Erland cannot lead the armies. He is not well. Even if
he could, the King would not allow it. Nor would he
give leave for Erland's Marshal, Dulanic. You have seen
Rodric at his best, of late. When the black moods are
upon him, he fears for his life. None dare say it, but the
King suspects his uncle of plotting for the crown."

"Ridiculous!" exclaimed Borric. "The crown was
Erland's for the asking thirteen years ago. There was no
clear succession. Rodric's father had not yet named him
heir apparent, and Erland's claim was as clear as the
King's, perhaps more so. Only Guy and those who
sought to use the boy pressed Rodric's claim. Most of
the congress would have sustained Erland as King."

"I know, but times are different, and the boy is a
boy no longer. He is now a frightened young man who
is sick from fear. Whether it is due to Guy's and the
others' influence or from some illness of the mind, I do
not know. The King does not think as other men do.
No king does, and Rodric less than most. Ridiculous as
it may seem, he will not give the Armies of the West to
his uncle. I am also afraid that once Guy has his ear, he
will not give them to you either."

Borric opened his mouth to say something, but
Kulgan interrupted. "Excuse me, Your Graces, but may
I suggest something?"

Caldric looked at Borric, who nodded. Kulgan
cleared his throat and said, "Would the King give the
Armies of the West to Duke Brucal of Yabon?"

Comprehension slowly dawned on Borric's and
Caldric's faces, until the Duke of Crydee threw back
his head and laughed. Slamming his fist on the table,
he nearly shouted, "Kulgan! If you had not served me
well in all the years I have known you, tonight you
have." He turned to Caldric. "What do you think?"

Caldric smiled for the first time since entering the
room. "Brucal? That old war dog? There is no more

honest man in the Kingdom. And he is not in the line of succession. He would be beyond even Guy's attempts to discredit. Should he receive the command of the armies . . ."

Arutha finished the thought. "He would call Father to be his chief adviser. He knows Father is the finest commander in the West."

Caldric sat up straight in his chair, excitement on his face. "You would even have command of the armies of Yabon."

"Yes," said Arutha, "and LaMut, Zūn, Ylith, and the rest."

Caldric stood. "I think it will work. Say nothing to the King tomorrow. I will find the proper time to make the 'suggestion.' Pray that His Majesty approves."

Caldric took his leave, and Pug could see that for the first time there was hope for a good ending to this journey. Even Arutha, who had fumed like black thunder all week, looked nearly happy.

Pug WAS AWAKENED by a pounding on his door. He sleepily called out for whoever was out there to enter, and the door opened. A royal steward peeked in. "Sir, the King commands all in the Duke's party to join him in the throne room. At once." He held a lantern for Pug's convenience.

Pug said he would come straight away and hurriedly got dressed. Outside it was still dark, and he felt anxious about what had caused this surprise summons. The hopeful feeling of the night before, after Caldric had left, was replaced by a gnawing worry that the unpredictable King had somehow learned of the plan to circumvent the arrival of the Duke of Bas-Tyra.

He was still buckling his belt about his tunic when he left his room. He hurried down the hall, with the steward beside him holding a lantern against the dark, as the torches and candles usually lit in the evening had all been extinguished.

When they reached the throne room, the Duke, Arutha, and Kulgan were arriving, all looking apprehensively toward Rodric, who paced by his throne, still in his night-robes. Duke Caldric stood to one side, a grave expression on his face. The room was dark, save for the lanterns carried by the stewards.

As soon as they were gathered before the throne, Rodric flew into a rage. "Cousin! Do you know what I have here?" he screamed, holding out a sheaf of parchment.

Borric said he didn't. Rodric's voice lowered only a little. "It is a message from Yabon! That old fool Brucal has let those Tsurani aliens attack and destroy one of his garrisons. Look at these!" he nearly shrieked, throwing the parchments toward Borric. Kulgan picked them up and handed them to the Duke. "Never mind," said the King, his voice returning to near-normalcy. "I'll tell you what they say.

"These invaders have attacked into the Free Cities, near Walinor. They have attacked into the elven forests. They have attacked Stone Mountain. They have attacked Crydee."

Without thinking, Borric said, "What news from Crydee?"

The King stopped his pacing. He looked at Borric, and for a moment Pug saw madness in his eyes. He closed them briefly, then opened them, and Pug could see the King was himself again. He shook his head slightly and raised his hand to his temple. "I have only secondhand news from Brucal. When those messages left six weeks ago, there had only been one attack at Crydee. Your son Lyam reports the victory was total, driving the aliens deep into the forest."

Caldric stepped forward. "All reports say the same

thing. Heavily armed companies of foot soldiers attacked during the night, before the snows had melted, taking the garrisons by surprise. Little is known save that a garrison of LaMutians near Stone Mountain was overrun. All other attacks seem to have been driven back." He looked at Borric meaningfully. "There is no word of the Tsurani's using cavalry."

Borric said, "Then perhaps Tully was right, and they have no horses."

The King seemed to be dizzy, for he took a staggering step backward and sat on his throne. Again he placed a hand to his temple, then said, "What is this talk of horses? My Kingdom is invaded. These creatures dare to attack my soldiers."

Borric looked at the King. "What would Your Majesty have me do?"

The King's voice rose. "Do? I was going to wait for my loyal Duke of Bas-Tyra to arrive before I made any decision. But now I must act."

He paused, and his face took on a vulpine look, as his dark eyes gleamed in the lantern light. "I was considering giving the Armies of the West to Brucal, but the doddering old fool can't even protect his own garrisons."

Borric was about to protest on Brucal's behalf, but Arutha, knowing his father, gripped his arm, and the Duke remained silent.

The King said, "Borric, you must leave Crydee to your son. He is capable enough, I should think. He's given us our only victory so far." His eyes wandered and he giggled. He shook his head for a moment, and his voice lost its frantic edge. "Oh, gods, these pains. I think my head will burst." He closed his eyes briefly. "Borric, leave Crydee to Lyam and Arutha; I'm giving you the banner of the Armies of the West; go to Yabon. Brucal is sorely pressed, for most of the alien army strikes toward LaMut and Zūn. When you are there, request what you need. These invaders must be driven from our lands."

The King's face was pale, and perspiration gleamed on his forehead. "This is a poor hour to start, but I have sent word to the harbor to ready a ship. You must leave at once. Go now."

The Duke bowed and turned. Caldric said, "I will see His Majesty to his room. I will accompany you to the docks when you are ready."

The old Chancellor helped the King from the throne, and the Duke's party left the hall. They rushed back to their rooms to find stewards already packing their belongings. Pug stood around excitedly, for at last he was returning to his home.

THEY STOOD AT dockside, bidding farewell to Caldric. Pug and Meecham waited, and the tall franklin said, "Well, lad. It will be some time before we see home again, now that war is joined."

Pug looked up into the scarred face of the man who had found him in the storm, so long ago. "Why? Aren't we going home?"

Meecham shook his head. "The Prince will ship from Krondor through the Straits of Darkness to join his brother, but the Duke will ship for Ylith, then to Brucal's camp somewhere near LaMut. Where Lord Borric goes, Kulgan goes. And where my master goes, I go. And you?"

Pug felt a sinking in his stomach. What the franklin said was true. He belonged with Kulgan, not with the folk at Crydee, though he knew if he asked, he would be allowed to go home with the Prince. He resigned himself to another sign that his boyhood was ending. "Where Kulgan goes, I go."

Meecham clapped him on the shoulder and said,

"Well, at least I can teach you to use that bloody sword you swing like a fishwife's broom."

Feeling little cheer at the prospect, Pug smiled weakly. They soon boarded the ship and were under way toward Salador, and the first leg of the long journey west.

14

Invasion

The spring rains were heavy that year.

The business of war was hampered by the ever-present mud. It would stay wet and cold for nearly another month before the brief, hot summer came.

Duke Brucal of Yabon and Lord Borric stood looking over a table laden with maps. The rain hammered on the roof of the tent, the central part of the commander's pavilion. On either side of the tent two others were attached, providing sleeping quarters for the two nobles. The tent was filled with smoke, from lanterns and from Kulgan's pipe. The magician had proven an able adviser to the dukes, and his magical aid helpful. He could detect trends in the weather, and his wizard's sight could detect some of the Tsurani's troop movements, though not often. And over the years his reading of every book he encountered, including narratives of warfare, had made him a fair student of tactics and strategy.

Brucal pointed to the newest map on the table.

"They have taken this point here, and another here. They hold this point"—he indicated another spot on the map—"in spite of our every effort to dislodge them. They also seem to be moving along a line from here, to here." His finger swept down a line along the eastern face of the Grey Towers. "There is a coordinated pattern here, but I'm damned if I can anticipate where it's going next." The old Duke looked weary. The fighting had been going on sporadically for over two months now, and no distinct advantage could be seen on either side.

Borric studied the map. Red spots marked known Tsurani strongholds: hand-dug, earthen breastworks, with a minimum of two hundred men defending. There were also suspected reinforcement companies, their approximate location indicated with yellow spots. It was known that any position attacked was quick to get reinforcements, sometimes in a matter of minutes. Blue spots indicated the location of Kingdom pickets, though most of Brucal's forces were billeted around the hill upon which the commander's tent sat.

Until the heavy foot soldiers and engineers from Ylith and Tyr-Sog arrived to man and create permanent fortifications, the Kingdom was fighting a principally mobile war, for most of the troops assembled were cavalry. The Duke of Crydee agreed with the other man's assessment. "It seems their tactics remain the same: bring in a small force, dig in, and hold. They prevent our troops from entering, but refuse to follow when we withdraw. There is a pattern. But for the life of me, I can't see it either."

A guard entered. "My lords, an elf stands without, seeking entrance."

Brucal said, "Show him in."

The guard held aside the tent flap, and an elf entered. His red-brown hair was plastered to his head, and his cloak dripped water on the floor of the tent. He made a slight bow to the dukes.

"What news from Elvandar?" Borric asked.

"My Queen sends you greetings." He quickly turned to the map. He pointed at the pass between the Grey Towers on the south and Stone Mountain on the north, the same pass Borric's forces now bottled up at its east end. "The outworlders move many soldiers through this pass. They have advanced to the edge of the elven forests, but seek not to enter. They have made it difficult to get through." He grinned. "I led several a merry chase for half a day. They run nearly as well as the dwarves. But they could not keep up in the forest." He returned his attention to the map. "There is word from Crydee that skirmishes have been fought by out-riding patrols, but nothing close to the castle itself. There is no word of activity from the Grey Towers, Carse, or Tulan. They seem content to dig in along this pass. Your forces to the west will not be able to join you, for they could not break through now."

"How strong do the aliens appear to be?" asked Brucal.

"It is not known, but I saw several thousand along this route." His finger indicated a route along the northern edge of the pass, from the elven forests to the Kingdom camp. "The dwarves of Stone Mountain are left alone, so long as they do not venture south. The outworlders deny them the pass also."

Borric asked the elf, "Has there been any report of the Tsurani's having cavalry?"

"None. Every report refers only to infantry."

Kulgan said, "Father Tully's speculation on their being horseless seems to be borne out."

Brucal took brush and ink in hand and entered the information on the map. Kulgan stood looking over his shoulder.

Borric said to the elf, "After you've rested, carry my greetings to your mistress, and my wish for her good health and prosperity. If you should send runners to the west, please carry the same message to my sons."

The elf bowed. "As my lord wishes. I shall return to Elvandar at once." He turned and left the tent.

Kulgan said, "I think I see it." He pointed to the new red spots on the map. They formed a rough half circle, through the pass. "The Tsurani are trying to hold this area here. That valley is the center of the circle. I would guess they are attempting to keep anyone from getting close."

Both the dukes looked puzzled. Borric said, "But to what purpose? There is nothing there of any value militarily. It is as if they are inviting us to bottle them up in that valley."

Suddenly Brucal gasped. "It's a bridgehead. Think of it in terms of crossing a river. They have a foothold on this side of the rift, as the magician calls it. They have only as many supplies as their men can carry through. They don't have enough control of the area for foraging, so they need to expand the area under their control and build up supplies before they launch an offensive."

Brucal turned to the magician. "Kulgan, what do you think? This is more in your province."

The magician looked at the map as if trying to divine information hidden in it. "We know nothing of the magic involved. We don't know how fast they can pass supplies and men through, for no one has ever witnessed an appearance. They may require a large area, which this valley provides them. Or they may have some limit on the amount of time available to pass troops through."

Duke Borric considered this. "Then there is only

one thing to do. We must send a party into the valley to see what they are doing."

Kulgan smiled. "I will go too, if Your Grace permits. Your soldiers might not have the faintest idea of what they are seeing if it involves magic."

Brucal started to object, his gaze taking in the magician's ample size. Borric cut him off. "Don't let his look fool you. He rides like a trooper." He turned to Kulgan. "You had best take Pug, for if one should fall, then the other can carry the news."

Kulgan looked unhappy at that, but saw the wisdom in it. The Duke of Yabon said, "If we strike at the North Pass, then into this valley and draw their forces there, a small, fast company might break through here." He pointed at a small pass that entered the south end of the valley from the east.

Borric said, "It is a bold enough plan. We have danced with the Tsurani so long, holding a stable front, I doubt they will expect it." The magician suggested they retire for the rest of the evening, for it would be a long day on the morrow. He closed his eyes briefly, then informed the two leaders that the rain would stop and the next day would be sunny.

PUG LAY WRAPPED in a blanket, trying to nap, when Kulgan entered their tent. Meecham sat before the cook fire, preparing the evening meal and attempting to keep it from the greedy maw of Fantus. The firedrake had sought out his master a week before, eliciting startled cries from the soldiers as he swooped over the tents. Only Meecham's commanding shouts had kept a bowman from putting a cloth-yard arrow into the playful drake. Kulgan had been pleased to see his pet, but at a loss to explain how the creature had found them. The drake had moved right into the magician's tent, content to sleep next to Pug and steal food from under Meecham's watchful eye.

Pug sat up as the magician pulled off his sopping cloak. "There is an expedition going deep within Tsurani-held territory, to break the circle they've thrown up around a small valley and find out what they are up to. You and Meecham will be going with me on this trip, I would have friends at my back and side."

Pug felt excited by the news. Meecham had spent long hours schooling him in use of sword and shield, and the old dream of soldiering had returned. "I have kept my blade sharp, Kulgan."

Meecham gave forth a snort that passed for laughter, and the magician threw him a black look. "Good, Pug. But with any luck we'll not be fighting. We are to go in a smaller force attached to a larger one that will draw off the Tsurani. We will drive quickly into their territory and discover what they are hiding. We will then ride as fast as possible to bring back the news. I thank the gods they are without horses, or we could never hope to accomplish so bold a stroke. We shall ride through them before they know we have struck."

"Perhaps we may take a prisoner," the boy said hopefully.

"It would be a change," said Meecham. The Tsurani had proved to be fierce fighters, preferring to die rather than be captured.

"Maybe then we'd discover why they've come to Midkemia," ventured Pug.

Kulgan looked thoughtful. "There is little we understand about these Tsurani. Where is this place they come from? How do they cross between their world and ours? And as you've pointed out, the most vexing question of all, why do they come? Why invade our lands?"

"Metal."

Kulgan and Pug looked over at Meecham, who was spooning up stew, keeping one eye on Fantus. "They don't have any metal and they want ours." When Kulgan and Pug regarded him with blank expressions, he shook his head. "I'd thought you puzzled it out by now, so I didn't think to bring it up." He put aside the bowls of stew, reached behind himself, and drew a bright red arrow out from under his bedding. "Souvenir," he said, holding it out for inspection. "Look at the head. It's the same stuff their swords are made from, some kind of wood, hardened like steel. I picked over a lot of things fetched in by the soldiers, and I haven't seen one thing these Tsurani make with any metal in it."

Kulgan looked flabbergasted. "Of course! It's all so simple. They found a way to pass between their world and ours, sent through scouts, and found a land rich in metals they lack. So they sent in an invading army. It also explains why they marshal in a high valley of the mountains, rather than in the lower forests. It gives them free access to . . . the dwarven mines!" He jumped up. "I'd better inform the dukes at once. We must send word to the dwarves to be alert for incursions into the mines."

Pug sat thoughtfully as Kulgan vanished through the tent entrance. After a moment he said, "Meecham, why didn't they try trading?"

Meecham shook his head. "The Tsurani? From what I've seen, boy, it's a good bet trading never entered their minds. They are one very warlike bunch. Those bastards fight like six hundred kinds of demons. If they had cavalry, they would have chased this whole lot back to LaMut, then probably burned the city down around them. But if we can wear them down, like a bulldog does, just keep hanging on until they tire, we might settle this after a time. Look what happened to

Kesh. Lost half of Bosania to the Kingdom in the north 'cause the Confederacy just plain wore the Empire out with one rebellion after another in the south."

After a time, Pug gave up on Kulgan's returning soon, ate supper alone, and made ready for bed. Meecham quit trying to keep the magician's meal away from the drake, and also turned in.

In the dark, Pug lay staring up at the tent roof, listening to the sound of the rain and the drake's joyous chewing. Soon he drifted off into sleep, where he dreamed of a dark tunnel and a flickering light vanishing down it.

THE TREES WERE thick and the air hung heavy with mist as the column moved slowly through the forest. Outriders came and went every few minutes, checking for signs that the Tsurani were preparing an ambush. The sun was lost high in the trees overhead, and the entire scene had a greyish-green quality to it, making it difficult to see more than a few yards ahead.

At the head of the column rode a young captain of the LaMutian army, Vandros, son of the old Earl of LaMut. He was also one of the more level-headed and capable young officers in Brucal's army.

They rode in pairs, with Pug sitting next to a soldier, behind Kulgan and Meecham. The order to halt came down the line, and Pug reined in his horse and dismounted. Over a light gambeson, he wore a well-oiled suit of chain mail. Over that was a tabard of the LaMutian forces, with the grey wolf's head on a circle of blue in the center. Heavy woolen trousers were tucked into his high boots. He had a shield on his left arm, and his sword hung from his belt; he felt truly a soldier. The only discordant note was his helm, which was a little too large and gave him a slightly comic appearance.

Captain Vandros came back to where Kulgan stood waiting, and dismounted. "The scouts have spotted a camp about half a mile ahead. They think they were not seen by the guards."

The captain pulled out a map. "We are about here. I will lead my men and attack the enemy position. Cavalry from Zūn will support us on either side. Lieutenant Garth will command the column you will ride with. You will pass the enemy camp and continue on toward the mountains. We will try to follow if we can, but if we haven't rejoined you by sundown, you must continue alone.

"Keep moving, if only at a slow walk. Push the horses, but try to keep them alive. On horseback you can always outrun these aliens, but on foot I wouldn't give you much chance of getting back. They run like fiends.

"Once in the mountains, move through the pass. Ride into the valley one hour after sunrise. The North Pass will be attacked at dawn, so if you get safely into the valley you should, I hope, find little between you and the North Pass. Once in the valley, don't stop for anything. If a man falls, he is to be left. The mission is to get information back to the commanders. Now try to rest. It may be your last chance for some time. We attack in an hour."

He walked his horse back to the head of the line. Kulgan, Meecham, and Pug sat without speaking. The magician wore no armor because he claimed it would interfere with his magic. Pug was more inclined to believe it would interfere with his considerable girth. Meecham had a sword at his side, like the others, but held a horse bow. He preferred archery to close fighting, though Pug knew, from long hours of instruction at his hands, that he was no stranger to the blade.

The hour passed slowly, and Pug felt mounting

excitement, for he was still possessed by boyish notions of glory. He had forgotten the terror of the fighting with the Dark Brothers before they reached the Grey Towers.

Word was passed and they remounted. They rode slowly at first, until the Tsurani were in sight. As the trees thinned, they picked up speed, and when they reached the clearing, they galloped the horses. Large breastworks of earth had been thrown up as a defense against the charge of horsemen. Pug could see the brightly colored helmets of the Tsurani rushing to defend their camp. As the riders charged, the sounds of fighting could be heard echoing through the trees as the Zūnese troops engaged other Tsurani camps.

The ground shook under the horses as they rode straight at the camp, sounding like a rolling wave of thunder. The Tsurani soldiers stayed behind the earthworks, shooting arrows, most of which fell short. As the first element of the column hit the earthworks, the second element turned to the left, riding off at an angle past the camp. A few Tsurani soldiers were outside the breastworks here, and were ridden down like wheat before a scythe. Two came close to hitting the riders with the great two-handed swords they wielded, but their blows went wide. Meecham, guiding his horse with his legs, dropped both with two quick arrows.

Pug heard a horse scream among the sounds of the fighting behind, then suddenly found himself crashing through the brush as they entered the forest. They rode as hard as possible, cutting through the trees, ducking under low branches, the scene a passing kaleidoscope of greens and browns.

The column rode for nearly a half hour, then slackened pace as the horses began to tire. Kulgan called to Lieutenant Garth, and they halted to check their position against the map. If they moved slowly for the balance of the day and night, they would reach the mouth of the pass near daybreak.

Meecham peered over the heads of the lieutenant and Kulgan as they knelt on the ground. "I know this place. I hunted it as a boy, when I lived near Hūsh."

Pug was startled. This was the first time Meecham had ever mentioned anything about his past. Pug had supposed that Meecham was from Crydee, and was surprised to find he had been a youth in the Free Cities. But then he found it difficult to imagine Meecham as a boy.

The franklin continued. "There is a way over the crest of the mountains, a path that leads between two smaller peaks. It is little more than a goat trail, but if we led the horses all night, we could be in the valley by sunrise. This way is difficult to find on this side if you don't know where to seek it. From the valley side, it is nearly impossible. I would bet the Tsurani know nothing about it."

The lieutenant regarded Kulgan with a question in his eyes. The magician looked at Meecham, then said, "It might be worth a try. We can mark our trail for Vandros. If we move slowly, he might catch up before we reach the valley."

"All right," said the lieutenant, "our biggest advantage is mobility, so let's keep moving. Meecham, where will we come out?"

The large man leaned over the lieutenant's shoulder to point at a spot on the map near the south end of the valley. "Here. If we come out straight west for a half mile or so, then swing north, we can cut down the heart of the valley." He motioned with his finger as he spoke. "This valley's mostly woods at the north and south end, with a big meadow in the middle. That's where they'd be if they have a big camp. It's mostly open there, so if the aliens haven't come up with anything surprising, we should be able to ride right by them afore they can organize to stop us. The dicey part will be getting through the northern woods if they've garrisoned soldiers there. But if we get through them, we'll be free to the North Pass."

"All agreed?" asked the lieutenant. When no one said anything, he gave orders for the men to walk their horses, and Meecham took the lead as guide.

They reached the entrance to the pass, or what Pug thought Meecham had correctly called a goat trail, an hour before sundown. The lieutenant posted guards and ordered the horses unsaddled. Pug rubbed down his horse with handfuls of long grass, then staked it out. The thirty soldiers were busy tending to their horses and armor. Pug could feel the tension in the air. The run around the Tsurani camp had set the soldiers on edge, and they were anxious for a fight.

Meecham showed Pug how to muffle his sword and shield with rags torn from the soldiers' blankets. "We're not going to be using these bed rolls this night, and nothing will ring through the hills like the sound of metal striking metal, boy. Except maybe the clopping of hooves on the rock." Pug watched as he muffled the horses' hooves with leather stockings designed for just this purpose and carried in the saddlebags. Pug rested as the sun began to set. Through the short spring twilight, he waited until he heard the order to resaddle. The soldiers were beginning to pull their horses into a line when he finished.

Meecham and the lieutenant were walking down the line repeating instructions to the men. They would move in single file, Meecham taking the lead, the lieutenant second, down the line to the last soldier. They tied a series of ropes through the left stirrup of each horse, and each man gripped it tightly as he led his own horse. After everyone was in position, Meecham started off.

The path rose steeply, and the horses had to scramble in places. In the darkness they moved slowly, taking great care not to stray from the path. Occasionally Meecham stopped the line, to check ahead. After several such stops, the trail crested through a deep, narrow pass and started downward. An hour later it widened, and they stopped to rest. Two soldiers were sent ahead with Meecham to scout the way, while the rest of the tired line dropped to the ground to ease cramped legs. Pug realized the fatigue was as much the result of the tension created by the silent passage as of the climbing, but it didn't make his legs feel any better.

After what seemed to be much too short a rest they were moving again. Pug stumbled along, fatigue numbing his mind to the point where the world became an endless series of picking up one foot and placing it before the other. Several times the horse before him was literally towing him as he grasped the rope tied to its stirrup.

Suddenly Pug was aware that the line had stopped and that they were standing in a gap between two small hills, looking down at the valley floor. From here it would take only a few minutes to ride down the slope.

Kulgan walked back to where the boy stood next to his animal. The stout wizard seemed little troubled by the climb, and Pug wondered at the muscle that must lie hidden beneath the layers of fat. "How are you feeling, Pug?"

"I'll live, I expect, but I think next time I'll ride, if it's all the same to you." They were keeping their voices low, but the magician gave out with a soft chuckle anyway.

"I understand completely. We'll be staying here until first light. That will be slightly less than two hours. I suggest you get some sleep, for we have a great deal of hard riding ahead."

Pug nodded and lay down without a word. He used his shield for a pillow and, before the magician had taken a step away, was fast asleep. He never stirred as Meecham came and removed the leather muffles from his horse.

A GENTLE SHAKING brought Pug awake. He felt as if he had just closed his eyes a moment before. Meecham was squatting before him, holding something out. "Here, boy. Eat this."

Pug took the offered food. It was soft bread, with a nutty flavor. After two bites he began to feel better.

Meecham said, "Eat quickly, we're off in a few minutes." He moved forward to where the lieutenant and the magician stood by their horses. Pug finished the bread and remounted. The soreness had left his legs, and by the time he was astride his mount, he felt anxious to be off.

The lieutenant turned his horse and faced the men. "We will ride west—then, on my command, north. Fight only if attacked. Our mission is to return with information about the Tsurani. If any man falls, we cannot stop. If you are separated from the others, get back as best you can. Remember as much of what you see as possible, for you may be the only one to carry the news to the dukes. May the gods protect us all."

Several of the soldiers uttered quick prayers to various deities, chiefly Tith, the war god, then they were off. The column came down the hillside and reached the flat of the valley. The sun was cresting the hills behind, and a rosy glow bathed the landscape. At the foot of the hills they crossed a small creek and entered a plain of tall grass. Far ahead was a stand of trees, and another could be seen off to the north. At the north end of the valley the haze of campfire smoke hung in the air. The enemy was there all right, thought Pug, and from the volume of smoke there must be a large concentration of them. He hoped Meecham was right and they were all garrisoned out in the open, where the Kingdom soldiers stood a fair chance of outrunning them.

After a while the lieutenant passed the word, and the column turned north. They trotted along, saving the horses for when they would be sure to need the speed.

Pug thought he saw glimpses of color in the trees ahead, as they descended into the southern woods of the valley, but couldn't be sure. As they reached the woods, a shout went up from within the trees. The lieutenant cried, "All right, they've seen us. Ride hard and stay close." He spurred his horse forward, and soon the entire company was thundering through the woods. Pug saw the horses in front bear to the left and turned his to follow, seeing a clearing in the trees. The sound of voices grew louder as the first trees went flying past, and his eyes tried to adjust to the darkness of the woods. He hoped his horse could see more clearly than he could, or he might find himself inside a tree.

The horse, battle trained and quick, darted between the trunks, and Pug could begin to see flashes of color among the branches. Tsurani soldiers were rushing to intercept the horsemen, but were forced to weave through the trees, making it impossible. They were speeding through the woods faster than the Tsurani could pass the word and react. Pug knew that this advantage of surprise couldn't last much longer; they were making too great a commotion for the enemy not to realize what was happening.

After a mad dash through the trees, they broke

into another clear area where a few Tsurani soldiers stood waiting for them. The horsemen charged, and most of the defenders scattered to avoid being run down. One, however, stood his ground, in spite of the terror written on his face, and swung the blue two-handed sword he carried. A horse screamed, and the rider was thrown as the blade cut the horse's right leg from under him. Pug lost sight of the fight as he sped quickly past.

An arrow shot over Pug's shoulder, buzzing like an angry bee. He hunched over the withers of his mount, trying to give the archers behind him as small a target as possible. Ahead, a soldier fell backward out of his saddle, a red arrow through his neck.

Soon they were out of bow range and riding toward a breastwork thrown across an old road from the mines in the south. Hundreds of brightly colored figures scurried behind it. The lieutenant signaled for the riders to pass around it, to the west.

As soon as it was apparent they would pass the earthwork and not charge it, several Tsurani bowmen came tumbling over the top of the redoubt and ran to intercept the riders. As soon as they came within bowshot, the air filled with red and blue shafts. Pug heard a horse scream, but he couldn't see the stricken animal or its rider.

Riding quickly beyond the range of the bowmen, they entered another thick stand of trees. The lieutenant pulled up his mount for a moment and yelled, "From here on, make straight north. We're almost to the meadow, so there'll be no cover, and speed is your only ally. Then once you're in the woods to the north, keep moving. Our forces should have broken through up there, and if we can get past those woods, we should be all right." Meecham had described the woods as being about two or three miles across. From there it was three miles of open ground until the North Pass through the hills began.

They slowed to a walk, trying to rest the horses as much as possible. They could see the tiny figures of the Tsurani coming from behind, but they would never catch up before the horses were running again. Ahead Pug could see the trees of the forest, looming larger with each passing minute. He could feel the eyes that must be there, watching them, waiting.

"As soon as we are within bowshot, ride as fast as you can," shouted the lieutenant. Pug saw the soldiers pull their swords and bows out, and drew his own sword. Feeling uncomfortable with the weapon clutched in his right hand, he rode at a trot toward the trees.

Suddenly the air was filled with arrows. Pug felt one glance off his helm, but it still snapped his head back and brought tears to his eyes. He urged his horse ahead blindly, trying to blink his eyes clear. He had the shield in his left hand and a sword in his right, so that by the time he blinked enough to be able to see clearly, he found himself in the woods. His war-horse responded to leg pressure as he moved into the forest.

A yellow-garbed soldier burst from behind a tree and aimed a swing at the boy. He caught the sword blow on his shield, which sent a numbing shock up his left arm. He swung overhand and down at the soldier, who leaped away, and the blow missed. Pug spurred his horse on, before the soldier could get in position to swing again. All around, the forest rang with the sounds of battle. He could barely make out the other horsemen among the trees.

Several times he rode down Tsurani soldiers as they tried to block his passage. Once one tried to grab at the reins of the horse, but Pug sent him reeling with a blow on the potlike helmet. To Pug it seemed as if they were all engaged in some mad game of hide-and-go-seek, with foot soldiers jumping out from behind every other tree.

A sharp pain stung Pug on the right cheek. Feeling with the back of his sword hand as he bounded through the wood, he felt a wetness, and when he pulled his hand away, he could see blood on his knuckles. He felt a detached curiosity. He hadn't even heard the arrow that had stung him.

Twice more he rode down soldiers, the war-horse knocking them aside. Suddenly he burst out of the forest and was assaulted by a kaleidoscope of images. He pulled up for a moment and let the scene register. Less than a hundred yards to the west of where he exited the woodlands, a great device, some hundred feet in length, with twenty-foot-high poles at each end, stood. Around it were clustered several men, the first Tsurani Pug had seen who weren't wearing armor. These men wore long black robes and were completely unarmed. Between the poles a shimmering grey haze like the one they had seen in Kulgan's room filled the air, blocking out the view of the area directly behind. From out of the haze a wagon was being pulled by two grey, squat, six-legged beasts, who were prodded by two soldiers in red armor. Several more wagons were standing beyond the machines, and a few of the strange beasts could be seen grazing beyond the wagons.

Beyond the strange device, a mighty camp sprawled across the meadow, with more tents than Pug could count. Banners of strange design and gaudy colors fluttered in the wind above them, and the rising smoke of the campfires stung his nose with acrid pungency as it was carried off in the breeze.

More riders were coming through the trees, and Pug spurred his horse forward, angling away from the strange device. The six-legged beasts raised their heads and ambled away from the oncoming horses, seeming to move with little more than the minimum effort required to take them out of the path of the riders.

One of the black-robed men ran toward the riders. He stopped and stood off to one side as they sped past. Pug got a glimpse of his face, clean shaven, his lips moving and eyes fixed on something behind the boy. Pug heard a yell and, looking back, saw a rider on the ground, his horse rooted in place, like a statue. Several guards were rushing over to subdue the man when the boy turned away. Once beyond the strange device, he could see a series of large, brightly colored tents off to the left. Ahead, the way was clear.

Pug caught sight of Kulgan and reined his horse to bring himself closer to the magician. Thirty yards to the right, Pug could see other riders. As they dashed away, Kulgan shouted something at the boy that he couldn't make out. The magician pointed at the side of his face, then at Pug, who realized the mage was asking if he was all right. Pug waved his sword and smiled, and the magician smiled back.

Suddenly, about a hundred yards in front, a loud buzzing noise filled the air, and a black-robed man appeared, as if from thin air. Kulgan's horse bore straight for him, but the man had a queer-looking device in his hand that he pointed at the magician.

The air sizzled with energy. Kulgan's horse screamed and fell as if poleaxed. The fat magician was tossed over the horse's head and tucked his shoulder under as he hit the ground. With an amazing display of agility he rolled up onto his feet and bowled over the black-robed man.

Pug pulled up in spite of the order to keep going. He reined his horse around and charged back to find the magician sitting astride the chest of the smaller man, each grasping the left wrist of the other with his right hand. Pug could see that they were locked eye to eye in a contest of wills. Kulgan had explained this strange mental power to Pug before. It was a way in which a magician could bend the will of another to his own. It took great concentration and was very dangerous. Pug leaped from his own mount and rushed over to where the two men were locked in struggle. With the flat of his sword, he struck the black-robed figure on the temple. The man slumped unconscious.

Kulgan staggered to his feet. "Thank you, Pug. I don't think I could have bettered him. I've never encountered such mental strength." Kulgan looked to where his horse lay quivering on the ground. "It's useless." Turning to Pug, he said, "Listen well, for you'll have to carry word to Lord Borric. From the speed that wagon was coming through the rift, I estimate they can bring in several hundred men a day, perhaps a great deal more. Tell the Duke it would be suicide to try to take the machine. Their magicians are too powerful. I don't think we can destroy the machine they use to hold the rift open. If I had time to study it . . . He must call for reinforcements from Krondor, perhaps from the East."

Pug grabbed Kulgan by the arm. "I can't remember all that. We'll ride double."

Kulgan began to protest but was too weak to prevent the boy's pulling him to where his horse stood. Ignoring Kulgan's objections, he bullied his master up into the saddle. Pug hesitated a moment, noting the animal's fatigue, then came to a decision. "With both of us to carry, he'll never make it, Kulgan," he shouted as he struck the animal on the flank. "I'll find another."

Pug scanned the area as the horse bearing Kulgan sped away. A riderless mount was wandering about, less than twenty feet away, but as he approached, the animal bolted. Cursing, Pug turned and was confronted by the sight of the black-robed Tsurani regaining his feet. The man appeared confused and weak, and Pug charged him. Only one thought was in Pug's mind: to capture a prisoner, and, from his appearance, a Tsurani magician in the bargain. Pug took the magician by surprise, knocking him down.

The man scrambled backward in alarm as Pug raised his sword threateningly. The man put forth his hand in what Pug took as a sign of submission, and the boy hesitated. Suddenly a wave of pain passed through him, and he had to fight to keep his feet. He staggered about and through the agony saw a familiar figure riding toward him, shouting his name.

Pug shook his head, and suddenly the pain vanished. Meecham sped toward him, and Pug knew the franklin could carry the Tsurani to the Duke's camp if Pug could keep him from fleeing. So he spun, all pain forgotten, and closed upon the still-supine Tsurani. A look of shock crossed the magician's face when he saw the boy again advancing on him. Pug heard Meecham's voice calling his name from behind but didn't take his eyes from the Tsurani.

Several Tsurani soldiers ran across the meadow, seeking to aid their fallen magician, but Pug stood only a few feet away, and Meecham would reach them in a few more moments.

The magician jumped to his feet and reached into his robe. He pulled out a small device and activated it. A loud humming came from the object. Pug rushed the man, determined to knock the device from his hand, whatever it might be. The device hummed louder, and Pug could hear Meecham again shouting his name as he struck the magician, burying his shoulder in the man's stomach.

Suddenly the world exploded with white and blue lights, and Pug felt himself falling through a rainbow of colors into a pit of darkness.

PUG OPENED HIS eyes. For a moment he struggled to bring them into focus, for everything in his field of vision seemed to be flickering. He then came fully awake and realized it was still night and the flickering came from campfires a short distance from where he lay. He tried to sit up and found his hands tied behind him. A groan sounded next to him. In the dim light he could make out the features of a LaMutian horse soldier lying a few feet away. He was also bound. His face was drawn, and there was a nasty-looking cut running down from his hairline to his cheekbone, all crusted over with dried blood.

Pug's attention was distracted by the sound of voices speaking low, behind him. He rolled over and saw two Tsurani guards in blue armor standing watch. Several more tied prisoners lay about between the boy and the two aliens, who were speaking together in their strange, musical-sounding language. One noticed Pug's movement and said something to the other, who nodded and quickly hurried off.

In a moment he was back with another soldier, this one in red-and-yellow armor, with a large crest on his helm, who ordered the two guards to stand Pug up. He was pulled roughly to his feet, and the newcomer stood before him and took stock. This man was dark-haired and had the uptilted, wide-set eyes that Pug had seen before in the field among the Tsurani dead. His cheekbones were flat, and he had a broad brow, topped by thick dark hair. In the dim firelight, his skin looked nearly golden in color.

Except for their short stature, most of the Tsurani soldiers could pass for citizens of many of the nations of Midkemia, but these golden men, as Pug thought of them, resembled some Keshian traders Pug had seen in Crydee years before, from the distant trading city of Shing Lai.

The officer inspected the boy's clothing. Next he knelt and inspected the boots on Pug's feet. He stood and barked an order at the soldier who had fetched him, who saluted and turned to Pug. He seized the bound boy and led him away, on a winding course through the Tsurani camp.

At the center of the camp, large banners hung from the cross pieces of standards, all set in a circle around a large tent. All bore strange designs, creatures of outlandish configuration, depicted in bold colors. Several had glyphs of an unknown language on them. It was to this place Pug was half pulled, half dragged, through the hundreds of Tsurani soldiers who sat quietly polishing their leather armor and making repairs on weapons. Several watched as he passed, but the camp was free of the usual noise and bustle Pug was used to in the camp of his own army. There was more than just the strange and colorful banners to give this place an otherworld feeling. Pug tried to note the details, so if he could escape and report, he could tell Duke Borric something useful, but he found his senses betrayed by so many unfamiliar images. He didn't know what was important in all he saw.

At the entrance of the large tent, the guard who pulled Pug along was challenged by two others, wearing black-and-orange armor. A quick exchange of words resulted in the tent flap being held aside while Pug was thrust through. He fell forward onto a thick pile of furs and woven mats. From where he lay, Pug could see more banners hanging on the tent walls. The tent was richly fashioned, with silklike hangings and thick rugs and pillows.

Hands roughly pulled him upright, and he could see several men regarding him. All stood dressed in the gaudy armor and crested helms of the Tsurani officers except for two. They sat upon a raised dais covered with cushions. The first wore a simple black robe with cowl pulled back, revealing a thin, pale face and bald pate: a Tsurani magician. The other wore a rich-looking robe of orange with black trim, cut below knees and elbows, so that it gave the look of something worn for comfort. From his wiry, muscled appearance and several visible scars, Pug assumed that this man was a warrior who had put aside his armor for the night.

The man in black said something in a high-pitched, singsong language to the others. None of the other men said anything, but the one in the orange robe nodded. The great tent was lit by a single brazier near where the two robed men sat. The lean, black-robed one sat forward, and the light from the brazier cast upward on his face, giving him a decidedly demonic look. His words came haltingly, and thick with accent.

"I know only . . . little . . . of your speech. You understand?"

Pug nodded, his heart pounding while his mind worked furiously. Kulgan's training was coming into play. First he calmed himself, clearing the fog that had gripped his mind. Then he extended every sense, automatically, taking in every scrap of information available, seeking any useful bit of knowledge that might improve his chances of survival. The soldier nearest the door seemed to be relaxing, his left arm behind his head as he lay back on a pile of cushions, his attention only half focused on the captive. But Pug noticed that his other hand was never more than an inch from the hilt of a wicked-looking dagger at his belt. A brief gleam of light on lacquer revealed the presence of another dagger hilt, half protruding from a pillow at the right elbow of the man in orange.

The man in black said slowly, "Listen, for I tell you something. Then you asked questions. If you lie, you die. Slowly. Understand?" Pug nodded. There was no doubt in his mind.

"This man," said the black-robed one, pointing to the man in the short orange robe, "is a . . . great man. He is . . . high man. He is . . ." The man used a word Pug didn't understand. When Pug shook his head, the magician said, "He family great . . . Minwanabi. He second to . . ." He fumbled for a term, then moved his hand in a circle, as if indicating all the men in the tent, officers from their proud plumes. ". . . man who lead."

Pug nodded and softly said, "Your lord?"

The magician's eyes narrowed, as if he were about to object to Pug's speaking out of turn, but instead he paused, then said, "Yes. Lord of War. It is that one's will that we are here. This one is second to Lord of War." He pointed to the man in orange, who looked on impassively. "You are nothing to this man." It was obvious the man was feeling frustration in his inability to convey what he wished. It was plain this lord was something special by the lights of his own people, and the man translating was trying to impress this upon Pug.

The lord cut the translator off and said several things, then nodded toward Pug. The bald magician bobbed his head in agreement, then turned his attention toward Pug. "You are lord?"

Pug looked startled, then stammered out a negative. The magician nodded, translated, and was given instruction by the lord. He turned back to Pug. "You wear cloth like lord, true?"

Pug nodded. His tunic was of a finer fabric than the homespun of the common soldiers. He tried to explain his position as a member in the Duke's court. After several attempts he resigned himself to the presumption they made of his being some sort of highly placed servant.

The magician picked up a small device and held it out to Pug. Hesitating for a moment, the boy reached out and took it. It was a cube of some crystallike material, with veins of pink running throughout. After a moment in his hand, it took on a glow, softly pink. The man in orange gave an order, and the magician translated. "This lord says, how many men along pass to . . ." He faltered and pointed.

Pug had no idea of where he was, or what direction was being pointed to. "I don't know where I am," he said. "I was unconscious when I was brought here."

The magician sat in thought for a moment, then stood. "That way," he said, pointing at a right angle to the direction he had just indicated, "is tall mountain, larger than others. That way," he moved his hand a little, "in sky, is five fires, like so." His hands traced a pattern. After a moment Pug understood. The man had pointed to where Stone Mountain lay and where the constellation called the Five Jewels hung in the sky. He was in the valley they had raided. The pass indicated was the one used as an escape route.

"I . . . really, I don't know how many."

The magician looked closely at the cube in Pug's hand. It continued to glow in soft pink tones. "Good, you tell truth."

Pug then understood that he held some sort of device that would inform his captives if he tried to deceive them. He felt black despair wash over him. He knew that any survival hopes he entertained were going to involve some manner of betraying his homeland.

The magician asked several questions about the nature of the force outside the valley. When most went unanswered, for Pug had not been privy to meetings on strategy matters, the question changed to a more general nature, about common things in Midkemia, but which seemed to hold a fascination for the Tsurani.

The interview continued for several hours. Pug began to feel faint on several occasions as the pressure of the situation combined with his general exhaustion. He was given a strong drink one of these times, which restored his energy for a while but left him light-headed.

He answered every question. Several times he got around the truth device by telling only some of the information requested, not volunteering anything. On several of these occasions, he could tell both the lord and magician were nettled by their inability to deal with answers that were incomplete or complex. Finally the lord indicated the interview was over, and Pug was dragged outside. The magician followed.

Outside the tent the magician stood before Pug. "My lord says, 'I think this servant' "—he pointed at Pug's chest—" 'he is . . .' " He groped for a word. " 'He is clever.' My lord does not mind clever servants, for they work well. But he thinks you are too clever. He says to tell you to be careful, for you are now slave. Clever slave may live long time. Too clever slave, dies quickly if . . ." Again the pause. Then a broad smile crossed the magician's face. "If he is fortun . . . fortunate. Yes . . . that is the word." He rolled the word around his mouth one more time, as if savoring the taste of it. "Fortunate."

Pug was led back to the holding area and left with

his own thoughts. He looked around and saw that a few other captives were awake. Most looked confused and dispirited. One openly wept. Pug turned his eyes skyward and saw the pink edge along the mountains in the east, heralding the coming dawn.

15

Conflicts

The rain was unceasing.

Huddled near the mouth of the cave, a group of dwarves sat around a small cook fire, the gloom of the day reflected upon their faces. Dolgan puffed upon his pipe, and the others were working on their armor, repairing cuts and breaks in leather, cleaning and oiling metal. A pot of stew simmered on the fire.

Tomas sat at the back of the cave, his sword set across his knees. He looked blankly past the others, his eyes focused on some point far beyond them.

Seven times the dwarves of the Grey Towers had ventured out against the invaders, and seven times they had inflicted heavy losses. But each time it was clear that the Tsurani's numbers were undiminished. Many dwarves were missing now, their lives bought at a dear price to the enemy, but dearer to the families of the Grey Towers. The long-lived dwarves had fewer children, years further apart, than did humans. Each loss diminished dwarvenkind at a much more damaging cost than could have been imagined by the humans.

Each time the dwarves had gathered and attacked through the mines into the valley, Tomas had been in the van. His golden helm would be a signal beacon for the dwarves. His golden broadsword would arc above the fray, then swing down to take its toll from the enemy. In battle the keep boy was transformed into a figure of power, a fighting hero whose presence on the field struck awe and fear into the Tsurani. Had he possessed any doubt about the magical nature of his arms and armor after driving off the wraith, they were dispelled the first time he wore them into battle.

They had gathered thirty fighting dwarves from Caldara and ventured through the mines to an entrance in the south portion of the captured valley. They surprised a Tsurani patrol not far from the mines and slew them. But during the course of the fighting, Tomas had been cut off from the dwarves by three Tsurani warriors. As they bore down on him, their swords raised high overhead, he felt something take hold of him. Darting between two of them, like some maddened acrobat, he had slain both with a single stroke from one side to the other. The third had been taken quickly from behind before he could recover from the sudden move.

After the fray, Tomas had been filled with an elation new to him, and somehow frightening as well. All the way back from the battle, he had felt suffused with an unknown energy.

Each subsequent battle had gained him the same power and skill of arms. But the elation had become something more urgent, and the last two times the visions had begun. Now for the first time the visions were coming unbidden. They were transparent, like an image laid upon another.

He could see the dwarves through it, as well as the forest beyond. But upon them played a scene of people long dead and places vanished from the memories of the living. Halls decked with golden trappings were lit with torches that threw dancing light from crystal set upon tables. Goblets that never knew human touch were raised to lips that curved in unfamiliar smiles. Great lords of some long-dead race supped at banquet before his eyes. Strange they were, yet also familiar. Humanlike, but with elven ears and eyes. Tall like the elvenfolk, but broader of shoulder and thicker of arm. The women were beautiful, but in alien ways.

The dream took shape and substance, more vivid than any he had experienced so far. Tomas strained to hear the faint laughter, the sound of alien music, and the spoken words of these people.

He was ripped from his reverie by Dolgan's voice. "Will you take some food, laddie?" He could answer with only a part of his awareness, as he rose and crossed the space between them to take the offered bowl of meat stew. When his hand touched the bowl, the vision vanished, and he shook his head to clear it.

"Are you all right, Tomas?"

Slowly sitting, Tomas looked at his friend for a moment. "I'm not sure," he said hesitantly. "There is something. I . . . I'm not really sure. Just tired, I guess."

Dolgan looked at the boy. The ravages of battle were showing on his young face. Already he looked less the boy and more the man. But beyond the normal hardening of character expected from battle, something else was occurring in Tomas. Dolgan had not as yet decided if the change was fully for good or ill—or if it could even be considered in those terms. Six months of watching Tomas was not long enough to come to any sort of conclusion.

Since donning the dragon's gift armor, Tomas had become a fighter of legendary capabilities. And the boy . . . no, the young man, was taking on weight, even though food was often scarce. It was as if something were acting to bring him to a growth sufficient to fit the cut of the armor. And his features were gaining a strange cast. His nose had taken on a slightly more angular shape, more finely chiseled than before. His brows had become more arched, his eyes deeper set. He was still Tomas, but Tomas with a slight change in appearance, as if wearing someone else's expression.

Dolgan pulled long on his pipe and looked at the white tabard Tomas wore. Seven times in battle, and free from stain. Dirt, blood, and all other manner of contamination were refused purchase in its fabric. And the device of the golden dragon gleamed as brightly as when they had first found it. So it was also with the shield he wore in battle. Many times struck, still it was free of any scar. The dwarves were circumspect in this matter, for their race had long ago used magic in the fashioning of weapons of power. But this was something else. They would wait and see what it brought before they would judge.

As they finished their meager meal, one of the guards on the edge of camp came into the clearing before the cave. "Someone comes."

The dwarves quickly armed themselves and stood ready. Instead of the strangely armored Tsurani soldiers, a single man dressed in the dark grey cloak and tunic of a Natalese Ranger appeared. He walked directly into the center of the clearing and announced in a voice hoarse from days running through wet forests, "Hail, Dolgan of the Grey Towers."

Dolgan stepped forward. "Hail, Grimsworth of Natal."

The rangers were serving as scouts and runners since the invaders had taken the Free City of Walinor. The man walked into the cave mouth and sat down.

He was given a bowl of stew, and Dolgan asked, "What news?"

"None good, I'm afraid," he said, between mouthfuls of stew. "The invaders hold a hard front from out of the valley, northeast toward LaMut. Walinor has been reinforced with fresh troops from their homeland and stands like a knife between the Free Cities and the Kingdom. They had thrice raided the main camp of the Kingdom's host when I left two weeks ago, probably again since. They harry patrols from Crydee. I am to tell you that it is believed they will start a drive into your area soon."

Dolgan looked perplexed. "Why do the dukes think that? Our lookouts have seen no increase in the aliens' activity in these parts. Every patrol they send out we attack. If anything, they seem to be leaving us alone."

"I am not sure. I heard that the magician Kulgan thinks the Tsurani seek metals from your mines, though why I do not know. In any event, this is what the dukes have said. They think there will be an assault on the mine entrances in the valley. I am to tell you that new Tsurani troops may be coming into the southern end of the valley, for there has been no new major assault in the north, only the small raids.

"Now you must do what you think is best." So saying, he turned his full attention to the stew.

Dolgan thought. "Tell me, Grimsworth, what news of the elvenfolk?"

"Little. Since the aliens have invaded the southern part of the elven forests, we are cut off. The last elven runner came through over a week before I left. At last word, they had stopped the barbarians at the fords of the river Crydee where it passes through the forest.

"There are also rumors of alien creatures fighting with the invaders. But as far as I know, only a few burned out village folk have seen these creatures, so I wouldn't place too much stock in what they say.

"There is one interesting piece of news, though. It seems a patrol from Yabon made an unusually broad sweep to the edge of the Lake of the Sky. On the shore they found what was left of some Tsurani and a band of goblins raiding south from the Northlands. At least we don't have to worry about the northern borders. Perhaps we could arrange for them to battle each other for a while and leave us alone."

"Or take up common cause against us," said Dolgan. "Still, I think that unlikely, as the goblins tend to kill first and negotiate later."

Grimsworth chuckled deeply. "It is somehow meet that these two bloody-handed folk should run across one another."

Dolgan nodded. He hoped Grimsworth correct, but was disquieted by the thought of the Nations of the North—as the dwarves thought of the Northlands—joining the fray.

Grimsworth wiped his mouth with the back of his hand. "I will stay this night only, for if I am to pass safely through their lines, I must move quickly. They step up their patrols to the coast, cutting off Crydee for days at a time. I will spend some time there, then start the long run for the dukes' camp."

"Will you return?" asked Dolgan.

The ranger smiled, his grin showing up brightly against his dark skin. "Perhaps, if the gods are obliging. If not I, then one of my brothers. It might be that you'll see Long Leon, for he was sent to Elvandar and, if he is a'right, may be bound here with missives from the Lady Aglaranna. It would be good to know how the elvenfolk fare." Tomas's head came up from his musing at the mention of the Elf Queen's name.

Dolgan puffed on his pipe and nodded. Grimsworth turned to Tomas and spoke directly to him for the first time. "I bring you a message from Lord Borric, Tomas." It had been Grimsworth who carried the first messages from the dwarves along with the news that Tomas was alive and well. Tomas had wanted to return to the Kingdom forces with Grimsworth, but the Natalese Ranger had refused to have him along, citing his need to travel fast and quietly. Grimsworth continued his message. "The Duke rejoices at your good fortune and your good health. But he sends grave news as well. Your friend Pug fell in the first raid into the Tsurani camp and was taken by them. Lord Borric shares your loss."

Tomas stood without a word and moved deep into the cave. He sat in the rear, for a few moments as still as the rock around him, then a faint trembling started in his shoulders. It grew in severity until he shook violently, teeth chattering as if from bitter cold. Then tears came unbidden to his cheeks, and he felt a hot pain rush up from his bowels to his throat, constricting his chest. Without a sound he gasped for breath, and great silent sobs shook him. As the pain grew near-unbearable, a seed of cold fury formed in the center of his being, pushing upward, displacing the hot pain of grief.

Dolgan, Grimsworth, and the rest looked up when Tomas reentered the light of the fire. "Would you please tell the Duke that I thank him for thinking of me?" he asked the ranger.

Grimsworth nodded. "Yes, I will, lad. I think it would be a'right for you to make the run to Crydee, if you wish to return home. I'm sure Prince Lyam could use your sword."

Tomas thought. It would be good to see home again, but at the keep he would be just another apprentice, even if he did bear arms. They would let him fight if the keep was attacked, but they certainly wouldn't let him participate in raids.

"Thank you, Grimsworth, but I will remain. There is much yet to be done here, and I would be a part of it. I would ask you to give word to my mother and father that I am well enough and think of them." Sitting down, he added, "If it is my destiny to return to Crydee, I shall."

Grimsworth looked hard at Tomas, seemed about to speak, then noticed a slight shake of Dolgan's head. More than any other humans in the West, the Rangers of Natal were sensitive to the ways of the elves and dwarves. Something was occurring here that Dolgan thought best left unexplored for the time being, and Grimsworth would bow before the dwarven chief's wisdom.

As soon as the meal was finished, guards were posted, and the rest made ready for sleep. As the fire died down, Tomas could hear the faint sounds of inhuman music and again saw the shadows dance. Before sleep claimed him, he plainly saw one figure stand apart from the rest, a tall warrior, cruel of face and powerful in countenance, dressed in a white tabard emblazoned with a golden dragon.

TOMAS STOOD WITH his back pressed against the wall of the passage. He smiled, a cruel and terrible smile. His eyes were wide, whites vivid around pale blue irises. His body was nearly rigid as he stood motionless. His fingers clenched and unclenched on the hilt of his sword of white and gold.

Images shimmered before his eyes: tall, graceful people who rode on the backs of dragons and lived in halls deep in the earth. Music could be faintly heard in his mind's ear, and strange tongues. The long-dead race called to him, a mighty race who had fashioned this armor, never meant for human use.

More and more the visions came. He could keep his mind free of them most times, but when he felt the battle lust rise, as it did now, the images took on dimension, color, and sound. He would strain to hear the words. They came faintly, and he could almost understand them.

He shook his head, bringing himself back to the present. He looked around the dark passage, no longer surprised at his ability to see in the dark. He signaled across the intersecting tunnel to Dolgan, who stood quietly waiting in position with his men forty feet away and acknowledged him with a wave. On each side of the large tunnel sixty dwarves waited to spring the trap. They waited for the handful of dwarves who were running before a Tsurani force, leading the enemy into the trap.

The sound of footfalls pounding down the tunnel alerted them. In a moment it was joined by the sounds of clashing arms. Tomas tensed. Several dwarves came into view, moving backward as they fought a rearward action. Passing the side tunnels, the fighting dwarves gave no indication they were aware of their brethren waiting on either side.

As soon as the first Tsurani warriors were past, Tomas cried, "Now!" and leaped forward. Suddenly the tunnel was filled with turning, slashing bodies. The Tsurani were mostly armed with broadswords, ill fitted for close quarters, and the dwarves wielded hand axes and hammers with expertise. Tomas laid about himself, and several bodies fell. The flickering Tsurani torches threw mad, dancing shadows high on the passage walls, creating confusion for the eye.

A shout from the rear of the Tsurani force sounded, and the aliens began to back down the tunnel. Those with shields came to the fore, forming a wall over which the swordsmen could strike. The dwarves were unable to reach far enough to do any damage. Each time a dwarf attacked, the shield wall would stand, and the attacker would be answered by sword blows from behind the shield. In short spurts the enemy backed away.

Tomas moved to the fore, since his reach was long enough to strike at the shield holders. He felled two, but as quickly as each dropped, another took his place. Still the dwarves pressed them and they retreated.

They reached a glory hole, entering it at the lowest level, and the Tsurani rapidly took position in the center of the great cavern, forming a rough circle of shields. The dwarves paused for a moment, then charged the position.

A faint flicker of movement caught Tomas's eye, and he looked up to one of the ledges above. In the darkness of the mine it was impossible to see anything clearly, but a sudden feeling alerted him. "Look to the rear!" he shouted.

Most of the dwarves had broken through the shield wall and were too busy to heed him, but a few close by stopped their attack and looked up. One standing next to Tomas cried, "From above!"

Black shapes came pouring from above, seeming to crawl down the face of the rock. Other, human, shapes came running down the paths from the higher levels. Lights appeared above as Tsurani warriors on the upper levels opened shuttered lamps and lit torches.

Tomas stopped in shock. Directly behind the few surviving Tsurani in the center of the cavern he could see creatures entering from every opening above, like a herd of ants, which they closely resembled. Unlike ants, though, they were upright from the center of their bodies, with humanlike arms bearing weapons. Their faces, insectlike, had large multifaceted eyes but very human-like mouths. They moved with incredible speed, dodging forward to strike at the dwarves, who, surprised though they were, responded without hesitation, and the battle was joined.

The fray increased in intensity, and several times Tomas faced two opponents, Tsurani, or monster, or both. The creatures were obviously intelligent, for they fought in an organized manner, and their inhuman voices could be heard crying out in the Tsurani tongue.

Tomas looked up after dispatching one of the creatures and saw a new influx of warriors from above. "To me! To me!" he shouted, and the dwarves started fighting toward him. When most were close by, Dolgan could be heard shouting, "Back, fall back! They are too many."

The dwarves slowly began to move toward the tunnel they had entered from, with its relative safety. There they could face a smaller number of creatures and Tsurani and, they hoped, lose them in the mines. Seeing the dwarves moving back, the Tsurani and their allies pressed the attack. Tomas saw a large number of the creatures interpose themselves between the dwarves and the escape route. He sprang forward and heard a strange war cry escape from his lips, words he didn't understand. His golden sword flashed, and with a shriek one of the strange creatures fell. Another wielded a broadsword at him, and he caught it on his shield. A lesser being's arm would have been broken, but the blow rang out on the white shield and the creature backed away, then struck again.

Again he blocked it, and with a looping overhand swing struck through its neck, severing head from body. It stiffened for a moment, then collapsed at his feet. He leaped over its fallen body and landed before three startled Tsurani warriors. One held two lanterns and the others were armed. Before the man with the lanterns could drop them, Tomas jumped forward and struck down the other two men. The third died trying to draw his sword.

Letting his shield hang on his arm, Tomas reached down and grabbed a lantern. He turned and saw the dwarves scrambling over the bodies of the fallen creatures he had killed. Several carried wounded comrades. A handful of dwarves, with Dolgan at their head, held their enemies at bay while the others made good their escape. The dwarves who carried wounded hurried past Tomas.

One, who had stayed behind in the tunnel during the fighting, hastened forward when his comrades were obviously in retreat. Instead of weapons he carried two bulging skins filled with liquid.

The rear guard was pressed back toward the escape tunnel, and twice soldiers tried to circle to cut them off. Both times Tomas struck out, and they fell. When Dolgan and his fighters stood atop the bodies of the fallen monsters, Tomas yelled, "Be ready to jump."

He took the two heavy skins from the dwarf. "Now!" he shouted. Dolgan and the others leaped back, and the Tsurani were left standing on the other side of the corpses. Without hesitation, the dwarves sped up the tunnel while Tomas threw the skins at the bodies. They had been carried carefully, for they were fashioned to rupture on impact. Both contained naphtha, which the dwarves had gathered from deep black pools under the mountain. It would burn without a wick, as oil would not.

Tomas raised the lantern and smashed it in the midst of the pools of volatile liquid. The Tsurani, hesitating only briefly, were moving forward as the lantern burst. White heat exploded in the tunnel as the naphtha burst into flame. The dwarves, blinded, could hear the screams of the Tsurani who had been caught. When their vision recovered, they could see a single figure striding down the tunnel. Tomas appeared black, outlined against the near-white flames.

When he reached them, Dolgan said, "They'll be upon us when the flames die."

They quickly made their way through a series of tunnels and headed back toward the exit on the western side of the mountains. After they had traveled a short distance, Dolgan halted the party. He and several others stood still, listening to the silence in the tunnels. One dropped to the floor and placed his ear on the ground, but immediately jumped to his feet. "They come! By the sound, hundreds of them, and the creatures too. They must be mounting a major offensive."

Dolgan took stock. Of the hundred and fifty dwarves who had begun the ambush, only seventy or so stood here, and of these, twelve were injured. It could be hoped that others had escaped through other passages, but for the moment they were all in danger.

Dolgan acted quickly. "We must make for the forest." He started to trot along with the others following behind.

Tomas ran easily, but his mind reeled with images. In the heat of battle they assaulted him, more vivid and clear than before. He could see the bodies of his fallen enemies, yet they looked nothing like the Tsurani. He could taste the blood of the fallen, the magic energies that came with him as he drank from their open wounds in the ceremony of victory. He shook his head to clear the images. What ceremony? he wondered.

Dolgan spoke, and Tomas forced his attention to the dwarf's words. "We must find another stronghold," he said as they ran. "Perhaps it would be best to try for Stone Mountain. Our villages here are safe, but we have no base to fight from, for I think the Tsurani will have control of these mines soon. Those creatures of theirs fight well in the dark, and if they have many of them, they can ferret us out of the deeper passages."

Tomas nodded, unable to speak. He was burning inside, a cold fire of hatred for these Tsurani. They had savaged his homeland and taken his brother in all but name, and now many dwarven friends lay dead under the mountain because of them. His face was grim as he made a silent vow to destroy these invaders, whatever the cost.

THEY MOVED CAUTIOUSLY through the trees, watching for signs of the Tsurani. Three times in six days they had skirmished, and now the dwarves numbered fifty-two. The more seriously wounded had been carried to the relative safety of the high villages, where the Tsurani were unlikely to follow.

Now they approached the southern part of the elven forests. At first they had tried to turn eastward toward the pass, seeking a way toward Stone Mountain. The route was thick with Tsurani camps and patrols, and they had been constantly turned northward. Finally it had been decided to try for Elvandar, where they could find rest from the constant flight.

A scout returned from his position twenty yards ahead and said softly, "A camp, at the ford."

Dolgan considered. The dwarves were not swimmers, and they would need to cross at a ford. It was likely the Tsurani would hold all the fords on this side. They would have to find a place free of guards, if one existed.

Tomas looked around. It was nearly nightfall, and if they were to sneak across the river this close to the Tsurani lines, it would best be done in the dark. Tomas whispered this to Dolgan, who nodded. He signaled the guard to head off to the west of the espied camp, to find a likely looking place to hole up.

After a short wait the guide returned with word of a thicket facing a hollowed rock, where they could wait for nightfall. They hurried to the place and found a boulder of granite extruding from the ground, twelve feet tall, and broadening to a base twenty-five or thirty feet across. When they pulled back the brush, they found a hollow in which they could tightly fit. It was only twenty feet across, but it reached back under the rock shelf for over forty feet, angling down. When they were all safely tucked in, Dolgan observed, "This must have been under the river at one time—see how it is worn smooth on the underside. It is cramped, but we should be safe for a bit."

Tomas barely heard, for he was once again fighting his battle against the images, the waking dreams, as he thought of them. He closed his eyes, and again the visions came, and the faint music.

THE VICTORY HAD been swift, but Ashen-Shugar brooded. Something troubled the Ruler of the Eagles' Reaches. The blood of Algon Kokoon, Tyrant of Wind Valley, was still salty upon his lips, and his consorts were now Ashen-Shugar's. Still there was something lacking.

He studied the moredhel dancers, moving in perfect time with the music for his amusement. That was as it should be. No, the lack was felt deep within Ashen-Shugar.

Alengwan, one whom the elves called their Princess, and his latest favorite, sat on the floor beside his throne, awaiting his pleasure. He barely noticed her lovely face and her supple body, clothed in silken garments that served to accent her beauty rather than conceal it.

"Art thou troubled, master?" she asked faintly, her terror of him as thinly veiled as her body.

He glanced away. She had glimpsed his uncertainty; that earned her death, but he would kill her later. Appetites of the flesh had fled lately, both the pleasure of the bed and that of killing. Now he thought upon his nameless feeling, that phantom emotion so strange within. Ashen-Shugar raised his hand, and the dancers were on the floor, foreheads pressed to the stone. The musicians had ceased playing in midnote, it seemed, and the cavern was silent. With a flickering of his hand he dismissed them, and they fled out of the great hall, past the mighty golden dragon, Shuruga, who patiently awaited his master. . . .

"Tomas," came the voice.

Tomas's eyes opened with a snap. Dolgan had his hand upon the young man's arm. "It is time. Night has fallen. You've been asleep, laddie."

Tomas shook his head to clear it, and the lingering images fled. He felt a churning in his stomach as the last flickering vision of a warrior in white and gold standing over the bloody body of an elven princess vanished.

With the others, he crawled out from under the overhanging rock, and they set out once more toward the river. The forest was silent, even the night birds seemingly cautious about revealing their whereabouts.

They reached the river without incident, save that they had to lie hidden while a patrol of Tsurani passed. They followed the river, with a scout in front. After a few minutes, the scout returned. "A sandbar crosses the river."

Dolgan nodded; the dwarves moved quietly forward and entered the water in single file. Tomas waited with Dolgan while the others crossed. When the last dwarf entered the water, an inquiring shout sounded from farther up the bank. The dwarves froze. Tomas moved quickly forward and surprised a Tsurani guard who was trying to peer through the gloom. The man cried out as he was felled, and shouting erupted a short way off.

Tomas saw lantern light rapidly approaching him, turned, and ran. He found Dolgan waiting on the bank and shouted, "Fly! They are upon us."

Several dwarves stood indecisively as Tomas and Dolgan splashed into the river. The water was cold, moving rapidly over the sandbar. Tomas had to steady himself as he waded through. The water was only waist deep for him, but the dwarves were covered nearly to their chins. They would never be able to fight in the river.

As the first Tsurani guards leaped into the water, Tomas turned to hold them off while the dwarves made good their escape. Two Tsurani attacked, and he struck them both down. Several more jumped into the river, and he had only a brief moment to see to the dwarves. They were almost at the opposite bank, and he caught sight of Dolgan, helpless frustration clearly marked on his face in the Tsurani lamplight.

Tomas struck out again at the Tsurani soldiers. Four or five were trying to surround him, and the best he could manage was to keep them at bay. Each time he tried for a kill, he would leave himself open from a different quarter.

The sound of new voices told him it was only a matter of moments before he would be overwhelmed. He vowed to make them pay dearly and lashed out at one man, splitting his shield and breaking his arm. The man went down with a cry.

Tomas barely caught an answering blow on his shield when a whistling sound sped past his ear, and a

Tsurani guard fell screaming, a long arrow protruding from his chest. The air was at once full of arrows. Several more Tsurani fell, and the rest pulled back. Every soldier in the water died before he could reach the shore.

A voice called out, "Quickly, man. They will answer in kind." As if to demonstrate the truth of the warning, an arrow sped past Tomas's face from the other direction. He hurried toward the safety of the opposite bank. A Tsurani arrow struck him in the helm, and he stumbled. As he righted himself, another took him in the leg. He pitched forward and felt the sandy soil of the riverbank below him. Hands reached down and pulled him unceremoniously along.

A dizzy, swimming sensation swept over him, and he heard a voice say, "They poison their arrows. We must . . ." The rest trailed away into blackness.

TOMAS OPENED HIS eyes. For a moment he had no idea of where he was. He felt light-headed and his mouth was dry. A face loomed over him, and a hand lifted his head as water was placed at his lips. He drank deeply, feeling better afterward. He turned his head a little and saw two men sitting close by. For a moment he feared he had been captured, but then he saw that these men wore dark green leather tunics.

"You have been very ill," said the one who had given him water. Tomas then realized these men were elves.

"Dolgan?" he croaked.

"The dwarves have been taken to council with our mistress. We could not chance moving you, for fear of the poison. The outworlders have a venom unknown to us, which kills rapidly. We treat it as best we can, but those wounded die as often as not."

He felt his strength returning slowly. "How long?"

"Three days. You have hovered near death since we fished you from the river. We carried you as far as we dared."

Tomas looked around and saw that he had been undressed and was lying under a shelter fashioned from tree branches, a blanket over him. He smelled food cooking over a fire and saw the pot the savory aroma came from. His host noticed and signaled for a bowl to be brought over.

Tomas sat up, and his head swam for a moment. He was given a large piece of bread and used it in place of a spoon. The food was delicious, and every bite seemed to fill him with increasing strength. As he ate, he took stock of the others sitting nearby. The two silent elves regarded him with blank expressions. Only the speaker showed any signs of hospitality.

Tomas looked at him and said, "What of the enemy?"

The elf smiled. "The outworlders still fear to cross the river. Here our magic is stronger, and they find themselves lost and confused. No outworlder has reached our shore and returned to the other side."

Tomas nodded. When he finished eating, he felt surprisingly well. He tried to stand and found he was only a little shaky. After a few steps, he could feel the strength returning to his limbs, and that his leg was already healed. He spent a few minutes stretching and working out the stiffness of three days sleeping on the ground, then dressed.

"You're Prince Calin. I remember you from the Duke's court."

Calin smiled in return. "And I you, Tomas of Crydee, though you have changed much in a year's time. These others are Galain and Algavins. If you feel up to it, we can rejoin your friends at the court of the Queen."

Tomas smiled. "Let's go."

They broke camp and set out. At first they moved slowly, giving Tomas plenty of time to gain his wind, but after a while it was evident he was remarkably fit in light of his recent brush with death.

Soon the four figures were running through the trees. Tomas, in spite of his armor, kept pace. His hosts glanced questioningly at each other.

They ran most of the afternoon before stopping. Tomas looked around the forest and said, "What a wonderful place."

Galain said, "Most of your race would disagree, man. They find the forest frightening, full of strange shapes and fearful sounds."

Tomas laughed. "Most men lack imagination, or possess too much. The forest is quiet and peaceful. It is the most peaceful place I think I have known."

The elves said nothing, but a look of mild surprise crossed Calin's face. "We had best continue, if we are to reach Elvandar before dark."

As night fell, they reached a giant clearing. Tomas stopped and stood rooted by the sight before him. Across the clearing a huge city of trees rose upward. Gigantic trees, dwarfing any oaks imagined, stood together. They were linked by gracefully arching bridges of branches, flat across the tops, on which elves could be seen crossing from bole to bole. Tomas looked up and saw the trunks rise until they were lost in a sea of leaves and branches. The leaves were deep green, but here and there a tree with golden, silver, or even white foliage could be seen, sparkling with lights. A soft glow permeated the entire area, and Tomas wondered if it ever became truly dark here.

Calin placed his hand on Tomas's shoulder and simply said, "Elvandar."

They hurried across the clearing, and Tomas could see the elven tree city was even larger than he had first imagined. It spread away on all sides and must have been over a mile across. Tomas felt a thrill of wonder at this magic place, a singular exaltation.

They reached a stairway, carved into the side of a tree, that wound its way upward, into the branches. They started up the steps, and Tomas again felt a sensation of joy, as if the mad frenzy that filled him during a battle had a harmonious aspect of gentler nature.

Upward they climbed, and as they passed the large branches that served as roadways for the elves, Tomas could see elven men and women on all sides. Many of the men wore fighting leather like his guides, but many others wore long, graceful robes or tunics of bright and rich colors. The women were all beautiful, with their hair worn long and down, unlike the ladies of the Duke's court. Many had jewels woven into their tresses that sparkled when they passed. All were tall and graceful.

They reached a gigantic branch and left the stairs. Calin began to warn him about not looking down, for he knew humans had difficulty on the high pathways, but Tomas stood near the edge, looking down with no sign of discomfort or vertigo.

"This is a marvelous place," he said. The three elves exchanged questioning glances, but no words were spoken.

They set off again, and when they came to an intersection of branches, the two elves turned off the path, leaving Tomas and Calin to travel alone. Deeper and deeper they moved, Tomas as surefooted on the branch road as the elf, until they reached a large opening. Here a circle of trees formed a central court for the

Elf Queen. A hundred branches met and merged into a huge platform. Aglaranna was sitting upon a wooden throne, surrounded by her court. A single human, in the grey of a Natalese Ranger, stood near the Queen, his black skin gleaming in the night glow. He was the tallest man Tomas had ever seen, and the young man from Crydee knew this must be Long Leon, the ranger Grimsworth had spoken of.

Calin led Tomas into the center of the clearing and presented him to Queen Aglaranna. She showed slight surprise as she saw the figure of the young man in white and gold, but quickly composed her features. In her rich voice she welcomed Tomas to Elvandar, and bade him stay as long as he wished.

The court adjourned, and Dolgan came to where Tomas stood. "Well, laddie, I am glad to see you recovered. It was an undecided issue when we left you. I hated to do so, but I think you understand. I was in need of getting word on the fighting near Stone Mountain."

Tomas nodded. "I understand. What news?"

Dolgan shook his head. "Bad, I fear. We are cut off from our brethren. I think we will be staying with the elvenfolk for a while, and I have little love for these heights."

Tomas broke into open laughter at that. Dolgan smiled, for it was the first time since the boy had donned the dragon's armor he had heard the sound.

16

Raid

Wagons groaned under heavy loads.

Whips cracked and wheels creaked as lumbering oxen pulled their burdens down the road toward the beach. Arutha, Fannon, and Lyam rode before soldiers protecting the wagons traveling between the castle and the shore. Behind the wagons a ragged crowd of townspeople followed. Many carried bundles or pulled carts, following the Duke's sons toward the waiting ships.

They turned down the road that split off from the town road, and Arutha's gaze swept over the signs of destruction. The once-thriving town of Crydee was now covered in an acrid blue haze. The sounds of hammering and sawing rang through the morning air as workmen labored to repair what they could of the damage.

The Tsurani had raided at sundown two days before, racing through the town, overwhelming the few guards at their posts before an alarm was raised by terrified women, old men, and children. The aliens had run riot through the town, not pausing until they reached dockside, where they had fired three ships, heavily damaging two. The damaged ships were already limping toward Carse, while the undamaged ships in the harbor had moved down the coast to their present location, north of Sailor's Grief.

The Tsurani had put most of the buildings near the quay to the torch, but while heavily damaged, they were reparable. The fire had spread into the heart of town, resulting in the heaviest loss there. The Hall of the Craftmasters, the two inns, and dozens of lesser buildings were now only smoldering ruins. Blackened timbers, cracked roof tiles, and scorched stones marked their locations. Fully one third of Crydee had burned before the fire had been brought under control.

Arutha had stood on the wall, watching the hellish glow reflected on the clouds above the town as the flames spread. Then at first light he had led the garrison out, finding the Tsurani already vanished into the forests.

Arutha still chafed at the memory. Fannon had advised Lyam not to allow the garrison out until dawn—fearing it was a ruse to get the castle gates open or to lure the garrison into the woods where a larger force waited in ambush—and Lyam had acceded to the old Swordmaster's request. Arutha was sure he could have prevented much of the damage had he been allowed to rout the Tsurani at once.

As he rode down the coast road, Arutha was lost in thought. Orders arrived the day before instructing Lyam to leave Crydee. The Duke's aide-de-camp had been killed, and with the war beginning its third year this spring, he wished Lyam to join him at his camp in Yabon. For reasons Arutha didn't understand, Duke Borric had not given command to him as expected;

instead Borric had named the Swordmaster garrison commander. But, thought the younger Prince, at least Fannon will be less ready to order me about without Lyam's backing. He shook his head slightly in an attempt to dislodge his irritation. He loved his brother, but wished Lyam had shown more willingness to assert himself. Since the beginning of the war, Lyam had commanded in Crydee, but it had been Fannon making all the decisions. Now Fannon had the office as well as the influence.

"Thoughtful, brother?"

Lyam had pulled his own horse up and was now beside Arutha, who shook his head and smiled faintly. "Just envious of you."

Lyam smiled his warmest at his younger brother. "I know you wish to be going, but Father's orders were clear. You're needed here."

"How needed can I be where every suggestion I make has been ignored?"

Lyam's expression was conciliatory. "You're still disturbed by Father's decision to name Fannon commander of the garrison."

Arutha looked hard at his brother. "I am now the age you were when Father named you commander at Crydee. Father was full commander and second Knight-General in the West at my age, only four years shy of being named King's Warden of the West. Grandfather trusted him enough to give him full command."

"Father's not Grandfather, Arutha. Remember, Grandfather grew up in a time when we were still warring in Crydee, pacifying newly conquered lands. He grew up in war. Father did not. He learned all his warcraft down in the Vale of Dreams, against Kesh, not defending his own home as Grandfather had. Times change."

"How they change, brother," Arutha said dryly.

"Grandfather, like his father before him, would not have sat behind safe walls. In the two years since the war began, we have not mounted one major offensive against the Tsurani. We cannot continue letting them dictate the course of the war, or surely they will prevail."

Lyam regarded his brother with concern mirrored in his eyes. "Arutha, I know you are restless to harry the enemy, but Fannon is right in saying we dare not risk the garrison. We must hold here and protect what we have."

Arutha cast a quick glance at the ragged townspeople behind. "I'll tell those who follow how well they're protected."

Lyam saw the bitterness in Arutha. "I know you blame me, brother. Had I taken your advice, rather than Fannon's . . ."

Arutha lost his harsh manner. "It is not your doing," he conceded. "Old Fannon is simply cautious. He also is of the opinion a soldier's worth is measured by the grey in his beard. I am still only the Duke's boy. I fear my opinions from now on will receive short shrift."

"Curb thy impatience, youngster," he said in mock seriousness. "Perhaps between your boldness and Fannon's caution, a safe middle course will be followed." Lyam laughed.

Arutha had always found his brother's laughter infectious and couldn't repress a grin. "Perhaps, Lyam," he said with a laugh.

They came to the beach where longboats waited to haul the refugees out to the ships anchored offshore. The captains would not return to the quayside until they were assured their ships would not again come under attack, so the fleeing townspeople were forced to walk through the surf to board the boats. Men and women began to wade to the boats, bundles of belongings and small children held safely overhead. Older children swam playfully, turning the event into sport. There were many tearful partings, for most of the townsmen were remaining to rebuild their burned homes and serve as levies in the dukes' army. The women, children, and old men who were leaving would be carried down the coast to Tulan, the southernmost town in the Duchy, as yet untroubled by either the Tsurani or the rampaging Dark Brothers in the Green Heart.

Lyam and Arutha dismounted, and a soldier took their horses. The brothers watched as soldiers carefully loaded crates of messenger pigeons onto the sole long-boat pulled up on shore. The birds would be shipped through the Straits of Darkness to the dukes' camp. Pigeons trained to fly to the camp were now on their way to Crydee, and with their arrival some of the responsibility for carrying information to and from the dukes' camp would be lifted from Martin Longbow's trackers and the Natalese Rangers. This was the first year mature pigeons raised in the camp—necessary for them to develop the homing instinct—were available.

Soon the baggage and refugees were loaded, and it was time for Lyam to depart. Fannon bid him a stiff and formal farewell, but it was apparent from his controlled manner that the old Swordmaster felt concern for the Duke's older son. With no family of his own, Fannon had been something of an uncle to the boys when they were growing, personally instructing them in swordsmanship, the maintenance of armor, and the theories of warcraft. He maintained his formal pose, but both brothers could see the genuine affection there.

When Fannon left, the brothers embraced. Lyam said, "Take care of Fannon." Arutha looked surprised. Lyam grinned and said, "I'd not care to think what would happen here should Father pass you over once more and name Algon commander of the garrison."

Arutha groaned, then laughed with his brother. As Horsemaster, Algon was technically second-in-command behind Fannon. All in the castle shared genuine affection for the man, and deep respect for his vast knowledge of horses, but everyone conceded his general lack of knowledge about anything *besides* horses. After two years of warfare, he still resisted the idea the invaders came from another world, an attitude that caused Tully no end of irritation.

Lyam moved into the water, where two sailors held the longboat for him. Over his shoulder he shouted, "And take care of our sister, Arutha."

Arutha said he would. Lyam leaped into the longboat, next to the precious pigeons, and the boat was pushed away from shore. Arutha watched as the boat dwindled into the distance.

Arutha walked slowly back to where a soldier held his mount. He paused to stare down the beach. To the south, the high bluffs reared, dominated by Sailor's Grief, which stood upthrust against the morning sky. Arutha silently cursed the day the Tsurani ship crashed against those rocks.

CARLINE STOOD ATOP the southern tower of the keep, watching the horizon, gathering her cloak around her against the sea breeze. She had stayed at the castle, bidding Lyam good-bye earlier, not wishing to ride to the beach. She preferred that her fears not becloud Lyam's happiness at joining their father in the dukes' camp. Many times over the last two years she had chided herself over such feelings. Her men were soldiers, all trained since boyhood for war. But since word had reached Crydee of Pug's capture, she had remained afraid for them.

A feminine clearing of the throat made Carline turn. Lady Glynis, the Princess's companion for the last four years, smiled slightly and indicated with a nod of her head the newcomer who appeared at the trapdoor leading down into the tower.

Roland emerged from the doorway in the floor. The last two years had added to his growth, and now he stood as tall as Arutha. He was still thin, but his boyish features were resolving into those of a man.

He bowed and said, "Highness."

Carline acknowledged the greeting with a nod and gestured that Lady Glynis should leave them alone. Glynis fled down the stairway into the tower.

Softly Carline said, "You did not ride to the beach with Lyam?"

"No, Highness."

"You spoke with him before he left?"

Roland turned his gaze to the far horizon. "Yes, Highness, though I must confess to a foul humor at his going."

Carline nodded understanding. "Because you have to stay."

He spoke with bitterness, "Yes, Highness."

Carline said gently, "Why so formal, Roland?"

Roland looked at the Princess, seventeen years old just this last Midsummer's Day. No longer a petulant little girl given to outbursts of temper, she was changing into a beautiful young woman of thoughtful introspection. Few in the castle were unaware of the many nights' sobbing that issued from Carline's suite after news of Pug had reached the castle. After nearly a week of solitude, Carline had emerged a changed person, more subdued, less willful. There was little outward to show how Carline felt, but Roland knew she carried a scar.

After a moment of silence, Roland said, "Highness, when . . ." He halted, then said, "It is of no consequence."

Carline placed her hand upon his arm. "Roland, whatever else, we have always been friends."

"It pleases me to think that is true."

"Then tell me, why has a wall grown between us?"

Roland sighed, and there was none of his usual roguish humor in his answer. "If there has, Carline, it is not of my fashioning."

A spark of the girl's former self sprang into being, and with a temperamental edge to her voice she said, "Am I, then, the architect of this estrangement?"

Anger erupted in Roland's voice. "Aye, Carline!" He ran his hand through his wavy brown hair and said, "Do you remember the day I fought with Pug? The very day before he left."

At the mention of Pug's name she tensed. Stiffly she said, "Yes, I remember."

"Well, it was a silly thing, a boys' thing, that fight. I told him should he ever cause you any hurt, I'd thrash him. Did he tell you that?"

Moisture came unbidden to her eyes. Softly she said, "No, he never mentioned it."

Roland looked at the beautiful face he had loved for years and said, "At least then I knew my rival." He lowered his voice, the anger slipping away. "I like to think then, near the end, he and I were fast friends. Still, I vowed I'd never stop my attempts to change your heart."

Shivering, Carline drew her cloak about her, though the day was not that cool. She felt conflicting emotions within, confusing emotions. Trembling, she said, "Why did you stop, Roland?"

Sudden harsh anger burst within Roland. For the first time he lost his mask of wit and manners before the Princess. "Because I can't contend with a memory,

Carline." Her eyes opened wide, and tears welled up and ran down her cheeks. "Another man of flesh I can face, but this shade from the past I cannot grapple with." Hot anger exploded into words. "He's dead, Carline. I wish it were not so; he was my friend and I miss him, but I've let him go. Pug is dead. Until you grant that this is true, you are living with a false hope."

She put her hand to her mouth, palm outward, her eyes regarding him in wordless denial. Abruptly she turned and fled down the stairs.

Alone, Roland leaned his elbows on the cold stones of the tower wall. Holding his head in his hands, he said, "Oh, what a fool I have become!"

"PATROL!" SHOUTED THE guard from the wall of the castle. Arutha and Roland turned from where they watched soldiers giving instructions to levies from the outlying villages.

They reached the gate, and the patrol came riding slowly in, a dozen dirty, weary riders, with Martin Longbow and two other trackers walking beside. Arutha greeted the Huntmaster and then said, "What have you there?"

He indicated the three men in short grey robes who stood between the line of horsemen. "Prisoners, Highness," answered the hunter, leaning on his bow.

Arutha dismissed the tired riders as other guards came to take position around the prisoners. Arutha walked to where they waited, and when he came within touching distance, all three fell to their knees, putting their foreheads to the dirt.

Arutha raised his eyebrows in surprise at the display. "I have never seen such as these."

Longbow nodded in agreement. "They wear no armor, and they didn't give fight or run when we found them in the woods. They did as you see now, only then they babbled like fishwives."

Arutha said to Roland, "Fetch Father Tully. He may be able to make something of their tongue." Roland hurried off to find the priest. Longbow dismissed his two trackers, who headed for the kitchen. A guard was dispatched to find Swordmaster Fannon and inform him of the captives.

A few minutes later Roland returned with Father Tully. The old priest of Astalon was dressed in a deep blue, nearly black, robe, and upon catching a glimpse of him, the three prisoners set up a babble of whispers. When Tully glanced in their direction, they fell completely silent. Arutha looked at Longbow in surprise.

Tully said, "What have we here?"

"Prisoners," said Arutha. "As you are the only man here to have had some dealings with their language, I thought you might get something out of them."

"I remember little from my mind contact with the Tsurani Xomich, but I can try." The priest spoke a few halting words, which resulted in a confusion as all three prisoners spoke at once. The centermost snapped at his companions, who fell silent. He was short, as were the others, but powerfully built. His hair was brown, and his skin swarthy, but his eyes were a startling green. He spoke slowly to Tully, his manner somehow less deferential than his companions'.

Tully shook his head. "I can't be certain, but I think he wishes to know if I am a Great One of this world."

"Great One?" asked Arutha.

"The dying soldier was in awe of the man aboard ship he called 'Great One.' I think it was a title rather than a specific individual. Perhaps Kulgan was correct in his suspicion these people hold their magicians or priests in awe."

"Who are these men?" asked the Prince.

Tully spoke to them again in halting words. The man in the center spoke slowly, but after a moment Tully cut him off with a wave of his hand. To Arutha he said, "These are slaves."

"Slaves?" Until now there had been no contact with any Tsurani except warriors. It was something of a revelation to find they practiced slavery. While not unknown in the Kingdom, slavery was not widespread and was limited to convicted felons. Along the Far Coast, it was nearly nonexistent. Arutha found the idea strange and repugnant. Men might be born to low station, but even the lowliest serf had rights the nobility were obligated to respect and protect. Slaves were property. With a sudden disgust, Arutha said, "Tell them to get up, for mercy's sake."

Tully spoke and the men slowly rose, the two on the flanks looking about like frightened children. The other stood calmly, eyes only slightly downcast. Again Tully questioned the man, finding his understanding of their language returning.

The centermost man spoke at length, and when he was done Tully said, "They were assigned to work in the enclaves near the river. They say their camp was overrun by the forest people—he refers to the elves, I think—and the short ones."

"Dwarves, no doubt," added Longbow with a grin.

Tully threw him a withering look. The rangy forester simply continued to smile. Martin was one of the few young men of the castle never intimidated by the old cleric, even before becoming one of the Duke's staff.

"As I was saying," continued the priest, "the elves

and dwarves overran their camp. They fled, fearing they would be killed. They wandered in the woods for days until the patrol picked them up this morning."

Arutha said, "This fellow in the center seems a bit different from the others. Ask why this is so."

Tully spoke slowly to the man, who answered with little inflection in his tones. When he was done, Tully spoke with some surprise. "He says his name is Tchakachakalla. He was once a Tsurani officer!"

Arutha said, "This may prove most fortunate. If he'll cooperate, we may finally learn some things about the enemy."

Swordmaster Fannon appeared from the keep and hurried to where Arutha was questioning the prisoners. The commander of the Crydee garrison said, "What have you here?"

Arutha explained as much as he knew about the prisoners, and when he was finished, Fannon said, "Good, continue with the questioning."

Arutha said to Tully, "Ask him how he came to be a slave."

Without sign of embarrassment, Tchakachakalla told his story. When he was done, Tully stood shaking his head. "He was a Strike Leader. It may take some time to puzzle out what his rank was equivalent to in our armies, but I gather he was at least a Knight-Lieutenant. He says his men broke in one of the early battles and his 'house' lost much honor. He wasn't given permission to take his own life by someone he calls the Warchief. Instead he was made a slave to expiate the shame of his command."

Roland whistled low. "His men fled and he was held responsible."

Longbow said, "There's been more than one earl who's bollixed a command and found himself ordered by his Duke to serve with one of the Border Barons along the Northern Marches."

Tully shot Martin and Roland a black look. "If you are finished?" He addressed Arutha and Fannon: "From what he said, it is clear he was stripped of everything. He may prove of use to us."

Fannon said, "This may be some trick. I don't like his looks."

The man's head came up, and he fixed Fannon with a narrow gaze. Martin's mouth fell open. "By Kilian! I think he understands what you said."

Fannon stood directly before Tchakachakalla. "Do you understand me?"

"Little, master." His accent was thick, and he spoke with a slow singsong tone alien to the King's Tongue. "Many Kingdom slaves on Kelewan. Know little King's Tongue."

Fannon said, "Why didn't you speak before?"

Again without any show of emotion, he answered, "Not ordered. Slave obey. Not . . ." He turned to Tully and spoke a few words.

Tully said, "He says it isn't a slave's place to show initiative."

Arutha said, "Tully, do you think he can be trusted?"

"I don't know. His story is strange, but they are a strange people by our standards. My mind contact with the dying soldier showed me much I still don't understand." Tully spoke to the man.

To Arutha the Tsurani said, "Tchakachakalla tell." Fighting for words, he said, "I Wedewayo. My house, family. My clan Hunzan. Old, much honor. Now slave. No house, no clan, no Tsuranuanni. No honor. Slave obey."

Arutha said, "I think I understand. If you go back to the Tsurani, what would happen to you?"

Tchakachakalla said, "Be slave, maybe. Be killed, maybe. All same."

"And if you stay here?"

"Be slave, be killed?" He shrugged, showing little concern.

Arutha said, slowly, "We keep no slaves. What would you do if we set you free?"

A flicker of some emotion passed over the slave's face, and he turned to Tully and spoke rapidly. Tully translated. "He says such a thing is not possible on his world. He asks if you can do such a thing."

Arutha nodded. Tchakachakalla pointed to his companions. "They work. They always slaves."

"And you?" said Arutha.

Tchakachakalla looked hard at the Prince and spoke to Tully, never taking his eyes from Arutha. Tully said, "He's recounting his lineage. He says he is Tchakachakalla, Strike Leader of the Wedewayo, of the Hunzan Clan. His father was a Force Leader, and his great-grandfather Warchief of the Hunzan Clan. He has fought honorably, and only once has he failed in his duty. Now he is only a slave, with no family, no clan, no nation, and no honor. He asks if you mean to give him back his honor."

Arutha said, "If the Tsurani come, what will you do?"

Tchakachakalla indicated his companions. "These men slaves. Tsurani come, they do nothing. Wait. Go with . . ." He and Tully exchanged brief remarks and Tully supplied him with the word he wished. ". . . victors. They go with victors." He looked at Arutha, and his eyes came alive. "You make Tchakachakalla free. Tchakachakalla be your man, lord. Your honor is Tchakachakalla's honor. Give life if you say. Fight Tsurani if you say."

Fannon spoke. "Likely story that. More's the odds he's a spy."

The barrel-chested Tsurani looked hard at Fannon, then with a sudden motion stepped before the Swordmaster, and before anyone could react, pulled Fannon's knife from his belt.

Longbow had his own knife out an instant later, as Arutha's sword was clearing its scabbard. Roland and the other soldiers were only a moment behind. The Tsurani made no threatening gesture, but simply flipped the knife, reversing it and handing it to Fannon hilt first. "Master think Tchakachakalla enemy? Master kill. Give warrior's death, return honor."

Arutha returned his sword to his scabbard and took the knife from Tchakachakalla's hand. Returning the knife to Fannon, he said, "No, we will not kill you." To Tully he said, "I think this man may prove useful. For now, my inclination is to believe him."

Fannon looked less than pleased. "He may be a very clever spy, but you're right. There's no harm if we keep a close watch on him. Father Tully, why don't you take these men to soldiers' commons and see what you can learn from them. I'll be along shortly."

Tully spoke to the three slaves and indicated they should follow. The two timid slaves moved at once, but Tchakachakalla bent his knee before Arutha. He spoke rapidly in the Tsurani tongue; Tully translated. "He's just demanded you either kill him or make him your man. He asked how a man can be free with no house, clan, or honor. On his world such men are called grey warriors and have no honor."

Arutha said, "Our ways are not your ways. Here a man can be free with no family or clan and still have honor."

Tchakachakalla bent his head slightly while listening, then nodded. He rose and said, "Tchakachakalla understand." Then with a grin he added, "Soon, I be your man. Good lord need good warrior. Tchakachakalla good warrior."

"Tully, take them along, and find out how much Tchak . . . Tchakal . . ." Arutha laughed. "I can't pronounce that mouthful." To the slave he said, "If you're to serve here, you need a Kingdom name."

The slave looked about and then gave a curt nod.

Longbow said, "Call him Charles. It's as close a name as I can imagine."

Arutha said, "As good a name as any. From now on, you will be called Charles."

The newly named slave said, "Tcharles?" He shrugged and nodded. Without another word he fell in beside Father Tully, who led the slaves toward the soldiers' commons.

Roland said, "What do you make of that?" as the three slaves vanished around the corner.

Fannon said, "Time will tell if we've been duped."

Longbow laughed. "I'll keep an eye on Charles, Swordmaster. He's a tough little fellow. He traveled at a good pace when we brought them in. Maybe I'll turn him into a tracker."

Arutha interrupted. "It will be some time before I'll be comfortable letting him outside the castle walls."

Fannon let the matter drop. To Longbow he said, "Where did you find them?"

"To the north, along the Clearbrook branch of the river. We were following the signs of a large party of warriors heading for the coast."

Fannon considered this. "Gardan leads another patrol near there. Perhaps he'll catch sight of them and we'll find out what the bastards are up to this year." Without another word he walked back toward the keep.

Martin laughed; Arutha was surprised to hear him. "What in this strikes you as funny, Huntmaster?"

Martin shook his head. "A little thing, Highness. It's the Swordmaster himself. He'll not speak of it to anyone, but I wager he would give all he owns to have your father back in command. He's a good soldier, but he dislikes the responsibility."

Arutha regarded the retreating back of the Swordmaster, then said, "I think you are right, Martin." His voice carried a thoughtful note. "I have been at odds with Fannon so much of late, I lost sight of the fact he never requested this commission."

Lowering his voice, Martin said, "A suggestion, Arutha."

Arutha nodded. Martin pointed to Fannon. "Should anything happen to Fannon, name another Swordmaster quickly; do not wait for your father's consent. For if you wait, Algon will assume command, and he is a fool."

Arutha stiffened at the Huntmaster's presumption, while Roland tried to silence Martin with a warning look. Arutha coldly said, "I thought you a friend of the Horsemaster."

Martin smiled, his eyes hinting at strange humor. "Aye, I am, as are all in the castle. But anyone you ask will tell you the same: take his horses away, and Algon is an indifferent thinker."

Nettled by Martin's manner, Arutha said, "And who should take his place? The Huntmaster?"

Martin laughed, a sound of such open, clear amusement at the thought, Arutha found himself less angry at his suggestion.

"I?" said the Huntmaster. "Heaven forfend, Highness. I am a simple hunter, no more. No, should the need come, name Gardan. He is by far the most able soldier in Crydee."

Arutha knew Martin was correct, but gave in to impatience. "Enough. Fannon is well, and I trust will remain so."

Martin nodded. "May the gods preserve him . . . and us all. Please excuse me, it was but a passing concern. Now, with Your Highness's leave, I've not had a hot meal in a week."

Arutha indicated he could leave, and Martin walked away toward the kitchen. Roland said, "He is wrong on one account, Arutha."

Arutha stood with his arms folded across his chest, watching Longbow as he vanished around the corner. "What is that, Roland?"

"That man is much more than the simple hunter he pretends."

Arutha was silent for a moment. "He is. Something about Martin Longbow has always made me uneasy, though I have never found fault with him."

Roland laughed, and Arutha said, "Now something strikes you as funny, Roland?"

Roland shrugged. "Only that many think you and he are much alike."

Arutha turned a black gaze upon Roland, who shook his head. "It's often said we take offense most in what we see of ourselves in others. It's true, Arutha. You both have that same cutting edge to your humor, almost mocking, and neither of you suffers foolishness." Roland's voice became serious. "There's no mystery to it, I should think. You're a great deal like your father, and with Martin having no family, it follows he would pattern himself after the Duke."

Arutha became thoughtful. "Perhaps you're right. But something else troubles me about that man." He left the thought unfinished and turned toward the keep.

Roland fell into step beside the thoughtful Prince and wondered if he had overstepped himself.

THE NIGHT THUNDERED. Ragged bolts of lightning shattered the darkness as clouds rolled in from the west. Roland stood on the southern tower watching the display. Since dinner his mood had been as dark as the western sky. The day had not gone well. First he had felt troubled by his conversation with Arutha by the gate. Then Carline had treated him at dinner with the same stony silence he had endured since their meeting on this very tower two weeks earlier. Carline had seemed more subdued than usual, but Roland felt a stab of anger at himself each time he chanced a glance in her direction. Roland could still see the pain in the Princess's eyes. "What a witless fool I am," he said aloud.

"Not a fool, Roland."

Carline was standing a few paces away, looking toward the coming storm. She clutched a shawl around her shoulders, though the air was temperate. The thunder had masked her footfalls, and Roland said, "It is a poor night to be upon the tower, my lady."

She came to stand beside him and said, "Will it rain? These hot nights bring thunder and lightning, but usually little rain."

"It will rain. Where are your ladies?"

She indicated the tower door. "Upon the stairs. They fear the lightning, and besides, I wished to speak with you alone."

Roland said nothing, and Carline remained silent for a time. The night was sundered with violent displays of energy tearing across the heavens, followed by cracking booms of thunder. "When I was young," she said at last, "Father used to say on nights such as this the gods were sporting in the sky."

Roland looked at her face, illuminated by the single lantern hanging on the wall. "My father told me they made war."

She smiled. "Roland, you spoke rightly on the day Lyam left. I have been lost in my own grief, unable to see the truth. Pug would have been the first to tell me that nothing is forever. That living in the past is foolish and robs us of the future." She lowered her head a little. "Perhaps it has something to do with Father. When Mother died, he never fully recovered. I was very young, but I can still remember how he was. He used to laugh a great deal before she died. He was more like Lyam then. After . . . well, he became more like Arutha. He'd laugh, but there'd be a hard edge to it, a bitterness."

"As if somehow mocking?"

She nodded thoughtfully. "Yes, mocking. Why did you say that?"

"Something I noticed . . . something I pointed out to your brother today. About Martin Longbow."

She sighed. "Yes, I understand. Longbow is also like that."

Softly Roland said, "Nevertheless, you did not come to speak of your brother or Martin."

"No, I came to tell you how sorry I am for the way I've acted. I've been angry with you for two weeks, but I'd no right. You only said what was true. I've treated you badly."

Roland was surprised. "You've not treated me badly, Carline. I acted the boor."

"No, you have done nothing but be a friend to me, Roland. You told me the truth, not what I wanted to hear. It must have been hard . . . considering how you feel." She looked out at the approaching storm. "When I first heard of Pug's capture, I thought the world ended."

Trying to be understanding, Roland quoted, " 'The first love is the difficult love.' "

Carline smiled at the aphorism. "That is what they say. And with you?"

Roland mustered a carefree stance. "So it seems, Princess."

She placed her hand upon his arm. "Neither of us is free to feel other than as we do, Roland."

His smile became sadder. "That is the truth, Carline."

"Will you always be my good friend?"

There was a genuine note of concern in her voice that touched the young Squire. She was trying to put matters right between them, but without the guile she'd used when younger. Her honest attempt turned aside any frustration he felt at her not returning his affections fully. "I will, Carline. I'll always be your good friend."

She came into his arms and he held her close, her head against his chest. Softly she said, "Father Tully says that some loves come unbidden like winds from the sea, and others grow from the seeds of friendship."

"I will hope for such a harvest, Carline. But should it not come, still I will remain your good friend."

They stood quietly together for a time, comforting each other for different causes, but sharing a tenderness each had been denied for two years. Each of them was lost in the comfort of the other's nearness, and neither saw what the lightning flashes revealed for brief instants. On the horizon, beating for the harbor, came a ship.

THE WINDS WHIPPED the banners on the palisades of the castle walls as rain began to fall. As water gathered in small pools, the lanterns cast yellow reflections up-

ward off the puddles to give an otherworldly look to
the two men standing on the wall.

A flash of lightning illuminated the sea, and a
soldier said, "There! Highness, did you see? Three
points south of the Guardian Rocks." He extended his
arm, pointing the way.

Arutha peered into the gloom, his brow furrowed
in concentration. "I can see nothing in this darkness.
It's blacker than a Guis-wan priest's soul out there."
The soldier absently made a protective sign at the mention of the killer god. "Any signal from the beacon
tower?"

"None, Highness. Not by beacon, nor by messenger."

Another flash of lightning illuminated the night,
and Arutha saw the ship outlined in the distance. He
swore. "It will need the beacon at Longpoint to reach
the harbor safely." Without another word, he ran down
the stairs leading to the courtyard. Near the gate he
instructed a soldier to get his horse and two riders to
accompany him. As he stood there waiting, the rain
passed, leaving the night with a clean but warm, moist
feeling. A few minutes later, Fannon appeared from the
direction of the soldiers' commons. "What's this? Riding?"

Arutha said, "A ship makes for the harbor, and
there is no beacon at Longpoint."

As a groom brought Arutha's horse, followed by
two mounted soldiers, Fannon said, "You'd best be off,
then. And tell those stone-crowned layabouts at the
lighthouse I'll have words for them when they finish
duty."

Arutha had expected an argument from Fannon
and felt relieved there would be none. He mounted and
the gates were opened. They rode through and headed
down the road toward town.

The brief rain had made the night rich with fresh odors: the flowers along the road, and the scent of salt from the sea, soon masked by the acrid odor of burned wood from the charred remnants of gutted buildings as they neared town.

They sped past the quiet town, taking the road along the harbor. A pair of guards stationed by the quayside hastily saluted when they saw the Prince fly past. The shuttered buildings near the docks bore mute testimony to those who had fled after the raid.

They left the town and rode out to the lighthouse, following a bend in the road. Beyond the town they gained their first glimpse of the lighthouse, upon a natural island of rock joined to the mainland by a long causeway of stone, topped by a compacted dirt road. The horses' hooves beat a dull tattoo upon the dirt as they approached the tall tower. A lightning flash lit up the sky, and the three riders could see the ship running under full sail toward the harbor.

Shouting to the others, Arutha said, "They'll pile upon the rocks without a beacon."

One of the guards shouted back, "Look, Highness. Someone signals!"

They reined in and saw figures near the base of the tower. A man dressed in black stood swinging a shuttered lantern back and forth. It could be clearly seen by those on the ship, but not by anyone upon the castle walls. In the dim light, Arutha saw the still forms of Crydee soldiers lying on the ground. Four men, also attired in black with head coverings that masked their faces, ran toward the horsemen. Three drew long swords from back scabbards, while the fourth aimed a bow. The soldier to Arutha's right cried out as an arrow struck him in the chest. Arutha charged his horse among the three who closed, knocking over two while

his sword slashed out, raking the third across the face.
The man fell without a sound.

The Prince wheeled around and saw his other
companion also engaged, hacking downward at the
bowman. More men in black dashed from within the
tower, rushing forward silently.

Arutha's horse screamed. He could see an arrow
protruding from its neck. As it collapsed beneath him,
he freed his feet from the stirrups and lifted his left leg
over the dying animal's neck, jumping free as it struck
the ground. He hit and rolled, coming to his feet before
a short figure in black with a long sword held high
overhead with both hands. The long blade flashed
down, and Arutha jumped to his left, thrusting with his
own sword. He took the man in the chest, then yanked
his sword free. Like the others before, the man in black
fell without uttering a cry.

Another flash of lightning showed men rushing
toward Arutha from the tower. Arutha turned to order
the remaining rider back to warn the castle, but the
shouted command died aborning when he saw the man
pulled from his saddle by swarming figures in black.
Arutha dodged a blow from the first man to reach him
and ran past three startled figures. He smashed at the
face of a fourth man with his sword hilt, trying to
knock the man aside. His only thought was to open a
pathway so he might flee to warn the castle. The struck
man reeled back, and Arutha attempted to jump past
him. The falling man reached out with one hand,
catching Arutha's leg as he sprang.

Arutha struck hard stone and felt hands frantically
grab at his right foot. He kicked backward with his left
and took the man in the throat with his boot. The
sound of the man's windpipe being crushed was followed by a convulsion of movement.

Arutha came to his feet as another attacker

reached him, others only a step behind. Arutha sprang backward, trying to gain some distance. His boot heel caught on a rock, and suddenly the world tilted crazily. He found himself suspended in space for an instant, then his shoulders met rock as he bounced down the side of the causeway. He hit several more rocks, and icy water closed over him.

The shock of the water kept him from passing into unconsciousness. Dazed, he reflexively held his breath, but had little wind. Without thinking, he pushed upward and broke the surface with a loud, ragged gasp. Still groggy, he nevertheless possessed enough wits to duck below the surface when arrows struck the water near him. He couldn't see a thing in the murky darkness of the harbor, but clung to the rocks, pulling himself along more than swimming. He moved back toward the tower end of the causeway, hoping the raiders would think him headed in the other direction.

He quietly surfaced and blinked the salt water from his eyes. Peering around the shelter of a large rock, he saw black figures searching the darkness of the water. Arutha moved quietly, nestling himself into the rocks. Bruised muscles and joints made him wince as he moved, but nothing seemed broken.

Another flash of lightning lit the harbor. Arutha could see the ship speeding safely into Crydee harbor. It was a trader, but rigged for speed and outfitted for war. Whoever piloted the ship was a mad genius, for he cleared the rocks by a scant margin, heading straight for the quayside around the bend of the causeway. Arutha could see men in the rigging, frantically reefing in sails. Upon the deck a company of black-clad warriors stood with weapons ready.

Arutha turned his attention to the men on the causeway and saw one motion silently to the others. They ran off in the direction of the town. Ignoring the pain in his body, Arutha pulled himself up, negotiating the slippery rocks to regain the dirt road of the causeway. Staggering a bit, he came to his feet and looked off toward the town. There was still no sign of trouble, but he knew it would erupt shortly.

Arutha half staggered, half ran to the lighthouse tower and forced himself to climb the stairs. Twice he came close to blacking out, but he reached the top of the tower. He saw the lookout lying dead near the signal fire. The oil-soaked wood was protected from the elements by a hood that hung suspended over it. The cold wind blew through the open windows on all sides of the building.

Arutha found the dead sentry's pouch and removed flint, steel, and tinder. He opened the small door in the side of the metal hood, using his body to shield the wood from the wind. The second spark he fired caught in the wood, and a small flame sprang into existence. It quickly spread, and when it was burning fully, Arutha pulled on the chain hoist that elevated the hood. With an audible whoosh, the flames sprang fully to the ceiling as the wind struck the fire.

Against one wall stood a jar of powder mixed by Kulgan against such an emergency. Arutha fought down dizziness as he bent again to pull the knife from the dead sentry's belt. He used it to pry the lid off the jar and then tossed the entire contents into the fire.

Instantly the flames turned bright crimson, a warning beacon none could confuse with a normal light. Arutha turned toward the castle, standing away from the window so as not to block the light. Brighter and brighter the flames burned as Arutha found his mind going vague again. For a long moment there was silence in the night, then suddenly an alarm sounded from the castle. Arutha felt relief. The red beacon was the signal for reavers in the harbor, and the castle garrison had been well drilled to meet such raids. Fannon might be cautious with chasing Tsurani raiders into the woods at night, but a pirate ship in his harbor was something he would not hesitate to answer.

Arutha staggered down the stairs, stopping to support himself at the door. His entire body hurt, and he was nearly overcome by dizziness. He drew a deep breath and headed for the town. When he came to where his dead horse lay, he looked about for his sword, then remembered he had carried it with him into the harbor. He stumbled to where one of his riders lay, next to a black-clad bowman. Arutha bent down to pick up the fallen soldier's sword, nearly blacking out as he stood. He held himself erect for a moment, fearing he might lose consciousness if he moved, and waited as the ringing in his head subsided. He slowly reached up and touched his head. One particularly sore spot, with an angry lump forming, told him he had struck his head hard at least once as he fell down the causeway. His fingers came away sticky with clotting blood.

Arutha began to walk to town, and as he moved, the ringing in his head resumed. For a time he staggered, then he tried to force himself to run, but after only three wobbly strides he resumed his clumsy walk. He hurried as much as he could, rounding the bend in the road to come in sight of town. He heard faint sounds of fighting. In the distance he could see the red light of fires springing heavenward as buildings were put to the torch. Screams of men and women sounded strangely remote and muted to Arutha's ears.

He forced himself into a trot, and as he closed upon the town, anticipation of fighting forced away much of the fog clouding his mind. He turned along the harborside; with the dockside buildings burning, it was bright as day, but no one was in sight. Against the quayside the raiders' ship rested, a gangway leading down to the dock. Arutha approached quietly, fearing guards had been left to protect it. When he reached the gangway, all was quiet. The sounds of fighting were distant, as if all the raiders had attacked deeply into the town.

As he began to move away, a voice cried out from the ship, "Gods of mercy! Is anyone there?" The voice was deep and powerful, but with a controlled note of terror.

Arutha hurried up the gangway, sword ready. He stopped when he reached the top. From the forward hatch cover he could see fire glowing brightly below-decks. He looked about: everywhere his eyes traveled he saw seamen lying dead in their own blood. From the rear of the ship the voice cried out, "You, man. If you're a godsfearing man of the Kingdom, come help me."

Arutha made his way amid the carnage and found a man sitting against the starboard rail. He was large, broad-shouldered, and barrel-chested. He could have been any age between twenty and forty. He held the side of an ample stomach with his right hand, blood seeping through his fingers. Curly dark hair swept back from a receding hairline, and he wore his black beard cut short. He managed a weak smile as he pointed to a black-clothed figure lying nearby. "The bastards killed my crew and fired my ship. That one made the mistake of not killing me with the first blow." He pointed at the section of a fallen yard pinning his legs. "I can't manage to budge that damned yard and hold my guts in at the same time. If you'd lift it a bit, I think I can pull myself free."

Arutha saw the problem: the man was pinned down at the short end of the yard, tangled in a mass of ropes and blocks. He gripped the long end and heaved upward, moving it only a few inches, but enough. With a half grunt, half groan, the wounded man pulled his legs out. "I don't think my legs are broken, lad. Give me a hand up and we'll see."

Arutha gave him a hand and nearly lost his footing pulling the bulky seaman to his feet. "Here, now," said the wounded man. "You're not in much of a fighting trim yourself, are you?"

"I'll be all right," said Arutha, steadying the man while fighting off an attack of nausea.

The seaman leaned upon Arutha. "We'd better hurry, then. The fire is spreading." With Arutha's help, he negotiated the gangway. When they reached the quayside, gasping for breath, the heat was becoming intense. The wounded seaman gasped, "Keep going!"

Arutha nodded and slung the man's arm over his shoulder. They set off down the quay, staggering like a pair of drunken sailors on the town.

Suddenly there came a roar, and both men were slammed to the ground. Arutha shook his dazed head and turned over. Behind him a great tower of flames leaped skyward. The ship was a faintly seen black silhouette in the heart of the blinding yellow-and-white column of fire. Waves of heat washed over them, as if they were standing at the door of a giant oven.

Arutha managed to croak, "What was that?"

His companion gave out with an equally feeble reply: "Two hundred barrels of Quegan fire oil."

Arutha spoke in disbelief. "You didn't say anything about fire oil back aboard ship."

"I didn't want you getting excited. You looked half-gone already. I figured we'd either get clear or we wouldn't."

Arutha tried to rise, but fell back. Suddenly he felt very comfortable resting on the cool stone of the quay. He saw the fire begin to dim before his eyes, then all went dark.

. . .

ARUTHA OPENED HIS eyes and saw blurred shapes over him. He blinked and the images cleared. Carline hovered over his sleeping pallet, looking anxiously on as Father Tully examined him. Behind Carline, Fannon watched, and next to him stood an unfamiliar man. Then Arutha remembered him. "The man from the ship."

The man grinned. "Amos Trask, lately master of the *Sidonie* until those bast—begging the Princess's pardon—those cursed land rats put her to the torch. Standing here thanks to Your Highness."

Tully interrupted. "How do you feel?"

Arutha sat up, finding his body a mass of dull aches. Carline placed cushions behind her brother. "Battered, but I'll survive." His head swam a little. "I'm a bit dizzy."

Tully looked down his nose at Arutha's head. "Small wonder. You took a nasty crack. You may find yourself occasionally dizzy for a few days, but I don't think it is serious."

Arutha looked at the Swordmaster. "How long?"

Fannon said, "A patrol brought you in last night. It's morning."

"The raid?"

Fannon shook his head sadly. "The town's gutted. We managed to kill them all, but there's not a whole building left standing in Crydee. The fishing village at the south end of the harbor is untouched, but otherwise everything was lost."

Carline fussed around near Arutha, tucking in covers and fluffing his cushions. "You should rest."

He said, "Right now, I'm hungry."

She brought over a bowl of hot broth. He submitted to the light broth in place of solid food, but refused to let her spoon-feed him. Between mouthfuls he said, "Tell me what happened."

Fannon looked disturbed. "It was the Tsurani."

Arutha's hand stopped, his spoon poised halfway between bowl and mouth. "Tsurani? I thought they were reavers, from the Sunset Islands."

"At first so did we, but after talking to Captain Trask here, and the Tsurani slaves who are with us, we've pieced together a picture of what's happened."

Tully picked up the narrative. "From the slaves' story, these men were specially chosen. They called it a death raid. They were selected to enter the town, destroy as much as possible, then die without fleeing. They burned the ship as much as a symbol of their commitment as to deny it to us. I gather from what they say it's considered something of a great honor."

Arutha looked at Amos Trask. "How is it they managed to seize your ship, Captain?"

"Ah, that is a bitter story, Highness." He leaned to his right a little, and Arutha remembered his wound. "How is your side?"

Trask grinned, his dark eyes merry. "A messy wound, but not a serious one. The good father put it right as new, Highness."

Tully made a derisive sound. "That man should be in bed. He is more seriously injured than you. He would not leave until he saw you were all right."

Trask ignored the comment. "I've had worse. We once had a fight with a Quegan war galley turned rogue pirate and—well, that's another story. You asked about my ship." He limped over closer to Arutha's pallet. "We were outward bound from Palanque with a load of weapons and fire oil. Considering the situation here, I thought to find a ready market. We braved the straits early in the season, stealing the march on other ships, or so we hoped.

"But while we made the passage early, we paid the price. A monstrous storm blew up from the south, and we were driven for a week. When it was over, we headed east, striking for the coast. I thought we'd have no trouble plotting our position from landmarks. When we sighted land, not one aboard recognized a single feature. As none of us had ever been north of Crydee, we judged rightly we had gone farther than we had thought.

"We coasted by day, heaving to at night, for I'd not risk unknown shoals and reefs. On the third night the Tsurani came swimming out from shore like a pod of dolphins. Dived right under the ship, and came up on both sides. By the time I was awake from the commotion on deck, there was a full half dozen of the bast—begging the Princess's pardon—them Tsurani swarming over me. It took them only minutes to take my ship." His shoulders sagged a bit. "It's a hard thing to lose one's ship, Highness."

He grimaced and Tully stood, making Trask sit on the stool next to Arutha. Trask continued his story. "We couldn't understand what they said; their tongue is more suited for monkeys than men—I myself speak five civilized languages and can do 'talk-see' in a dozen more. But as I was saying, we couldn't understand their gibberish, but they made their intentions clear enough.

"They pored over my charts." He grimaced in remembering. "I purchased them legal and aboveboard from a retired captain down in Durbin. Fifty years of experience in those charts, there were, from here in Crydee to the farthest eastern shores of the Keshian Confederacy, and they were tossing them around my cabin like so much old canvas until they found the ones they wanted. They had some sailors among them, for as soon as they recognized the charts, they made their plans known to me.

"Curse me for a freshwater fisherman, but we had heaved to only a few miles north of the headlands above your lighthouse. If we'd sailed a little longer, we would have been safely in Crydee harbor two days ago."

Arutha and the others said nothing. Trask continued, "They went through my cargo holds and started tossing things overboard, no matter what. Over five hundred fine Quegan broadswords, over the side. Pikes, lances, longbows, everything—I guess to keep any of it from reaching Crydee somehow. They didn't know what to do with the Quegan fire oil—the barrels would've needed a dock hoist to get them out of the hold—so they left it alone. But they made sure there wasn't a weapon aboard that wasn't in their hands. Then some of the little land rats got dressed up in those black rags, swam ashore, and started down the coast toward the lighthouse. While they were going, the rest were praying, on their knees rocking back and forth, except for a few with bows watching my crew. Then all of a sudden, about three hours after sundown, they're up and kicking my men around, pointing to the harbor on the map.

"We set sail and headed down the coast. The rest you know. I guess they judged you would not expect an attack from seaward."

Fannon said, "They judged correctly. Since their last raid we've patrolled the forests heavily. They couldn't get within a day's march of Crydee without our knowing. This way they caught us unawares." The old Swordmaster sounded tired and bitter. "Now the town is destroyed, and we've a courtyard filled with terrified townsmen."

Trask also sounded bitter. "They put most of their men ashore quickly, but left two dozen to slaughter my men." An expression of pain crossed his face. "They were a hard lot, my lads, but on the whole good enough men. We didn't know what was happening until the first of my boys began to fall from the spars with Tsurani arrows in them, waving like little flags as they hit the water. We thought they were going to have us take them out again. My boys put up a struggle then, you can bet. But they didn't start soon enough. Marlinspikes and belayin' pins can't stand up to men with swords and bows."

Trask sighed deeply, the pain on his face as much from his story as from his injury. "Thirty-five men. Dock rats, cutthroats, and murderers all, but they were *my* crew. I was the only one allowed to go killing them. I cracked the skull of the first Tsurani who came at me, took his sword, and killed another. But the third one knocked it from my hand and ran me through." He barked a short, harsh-sounding laugh. "I broke his neck. I passed out for a time. They must have thought me dead. The next I knew, the fires were going and I started yelling. Then I saw you come up the gangway."

Arutha said, "You're a bold man, Amos Trask."

A look of deep pain crossed the large man's face. "Not bold enough to keep my ship, Highness. Now I'm nothing more than another beached sailor."

Tully said, "Enough for now. Arutha, you need rest." He put his hand on Amos Trask's shoulder. "Captain, you'd do well to follow his example. Your wound is more serious than you admit. I'll take you to a room where you can rest."

The captain rose, and Arutha said, "Captain Trask."

"Yes, Highness?"

"We have need of good men here in Crydee."

A glimmer of humor crossed the seaman's face. "I thank you, Highness. Without a ship, though, I don't know what use I could be."

Arutha said, "Between Fannon and myself, we'll find enough to keep you busy."

The man bowed slightly, restricted by his wounded side. He left with Tully. Carline kissed Arutha on the cheek, saying, "Rest now." She took away the broth and was escorted from the room by Fannon. Arutha was asleep before the door closed.

17

Attack

*C*arline lunged.

She thrust the point of her sword in a low line, aiming a killing blow for the stomach. Roland barely avoided the thrust by a strong beat of his blade, knocking hers out of line. He sprang back and for a moment was off balance. Carline saw the hesitation and lunged forward again.

Roland laughed as he suddenly leaped away, knocking her blade aside once more, then stepping outside her guard. Quickly tossing his sword from right hand to left, he reached out and caught her sword arm at the wrist, pulling her, in turn, off balance. He swung her about, stepping behind her. He wrapped his left arm around her waist, being careful of his sword edge, and pulled her tightly to him. She struggled against his superior strength, but while he was behind her, she could inflict no more than angry curses on him. "It was a trick! A loathsome trick," she spat.

She kicked helplessly as he laughed. "Don't overextend yourself that way, even when it looks like a clean kill. You've good speed, but you press too much. Learn patience. Wait for a clear opening, then attack. You overbalance that much and you're dead." He gave her a quick kiss on the cheek and pushed her unceremoniously away.

Carline stumbled forward, regained her balance, and turned. "Rogue! Make free with the royal person, will you?" She advanced on him, sword at the ready, slowly circling to the left. With her father away, Carline had pestered Arutha into allowing Roland to teach her swordplay. Her final argument had been, "What do I do if the Tsurani enter the castle? Attack them with embroidery needles?" Arutha had relented more from tiring of the constant nagging than from any conviction she would have to use the weapon.

Suddenly Carline launched a furious attack in high line, forcing Roland to retreat across the small court behind the keep. He found himself backed against a low wall and waited. She lunged again, and he nimbly stepped aside, the padded point of her rapier striking the wall an instant after he vacated the spot. He jumped past her, playfully swatting her across the rump with the flat of his blade as he took up position behind her. "And don't lose your temper, or you'll lose your head as well."

"Oh!" she cried, spinning to face him. Her expression was caught halfway between anger and amusement. "You monster!"

Roland stood ready, a look of mock contrition on his face. She measured the distance between them and began to advance slowly. She was wearing tight-fitting men's trousers—to the despair of Lady Marna—and a man's tunic cinched at the waist by her sword belt. In the last year her figure had filled out, and the snug costume bordered on the scandalous. Now eighteen years of age, there was nothing about Carline that was girlish. The specially crafted boots she wore, black, ankle-high, carefully beat upon the ground as she stepped the distance between them, and her long, lustrous dark hair was tied into a single braid that swung freely about her shoulders.

Roland welcomed these sessions with her. They had rediscovered much of their former playful fun in them, and Roland held the guarded hope her feelings for him might be developing into something more than friendship. In the year since Lyam's departure they had practiced together, or had gone riding when it was considered safe, near the castle. The time with her had nourished a sense of companionship between them he had previously been unable to bring about. While more serious than before, she had regained her spark and sense of humor.

Roland stood lost in reflection a moment. The little-girl Princess, spoiled and indulged, was gone. The child grown petulant and demanding from the boredom of her role was now a thing of the past. In her stead was a young woman of strong mind and will, tempered by harsh lessons.

Roland blinked and found himself with her sword's point at his throat. He playfully threw down his own weapon and said, "Lady, I yield!"

She laughed. "What were you daydreaming about, Roland?"

He gently pushed aside the tip of her sword. "I was remembering how distraught Lady Marna became when you first went riding in those clothes and came back all dirty and very unladylike."

Carline smiled at the memory. "I thought she would stay abed for a week." She put up her sword. "I wish I could find reasons to wear these clothes more often. They are so comfortable."

Roland nodded, grinning widely. "And very fetching." He made a display of leering at the way they hugged Carline's curvaceous body. "Though I expect that is due to the wearer."

She tilted her nose upward in a show of disapproval. "You are a rogue and a flatterer, sir. And a lecher."

With a chuckle, he picked up his sword. "I think that is enough for today, Carline. I could endure only one defeat this afternoon. Another, and I shall have to quit the castle in shame."

Her eyes widened as she drew her weapon, and he saw the dig had struck home. "Oh! Shamed by a mere girl, is it?" she said, advancing with her sword ready.

Laughing, he brought his own to the ready, backing away. "Now, Lady. This is most unseemly."

Leveling her sword, she fixed him with an angry gaze. "I have Lady Marna to be concerned with my manners, Roland. I don't need a buffoon like you to instruct me."

"Buffoon!" he cried, leaping forward. She caught his blade and riposted, nearly striking. He took the thrust on his blade, sliding his own along hers until they stood *corps a corps*. He seized her sword wrist with his free hand and smiled. "You never want to find yourself in this position." She struggled to free herself, but he held her fast. "Unless the Tsurani start sending their women after us, most anyone you fight will prove stronger than yourself, and from here have his way with you." So saying, he jerked her closer and kissed her.

She pulled back, an expression of surprise on her face. Suddenly the sword fell from her fingers and she grabbed him. Pulling him with surprising force, she kissed him with a passion that answered his.

When he pulled back, she regarded him with a look of surprise mixed with longing. A smile spread on her face, as her eyes sparkled. Quietly she said, "Roland, I—"

Alarm sounded throughout the castle, and the shout of "Attack!" could be heard from the walls on the other side of the keep.

Roland swore softly and stepped back. "Of all the gods-cursed, ill-timed luck." He headed into the hall that led to the main courtyard. With a grin he turned and said, "Remember what you were going to say, Lady." His humor vanished when he saw her following after, sword in hand. "Where are you going?" he asked, all lightness absent from his voice.

Defiantly she said, "To the walls. I'm not going to sit in the cellars any longer."

Firmly he said, "No. You've never experienced true fighting. As a sport, you do well enough with a sword, but I'll not risk your freezing the first time you smell blood. You'll go to the cellars with the other ladies and lock yourself safely in."

Roland had never spoken to her in this manner before, and she was amazed. Always before he had been the teasing rogue, or the gentle friend. Now he was suddenly a different man. She began to protest, but he cut her off. Taking her by the arm, half leading, half dragging her, he walked in the direction of the cellar doors. "Roland!" she cried. "Let me go!"

Quietly he said, "You'll go where you were ordered. And I'll go where I'm ordered. There will be no argument."

She pulled against his hold, but the grip was unyielding. "Roland! Take your hand from me this instant!" she commanded.

He continued to ignore her protests and dragged her along the hall. At the cellar door a startled guard watched the approaching pair. Roland came to a stop and propelled Carline toward the door with a less than gentle shove. Her eyes wide in outrage, Carline turned to the guard. "Arrest him! At once! He"—anger elevated her voice to a most unladylike volume—"laid *hands* on me!"

The guard hesitated, looking from one to another, then tentatively began to step toward the Squire. Roland raised a warning finger and pointed it at the guard, less than an inch from his nose. "You will see Her Highness to her appointed place of safety. You will ignore her objections, and should she try to leave, you will restrain her. Do you understand?" His voice left no doubt he was deadly serious.

The guard nodded, but still was reluctant to place hands upon the Princess. Without taking his eyes from the soldier's face, Roland pushed Carline gently toward the door and said, "If I find she has left the cellar before the signal that all is safe has sounded, I will ensure that the Prince and the Swordmaster are informed you allowed the Princess to step in harm's way."

That was enough for the guard. He might not understand who had right of rank between Princess and Squire during attacks, but there was no doubt at all in his mind of what the Swordmaster would do to him under such circumstances. He turned to the cellar door before Carline could return and said, "Highness, this way," forcing her down the steps.

Carline backed down the stairs, fuming. Roland closed the door behind them. She turned after another backward step, then haughtily walked down. When they reached the room set aside for the women of the castle and town in time of attack, Carline found the other women waiting, huddled together, terrified.

The guard hazarded an apologetic salute and said, "Begging the Princess's pardon, but the Squire seemed most determined."

Suddenly Carline's scowl vanished, and in its place a small smile appeared. She said, "Yes, he did, didn't he?"

RIDERS SPED INTO the courtyard, the massive gates swinging shut behind. Arutha watched from the walls and turned to Fannon.

Fannon said, "Of all the worst possible luck."

Arutha said, "Luck has nothing to do with it. The Tsurani would certainly not be attacking when the advantage is ours." Everything looked peaceful, except the burned town standing as a constant reminder of the war. But he also knew that beyond the town, in the forests to the north and northeast, an army was gathering. And by all reports as many as two thousand more Tsurani were on the march toward Crydee.

"Get back inside, you rat-bitten, motherless dog."

Arutha looked downward into the courtyard and saw Amos Trask kicking at the panic-stricken figure of a fisherman, who dashed back into one of the many rude huts erected inside the wall of the castle to house the last of the displaced townsfolk who had not gone south. Most of the townspeople had shipped for Carse after the death raid, but a few had stayed the winter. Except for some fishermen who were to stay to help feed the garrison, the rest were due to be shipped south to Carse and Tulan this spring. But the first ships of the coming season were not due in for weeks. Amos had been put in charge of these folk since his ship had been burned the year before, keeping them from getting underfoot and from causing too much disruption in the castle. The former sea captain had proved a gift during the first weeks after the burning of the town. Amos had the necessary talent for command and kept the tough, ill-mannered, and individualistic fisherfolk in line. Arutha judged him a braggart, a liar, and most probably, a pirate, but generally likable.

Gardan came up the stairs from the court, Roland following. Gardan saluted the Prince and Swordmaster, and said, "That's the last patrol, sir."

"Then we must only wait for Longbow," said Fannon.

Gardan shook his head. "Not one patrol caught sight of him, sir."

"That's because Longbow is undoubtedly closer to the Tsurani than any soldier of sound judgment is likely to get," ventured Arutha. "How soon, do you think, before the rest of the Tsurani arrive?"

Pointing to the northeast, Gardan said, "Less than an hour, if they push straight through." He looked skyward. "They have less than four hours of light. We might expect one attack before nightfall. Most likely they'll take position, rest their men, and attack at first light."

Arutha glanced at Roland. "Are the women safe?"

Roland grinned. "All, though your sister might have a few harsh words about me when this is over."

Arutha returned the grin. "When this is over, I'll deal with it." He looked around. "Now we wait."

Swordmaster Fannon's eyes swept the deceptively peaceful scene before them. There was a note of worry mixed with determination in his voice as he said, "Yes, now we wait."

MARTIN RAISED HIS hand. His three trackers stopped moving. The woods were quiet as far as they could tell, but the three knew Martin possessed more acute senses than they. After a moment he moved along, scouting ahead.

For ten hours, since before dawn, they had been marking the Tsurani line of march. As well as he could judge, the Tsurani had been repulsed once more from Elvandar at the fords along the river Crydee and were now turning their attention to the castle at Crydee. For three years the Tsurani had been occupied along four fronts: against the Duke's armies in the east, the elves and dwarves along the north, the hold at Crydee in the west, and the Brotherhood of the Dark Path and the goblins in the south.

The trackers had stayed close to the Tsurani trail-breakers, occasionally too close. Twice they had been forced to run from attackers, Tsurani warriors tenaciously willing to follow the Huntmaster of Crydee and his men. Once they had been overtaken, and Martin had lost one of his men in the fighting.

Martin gave the raucous caw of a crow, and in a few minutes his three remaining trackers joined him. One, a long-faced young man named Garret, said, "They move far west of where I thought they would turn."

Longbow considered. "Aye, it seems they may be planning to encircle all of the lands around the castle. Or they may simply wish to strike from an unexpected quarter." Then with a wry grin he said, "But most likely, they simply sweep the area before the attack begins, ensuring they have no harrying forces at their backs."

Another tracker said, "Surely they know we mark their passing."

Longbow's crooked grin widened. "No doubt. I judge them unconcerned with our comings and goings." He shook his head. "These Tsurani are an arrogant crew." Pointing, he said, "Garret will come with me. You two will make straight for the castle. Inform the Swordmaster some two thousand more Tsurani march on Crydee." Without a word the two men set off at a brisk pace toward the castle.

To his remaining companion he spoke lightly. "Come, let us return to the advancing enemy and see what he is about now."

Garret shook his head. "Your cheerful manner does little to ease my worrisome mind, Huntmaster."

Turning back the way they had come, Longbow said, "One time is much like another to death. She comes when she will. So why give over your mind to worry?"

"Aye," said Garret, his long face showing he was unconvinced. "Why, indeed? It's not death arriving when she will that worries me; it's your inviting her to visit that gets me shivering."

Martin laughed softly. He motioned for Garret to follow. They set off at a trot, covering ground with long, loose strides. The forest was bright with sunlight, but between the thick boles were many dark places wherein a watchful enemy could lurk. Garret left it to Longbow's able judgment whether these hiding places were safe to pass. Then, as one, both men stopped in their tracks at the sound of movement ahead. Noiselessly they melted into a shadowy thicket. A minute passed slowly with neither man speaking. Then a faint whispering came to them, the words unclear.

Into their field of vision came two figures, moving cautiously along a north-south path that intersected the one Martin followed. Both were dressed in dark grey cloaks, with bows held ready. They stopped, and one kneeled down to study the signs left by Longbow and his trackers. He pointed down the trail and spoke to his companion, who nodded and returned the way they had come.

Longbow heard Garret hiss as he drew in his breath. Peering around the area was a tracker of the Brotherhood of the Dark Path. After a moment of searching he followed his companion.

Garret began to stir and Martin gripped his arm. "Not yet," Longbow whispered.

Garret whispered back, "What are they doing this far north?"

Martin shook his head. "They've slipped in behind our patrols along the foothills. We've grown lax in the south, Garret. We never thought they'd move north this far west of the mountains." He waited silently for a moment, then whispered, "Perhaps they tire of the Green Heart and are trying for the Northlands to join their brothers."

Garret started to speak, but stopped when another Dark Brother entered the spot vacated by the others a moment before. He looked around, then raised his hand in signal. Other figures appeared along the trail intersecting the one Martin's men had traveled. In ones, twos, and threes, Dark Brothers crossed the path, disappearing into the trees.

Garret sat holding his breath. He could hear Martin counting faintly as the figures crossed their field of vision: ". . . ten, twelve, fifteen, sixteen, eighteen . . ."

The stream of dark-cloaked figures continued, seemingly unending to Garret. ". . . thirty-one, thirty-two, thirty-four . . ."

As the crossing continued, larger numbers of Brothers appeared, and after a time Martin whispered, "There are more than a hundred."

Still they came, some now carrying bundles on their backs and shoulders. Many wore the dark grey mountain cloaks, but others were dressed in green, brown, or black clothing. Garret leaned close to Martin and whispered, "You are right. It is a migration north. I mark over two hundred."

Martin nodded. "And still they come."

For many more minutes the Dark Brothers

crossed the trail, until the flood of warriors was replaced by ragged-looking females and young. When they had passed, a company of twenty fighters crossed the trail, and then the area was quiet.

They waited a moment in silence. Garret said, "They are elven-kin to move so large a number through the forest undetected so long."

Martin smiled. "I'd advise you not mention that fact to the next elf you encounter." He stood slowly, unbending cramped muscles from the long sitting in the brush. A faint sound echoed from the east, and Martin got a thoughtful look on his face. "How far along the trail do you judge the Dark Brothers' march?"

Garret said, "At their rear, a hundred yards; at the van, perhaps a quarter mile or less. Why?"

Martin grinned, and Garret became discomforted by the mocking humor in his eyes. "Come, I think I know where we can have some fun."

Garret groaned softly, "Ah, Huntmaster, my skin gets a poxy feeling when you mention fun."

Martin struck the man a friendly blow to the chest with the back of his hand. "Come, stout fellow." The Huntmaster broke trail, with Garret behind. They loped along through the woods, easily avoiding obstacles that would have hindered less experienced woodsmen.

They came to a break in the trail, and both men halted. Just down the trail, at the edge of their vision in the gloom of the forest, came a company of Tsurani trailbreakers. Martin and Garret faded into the trees, and the Huntmaster said, "The main column is close behind. When they reach the crossing where the Dark Brothers passed, they might chance to follow."

Garret shook his head. "Or they might not, so we will make certain they do." Taking a deep breath, he added, "Oh well," then made a short silent prayer to Kilian, the Singer of Green Silences, Goddess of Foresters, as they unshouldered their bows.

Martin stepped out onto the trail and took aim, and Garret followed his example. The Tsurani trailbreakers came into view, cutting away the thick underbrush along the trail so the main body could more easily follow. Martin waited until the Tsurani were uncomfortably close, then he let fly, just as the first trailbreaker took notice of them. The first two men fell, and before they hit the ground, two more arrows were loosed. Martin and Garret pulled arrows from back quivers in fluid motions, set arrow to bowstring, and let fly with uncommon quickness and accuracy. It was not from any act of kindness Martin had selected Garret five years before. In the eye of the storm, he would stand calmly, do as ordered, and do it with skill.

Ten stunned Tsurani fell before they could raise an alarm. Calmly Martin and Garret shouldered their bows and waited. Then along the trail appeared a veritable wall of colored armor. The Tsurani officers in the van stopped in shocked silence as they regarded the dead trailbreakers. Then they saw the two foresters standing quietly down the trail and shouted something. The entire front of the column sprang forward, weapons drawn.

Martin leaped into the thicket on the north side of the trail, Garret a step behind. They dashed through the trees, the Tsurani in close pursuit.

Martin's voice filled the forest with a wild hunter's call. Garret shouted as much from some nameless, crazy exhilaration as from fear. The noise behind was tremendous as a horde of Tsurani pursued them through the trees.

Martin led them northward, paralleling the course taken by the Dark Brotherhood. After a time he stopped and between gasping breaths said, "Slowly, we don't want to lose them."

Garret looked back and saw the Tsurani were out of sight. They leaned against a tree and waited. A moment later the first Tsurani came into view, hurrying along on a course that angled off to the northwest.

With a disgusted look, Martin said, "We must have killed the only skilled trackers on their whole bloody world." He took his hunter's horn from his belt and let forth with such a loud blast the Tsurani soldier froze, an expression of shock clearly evident on his face even from where Martin and Garret stood.

The Tsurani looked around and caught sight of the two huntsmen. Martin waved for the man to follow, and he and Garret were off again. The Tsurani shouted for those behind and gave chase. For a quarter mile they led the Tsurani through the woods, then they angled westward. Garret shouted, between heaving breaths, "The Dark Brothers . . . they'll know . . . we come."

Martin shouted back, "Unless they've . . . suddenly all . . . gone deaf." He managed a smile. "The Tsurani . . . hold a six-to-one . . . advantage. I . . . think it . . . only fair to let . . . the Brotherhood . . . have the . . . ambush."

Garret spared enough breath for a low groan and continued to follow his master's lead. They crashed out of a thicket and Martin stopped, grabbing Garret by the tunic. He cocked his head and said, "They're up ahead."

Garret said, "I don't know . . . how you can hear a thing with . . . all that cursed racket behind." It sounded as if most of the Tsurani column had followed, though the forest amplified the noise and confused its source.

Martin said, "Do you still wear that . . . ridiculous red undertunic?"

"Yes, why?"

"Tear off a strip." Garret pulled his knife without question and lifted up his green forester's tunic. Underneath was a garish red cotton undertunic. He cut a long strip off the bottom, then hastily tucked the undertunic in. While Garret ordered himself, Martin tied the strip to an arrow. He looked back to where the Tsurani thrashed in the brush. "It must be those stubby legs. They may be able to run all day, but they can't keep up in the woods." He handed the arrow to Garret. "See that large elm across that small clearing?"

Garret nodded. "See the small birch behind, off to the left?" Again Garret nodded. "Think you can hit it with that rag dragging at your arrow?"

Garret grinned as he unslung his bow, notched the arrow, and let fly. The arrow sped true, striking the tree. Martin said, "When our bandy-legged friends get here, they'll see that flicker of color over there and go charging across. Unless I'm sadly mistaken, the Brothers are about fifty feet the other side of your arrow." He pulled his horn as Garret shouldered his bow again. "Once more we're off," he said, blowing a long, loud call.

Like hornets the Tsurani descended, but Longbow and Garret were off to the southwest before the note from the hunter's horn had died in the air. They dashed to be gone before the Tsurani caught sight of them, aborting the hoax. Suddenly they broke through a thicket and ran into a group of women and children milling about. One young woman of the Brotherhood was placing a bundle upon the ground. She stopped at the sight of the two men. Garret had to slide to a halt to keep from bowling her over.

Her large brown eyes studied him for an instant as

he stepped sideways to get around her. Without thinking, Garret said, "Excuse me, ma'am," and raised his hand to his forelock. Then he was off after the Huntmaster as shouts of surprise and anger erupted behind them.

Martin called a halt after they had covered another quarter mile and listened. To the northeast came the sounds of battle, shouts and screams, and the ring of weapons. Martin grinned. "They'll both be busy for a while."

Garret sank wearily to the ground and said, "Next time send me to the castle, will you, Huntmaster?"

Martin kneeled beside the tracker. "That should prevent the Tsurani from reaching Crydee until sundown or after. They won't be able to mount an attack until tomorrow. Four hundred Dark Brothers are not something they can safely leave at their rear. We'll rest a bit, then make for Crydee."

Garret leaned back against a tree. "Welcome news." He let out a long sigh of relief. "That was a close thing, Huntmaster."

Martin smiled enigmatically. "All life is a close thing, Garret."

Garret shook his head slowly. "Did you see that girl?"

Martin nodded. "What of her?"

Garret looked perplexed. "She was pretty . . . no, closer to being beautiful, in a strange sort of way, I mean. But she had long black hair, and her eyes were the color of otter's fur. And she had a pouty mouth and pert look. Enough to warrant a second glance from most men. It's not what I would have expected from the Brotherhood."

Martin nodded. "The moredhel are a pretty people, in truth, as are the elves. But remember, Garret," he said with a smile, "should you chance to find yourself exchanging pleasantries with a moredhel woman again, she'd as soon cut your heart out as kiss you."

They rested for a while as cries and shouts echoed from the northeast. Then slowly they stood and began the return to Crydee.

SINCE THE START of the war, the Tsurani had confined their activities to those areas immediately adjacent the valley in the Grey Towers. Reports from the dwarves and the elves revealed mining activities were taking place in the Grey Towers. Enclaves had been thrown up outside the valley, from which they raided Kingdom positions. Once or twice during the year they would mount an offensive against the Dukes' Armies of the West, the elves in Elvandar, or Crydee, but for the most part they were content to hold what they had already taken.

And each year they would expand their holdings, building more enclaves, expanding the area under their control, and gaining themselves a stronger position from which to conduct the next year's campaign. Since the fall of Walinor, the expected thrust toward the coast of the Bitter Sea had not materialized, nor had the Tsurani again tried for the LaMutian fortresses near Stone Mountain. Walinor and Crydee town were sacked and abandoned, more to deny them to the Kingdom and Free Cities than for any Tsurani gain. By the spring of the third year of the war, the leaders of the Kingdom forces despaired of a major attack, one that might break the stalemate. Now it came. And it came at the logical place, the allies' weakest front, the garrison at Crydee.

Arutha looked out over the walls at the Tsurani army. He stood next to Gardan and Fannon, with Martin Longbow behind. "How many?" he asked, not taking his eyes from the gathering host.

Martin spoke. "Fifteen hundred, two thousand, it is hard to judge. There were two thousand more coming yesterday, less whatever the Dark Brotherhood took with them."

From the distant woods the sounds of workmen felling trees rang out. The Swordmaster and Huntmaster judged the Tsurani were cutting trees to build scaling ladders.

Martin said, "I'd never thought to hear myself say such, but I wish there'd been four thousand Dark Brothers in the forest yesterday."

Gardan spat over the wall. "Still, you did well, Huntmaster. It is only fitting they should run afoul of each other."

Martin chuckled humorlessly. "It is also a good thing the Dark Brothers kill on sight. Though I am sure they do it out of no love for us, they do guard our southern flank."

Arutha said, "Unless yesterday's band was not an isolated case. If the Brotherhood is abandoning the Green Heart, we may soon have to fear for Tulan, Jonril, and Carse."

"I'm glad they've not parleyed," said Fannon. "If they should truce . . ."

Martin shook his head. "The moredhel will traffic only with weapons runners and renegades who will serve them for gold. Otherwise they have no use for us. And by all evidence, the Tsurani are bent on conquest. The moredhel are no more spared their ambition than we are."

Fannon looked back at the mounting Tsurani force. Brightly colored standards with symbols and designs strange to behold were placed at various positions along the leading edge of the army. Hundreds of warriors in different-colored armor stood in groups under each banner.

A horn sounded, and the Tsurani soldiers faced
the walls. Each standard was brought forward a dozen
paces and planted in the ground. A handful of soldiers
wearing the high-crested helmets that the Kingdom
forces took to denote officers walked forward and stood
halfway between the army and the standard-bearers.
One, wearing bright blue armor, called something and
pointed at the castle. A shout went up from the assembled Tsurani host, and then another officer, this one in
bright red armor, began to walk slowly up to the castle.

Arutha and the others watched in silence while the
man crossed the distance to the gate. He looked neither
right nor left, nor up at the people on the walls, but
marched with eyes straight ahead until he reached the
gate. There he took out a large hand ax and banged
three times upon it with the haft.

"What is he doing?" asked Roland, just come up
the stairs.

Again the Tsurani pounded on the gates of the
castle. "I think," said Longbow, "he's ordering us to
open up and quit the castle."

Then the Tsurani reached back and slammed his
ax into the gate, leaving it quivering in the wood.
Without hurrying, he turned and began walking away
to cheers from the watching Tsurani.

"What now?" asked Fannon.

"I think I know," said Martin, unshouldering his
bow. He drew out an arrow and fitted it to the bowstring. With a sudden pull, he let fly. The shaft struck
the ground between the Tsurani officer's legs and the
man halted.

"The Hadati hillmen of Yabon have rituals like
this," said Martin. "They put great store by showing
bravery in the face of an enemy. To touch one and live
is more honorable than killing him." He pointed toward the officer, who stood motionless. "If I kill him, I

have no honor, because he's showing us all how brave he is. But we can show we know how to play this game."

The Tsurani officer turned and picked up the arrow and snapped it in two. He faced the castle, holding the broken arrow high as he shouted defiance at those on the walls. Longbow sighted another arrow and let fly. The second arrow sped down and sliced the plume from the officer's helmet. The Tsurani fell silent as feathers began drifting down around his face.

Roland whooped at the shot, and then the walls of the castle erupted with cheers. The Tsurani slowly removed his helm.

Martin said, "Now he's inviting one of us either to kill him, showing we are without honor, or to come out of the castle and dare to face him."

Fannon said, "I will not allow the gates open over some childish contest!"

Longbow grinned as he said, "Then we'll change the rules." He leaned over the edge of the walkway and shouted down to the courtyard below. "Garret; fowling blunt!"

Garret, in the court below, drew a fowling arrow from his quiver and tossed it up to Longbow. Martin showed the others the heavy iron ball that served as the tip, used to stun game birds where a sharp arrow would destroy them, and then fitted it to his bow. Sighting the officer, he let fly.

The arrow took the Tsurani officer in the stomach, knocking him backward. All on the wall could imagine the sound made as the man had his breath knocked from him. The Tsurani soldiers shouted in outrage, then quieted as the man stood up, obviously stunned but otherwise showing no injury. Then he doubled over, his hands on his knees, and vomited.

Arutha said dryly, "So much for an officer's dignity."

"Well," said Fannon, "I think it is time to give them another lesson in Kingdom warfare." He raised his arm high above his head. "Catapults!" he cried.

Answering flags waved from the tops of the towers along the walls and atop the keep. He dropped his arm, and the mighty engines were fired. On the smaller towers, ballistae, looking like giant crossbows, shot spearlike missiles, while atop the keep, huge mangonels flung buckets of heavy stones. The rain of stones and missiles landed amid the Tsurani, crushing heads and limbs, tearing ragged holes in their lines. The screams of wounded men could be heard by the defenders, while the catapult crew quickly rewound and loaded their deadly engines.

The Tsurani milled about in confusion and, when the second flight of stones and missiles struck, broke and ran. A cheer went up from the defenders on the wall, then died when the Tsurani regrouped beyond the range of the engines.

Gardan said, "Swordmaster, I think they mean to wait us out."

"I think you're wrong," said Arutha, pointing. The other looked: a large number of Tsurani detached themselves from the main body, moving forward to stop just outside missile range.

"They look to be readying an attack," said Fannon, "but why with only a part of their force?"

A soldier appeared and said, "Highness, there are no signs of Tsurani along any of the other positions."

Arutha looked to Fannon. "And why attack only one wall?" After a few minutes, Arutha said, "I'd judge a thousand."

"More likely twelve hundred," said Fannon. He

saw scaling ladders appearing at the rear of the attackers, moving forward. "Anytime now."

A thousand defenders waited inside the walls. Other men of Crydee still manned outlying garrisons and lookout positions, but the bulk of the Duchy's strength was here. Fannon said, "We can withstand this force as long as the walls remain unbreached. Less than a ten-to-one advantage we can deal with."

More messengers came from the other walls. "They still mount nothing along the east, north, and south, Swordmaster," one reported.

"They seem determined to do this the hard way." Fannon looked thoughtful for a moment. "Little of what we've seen is understandable. Death raids, marshaling within catapult range, wasting time with games of honor. Still, they are not without skill, and we can take nothing for granted." To the guard he said, "Pass the word to keep alert on the other walls, and be ready to move to defend should this prove a feint."

The messengers left, and the waiting continued. The sun moved across the sky, until an hour before sunset, when it sat at the backs of the attackers. Suddenly horns blew and drums beat, and in a rush the Tsurani broke toward the walls. The catapults sang, and great holes appeared in the lines of attackers. Still they came, until they moved within bow range of the patiently waiting defenders. A storm of arrows fell upon the attackers, and to a man the front rank collapsed, but those behind came on, large brightly colored shields held overhead as they rushed the walls. A half-dozen times men fell, dropping scaling ladders, only to have others grab them up and continue.

Tsurani bowmen answered the bowmen from the walls with their own shower of arrows, and men of Crydee fell from the battlements. Arutha ducked behind the walls of the castle as the arrows sped overhead, then he risked a glance between the merlons of the wall. A horde of attackers filled his field of vision, and a ladder top suddenly appeared before him. A soldier near the Prince grabbed the ladder top and pushed it away, aided by a second using a pole arm. Arutha could hear the screams of the Tsurani as they fell from the ladder. The first soldier to the ladder then fell backward, a Tsurani arrow protruding from his eye, and disappeared into the courtyard.

A sudden shout went up from below, and Arutha sprang to his feet, risking a bowshaft by looking down. All along the base of the wall, Tsurani warriors were withdrawing, running back to the safety of their own lines.

"What are they doing?" wondered Fannon.

The Tsurani ran until they were safe from the catapults, then stopped, turned, and formed up ranks. Officers were walking up and down before the men, exhorting them. After a moment the assembled Tsurani cheered.

"Damn me!" came from Arutha's left, and he glimpsed Amos Trask at his shoulder, a seaman's cutlass in his hand. "The maniacs are congratulating themselves on getting slaughtered."

The scene below was grisly. Tsurani soldiers lay scattered around like toys thrown by a careless giant child. A few moved feebly and moaned, but most were dead.

Fannon said, "I'd wager they lost a hundred or more. This makes no sense." He said to Roland and Martin, "Check the other walls." They both hurried off. "What are they doing now?" he said as he watched the Tsurani. In the red glow of sunset, he could see them still in lines, while men lit torches and passed them around. "Surely they don't intend to attack after sunset? They'll fall over themselves in the dark."

"Who knows what they plan?" said Arutha. "I've never heard of an attack being staged this badly."

Amos said, "Beggin' the Prince's pardon, but I know a thing or two about warcraft—from my younger days—and I've also never heard of this like before. Even the Keshians, who'll throw away dog soldiers like a drunken seaman throws away his money, even they wouldn't try a frontal assault like this. I'd keep a weather eye out for trickery."

"Yes," answered Arutha. "But of what sort?"

THROUGHOUT THE NIGHT the Tsurani attacked, rushing headlong against the walls, to die at the base. Once a few made the top of the walls, but they were quickly killed and the ladders thrown back. With dawn the Tsurani withdrew.

Arutha, Fannon, and Gardan watched as the Tsurani reached the safety of their own lines, beyond catapult and bow range. With the sunrise a sea of colorful tents appeared, and the Tsurani retired to their campsites. The defenders were astonished at the number of Tsurani dead along the base of the castle walls.

After a few hours the stink of the dead became overpowering. Fannon consulted with an exhausted Arutha as the Prince was readying for an overdue sleep. "The Tsurani have made no attempt to reclaim their fallen."

Arutha said, "We have no common language in which to parley, unless you mean to send Tully out under a flag of truce."

Fannon said, "He'd go, of course, but I'd not risk him. Still, the bodies could be trouble in a day or two. Besides the stink and flies, with unburied dead comes disease. It's the gods' way of showing their displeasure over not honoring the dead."

"Then," said Arutha, pulling on the boot he had just taken off, "we had best see what can be done."

He returned to the gate and found Gardan already making plans to remove the bodies. A dozen volunteers were waiting by the gate to go and gather the dead for a funeral pyre.

Arutha and Fannon reached the walls as Gardan led the men through the gate. Archers lined the walls to cover the retreat of the men outside the walls if necessary, but it soon became evident the Tsurani were not going to trouble the party. Several came to the edge of their lines, to sit and watch the Kingdom soldiers working.

After a half hour it was clear the men of Crydee would not be able to complete the work before they were exhausted. Arutha considered sending more men outside, but Fannon refused, thinking it what the Tsurani were waiting for. "If we have to move a large party back through the gate, it might prove disastrous. If we close the gate, we lose men outside, and if we leave it open too long, the Tsurani breach the castle." Arutha was forced to agree, and they settled down to watch Gardan's men working in the hot morning.

Then, near midday, a dozen Tsurani warriors, unarmed, walked casually across their lines and approached the work party. Those on the wall watched tensely, but when the Tsurani reached the spot where Crydee men worked, they silently began picking up bodies and carrying them to where the pyre was being erected.

With the help of the Tsurani, the bodies were stacked upon the huge pyre. Torches were set, and soon the bodies of the slain were consumed in fire. The Tsurani who had helped place the bodies upon the pyre watched as the soldier who led the volunteers stood away from the mounting flames. Then one Tsurani soldier spoke a word, and he and his companions bowed in respect to those upon the fire. The soldier who led the Crydee soldiers said, "Honors to the dead!" The twelve men of Crydee assumed a posture of attention and saluted. Then the Tsurani turned to face the Kingdom soldiers and again they bowed. The commanding soldier called out, "Return salute!" and the twelve men of Crydee saluted the Tsurani.

Arutha shook his head, watching men who had tried to kill one another working side by side as if it were the most natural thing in the world, then saluting one another. "Father used to say that, among man's strange undertakings, war stood clearly forth as the strangest."

AT SUNDOWN THEY came again, wave after wave of attackers, rushing the west wall, to die at the base. Four times during the night they struck, and four times they were repulsed.

Now they came again, and Arutha shrugged off his fatigue to fight once more. They could see more Tsurani joining those before the castle, long snakes of torchlight coming from the forest to the north. After the last assault, it was clear the situation was shifting to the Tsurani's favor. The defenders were exhausted from two nights of fighting, and the Tsurani were still throwing fresh troops into the fray.

"They mean to grind us down, no matter what the cost," said a fatigued Fannon. He began to say something to a guard when a strange expression crossed his face. He closed his eyes and collapsed. Arutha caught him. An arrow protruded from his back. A panicky-looking soldier kneeling on the other side looked at Arutha, clearly asking: What do we do?

Arutha shouted, "Get him into the keep, to Father Tully," and the man and another soldier picked up the unconscious Swordmaster and carried him down. A third soldier asked, "What orders, Highness?"

Arutha spun around, seeing the worried faces of Crydee's soldiers nearby, and said, "As before. Defend the wall."

The fighting went hard. A half-dozen times Arutha found himself dueling with Tsurani warriors who topped the wall. Then, after a timeless battling, the Tsurani withdrew.

Arutha stood panting, his clothing drenched with perspiration beneath his chest armor. He shouted for water, and a castle porter arrived with a bucket. He drank, as did the others around, and turned to watch the Tsurani host.

Again they stood just beyond catapult range, and their torchlights seemed undiminished. "Prince Arutha," came a voice behind. He spun around. Horsemaster Algon was standing before him. "I just heard of Fannon's wound."

Arutha said, "How is he?"

"A close thing. The wound is serious, but not yet fatal. Tully thinks should he live another day, he will recover. But he will not be able to command for weeks, perhaps longer."

Arutha knew Algon was waiting for a decision from him. The Prince was Knight-Captain of the King's army and, without Fannon, the commander of the garrison. He was also untried and could turn over command to the Horsemaster. Arutha looked around. "Where is Gardan?"

"Here, Highness," came a shout from a short way down the wall. Arutha was surprised at the sergeant's appearance. His dark skin was nearly grey from the dust that stuck to it, held fast by the sheen of perspiration. His tunic and tabard were soaked with blood, which also covered his arms to the elbows.

Arutha looked down at his own hands and arms and found them likewise covered. He shouted, "More water!" and said to Algon, "Gardan will act as my second commander. Should anything happen to me, he will take command of the garrison. Gardan is acting Swordmaster."

Algon hesitated as if about to say something, then a look of relief crossed his face. "Yes, Highness. Orders?"

Arutha looked back toward the Tsurani lines, then to the east. The first light of the false dawn was coming, and the sun would rise over the mountains in less than two hours. He seemed to weigh facts for a time, as he washed away the blood on his arms and face. Finally he said, "Get Longbow."

The Huntmaster was called for and arrived a few minutes later, followed by Amos Trask, who wore a wide grin. "Damn me, but they can fight," said the seaman.

Arutha ignored the comment. "It is clear to me they plan to keep constant pressure upon us. With as little regard as they show for their own lives, they can wear us down in a few weeks. This is one thing we didn't count upon, this willingness of their men to go to certain death. I want the north, south, and east walls stripped. Leave enough men to keep watch, and hold any attackers until reinforcements can arrive. Bring the men from the other walls here, and order those here to stand down. I want six-hour watches rotated throughout the rest of the day. Martin, has there been any more word of Dark Brother migration?"

Longbow shrugged. "We've been a little busy, Highness. My men have all been in the north woods the last few weeks."

Arutha said, "Could you slip a few trackers over the walls before first light?"

Longbow considered. "If they leave at once, and if the Tsurani aren't watching the east wall too closely, yes."

"Do so. The Dark Brothers aren't foolish enough to attack this force, but if you could find a few bands the size of the one you spotted three days ago and repeat your trap . . ."

Martin grinned. "I'll lead them out myself. We'd best leave now, before it gets much lighter." Arutha dismissed him, and Martin ran down the stairs. "Garret!" he shouted. "Come on, lad. We're off for some fun." A groan could be heard by those on the wall as Martin gathered his trackers around him.

Arutha said to Gardan, "I want messages sent to Carse and Tulan. Use five pigeons for each. Order Barons Bellamy and Tolburt to strip their garrisons and take ship for Crydee at once."

Gardan said, "Highness, that will leave those garrisons nearly undefended."

Algon joined in the objection. "If the Dark Brotherhood moves toward the Northlands, the Tsurani will have an open path to the southern keeps next year."

Arutha said, "If the Dark Brothers are moving en masse, which they may not be, and if the Tsurani learn they have abandoned the Green Heart, which they may not. I am concerned by this known threat, not a possible one next year. If they keep this constant pressure upon us, how long can we withstand?"

Gardan said, "A few weeks, perhaps a month. No longer."

Arutha once more studied the Tsurani camp. "They boldly pitch their tents near the edge of town. They range through our forests, building ladders and siege engines no doubt. They know we cannot sally forth in strength. But with eighteen hundred fresh soldiers from the southern keeps attacking up the coast road from the beaches and the garrison sallying forth, we can rout them from Crydee. Once the siege is broken, they will have to withdraw to their eastern enclaves. We can harry them continuously with horsemen, keep them from regrouping. Then we can return those forces to the southern keeps, and they'll be ready for any Tsurani attacks against Carse or Tulan next spring."

Gardan said, "A bold enough plan, Highness." He saluted and left the wall, followed by Algon.

Amos Trask said, "Your commanders are cautious men, Highness."

Arutha said, "You agree with my plan?"

"Should Crydee fall, what matters when Carse or Tulan falls? If not this year, then next for certain. It might as well be in one fight as two or three. As the sergeant said, it is a bold plan. Still, a ship was never taken without getting close enough to board. You have the makings of a fine corsair should you ever grow tired of being a Prince, Highness."

Arutha regarded Amos Trask with a skeptical smile. "Corsair, is it? I thought you claimed to be an honest trader."

Amos looked slightly discomposed. Then he broke out in a hearty laugh. "I only said I had a cargo for Crydee, Highness. I never said how I came by it."

"Well, we have no time for your piratical past now."

Amos looked stung. "No pirate, Sire. The *Sidonie* was carrying letters of marque from Great Kesh, given by the governor of Durbin."

Arutha laughed. "Of course! And everyone knows there is no finer, more law-abiding group upon the high seas than the captains of the Durbin coast."

Amos shrugged. "They tend to be a crusty lot, it's true. And they sometimes make free with the concept of free passage on the high seas, but we prefer the term *privateer.*"

Horns blew and drums beat, and with shrieking war cries the Tsurani came. The defenders waited, then as the attacking host crossed the invisible line marking the outer range of the castle's war engines, death rained down upon the Tsurani. Still they came.

The Tsurani crossed the second invisible line marking the outer range of the castle's bowmen, and scores more died. Still they came.

The attackers reached the walls, and defenders dropped stones and pushed over scaling ladders, dealing out death to those below. Still they came.

Arutha quickly ordered a redeployment of his reserves, directing them to be ready near the points of heaviest attack. Men hurried to carry out his orders.

Standing atop the west wall, in the thick of the fight, Arutha answered attack with attack, repulsing warrior after warrior as they reached the top of the wall. Even in the midst of battle, Arutha was aware of the scene around him, shouting orders, hearing replies, catching glimpses of what others were doing. He saw Amos Trask, disarmed, strike a Tsurani full in the face with his fist, knocking the man from the wall. Trask then carefully bent down and picked up his cutlass as if he had simply dropped it while strolling along the wall. Gardan moved among the men, exhorting the defenders, bolstering sagging spirits, and driving the men beyond the point where they would normally have given in to exhaustion.

Arutha helped two soldiers push away another scaling ladder, then stared in momentary confusion as one of the men slowly turned and sat at his feet, surprise on his face as he looked down at the Tsurani bowshaft in his chest. The man leaned back against the wall and closed his eyes as if deciding to sleep for a time.

Arutha heard someone shout his name. Gardan stood a few feet away, pointing to the north section of the west wall. "They've crested the wall!"

Arutha ran past Gardan, shouting, "Order the reserves to follow!" He raced along the wall until he reached the breach in the defenses. A dozen Tsurani held each end of a section of the wall, pushing forward to clear room for their comrades to follow. Arutha hurled himself into the front rank, past weary and surprised guards who were being forced back along the battlement. Arutha thrust over the first Tsurani shield, taking the man in the throat. The Tsurani's face registered shock, then he keeled over and fell into the courtyard below. Arutha attacked the man next to the first and shouted, "For Crydee! For the Kingdom!"

Then Gardan was among them, like a towering black giant, dealing blows to all who stood before. Suddenly the men of Crydee pressed forward, a wave of flesh and steel along the narrow rampart. The Tsurani stood their ground, refusing to yield the hard-won breach, and to a man were killed.

Arutha struck a Tsurani warrior with the bell guard of his rapier, knocking him to the ground below, and turned to find the wall once more in the possession of the defenders. Horns blew from the Tsurani lines, and the attackers withdrew.

Arutha became aware the sun had cleared the mountains to the east. The morning had finally come. He surveyed the scene below and felt suddenly more fatigued than he could ever remember. Turning slowly, he saw every man on the wall was watching him. Then one of the soldiers shouted, "Hail, Arutha! Hail, Prince of Crydee!"

Suddenly the castle was ringing with shouts as men chanted, "Arutha! Arutha!"

To Gardan, Arutha asked, "Why?"

With a satisfied look the sergeant replied, "They saw you personally take the fight to the Tsurani, Highness, or heard from others. They are soldiers and expect certain things from a commander. They are now truly your men, Highness."

Arutha stood quietly as the cheers filled the castle. Then he raised his hand and the courtyard fell silent. "You have done well. Crydee is served aright by her soldiers." He spoke to Gardan. "Change the watch upon the walls. We may have little time to enjoy the victory."

As if his words were an omen, a shout came from a guard atop the nearest tower. "Highness, 'ware the field."

Arutha saw the Tsurani lines had been re-formed. Wearily he said, "Have they no limit?"

Instead of the expected attack, a single man walked from the Tsurani line, apparently an officer by his crested helm. He pointed to the walls, and the entire Tsurani line erupted in cheers. He walked farther, within bow range, stopping several times to point at the wall. His blue armor glinted in the morning sun as the attackers cheered with his gestures toward the castle.

"A challenge?" said Gardan, watching the strange display as the man showed his back, unmindful of personal danger, and walked back to his own lines.

"No," said Amos Trask, who came to stand next to Gardan. "I think they salute a brave enemy." Amos shook his head slightly. "A strange people."

Arutha said, "Shall we ever understand such men?"

Gardan put his hand upon Arutha's shoulder. "I doubt it. Look, they quit the field."

The Tsurani were marching back toward their tents before the remains of Crydee town. A few watchmen were left to observe the castle, but it was clear the main force was being ordered to stand down again. Gardan said, "I would have ordered another assault." His voice betrayed his disbelief. "They have to know we are near exhaustion. Why not press the attack?"

Amos said, "Who can say. Perhaps they, too, are tired."

Arutha said, "This attacking through the night has some meaning I do not understand." He shook his head. "In time we will know what they plot. Leave a watch upon the walls, but have the men retire to the courtyard. It is becoming clear they prefer not to attack during the day. Order food brought from the kitchen, and water to bathe with." Orders were passed, and men left their posts, some sitting on the walks below the wall, too tired to trudge down the steps. Others reached the courtyard and tossed aside their weapons, sitting in the shade of the battlements while castle porters hurried among them with buckets of fresh water. Arutha leaned against the wall. He spoke silently to himself. "They'll be back."

They came again that night.

18

Siege

Wounded men groaned at sunrise.

For the twelfth straight night the Tsurani had assaulted the castle, only to retire at dawn. Gardan could not see any clear reason for the dangerous night attacks. As he watched the Tsurani gathering up their dead, then returning to their tents, he said, "They are strange. Their archers cannot fire at the walls once the ladders are up for fear of hitting their own men. We have no such problem, knowing everyone below is the enemy. I don't understand these men."

Arutha sat numbly washing the blood and dirt from his face, oblivious to the scene about him. He was too tired even to answer Gardan. "Here," a voice nearby said, and he pulled the damp cloth from his face to see a proffered drinking cup. He took the cup and drained it in one long pull, savoring the taste of strong wine.

Carline stood before him, wearing tunic and trousers, her sword hanging at her side. "What are you doing here?" Arutha asked, fatigue making his voice sound harsh in his own ears.

Carline's manner was brisk. "Someone must carry water and food. With every man on the walls all night long, who do you think is fit for duty in the morning? Not that pitiful handful of porters who are too old for fighting, that is certain."

Arutha looked about and saw other women, ladies of the castle as well as servants and fishwives, walking among the men, who thankfully took the offered food and drink. He smiled his crooked smile. "How fare you?"

"Well enough. Still, sitting in the cellar is as difficult in its own way as being on the wall, I judge. Each sound of battle that reaches us brings one or another of the ladies to tears." Her voice carried a tone of mild disapproval. "They huddle like rabbits. Oh, it is so tiresome." She stood quietly for a moment, then asked, "Have you seen Roland?"

He looked about. "Last night for a time." He covered his face in the soothing wetness of the cloth. Pulling it away after a moment, he added, "Or perhaps it was two nights past. I've lost track." He pointed toward the wall nearest the keep. "He should be over there somewhere. I put him in charge of the off watch. He is responsible for guarding against a flank attack."

Carline smiled. She knew Roland would be chafing to get into the fight, but with his responsibilities it would be unlikely unless the Tsurani attacked on all sides. "Thank you, Arutha."

Arutha feigned ignorance. "For what?"

She kneeled and kissed his wet cheek. "For knowing me better than I know myself sometimes." She stood and walked away.

· · · ·

ROLAND WALKED ALONG the battlements, watching the distant forest beyond the broad clearing that ran along the eastern wall of the castle. He approached a guard standing next to an alarm bell and said, "Anything?"

"Nothing, Squire."

Roland nodded. "Keep a watchful eye. This is the narrowest open area before the wall. If they come against a second flank, this is where I would expect the assault."

The soldier said, "In truth, Squire. Why do they come only against one wall, and why the strongest?"

Roland shrugged. "I don't pretend to know. Perhaps to show contempt, or bravery. Or for some alien reason."

The guard came to attention and saluted. Carline had come silently up behind them. Roland took her by the arm and hurried her along. "What do you think you're doing up here?" he said in ungentle tones.

Her look of relief at finding him alive and unhurt turned to one of anger. "I came to see if you were all right," she said defiantly.

Guiding her down the stairs to the courtyard below, he answered, "We're not so far removed from the forest a Tsurani bowman could not reduce the Duke's household by one. I'll not explain to your father and brothers what my reasons were for allowing you up there."

"Oh! Is that your only reason? You don't want to face Father."

He smiled and his voice softened. "No. Of course not."

She returned the smile. "I was worried."

Roland sat upon the lower steps and plucked at some weeds growing near the base of the stones, pulling them out and tossing them aside. "Little reason for that. Arutha has seen I'll not risk much."

Placatingly, Carline said, "Still, this is an important post. If they attack here, you'll have to hold with a small number until reinforcements come."

"If they attack. Gardan came by yesterday, and he thinks they may tire of this soon and dig in for a long siege, waiting for us to starve."

She said, "More's their hard luck, then. We've stores through the winter, and they'll find little to forage out there once the snows come."

Playfully mocking, he said, "What have we here? A student of tactics?"

She regarded him like an overtaxed teacher confronted with a particularly slow student. "I listen, and I have my wits about me. Do you think I do nothing but sit around waiting for you men to tell me what is occurring? If I did, I'd know nothing."

He put up his hands in sign of supplication. "I'm sorry, Carline. You are most definitely no one's fool." He stood and took her hand. "But you have made me your fool."

She squeezed his hand. "No, Roland, I have been the fool. It has taken me almost three years to understand just how good a man you are. And how good a friend." She leaned over and kissed him lightly. He returned the kiss with tenderness. "And more," she added quietly.

"When this is over . . ." he began.

She placed her free hand over his lips. "Not now, Roland. Not now."

He smiled his understanding. "I'd best be back to the walls, Carline."

She kissed him again and left for the main courtyard and the work to be done. He climbed back to the wall and resumed his vigil.

• • •

IT WAS LATE afternoon when a guard shouted, "Squire! In the forest!" Roland looked in the indicated direction and saw two figures sprinting across the open ground. From the trees the shouts of men came, and the clamor of battle.

Crydee bowmen raised their weapons, then Roland shouted, "Hold! It's Longbow!" To the guard next to him he said, "Bring ropes, quickly."

Longbow and Garret reached the wall as the ropes were being lowered and, as soon as they were secured, scrambled upward. When they were safely over the walls, they sank exhaustedly behind the battlements. Waterskins were handed the two foresters, who drank deeply.

"What now?" asked Roland.

Longbow gave him a lopsided smile. "We found another band of travelers heading northward about thirty miles southeast of here and arranged for them to visit with the Tsurani."

Garret looked up at Roland with eyes darkly circled from fatigue. "A band he calls it. Damn near five hundred moredhel moving in strength. Must have been a full hundred chasing us through the woods the last two days."

Roland said, "Arutha will be pleased. The Tsurani have hit us each night since you left. We could do with a little diverting of their attentions."

Longbow nodded. "Where's the Prince?"

"At the west wall, where all the fighting's been."

Longbow stood and pulled the exhausted Garret to his feet. "Come along. We'd better report."

Roland instructed the guards to keep a sharp watch and followed the two huntsmen. They found Arutha supervising the distribution of weapons to those in need of replacing broken or dulled ones. Gardell, the smith, and his apprentices gathered up those that were reparable and dumped them into a cart, heading for the forge to begin work.

Longbow said, "Highness, another band of moredhel have come north. I led them here, so the Tsurani could be too busy to attack tonight."

Arutha said, "That is welcome news. Come, we'll have a cup of wine, and you can tell of what you saw."

Longbow sent Garret off to the kitchen and followed Arutha and Roland into the keep. The Prince sent word asking Gardan to join them in the council room and, when they were all there, asked Longbow to recount his travels.

Longbow drank deeply from the wine cup placed before him. "It was touch and go for a while. The woods are thick with both Tsurani and moredhel. And there are many signs they have little affection for one another. We counted at least a hundred dead on both sides."

Arutha looked at the other three men. "We know little of their ways, but it seems foolish for them to travel so close to Crydee."

Longbow shook his head. "They have little choice, Highness. The Green Heart must be foraged clean, and they cannot return to their mountains because of the Tsurani. The moredhel are making for the Northlands and won't risk passing near Elvandar. With the rest of the way blocked by the Tsurani strength, their only path is through the forests nearby, then westward along the river toward the coast. Once they reach the sea, they can turn northward again. They must gain the Great Northern Mountains before winter to reach their brothers in the Northlands safely."

He drank the rest of his cup and waited while a servant refilled it. "From all signs, nearly every moredhel in the south is making for the Northlands. It looks as if over a thousand have already safely been by here. How many more will come this way through the summer and fall, we cannot guess." He drank again. "The Tsurani will have to watch their eastern flank and would do well to watch the south as well. The moredhel are starved and might chance a raid into the Tsurani camp while the bulk of the army is thrown against the walls of the castle. Should a three-way fight occur, it could get messy."

"For the Tsurani," said Gardan.

Martin hoisted his cup in salute. "For the Tsurani."

Arutha said, "You've done well, Huntmaster."

"Thank you, Highness." He laughed. "I'd never thought to see the day I'd welcome sight of the Dark Brotherhood in the forests of Crydee."

Arutha drummed his fingers upon the table. "It will be another two to three weeks before we can expect the armies from Tulan and Carse. If the Dark Brothers harry the Tsurani enough, we might have some respite." He looked at Martin. "What occurs to the east?"

Longbow spread his hands upon the table. "We couldn't get close enough to see much as we hurried past, but they are up to something. They've a good number of men scattered throughout the woods from the edge of the clearing back about a half mile. If it hadn't been for the moredhel hot on our heels, Garret and I might not have made it back to the walls."

"I wish I knew what they were doing out there," said Arutha. "This attacking only at night, it surely masks some trickery."

Gardan said, "We'll know soon enough, I fear."

Arutha stood, and the others rose as well. "We have much to do in any event. But if they do not come this night, we should all take advantage of the rest.

Order watches posted, and send the men back to the commons for sleep. If I'm needed, I'll be in my room."

The others followed him from the council hall, and Arutha walked slowly to his room, his fatigued mind trying to grasp what he knew were important matters, but failing. He threw off only his armor and fell fully clothed across his pallet. He was quickly asleep, but it was a troubled, dream-filled slumber.

For a week no attacks came, as the Tsurani were cautious of the migrating Brotherhood of the Dark Path. As Martin had foretold, the moredhel were emboldened by hunger and had twice struck into the heart of the Tsurani camp.

On the eighth afternoon after the first moredhel attack, the Tsurani were again gathering on the field before the castle, their ranks once more swelled by reinforcements from the east. Messages carried by pigeon between Arutha and his father told of increased fighting along the eastern front as well. Lord Borric speculated Crydee was being attacked by troops fresh from the Tsurani homeworld, as there had been no reports of any troop movements along his front. Other messages arrived with word of relief from Carse and Tulan. Baron Tolburt's soldiers had departed Tulan within two days of receiving Arutha's message, and his fleet would join with Baron Bellamy's at Carse. Depending upon the prevailing winds, it would be from one to two weeks before the relief fleet arrived.

Arutha stood at his usual place upon the west wall, Martin Longbow at his side. They watched the Tsurani taking position as the sun sank in the west, a red beacon bathing the landscape in crimson.

"It seems," said Arutha, "they mount a full attack tonight."

Longbow said, "They've cleared the area of troublesome neighbors by all appearances, at least for a time. The moredhel gained us a little time, Highness, but no more."

"I wonder how many will reach the Northlands?"

Longbow shrugged. "One in five perhaps. From the Green Heart to the Northlands is a long, difficult journey under the best of circumstances. Now . . ." He let his words trail off.

Gardan came up the stairs from the courtyard. "Highness, the tower watch reports the Tsurani are in formation."

As he spoke, the Tsurani sounded their battle calls and began to advance. Arutha drew his sword and gave the order for the catapults to fire. Bowmen followed, unleashing a storm of arrows upon the attackers, but still the Tsurani came.

Through the night, wave after wave of brightly armored aliens threw themselves at the west wall of Castle Crydee. Most died on the field before the wall, or at its base, but a few managed to crest the battlements. They, too, died. Still, more came.

Six times the Tsurani wave had broken upon the defenses of Crydee, and now they prepared for a seventh assault. Arutha, covered in dirt and blood, directed the disposition of rested troops along the wall. Gardan looked to the east. "If we hold one more time, the dawn will be here. Then we should have some respite," he said, his voice thick with fatigue.

"We will hold," answered Arutha, his own voice sounding just as tired in his ears as Gardan's.

"Arutha?"

Arutha saw Roland and Amos coming up the stairs, with another man behind. "What now?" asked the Prince.

Roland said, "We can see no activity on the other walls, but there is something here you should see."

Arutha recognized the other man, Lewis, the castle's Rathunter. It was his responsibility to keep vermin from the keep. He tenderly held something in his hands.

Arutha looked closely: it was a ferret, twitching slightly in the firelight. "Highness," said Lewis, his voice thick with emotion, "it's—"

"What, man?" said Arutha impatiently. With attack about to begin, he had little time to mourn a lost pet.

Roland spoke, for Lewis was obviously overcome at the loss of his ferret. "The Rathunter's ferrets didn't return two days ago. This one crawled into the storage room behind the kitchen sometime since. Lewis found it there a few minutes ago."

In choked tones, Lewis said, "They're all well trained, sire. If they didn't come back, it's because something kept them from returnin'. This poor lad's been stepped on. His back's broken. He must've crawled for hours to get back."

Arutha said, "I fail to see the significance of this."

Roland gripped the Prince's arm. "Arutha, he hunts them in the rat tunnels *under the castle.*"

Comprehension dawned upon Arutha. He turned to Gardan and said, "Sappers! The Tsurani must be digging under the east wall."

Gardan said, "That would explain the constant attacks upon the west wall—to draw us away."

Arutha said, "Gardan, take command of the walls. Amos, Roland, come with me."

Arutha ran down the steps and through the courtyard. He shouted for a group of soldiers to follow and bring shovels. They reached the small courtyard behind the keep, and Arutha said, "We've got to find that tunnel and collapse it."

Amos said, "Your walls are slanted outward at the plinth. They'll recognize they can't fire the timbers of the tunnels to bring it down to make a breach. They'll be trying to get a force inside the castle grounds or into the keep."

Roland looked alarmed. "Carline! She and the other ladies are in the cellars."

Arutha said, "Take some men and go to the cellars." Roland ran off. Arutha fell to his knees and placed his ear on the ground. The others followed his example, moving around, listening for sounds of digging from below.

CARLINE SAT NERVOUSLY next to the Lady Marna. The fat former governess made a show of calmly attending to her needlepoint despite the rustling and stirring of the other women in the cellar. The sounds of battle from the walls came to them as faint, distant echoes, muted by the thick walls of the keep. Now there was an equally unnerving quiet.

"Oh! To be sitting here like a caged bird," said Carline.

"The walls are no place for a lady," came the retort from Lady Marna.

Carline stood. As she paced the room, she said, "I can tie bandages and carry water. All of us could."

The other ladies of the court looked at one another as if the Princess had been bereft of her senses. None of them could imagine subjecting herself to such a trial.

"Highness, please," said Lady Marna, "you should wait quietly. There will be much to do when the battle's over. Now you should rest."

Carline began a retort, then stopped. She held up her hand. "Do you hear something?"

The others stopped their movement, and all listened. From the floor came a faint tapping sound. Carline knelt upon the flagstone. "My lady, this is most unseemly," began the Lady Marna.

Carline stopped the complaint with an imperious wave of her hand. "Quiet!" She placed her ear upon the flagstones. "There is something . . ."

Lady Glynis shuddered. "Probably rats scurrying about. There are hundreds of them down here." Her expression showed this revelation was about as unpleasant a fact as imaginable.

"Be quiet!" ordered Carline.

There came a cracking sound from the floor, and Carline leaped to her feet. Her sword came out of its scabbard as a fracture appeared in the stones of the floor. A chisel point broke through the flagstone, and suddenly the upturned stone was pushed up and outward.

Ladies screamed as a hole appeared in the floor. A startled face popped into the light, then a Tsurani warrior, hair filthy from the dirt of the tunnel, tried to scramble upward. Carline's sword took him in the throat as she shouted, "Get out! Call the guards!"

Most of the women sat frozen in terror, refusing to move. Lady Marna heaved her massive bulk from the bench upon which she sat and gave a shrieking town girl a backhanded slap. The girl looked at Lady Marna with wide-eyed fright for an instant, then broke toward the steps. As if at a signal, the others ran after, screaming for help.

Carline watched as the Tsurani slowly fell back, blocking the hole in the floor. Other cracks appeared around the hole, and hands pulled pieces of flagstone downward into the ever-widening entrance. Lady Marna was halfway to the steps when she saw Carline standing her ground. "Princess!" she shrieked.

Another man came scrambling upward, and Carline delivered a death blow to him. She was then forced back as the stones near her feet collapsed. The Tsurani had terminated their tunnel in a wide hole and were now broadening the entrance, pulling down stones so that they could swarm out, overwhelming any defenders.

A man fought upward, pushing Carline to one side, allowing another to start his climb upward. Lady Marna ran back to her former ward and grabbed up a large piece of loose stone, which she brought crashing down on the unhelmeted skull of the second man. Grunts and strange-sounding words came from the tunnel mouth as the man fell back upon those behind.

Carline ran the other man through and kicked another in the face. "Princess!" cried Lady Marna. "We must flee!"

Carline didn't answer. She dodged a blow at her feet delivered by a Tsurani who then sprang nimbly out of the hole. Carline thrust and the man dodged. Another came scrambling out of the hole, and the Lady Marna shrieked.

The first man turned reflexively at the sound, and Carline drove her sword into his side. The second man raised a serrated sword to strike Lady Marna, and Carline sprang for him, thrusting her sword point into his neck. The man shuddered and fell, his fingers releasing their grip on the sword. Carline grabbed Lady Marna's arm and propelled her toward the steps.

Tsurani came swarming out of the hole, and Carline turned at the bottom of the stairs. Lady Marna stood behind her beloved Princess, not willing to leave. The Tsurani approached warily. The girl had killed enough of their companions to warrant their respect and caution.

Suddenly a body crashed past the girl as Roland charged into the Tsurani, soldiers of the keep hurrying behind. The young Squire was in a frenzy to protect the

Princess, and he bowled over three Tsurani in his rush. They tumbled backward, disappearing into the hole, Roland with them.

As the Squire vanished from view, Carline screamed, "Roland!" Other guards leaped past the Princess to engage the Tsurani who still stood in the cellar, and more jumped boldly into the hole. Grunts and cries, shouts and oaths rang from the tunnel.

A guard took Carline by the arm and began to drag her up the stairs. She followed, helpless in the man's strong grip, crying, "Roland!"

GRUNTS OF EXERTION filled the dark tunnel as the soldiers from Crydee dug furiously. Arutha had found the Tsurani tunnel and had ordered a shaft sunk near it. They were now digging a countertunnel to intercept the Tsurani, near the wall. Amos had agreed with Arutha's judgment that they needed to force the Tsurani back beyond the wall before collapsing the tunnel, denying them any access to the castle.

A shovel broke through, and men began frantically clearing away enough dirt to allow passage into the Tsurani tunnel. Boards were hastily jammed into place, jury-rigged supports, preventing the earth above from caving in on them.

The men from Crydee surged into the low tunnel and entered a frantic, terrible melee. Tsurani warriors and Roland's squad of soldiers were locked in a desperate hand-to-hand struggle in the dark. Men fought and died in the gloom under the earth. It was impossible to bring order to the fray, with the fighting in such confinement. An overturned lantern flickered faintly, providing little illumination.

Arutha said to a soldier behind, "Get more men!"

"At once, Highness!" answered the soldier, turning toward the shaft.

Arutha entered the Tsurani tunnel. It was only five feet high, so he moved stooped over. It was fairly wide, with enough room for three men to negotiate closely. Arutha stepped on something soft, which groaned in pain. He continued past the dying man, toward the sound of fighting.

It was a scene from his worst nightmare, faintly lit by widely spaced torches. With little room only the first three men could engage the enemy at any one point. Arutha called out, "Knives!" and dropped his rapier. In close quarters the shorter weapons would prove more effective.

He came upon two men struggling in the darkness and grabbed at one. His hand closed on chitinous armor, and he plunged his knife into the man's exposed neck. Jerking the now lifeless body off the other man, he saw a jam of bodies a few feet away, where Crydee and Tsurani soldiers pressed against one another. Curses and cries filled the tunnel, and the damp earth smell was mixed with the odor of blood and excrement.

Arutha fought madly, blindly, lashing out at barely seen foes. His own fear kept threatening to overcome him as primitive awareness cried for him to quit the tunnel and the threatening earth above. He forced his panic down and continued to lead the attack on the sappers.

A familiar voice grunted and cursed at his side, and Arutha knew Amos Trask was near. "Another thirty feet, lad!" he shouted.

Arutha took the man at his word, having lost all sense of distance. The men of Crydee pressed onward, and many died killing the resisting Tsurani. Time became a blur and the fight a dim montage of images.

Abruptly Amos shouted, "Straw!" and bundles of dry straw were passed forward. "Torches!" he cried, and flaming torches were passed up. He piled the straw near a latticework of timbers and drove the torch into the pile. Flames burst upward, and he yelled, "Clear the tunnel!"

The fighting stopped. Every man, whether of Crydee or Tsurani, turned and fled the flames. The sappers knew the tunnel was lost without means to quench the flames and scrambled for their lives.

Choking smoke filled the tunnel, and men began to cough as they cleared the cramped quarters. Arutha followed Amos, and they missed the turn to the countertunnel, coming out in the cellar. Guardsmen, dirty and bloody, were collapsing on the stones of the cellar, gasping for air. A dull rumble sounded, and with a crash, a blast of air and smoke blew out of the hole. Amos grinned, his face streaked with dirt. "The timbers collapsed. The tunnel's sealed."

Arutha nodded dumbly, exhausted and still reeling from the smoke. A cup of water was handed to him, and he drank deeply, soothing his burning throat.

Carline appeared before him. "Are you all right?" she asked, concern on her face. He nodded. She looked around. "Where's Roland?"

Arutha shook his head. "It was impossible to see down there. Was he in the tunnel?"

She bit her lower lip. Tears welled up in her blue eyes as she nodded. Arutha said, "He might have cleared the tunnel and come up in the courtyard. Let us see."

He got to his feet, and Amos and Carline followed him up the stairs. They left the keep, and a soldier informed him the attack on the wall had been repulsed. Arutha acknowledged the report and continued around the keep until they came to the shaft he had ordered dug. Soldiers lay on the grass of the yard, coughing and spitting, trying to clear their lungs of the burning smoke. The air hung heavy with an acrid haze as fumes from the fire continued to billow from the shaft. Another rumble sounded, and Arutha could feel it through the soles of his boots. Near the wall a depression had appeared where the tunnel had fallen below. "Squire Roland!" Arutha shouted.

"Here, Highness," came an answering shout from a soldier.

Carline dashed past Arutha and reached Roland before the Prince. The Squire lay upon the ground, tended by the soldier who answered. His eyes were closed and his skin pale, and blood seeped from his side. The soldier said, "I had to drag him along the last few yards, Highness. He was out on his feet. I thought it might be smoke until I saw the wound."

Carline cradled Roland's head, while Arutha first cut the binding straps of Roland's breastplate, then tore away the undertunic. After a moment Arutha sat back upon his heels. "It's a shallow wound. He'll be all right."

"Oh, Roland," Carline said softly.

Roland's eyes opened and he grinned weakly. His voice was tired, but he forced a cheery note. "What's this? You'd think I'd been killed."

Carline said, "You heartless monster." She gently shook him but didn't release her hold as she smiled down at him. "Playing tricks at a time like this!"

He winced as he tried to move. "Ooh, that hurts." She placed a restraining hand upon his shoulder.

"Don't try to move. We must bind the wound," she said, caught between relief and anger.

Nestling his head into her lap, he smiled. "I'd not move for half your father's Duchy."

She looked at him in irritation. "What were you doing throwing yourself upon the enemy like that?"

Roland looked genuinely embarrassed. "In truth, I

tripped coming down the steps and couldn't stop myself."

She placed her cheek against his forehead as Arutha and Amos laughed. "You are a liar. And I do love you," she said softly.

Arutha stood and took Amos in tow, leaving Roland and Carline to each other. Reaching the corner, they encountered the former Tsurani slave, Charles, carrying water for the wounded. Arutha halted the man.

He stood with a yoke across his shoulders holding two large water buckets. He was bleeding from several small wounds and was covered with mire. Arutha said, "What happened to you?"

With a broad smile, Charles said, "Good fight. Jump in hole. Charles good warrior."

The former Tsurani slave was pale and weaved a little as he stood there. Arutha remained speechless, then indicated he should continue his work. Happily Charles hurried along. Arutha said to Amos, "What do you make of that?"

Amos chuckled. "I've had many dealings with rogues and scoundrels, Highness. I know little of these Tsurani, but I think that's a man to count on."

Arutha watched as Charles dispensed water to the other soldiers, ignoring his own wounds and fatigue. "That was no mean thing, jumping into the shaft without orders. I'll have to consider Longbow's offer to put that man in service."

They continued on their way, Arutha supervising the care of the wounded, while Amos was put in charge of the final destruction of the tunnel.

When dawn came, the courtyard was still, and only a patch of raw earth, where the shaft had been filled in, and a long depression running from the keep to the outer wall showed anything unusual had occurred in the night.

FANNON HOBBLED ALONG the wall, favoring his right side. The wound to his back was almost healed, but he was still unable to walk without aid. Father Tully supported the Swordmaster as they came to where the others waited.

Arutha gave the Swordmaster a smile and gently took him by the other arm, helping Tully hold him. Gardan, Amos Trask, Martin Longbow, and a group of soldiers stood nearby.

"What's this?" asked Fannon, his display of gruff anger a welcome sight to those on the wall. "Have you so little wits among you that you must haul me from my rest to take charge?"

Arutha pointed out to sea. On the horizon dozens of small flecks could be seen against the blue of sea and sky, flashes of brilliant white glinting as the morning sun was caught and reflected back to them. "The fleet from Carse and Tulan approaches the south beaches."

He indicated the Tsurani camp in the distance, bustling with activity. "Today we'll drive them out. By this time tomorrow we'll clear this entire area of the aliens. We'll harry them eastward, allowing them no respite. It will be a long time before they'll come in strength again."

Quietly Fannon said, "I trust you are right, Arutha." He stood without speaking for a time, then said, "I have heard reports of your command, Arutha. You've done well. You are a credit to your father, and to Crydee."

Finding himself moved by the Swordmaster's praise, Arutha tried to make light, but Fannon interrupted. "No, you have done all that was needed, and more. You were right. With these people we must not be cautious. We must carry the struggle to them." He sighed. "I am an old man, Arutha. It is time I retired and left warfare to the young."

Tully made a derisive noise. "You're not old. I was already a priest when you were still in swaddling."

Fannon laughed with the others at the obvious untruth of the statement, and Arutha said, "You must know, if I've done well, it is because of your teachings."

Tully gripped Fannon's elbow. "You may not be an old man, but you are a sick one. Back to the keep with you. You've had enough gadding about. You can begin walking regularly tomorrow. In a few weeks you'll be charging about, shouting orders at everyone like your old self."

Fannon managed a slight smile and allowed Tully to lead him back down the stairs. When he was gone, Gardan said, "The Swordmaster's right, Highness. You've done your father proud."

Arutha watched the approaching ships, his angular features fixed in an expression of quiet reflection. Softly he said, "If I have done well, it is because I have had the aid of good men, many no longer with us." He took a deep breath, then continued, "You have played a great part in our withstanding this siege, Gardan, and you, Martin."

Both men smiled and voiced their thanks. "And you, pirate." Arutha grinned. "You've also played a great part. We are deeply in your debt."

Amos Trask tried to look modest and failed. "Well, Highness, I was merely protecting my own skin as well as everyone else's." He then returned Arutha's grin. "It was a rousing good fight."

Arutha looked toward the sea once more. "Let us hope we can soon be done with rousing good fights." He left the walls and started down the stairs. "Give orders to prepare for the attack."

•   •   •

CARLINE STOOD ATOP the south tower of the keep, her arm around Roland's waist. The Squire was pale from his wound, but otherwise in hale spirits. "We'll be done with the siege, now the fleet's arrived," he said, clinging tightly to the Princess.

"It has been a nightmare."

He smiled down at her, gazing into her blue eyes. "Not entirely. There has been some compensation."

Softly she said, "You are a rogue," then kissed him. When they separated, she said, "I wonder if your foolish bravery was nothing more than a ploy to gain my sympathies."

Feigning a wince, he said, "Lady, I am wounded."

She clung to him. "I was so worried about you, not knowing if you lay dead in the tunnel. I . . ." Her voice dropped off as her gaze strayed to the north tower of the keep, opposite the one upon which they stood. She could see the window upon the second floor, the window to Pug's room. The funny little metal chimney, which would constantly belch smoke when he was at his studies, was now only a mute reminder of just how empty the tower stood.

Roland followed her gaze. "I know," he said. "I miss him, too. And Tomas as well."

She sighed. "That seems such a long time ago, Roland. I was a girl then, a girl with a girl's notion of what life and love were about." Softly she said, "Some love comes like a wind off the sea, while others grow slowly from the seeds of friendship and kindness. Someone once told me that."

"Father Tully. He was right." He squeezed her waist. "Either way, as long as you feel, you live."

She watched as the soldiers of the garrison prepared for the coming sortie. "Will this end it?"

"No, they will come again. This war is fated to last a long time."

They stood together, taking comfort in the simple fact of each other's existence.

KASUMI OF THE Shinzawai, Force Leader of the Armies of the Kanazawai Clan, of the Blue Wheel Party, watched the enemy upon the castle wall.

He could barely make out the figures walking along the battlements, but he knew them well. He could not put names to any, but they were each as familiar to him as his own men. The slender youth who commanded, who fought like a demon, who brought order to the fray when needed, he was there. The black giant would not be too far from his side, the one who stood like a bulwark against every attack upon the walls. And the green-clad one, who could race through the woods like an apparition, taunting Kasumi's men by the freedom with which he passed their lines, he would be there as well. No doubt the broad-shouldered one was nearby, the laughing man with the curved sword and maniacal grin. Kasumi quietly saluted them all as valiant foemen, even if only barbarians.

Chingari of the Omechkel, the Senior Strike Leader, came to stand at Kasumi's side. "Force Leader, the barbarian fleet is nearing. They will land their men within the hour."

Kasumi regarded the scroll he held in his hand. It had been read a dozen times since arriving at dawn. He glanced at it one more time, again studying the chop at the bottom, the crest of his father, Kamatsu, Lord of the Shinzawai. Silently accepting his personal fate, Kasumi said, "Order for march. Break camp at once and begin assembling the warriors. We are commanded to return to Kelewan. Send the trailbreakers ahead."

Chingari's voice betrayed his bitterness. "Now the tunnel is destroyed, do we quit so meekly?"

"There is no shame, Chingari. Our clan has withdrawn itself from the Alliance for War, as have the other clans of the Blue Wheel Party. The War Party is once more alone in the conduct of this invasion."

With a sigh Chingari said, "Again politics interferes with conquest. It would have been a glorious victory to take such a fine castle."

Kasumi laughed. "True." He watched the activities of the castle. "They are the best we have ever faced. We already learn much from them. Castle walls slanted outward at the plinth, preventing sappers from collapsing them, this is a new and clever thing. And those beasts they ride. Ayee, how they move, like Thūn racing across the tundras of home. I will somehow gain some of those animals. Yes, these people are more than simple barbarians."

After a moment's more reflection, he said, "Have our scouts and trailbreakers keep alert for signs of the forest devils."

Chingari spat. "The foul ones move in great number northward once more. They're as much a dagger in our side as the barbarians."

Kasumi said, "When this world is conquered, we shall have to see to these creatures. The barbarians make strong slaves. Some may even prove valuable enough to make free vassals who will swear loyalty to our houses, but those foul ones, they must be obliterated." Kasumi fell silent for a while. Then he said, "Let the barbarians think we flee in terror from their fleet. This place is now a matter for the clans remaining in the War Party. Let Tasio of the Minwanabi worry about a garrison at his rear should he move eastward. Until the Kanazawai once more realign themselves in the

High Council, we are done with this war. Order the march."

Chingari saluted his commander and left, and Kasumi considered the implications of the message from his father. He knew the withdrawal of all the forces of the Blue Wheel Party would prove a major setback for the Warlord and his party. The repercussions of such a move would be felt throughout the Empire for some years to come. There would be no smashing victories for the Warlord now, for with the departure of those forces loyal to the Kanazawai lords and the other clans of the Blue Wheel, other clans would reconsider before joining in an all-out push. No, thought Kasumi, it was a bold but dangerous move by his father and the other lords. This war would now be prolonged. The Warlord was robbed of a spectacular conquest; he was now overextended with too few men holding too much land. Without new allies he would remain unable to press forward with the war. His choices were now down to two: withdraw from Midkemia and risk humiliation before the High Council, or sit and wait, hoping for another shift in politics at home.

It was a stunning move on behalf of the Blue Wheel. But the risk was great. And the risk from the next series of moves in the Game of the Council would be even more dangerous. Silently he said: O my father, we are now firmly committed to the Great Game. We risk much: our family, our clan, our honor, and perhaps even the Empire itself.

Crumbling the scroll, he tossed it into a nearby brazier, and when it was totally consumed by flame, he put aside thoughts of risk and walked back toward his tent.

Be sure not to miss
Bantam Spectra's classic reissues of

THE NOVELS OF THE
RIFTWAR

BY

RAYMOND E. FEIST

Here are some special previews:

Magician: Apprentice

VOLUME I IN THE *NEW YORK TIMES* BESTSELLING *RIFTWAR* SAGA

The storm had broken.

Pug danced along the edge of the rocks, his feet finding scant purchase as he made his way among the tide pools. His dark eyes darted about as he peered into each pool under the cliff face, seeking the spiny creatures driven into the shallows by the recently passed storm. His boyish muscles bunched under his light shirt as he shifted the sack of sandcrawlers, rockclaws, and crabs plucked from this water garden.

The afternoon sun sent sparkles through the sea spray swirling around him, as the west wind blew his sun-streaked brown hair about. Pug set his sack down, checked to make sure it was securely tied, then squatted on a clear patch of sand. The sack was not quite full, but Pug relished the extra hour or so that he could relax. Megar the cook wouldn't trouble him about the time as long as the sack was almost full. Resting with his back against a large rock, Pug was soon dozing in the sun's warmth.

A cool wet spray woke him hours later. He opened his eyes with a start, knowing he had stayed much too long. Westward, over the sea, dark thunderheads were forming above the black outline of the Six Sisters, the small islands on the horizon. The roiling, surging clouds, with rain trailing below like some sooty veil, heralded another of the sudden storms common to this part of the coast in early summer. To the south, the high bluffs of Sailor's Grief reared up against the sky, as waves crashed against the base of that rocky pinnacle. Whitecaps started to form behind the breakers, a sure sign that the storm would quickly strike. Pug knew he was in danger, for the storms of summer could drown anyone on the beaches, or if severe enough, on the low ground beyond.

He picked up his sack and started north, toward the castle. As he moved among the pools, he felt the coolness in the wind turn to a deeper, wetter cold. The day began to be broken by a patchwork of shadows as the first clouds passed before the sun, bright colors fading to shades of grey. Out to sea, lightning flashed against the blackness of the clouds, and the distant boom of thunder rode over the noise of the waves.

Pug picked up speed when he came to the first stretch of open beach. The storm was coming in faster than he would have thought possible, driving the rising tide before it. By the time he reached the second stretch of tide pools, there was barely ten feet of dry sand between water's edge and cliffs.

Pug hurried as fast as was safe across the rocks, twice nearly catching his foot. As he reached the next expanse of sand, he mistimed his jump from the last rock and landed poorly. He fell to the sand, grasping his ankle. As if waiting for the mishap, the tide surged forward, covering him for a moment. He reached out blindly and felt his sack carried away. Frantically grabbing at it, Pug lunged forward, only to have his ankle fail. He went under, gulping water . . .

Magician: Master

VOLUME II IN THE *NEW YORK TIMES* BESTSELLING
RIFTWAR SAGA

The dying slave lay screaming.

The day was unmercifully hot. The other slaves went about their work, ignoring the sound as much as possible. Life in the work camp was cheap, and it did no good to dwell on the fate that awaited so many. The dying man had been bitten by a relli, a snakelike swamp creature. Its venom was slow-acting and painful; short of magic, there was no cure.

Suddenly there was silence. Pug looked over to see a Tsurani guard wipe off his sword. A hand fell on Pug's shoulder. Laurie's voice whispered in his ear, "Looks like our venerable overseer was disturbed by the sound of Toffston's dying."

Pug tied a coil of rope securely around his waist. "At least it ended quickly." He turned to the tall blond singer from the Kingdom city of Tyr-Sog and said, "Keep a sharp eye out. This one's old and may be rotten." Without another word, Pug scampered up the bole of the ngaggi tree, a firlike swamp tree the Tsurani harvested for wood and resins. With few metals, the Tsurani had become clever in finding substitutes. The wood of this tree could be worked like paper, then dried to an incredible hardness, useful in fashioning a hundred things. The resins were used to laminate woods and cure hides. Properly cured hides could produce a suit of leather armor as tough as Midkemian chain mail, and laminated wooden weapons were nearly the match of Midkemian steel.

Four years in the swamp camp had hardened Pug's

body. His sinewy muscles strained as he climbed the tree. His skin had been tanned deeply by the harsh sun of the Tsurani homeworld. His face was covered by a slave's beard.

Pug reached the first large branches and looked down at his friend. Laurie stood knee-deep in the murky water, absently swatting at the insects that plagued them while they worked. Pug liked Laurie. The troubadour had no business being here, but then he had no business tagging along with a patrol in the hope of seeing Tsurani soldiers, either. He said he wanted material for ballads that would make him famous throughout the Kingdom. He had seen more than he had hoped for. The patrol had ridden into a major Tsurani offensive, and Laurie had been captured. He had come to this camp over four months ago, and he and Pug had quickly become friends.

Pug continued climbing, keeping one eye always searching for the most dangerous tree dwellers of Kelewan. Reaching the most likely place for a topping, Pug froze as he caught a glimpse of movement. He relaxed when he saw it was only a needler, a creature whose protection was its resemblance to a clump of ngaggi needles. It scurried away from the presence of the human and made the short jump to the branch of a neighboring tree. Pug made another survey and started tying his ropes. His job was to cut away the tops of the huge trees, making the fall less dangerous to those below.

Pug took several cuts at the bark, then felt the edge of his wooden axe bite into the softer pulp beneath. A faint pungent odor greeted his careful sniffing. Swearing, he called down to Laurie, "This one's rotten. . . ."

Silverthorn

VOLUME III IN THE *NEW YORK TIMES* BESTSELLING *RIFTWAR* SAGA

The ship sped home.

The wind changed quarter and the captain's voice rang out; aloft, his crew scrambled to answer the demands of a freshening breeze and a captain anxious to get safely to port. He was a seasoned sailingmaster, nearly thirty years in the King's navy, and seventeen years commanding his own ship. And the *Royal Eagle* was the best ship in the King's fleet, but still the captain wished for just a little more wind, just a little more speed, since he would not rest until his passengers were safely ashore.

Standing upon the foredeck were the reasons for the captain's concern, three tall men. Two, one blond and one dark, were standing at the rail, sharing a joke, for they both laughed. Each stood a full four inches over six feet, and each carried himself with the sure step of a fighting man or hunter. Lyam, King of the Kingdom of the Isles, and Martin, his elder brother and Duke of Crydee, spoke of many things, of hunting and feasting, of travel and politics, of war and discord, and occasionally they spoke of their father, Duke Borric.

The third man, not as tall or as broad of shoulder as the other two, leaned against the rail a short way off, lost in his own thoughts. Arutha, Prince of Krondor and youngest of the three brothers, also dwelt upon the past, but his vision was not of the father killed during the war with the Tsurani, in what was now being called the Riftwar. Instead he watched the bow wake of the ship as it sliced through emerald-green waters, and in that green he saw two sparkling green eyes.

The captain cast a glance aloft, then ordered the sails trimmed. Again he took note of the three men upon the foredeck and again he gave a silent prayer to Kilian, Goddess of Sailors, and wished Rillanon's tall spires were in sight. For those three were the three most powerful and important men in the Kingdom, and the sailingmaster refused to think of the chaos that would befall the Kingdom should any ill chance visit his ship.

Arutha vaguely heard the captain's shouts and the replies of his mates and crew. He was fatigued by the events of the last year, so he paid little attention to what was occurring about him. He could keep his thoughts only upon one thing: he was returning to Rillanon, and to Anita.

Arutha smiled to himself. His life had seemed unremarkable for the first eighteen years. Then the Tsurani invasion had come and the world had been forever changed. He had come to be counted one of the finest commanders in the Kingdom, had discovered an unsuspected elder brother in Martin, and had seen a thousand horrors and miracles. But the most miraculous thing that had happened to Arutha had been Anita.

They had been parted after Lyam's coronation. For nearly a year Lyam had been displaying the royal banner to both eastern lords and neighboring kings, and now they were returning home . . .

A Darkness at Sethanon

VOLUME IV IN THE *NEW YORK TIMES* BESTSELLING *RIFTWAR* SAGA

Jimmy raced down the hall.

The last few months had been a time of growth for Jimmy. He would be counted sixteen years old the next Midsummer's Day, though no one knew his real age. Sixteen seemed a likely guess, although he might be closer to seventeen or even eighteen years old. Always athletic, he had begun to broaden in the shoulders and had gained nearly a head of height since coming to court. He now looked more the man than the boy.

But some things never change, and Jimmy's sense of responsibility remained one of them. While he could be counted upon for important tasks, his disregard of the trivial once again threatened to turn the Prince of Krondor's court into chaos. Duty prescribed that he, as Senior Squire of the Prince's court, be first at assembly, and as usual, he was likely to be last. Somehow, punctuality seemed to elude him. He arrived either late or early, but rarely on time.

Squire Locklear stood at the door to the minor hall used as the squire's assembly point, waving frantically for Jimmy to hurry. Of all the squires, only Locklear had become a friend to the Prince's Squire since Jimmy returned with Arutha from the quest for Silverthorn. Despite Jimmy's first, accurate judgment that Locklear was a child in many ways, the youngest son of the Baron of Land's End had displayed a certain taste for the reckless that had both surprised and pleased his friend. No matter how chancy a scheme Jimmy plotted, Locklear usually agreed.

When delivered up to trouble as a result of Jimmy's gambles with the patience of the court officials, Locklear took his punishment with good grace, counting it the fair price of being caught.

Jimmy sped into the room, sliding across the smooth marble floor as he sought to halt himself. Two dozen green-and-brown-clad squires formed a neat pair of lines in the hall. He looked around, noting everyone as where they were supposed to be. He assumed his own appointed place at the instant that Master of Ceremonies Brian deLacy entered.

When given the rank of Senior Squire, Jimmy had thought it would be all privilege and no responsibility. He had been quickly disabused of that notion. An integral part of the court, albeit a minor one, he was, when he failed his duty, confronted by the single most important fact known to all bureaucrats of any nation or epoch: those above were not interested in excuses, only in results. Jimmy lived and died with every mistake made by the squires. So far, it had not been a good year for Jimmy . . .

Prince of the Blood

THE *NEW YORK TIMES* BESTSELLING SEQUEL TO THE
RIFTWAR SAGA

The inn was quiet.

Walls darkened with years of fireplace soot drank in the lantern light, reflecting dim illumination. The dying fire in the hearth offered scant warmth and, from the demeanor of those who chose to sit before it, less cheer. In contrast to the mood of most establishments of its ilk, this inn was nearly somber. In murky corners, men spoke in hushed tones, discussing things best not overheard by the uninvolved. A grunt of agreement to a whispered proposal or a bitter laugh from a woman of negotiable virtue were the only sounds to intrude upon the silence. The majority of the denizens of the inn called the Sleeping Dockman were closely watching the game.

The game was pokiir, common to the Empire of Great Kesh to the south and now replacing lin-lan and pashawa as the gambler's choice in the inns and taverns of the Western Realm of the Kingdom. One player held his five cards before him, his eyes narrowed in concentration. An off-duty soldier, he kept alert for any sign of trouble in the room, and trouble was rapidly approaching. He made a display of studying his cards, while discreetly inspecting the five men who played at the table with him.

The first two on his left were rough men. Both were sunburned and the hands holding their cards were heavily callused; faded linen shirts and cotton trousers hung loosely on lank but muscular frames. Neither wore boots or even sandals, barefoot despite the cool night air, a certain sign they were sailors waiting for a new berth. Usually such men quickly lost their pay and were bound again for sea, but from the way they had bet all night, the soldier was certain they were working for the man who sat to the soldier's right.

The soldier had seen his sort many times before; a rich merchant's son, or a younger son of a minor noble, with too much time on his hands and too little sense. He was fashionably attired in the latest rage among the young men of Krondor, a short pair of breeches tucked into hose, allowing the pants legs above the calf to balloon out. A simple white shirt was embroidered with pearls and semi-precious stones, and the jacket was the new cutaway design, a rather garish yellow, with white and silver brocade at the wrists and collar. He was a typical dandy. And from the look of the Rodezian slamanca hanging from the loose baldric across his shoulder, a dangerous man. It was a sword only used by a master or someone seeking a quick death—in the hands of an expert it was a fearsome weapon; in the hands of the inexperienced it was suicide.

The man had probably lost large sums of money before and now sought to recoup his previous losses by cheating at cards. One or the other of the sailors would win an occasional hand, but the soldier was certain this was planned to keep suspicion from falling upon the young dandy. The soldier sighed, as if troubled by what choice to make. The other two players waited patiently for him to make his play.

They were twin brothers, tall—two inches over six feet, he judged—and fit in appearance. Both came to the table armed with rapiers, again the choice of experts or fools. Since Prince Arutha had come to the throne of Krondor twenty years before, rapiers had become the choice of men who wore weapons as a consideration of fashion rather than survival. But these two didn't look the type to sport weapons as decorative baubles. They were dressed as common mercenaries, just in from caravan duty from the look of them. Dust still clung to their tunic and leather vest, while their red-brown hair was lightly matted. Both needed a shave. Yet while their clothing was common and dirty, there was nothing that looked neglected about their armor or arms; they might not pause to bathe after weeks on a caravan, but they would take an hour to oil their leather and polish their steel. They looked genuine in their part, save for a feeling of vague familiarity which caused the soldier slight discomfort: both spoke with none of the rough speech common to mercenaries, but rather with the educated crispness of those used to spending their days in court . . .

The King's Buccaneer

A SPELLBINDING NOVEL SET IN THE WORLD OF THE
RIFTWAR SAGA

The lookout pointed.

"Boat dead ahead!"

Amos Trask, Admiral of the Prince's fleet of the Kingdom navy, shouted, "What?"

The harbor pilot who stood beside the Admiral, guiding the Prince of Krondor's flagship, the *Royal Dragon*, toward the palace docks, shouted to his assistant at the bow, "Wave them off!"

His assistant pilot, a sour-looking young man, shouted back, "They fly the royal ensign!"

Amos Trask unceremoniously pushed past the pilot. Still a barrel-chested, bull-necked man at past sixty years of age, he hurried toward the bow with the sure step of a man who'd spent most of his life at sea. After sailing Prince Arutha's flagship in and out of Krondor for nearly twenty years, he could dock her blindfolded, but custom required the presence of the harbor pilot. Amos disliked turning over command of his ship to anyone, least of all an officious and not very personable member of the Royal Harbormaster's staff. Amos suspected that the second requirement for a position in that office was an objectionable personality. The first seemed to be marriage to one of the Harbormaster's numerous sisters or daughters.

Amos reached the bow and looked ahead. His dark eyes narrowed as he observed the scene unfolding below. As the ship glided toward the quay, a small sailing boat, no more than fifteen feet in length, attempted to dart into the opening ahead of it. Clumsily tied to the top of the mast was a pennant, a small version of the Prince of Krondor's naval ensign. Two young men frantically worked the sails and tiller, one attempting to hold as strong a line to the dock as possible while the other furled a jib. Both laughed at the impromptu race.

"Nicholas!" shouted Amos, as the boy lowering the jib waved at him. "You idiot! We're cutting your wind! Turn about!" The boy at the helm turned to look at Amos and threw him an impudent grin. "I should have known," said Amos to the assistant pilot. To the grinning boy, Amos shouted, "Harry! You lunatic!" Glancing back, seeing the last of the sails reefed, Amos observed, "We're coasting to the docks, we don't have room to turn if we wanted to and we certainly can't stop."

All ships coming into Krondor dropped anchor in the middle of the harbor, waiting for longboats to tow them to the docks. Amos was the only man with rank enough to intimidate the harbor pilot into allowing him to drop sail at a proper moment and coast into the docks. He took pride in always reaching the proper place for the land lines to be thrown out and in having never crashed the docks or required a tow. He had coasted into this slip a hundred times in twenty years, but never before with a pair of insane boys playing games in front of the ship. Looking forward at the small boat, which was now slowing even more rapidly, Amos said, "Tell me, Lawrence, how does it feel to be the man on the bow when you drown the Prince of Krondor's youngest son . . . ?"

ABOUT THE AUTHOR

RAYMOND E. FEIST is the internationally bestselling author or co-author of twenty-one novels, including *Magician, Silverthorn, A Darkness at Sethanon, Faerie Tale, The King's Buccaneer, Talon of the Silver Hawk,* and *King of Foxes.* Feist is a graduate of the University of California, San Diego, and resides in southern California with his family. He travels, collects wine, and lives and dies with the San Diego Chargers.

RAYMOND E. FEIST

The King's Buccaneer   ___56373-4 $7.99/$11.99

Magician: Apprentice   ___26760-4 $7.99/$11.99

Magician: Master   ___26761-2 $7.99/$11.99

Silverthorn   ___27054-0 $7.99/$11.99

A Darkness at Sethanon   ___26328-5 $7.99/$11.99

Prince of the Blood   ___28524-6 $7.50/$10.99

Faerie Tale   ___27783-9 $7.99/$11.99

*Daughter of the Empire   ___27211-X $7.99/$11.99

*Servant of the Empire   ___29245-5 $7.99/$11.99

*Mistress of the Empire   ___56118-9 $7.99/$11.99

   *with Janny Wurts

....

Please enclose check or money order only, no cash or CODs. Shipping & handling costs: $5.50 U.S. mail, $7.50 UPS. New York and Tennessee residents must remit applicable sales tax. Canadian residents must remit applicable GST and provincial taxes. Please allow 4 - 6 weeks for delivery. All orders are subject to availability. This offer subject to change without notice. Please call 1-800-726-0600 for further information.

Bantam Dell Publishing Group, Inc.	
Attn: Customer Service	TOTAL AMT $_____
400 Hahn Road	SHIPPING & HANDLING $_____
Westminster, MD 21157	SALES TAX (NY, TN) $_____
	TOTAL ENCLOSED $_____

Name _____

Address _____

City/State/Zip _____

Daytime Phone (____) _____

SF 167 7/04